THE DEVILS TIGER

Other books by Robert Flynn

North to Yesterday
In the House of the Lord
The Sounds of Rescue, the Signs of Hope
Seasonal Rain
When I was Just Your Age
A Personal War in Vietnam
Wanderer Springs
The Last Klick
Living With the Hyenas

By Dan Klepper

The 13th Month
Pocketguide to Deer Hunting, from Kill to Kitchen

THE
DEVILS TIGER

by Robert Flynn *and* Dan Klepper

TCU Press/*Fort Worth*

Copyright © 2000 by Robert Flynn

Library of Congress Cataloging–in–Publication Data

Flynn, Robert, 1932-
    The devils tiger / by Robert Flynn and Dan Klepper.
    p.cm.
    ISBN 0-87565-224-7 (alk. paper)
1.Tigers—Russia—Siberia—Fiction. 2. Tigers—Texas—Fiction.
3. Texas—Fiction. I. Klepper, Dan. II. Title.

PS3556.L9D48 2000
813'.43—dc21
99-089180

Book design and linolium cut illustration by

Barbara M. Whitehead

In memory of
Dan Klepper
Husband, father, sportsman,
writer, friend

1

In West Texas where Jacob Trace made his way toward a dry camp after a fruitless day trailing a mountain lion, September dusk brought little relief from the heat and his mule kicked up dust from the parched, cracked earth. In Houston where Randolph Morgan, assistant director of the North American Zoological Association, and bored reporters awaited the arrival of World Air 17, dusk was hardly noticeable in the warm blanket of fog that wrapped the city.

At 24,000 feet and holding, World Air 17 was at last out of the storm. The flight across the Atlantic had been rough, even for the experienced crew aboard World Air 17. Storms had forced a detour, and severe turbulence had placed the DC-10 at the edge of control. A downdraft had dropped the wide-bodied jet several thousand feet. The altitude loss took seconds but gave the passengers time for screaming, vomiting, hyperventilating, and discovering suspect hearts.

The plane had groaned like a woman in labor and bottomed out with a jolt that tested every weld in the airplane and destroyed some electrical circuits, none of them crucial. The passengers had been belted down, but one stewardess, Claudette, had been assisting a sick child just aft of the first-class cabin when the aircraft went into its Jesus Christ mode, and she had been slammed against the overhead and knocked unconscious. The passengers wanted their feet on the ground. However, World Air 17 had arrived at Houston to find the airport wrapped in dense fog.

"World Air 17, this is Houston Center. Do you wish to declare an emergency?"

"Negative, Houston." Captain Robert Hansen had never declared an emergency in a long career, and he had no intention of declaring one now. He wanted everything routine, another flawless flight under the hands of Smiling Bob, doctor of the air. "Had a little turbulence. Stewardess with minor injuries. We'd like a priority landing."

"Houston still below minimums, expecting momentary improvement. Continue pattern. You'll be first to land."

"Roger. And thanks."

"Darryl," the captain said, "everything's under control here. Amble aft, tell the folks back there that we'll be landing number one as soon as we get clearance, and have the stews break out the medicinal alcohol. Check on Claudette and be sure the stews have cleaned up any blood. It only takes a drop to panic passengers when they're scared."

Darryl nodded. He had occupied the copilot's seat for half a dozen years and this had been his worst trip. He wouldn't admit it once he was on the ground, but he had made his peace with God, certain the airframe would warp under the stress. He had often yearned for the newer, faster airplanes—the Ten had been approved by the FAA in 1971 and, twenty years later, World Air and some others were still flying them. Today he was grateful for the tough, reliable, and unglamorous Ten. He removed his headset and harness and left the flight deck to smile at the passengers and assure them they had the best captain in the sky and would be safely on the ground by the time they finished their drinks.

He was pleased to see there was no blood in the cabin. Claudette had a cut on her head that would require stitches and was calm but dazed. He told Susan, chief stewardess, to keep her quiet and out of sight of the passengers. He continued aft, smiling, reassuring, promising they would be landing soon. The flight attendants had done a good job helping those who were bruised or sick and cleaning up the mess.

On his way back to the flight deck Susan reported that the elevator was not in the full up position and seemed to be jammed. Darryl opened the door of the elevator and leaned inside to try the buttons. *Nothing.* The elevator was at an awkward angle in the shaft, and he jumped back when something shifted in the pressurized cargo compartment below. *Structural damage.* Forcing a smile, he returned to the cockpit to tell the captain.

In Moscow, the Iron Curtain had cracked, and strange winds blew through the open spaces—democracy, chaos, anarchy. Mikhail Kuzakov was not a politician; he was a bureaucrat. He had done as he was told and he had done well, director of the Moscow zoo. Things had been simpler when the Communists ruled. Logical, practical, hard. Then, he had known what to say.

He did not know what to say when the minister telephoned to report that the police had found Adja Bayan dead. The old man tended felines at the zoo. "There was a cat in his apartment," the minister said.

"I don't understand."

"Perhaps you know that before democracy," the minister said the word carefully, "scientific experiments were conducted on zoo animals." Unofficially, Kuzakov had known about the secret labs and faceless scientists who experimented with infectious diseases, but the labs had been dismantled, the records destroyed, the scientists removed.

"Adja Bayan's death seems normal but suspicious. You will take appropriate action."

Accompanied by a technician, Kuzakov went directly to the remaining lab in the wooded area behind the zoo, the lab for testing samples from sick animals and preparing their medicines. Everything seemed to be in order. He led the technician to the small building shielded from view by the antelope compound and the patch of woods on the back side of the zoo on Bolshaya Gruzinskaya Street. Adja had a single room with a cot, washstand, kerosene stove for cooking, a table, and one chair.

They searched for the cat until they found it hiding under the bed. The technician, a small man with folds of skin in his face, slipped a net over the cat. The cat flattened its ears and hissed, but the technician, who was wearing thick leather gloves, grasped the cat across the shoulders and lifted it from the net. Taking the cat's head in his other gloved hand, he twisted until the vertebrae cracked and the cat went limp. He dropped it into a bag and and the two men left the room as they found it. Kuzakov had done something. Would someone tell him whether he had done the right thing?

The captain glared at Darryl. "I didn't send you aft to panic the passengers," he growled. "One of the food pods in the galley must have torn loose, knocked out some circuits and jammed the elevator."

Darryl looked at Kenneth, the thin, balding second officer, but Ken was glued to the instruments. Susan opened the door and walked onto the flight deck. "We have the passengers set-tled down with drinks in their hands. Claudette has a concussion, but we have the bleeding stopped." Hansen nodded. "Captain, there's something loose below."

Hansen looked at Susan to demonstrate his contempt of crew members who created panic. "We're going to be on the ground in five minutes. Now get a grip, and that goes for your crew too."

"Captain, there is something moving in the galley," Susan repeated. "I can hear it through the dumb waiter. I can smell something burning. Something electrical."

"Some of the circuits are out," Hansen snapped. "Nothing important. Probably the ovens."

Hansen didn't like excitement in a crew member, and he didn't want the crew running back and forth through the cabin when the passengers were watching for any sign of alarm. *The attendants had been pushed to the limit with sick and frightened passengers, but if Susan said something was moving in the galley, something was moving. And if the panicky passengers caught a whiff of smoke it would take the whole crew to calm them.* Susan waited, silently insisting that he do something. "Darryl, go back there and hold her hand," Hansen said without looking at him. "Before she upsets the 'official' passengers."

Susan led Darryl to the dumb waiter shaft. "Listen," she said.

Passengers within line of sight of the two watched them intently. He leaned into the dumb waiter shaft and sniffed. *Nothing. The captain was right, probably the ovens.* He listened, trying to identify the sound. It wasn't metal to metal or constant like something banging against the bulkhead. It was a soft, shuffling sound, one Darryl had never heard on an aircraft before.

The emergency hatch was on the starboard side at the front of the first-class cabin. There was no way to open it without creating fear in some passengers, but he had to know what was loose. They couldn't have something rolling around on their descent into Houston. "I'm going to open the emergency hatch and take a look. Want to give me a hand?"

Susan nodded and followed Darryl to the small emergency hatch in the first-class section. The hatch opened into the forward part of the twenty-foot galley. The elevator shaft, flanked by movable bulkheads separating the galley from the forward cargo hold, was at the aft end. Between the two bulkheads, lining either side of the galley, were the heavy food pods.

Darryl stopped at the emergency hatch in the aisle beside one of the first-class seats and smiled at the heavyset, orange-haired woman who occupied it. She was not amused. Susan came to his aid. "If we're going to have any coffee, we're going to have to get into the galley through here," she said. "And the captain wants his coffee."

"To hell with the coffee," the woman said. "Tell the captain to get this son of a bitch down."

Darryl was startled, but he broke into a wide grin. "Yes ma'am, I'll tell him. Just after I've given him his coffee."

"Orders are orders," Susan said, in her sweetest official voice.

"I'll have some of that coffee," said a thin, bald-headed man sitting next to the fat woman. They did not know each other, and they had been together long enough to know they did not want to know each other.

Darryl knelt in the aisle, pulled back the carpet covering the hatch, hooked his finger in the folding ring, and looked at Susan. If smoke boiled out of the hatch it would be her job to control the passengers. Susan nodded.

Darryl opened the hatch. *No smoke, thank God.* He could see nothing but the bare deck at the foot of the ladder eight feet below. He bent over, stuck his head into the hatch for a better view of the galley, and looked into the unblinking eyes of a Siberian tiger.

· · ·

Arina Yeroskin was exhausted from the long, rough flight and from the tension. She shifted uncomfortably in her seat, squeezed between two over-sized men who gripped drinks in one hand and the armrests in the other. No matter, she was going to get her first glimpse of America. The workers' paradise, according to Americans. Land of heartless capitalists who exploited workers and armed their country's enemies, the Communists had said. A government of hardhearted, hard-bargaining but trustworthy associates, the present democratic leaders said. Soon, she would know.

Andrei would want to know her impressions of America. She would tell him of the fat lady in first class with orange hair and enormous jewelry—heavy gold bracelets, gold necklace, and rings on every finger. The woman complained because in a small Russian town she couldn't find silver polish so that her black servant could shine her tea service.

What would she tell Andrei about the nasty American who rubbed his leg against hers and offered to show her Houston when they landed. Do you live in Houston? she had asked. No, we can discover it together, he said, showing her his credit cards. As though she were for sale. The storm had frightened romance out of him. Perhaps the story would make Andrei laugh.

It had not been a good time for her to leave Andrei. He was disillusioned with democracy, depressed by the breakup of the Soviet Union with all its hopes and promise. She would buy him a T-shirt with cowboys on it. She wanted to buy him a plastic replica of a gun so realistic that they were used in American holdups, but she feared she would not be able to take it home.

Jacob Trace climbed the rockslide toward his dogs. Somewhere above him, the hounds bayed, and Trace's dogs seldom lied, especially when joined by Red. Trace could hear the tinkling of the redbone's bell and the old hound's deep, melodious voice, and knew he would find the cougar crouched on a ledge in front of the dogs.

Jacob hoped the cat had no way to retreat. Lions usually ran after being darted and had to be brought to bay again, and he was tired and it was getting dark. He had given up the chase for the day when his hounds crossed a fresh trail. He didn't have much time before it was too dark to see.

Jacob felt all of his forty years, as though he had been carrying the mountains instead of climbing them. He had spent too much time on this cat already, on and off the trail for days in the rugged canyon country near Big Bend National Park, and he was ready to find his way out of the mountains to a bath and a good night's sleep.

He glanced down at his mule hobbled more than sixty feet below. Caliche dust caked the creases at the corners of his eyes, creases carved in his tanned skin by constant squinting in the desert country. *They ought to move those sheep,* he thought to himself. He had argued unsuccessfully that the state should select another site for a desert bighorn sheep restoration program, that the sanctuary of the huge park, more than 700,000 acres, not to mention Mexico, was too hazardous for the small band of sheep the state had obtained from Arizona. The sheep will attract lions like blood attracts flies, he said, but his arguments were ignored.

The mountain lions had proved him right. Even an eight-foot fence the state had erected around the sheep pasture had not stopped them. But the sheep restoration attempt had simplified Jacob's Federal research project. It had concentrated the cougars and made it easier for him to locate them so that he could capture, attach radio transmitter collars to their necks, and release them in distant areas. Some of the lions were caught quickly, some came hard. This one had been hard. It was not a big lion—by the size of the tracks it was a young adult female—but it was smart. It had been one of the most evasive he had encountered.

Trace rubbed his lower back with his free hand. The other hand held a gas-operated rifle, a Cap-Chur gun capable of accurately propelling a drug-loaded syringe for a distance of forty yards. The gun was loaded, and Trace carried extra darts with a tranquilizing drug in a small duffel bag slung from his shoulder.

He finished the climb as quietly as possible and saw the lion as he reached the ledge. The cat faced the hounds, back to the wall. The ledge played out behind the cat and the face of the mountain became sheer, vertical rock. There was no exit from the ledge except through the dogs.

Encouraged by Trace's arrival, all the hounds but Red renewed their baying with vigor and feinted at the lion, scrambling away at the last moment as the cat spat and hissed and raked its claws at its tormentors.

The redbone stood back and barked in short, choppy bawls, and Jacob wondered how many hunts the dog had left in him. He had owned the redbone for a dozen years, and the hound had developed into one of the best he had ever seen at following a cold trail. Red had gone deaf a couple of years earlier, so Trace ran him with a bell on his collar. The redbone was a methodical plodder that seldom made a sound on a cold trail, and the bell enabled Jacob to keep track of him.

Jacob shouldered the rifle, fired a dart into the side of the lion's neck and quickly reloaded. The cougar did not attempt to run through the hounds, and as its movements slowed, Trace used the short ropes he had wrapped around his waist to leash the dogs. Within five minutes the lion was down, and Jacob removed the barbed dart, gave it another injection to keep it immobile, and checked his dogs.

One of the dogs had a cut on his shoulder. Jacob got out

his waterproof kit containing matches, sutures, and antibiotic and examined the cut. Not deep, more likely from the brush than from the cat. He decided it didn't need stitches but disinfected the cut and stroked the dog's head before dragging the lion down the rockslide to the desert floor.

He could keep a lion immobile for hours with the tranquilizer and if the lion were small enough, he could carry it draped over his lap in front of the saddle. Larger lions were tied behind the saddle. Loading a drugged lion on the small mule was no easy chore although Jacob was six feet tall and in good condition.

"Don't give me any trouble, Huevon," he said to the mule. "I'm going to load this cat if I have to tranquilize you to do it." The mule had never gotten accustomed to the smell of lion, and eyes wide and nostrils flared, it shied although snubbed to the base of a creosote bush. The young lion weighed no more than sixty pounds, and Trace slid its limp body over the saddle with the trembling mule trying to shy out from under it.

Once the lion was in place, Jacob draped an arm over the mule's neck and paused to catch his breath and enjoy this moment of fulfillment. "Thank you, Lord, for this day," he said. It wasn't exactly a prayer and not exactly a habit. It had gone well. No dogs had been torn by the lion, and the cat had not been injured. It was hard work but it had its moments—sitting beside a campfire with the dogs and the mule for company, going to sleep beneath a blanket of stars, awakening to the promise of first light, the music of the hounds on the trail. And the chase. Always, there was that leap of joy when the dogs found a hot trail. Above all else, there was the pleasure and pride that came with returning home from a job well done. Jacob was grateful for his life.

He unleashed the dogs and climbed into the saddle, slipping his knees under the lion. He urged Huevon toward the hills where the highway from Marathon cut south toward the park. The exhausted hounds, their tongues lolling, followed at the heels of the mule. Tired as they were the dogs seemed pleased with themselves. Old Red looked at him as if to say, "See, I'm not through yet."

It was a good five miles back to the pickup and trailer in the dark through rugged country, but Jacob wanted to get the lion in a cage where it would be less likely to injure itself.

"The tiger, as you are all aware, is a formidable killing machine," said Randolph Morgan to the reporters. Stuart Johnson, director of the North American Zoological Association, thought the September temperature and humidity in Houston above and the press coverage below his comfort level. He had sent one of his assistant directors, Randolph Morgan, who was competent, informed, and dull. Morgan would make the association look efficient without causing anyone to suggest that it was time for Johnson to step aside for a younger man. Morgan would conduct the press conference and oversee the transfer of the tigers. Johnson would welcome the tiger to the zoo in Seattle. Seattle was pleasant in September.

"The tiger is a stalker. It tries to get as close as possible to its victim undetected, then charges in for a kill," Morgan said. He knew some of the reporters didn't know a tiger from a lion, but he did not want to talk down to them. He wanted them on his side, and he wanted their attention. The interview had a chance of making the networks, and a good performance could make him the next director. He twisted the thin gold ring on his little finger. It was his late mother's wedding ring.

Randolph Morgan was in his early fifties, not quite six feet tall, a bit paunchy, balding, and he hated his first name. When he enrolled in college he introduced himself as Rand Morgan. It was short, crisp, and masculine.

"An observer compared a stalking tiger to a huge snake, its head extended until its throat touches the ground, every muscle taut, moving with surprising speed yet with no apparent motion. The tiger kills by grasping the throat of its victim in its powerful jaws or by biting through the nape of the neck. If the victim's neck is not broken in the ensuing fall or by the tiger's canines, the grip on the windpipe causes strangulation."

Morgan paused to observe the reaction of his audience. They were listening. When he graduated from state college with a degree in business, his only job offer was from a zoo. He had done well with the business end of the zoo, and he had studied zoology and public relations. If he could hold the interest of the reporters, he could earn the approval of Stuart Johnson.

Morgan wanted to wipe the perspiration from his forehead. Although the lounge was air-conditioned, the television lights were hot, his tie was too tight, his shirt stuck to his back and his suit wilted—not the image he wanted to convey. This was the most important moment of his life. He tried to radiate confidence.

"The tiger usually has a distinctive feeding routine. The tiger will consume the hindquarters at the time of the kill, then hide the carcass until it feeds again. During its second visit, the tiger eats the remainder of the body, usually up to the head. If there is a third visit, the head and the bones are consumed. If unmolested, a tiger seldom leaves much evidence of its victim." He had intentionally used victim rather than prey, and the ploy worked.

"Are the Russians sending us any man-eaters?" a reporter asked. The question was followed by chuckles, but Morgan welcomed the interruption. Nothing like discussing a man-eater to grab headlines.

"There are three tigers aboard the aircraft. To my knowledge none are man-eaters." Morgan smiled, remembering to look at the television camera instead of the reporter. "Although we often associate man-eating tigers with the days of Britain's rule over India, one of the more famous cases occurred in the late 1960s when a single tiger was credited with killing five hundred people. More than a dozen villages were abandoned before the tiger was hunted down."

Morgan paused for effect while the reporters scribbled their notes. "One authority estimates that as many as a million people have been killed by tigers over the last four centuries on the Asian continent. A million victims stalked by an animal that can glide through tall grass like a snake—" He paused to let them picture the horror of being stalked and eaten by the deadliest creature on earth, except for man. "You can understand man's fascination with this animal, and why it must be preserved."

"Hurry up, asshole," Hailee White muttered, irritated that the news director of KHTX-TV had sent her crew to Houston Intercontinental Airport to cover a story about a new animal for the zoo. A freighter carrying ammonium nitrate had collided with a string of oil barges in the ship channel. There had been no reports of fire, but if one did occur, it could explode into a major disaster. That was where Hailee White should be.

Houston was but a step on Hailee's road to New York, and the sooner she got there, the better. Anchor on a national network. She had the looks, she had the voice, all she needed was a chance. In a profession where her face was her fortune, she was a striking brunette with defined features, big brown eyes, a full mouth. She would blossom into an attractive professional woman, unlike the cute, vacuous, blond reporters who sagged into waxy sellers of household products. She was tall and slender with great legs, but on TV no one ever saw her legs, and her breasts were not as large as she would have liked. But she had a smile, she had a look, she had a brain, and she stood poised with the microphone, praying for a miracle. There are no small stories, there are only small-minded reporters, she told herself.

". . . Siberian tigers, destined for zoos in Houston, San Diego and Seattle. For several years NAZA, the North American Zoological Association, has been developing a captive propagation survival plan for a number of endangered species of wildlife, and the loan of these Siberian tigers marks the fruition. . . ."

Hailee groaned. There was a tanker in the channel that might explode, and a lot of people along the channel who might die, and this hype whore was yakking about the propagation of tigers. She cursed the reporters who asked questions, and she cursed the fog that kept World Air 17 circling overhead when it should have been on the ground twenty minutes ago. She wanted to get a videotape of the tigers, return to the station, and talk the assignments director into sending her to the docks where she could cover the freighter collision live.

"I thought these were Russian tigers," one of the reporters said, stepping in front of Hailee. "Exactly what do you mean by Siberian?"

"They are Russian in that they are on loan from the Moscow zoo," Morgan explained with a smile. "The Siberian tiger is a subspecies. In the wild it survives today only in the Amur region of southeastern Siberia, in Manchuria in northeast China, and in Korea. We estimate there are fewer than five hundred in the wild today. The Siberian is the largest of all cats. Males have been known to weigh up to 650 pounds and measure twelve feet in length, including the tail. There is the record of a thirteen-foot tiger, but that's another tale."

Morgan laughed at his own joke while Hailee turned to Tony Garcia, her cameraman, to show her disgust. The print boys were after details to fill pages. She needed a few seconds of pithy remarks, and this flack was blurbing "everything you need to know about tigers."

" . . . male will approach 600 pounds. We have two females, one mature tigress weighing perhaps 400 pounds. The other female is younger and smaller but has the potential to be an excellent breeding animal. I might add, however . . ."

Hailee's question regarding whether borrowing the tigers would improve relations between the two countries was lost as another reporter asked, "American zoos have tigers; why bring in more?"

"Most of the zoo tigers are Bengals, a different sub-species," Morgan said. "There are about 250 Siberians in our zoos, and about three times that many in other zoos through-out the world. We have problems with zoo animals because inbreeding results in higher infant mortality rates and shorter life spans for adults. These tigers will infuse fresh genes into the pool, and we hope, enable us to guarantee—"

"So these tigers are to be used for breeding purposes?" a reporter asked, causing Hailee to roll her eyes in open-mouthed disgust.

"Yes," Morgan said, "but they will be placed on display."

"How do you transport cats of this size? Keep them drugged all the way?" the reporter asked.

"The tigers were given tranquilizers in Moscow. The drug keeps them sedated for about eighteen hours, but they are on their feet. A drugged cat is unpredictable, but generally tigers will remain calm and quiet."

"What if they don't?" a reporter asked.

Morgan laughed. "A veterinarian from the Moscow zoo,

Dr. Arina Yeroskin, has accompanied the tigers from Moscow, and I am confident she is equipped to handle any situation."

"How long will the tigers remain in Houston, and do you have any idea when the plane will land?" Hailee blurted, hoping to end the interview.

Morgan twisted the ring on his little finger. The young woman had not been paying attention. He smiled at Hailee and started to speak when a man wearing a World Air uniform sidled up so that Morgan was between him and the camera and whispered, "The World Air supervisor would like to speak to you in his office. It's urgent."

Morgan was furious at the interruption. His complexion was ruddy, and when he became angry or embarrassed, he flushed. Now the redness of his face rose up his forehead and into the sparse blond hairs of his scalp. Morgan feared he looked ridiculous when the top of his head was red. He twisted the ring on his little finger and tried to smile. "I hope to have an answer for you when I return."

As Rand Morgan walked away the TV cameramen switched off their lights, and Hailee made no effort to conceal her disgust. This half-minute story was taking hours. "Shit," she said, loudly enough for everyone in the lounge to hear.

Darryl Wenthorp froze. He was close enough to smell the tiger, close enough to see the tiny beads of moisture dotting the cat's pink tongue, to hear the beginning of the growl deep in the animal's throat. The cat was sitting on its haunches four feet from the foot of the ladder. Behind it lay a piece of twisted bulkhead that had once separated the galley from the pressurized cargo compartment.

Beyond the broken panel was the wooden, metal-lined crate that had held the tiger. The crate had ripped the tie-downs from the deck, jumped the steel deck stops and smashed into the bulkhead and the elevator shaft, pushing the

16

four large food pods on the port side forward. The first pod had smashed into the forward bulkhead of the galley and into the small compartment below the cockpit where the bulk of the electrical circuitry of the aircraft was located. The collision had ruptured the tiger's crate.

Darryl jerked back his head and, still kneeling, blindly groped for the hatch cover. The moment he moved, the tiger bounded forward, reaching a muscular forepaw through the hatch.

"Sorry about the interruption, Mr. Morgan," the supervisor said. He was standing, his fingertips on the desk, but he did not meet Morgan's eyes. "We have a problem on flight 17."

"What kind of problem?" Morgan asked.

"We're not certain," the supervisor said, which was not a lie but not the truth either. "We have the airplane on radar and have been in radio communication with the pilot. The tigers have been sedated?"

"Yes, of course."

"Could they . . . uh . . . recover?"

"They're not unconscious if that's what you mean."

"But are they tranquilized? Suppose one were to get loose—"

"It could be excited or it could be docile. Tigers are unpredictable, very unpredictable when they're drugged."

"—in the passenger cabin."

It took a moment for Morgan to comprehend the question. He stared at the supervisor, his mouth working but forming no words. "Loose in the passenger cabin?" Morgan stepped back, reaching behind him for some support. "I—" He tried to swallow but couldn't. "These are zoo animals. They have no fear of man."

. . .

Susan was chatting with the passengers to reassure them when their attention shifted to Darryl. She turned in time to see a claw reach through the hatch, catch Darryl by the throat and jerk him forward, slamming his upper body over the hatch opening. His head struck the hatch cover and knocked it flat against the carpeted deck.

Susan gasped and stumbled backward as Darryl's arms and legs flailed. The orange-haired woman in the aisle seat screamed, lunged over the man beside her, and clawed at the window. Darryl's legs and arms stopped flailing and his body moved backward a few inches until his head dropped limply into the hatch opening. A huge hairy head took Darryl's head between its jaws and slowly dragged Darryl's body through the opening.

Susan stood paralyzed as the passengers stumbled over each other in an effort to get to the rear of the plane. A woman sitting on the port side fainted, while her four-year-old son stood in his seat and watched Darryl slide into the hatch. Susan leaned forward to close the hatch when the tigress' head appeared in the opening.

Susan backed toward the cockpit. Fixed by its cold, intense stare, she watched the cat climb out, almost in slow motion. One great paw, claws extended, gripped the carpet and pulled. The cat's shoulders squeezed through the hatch, leaving short orange and black hairs on the aluminum edges. Then the left foreleg appeared. The cat reached forward, digging a second set of sharp claws into the carpet and pulled.

The tiger emerged from the hatch in fluid motion. It ignored the orange-haired woman, who turned from clawing the window and curled, as best she could, into the lap of her thin, bald neighbor. Susan stood frozen in the tiger's unblinking stare as it stretched on its stomach before her and wrapped a powerful paw around her leg. She stifled a scream as the cockpit door opened behind her.

The captain, noting the shift in the balance of the aircraft as passengers fled to the rear, had automatically thumbed in compensation on the trim tab. The second officer opened the cockpit door to see what was going on. He started to step around the stewardess, then stopped. "Captain," he said. "One of the tigers—"

Over his shoulder Hansen could see nothing but Kenneth and apparently one of the stews standing in the door, but he could hear screams in the passenger section. "Houston, World Air 17, we have a tiger in the passenger cabin. Repeat, tiger in the passenger cabin."

"Roger, Seventeen. Uh, we are still below minimums. San Antonio reports 700 and two, New Orleans—"

Hansen didn't know what a tiger would do, but he knew passengers. "Houston, World Air 17 is shooting an emergency approach. Request emergency vehicles standby."

Kenneth, the second officer, stared at the tiger. Nothing in his training or experience had prepared him for this. The tiger did not dig in its claws, but held Susan's leg firmly in its grasp and licked the stewardess' calf. "It's tame," he said. *They were zoo tigers, weren't they?*

"Oh, God, oh, God, do something," Susan sobbed. "Somebody—"

"Don't move," Ken said. His training taught him to remain calm.

No one moved. Susan bit her lip, fighting to remain still. Passengers jammed the aisle and seats behind the first-class section and either stared or screamed. Some did both. But no one moved. Except Susan, and she didn't move far. The instant the muscles in her calf tightened, the tiger extended the tips of its claws, almost enough to puncture the skin. A low growl rumbled in its throat as it looked into her eyes.

Susan relaxed to keep the claws from digging deeper. She

slowly raised her right hand to her mouth and bit her knuckles as the tiger licked her leg again. The cat's tongue, rough as a wood rasp, abraded the skin on her leg. The skin turned pink, then red as tiny capillaries ruptured and droplets of blood mixed with the saliva of the tiger's tongue.

The tiger turned her head to glare over her shoulder at the bedlam behind her. The passengers quieted and pressed toward the rear of the airplane. The cat ran its wide, pink tongue over its lips and turned back to the raw skin where blood welled faster and thicker.

"Pull your leg away. It is the only chance. The more blood, the more aggressive it will become," said Arina, who had fought her way through the hysterical passengers to the first-class section. "Quickly. It is the only way. You," she said, pointing at Kenneth. "Distract the tiger."

Kenneth looked at the woman as if she were daft.

"Do something," the woman yelled. "Do it now."

Kenneth started to mouth the word "what?" when Arina grabbed the tiger's tail with one hand and yanked. The startled cat sprang half around. Kenneth jerked Susan toward the cockpit. Susan fell against the door. Kenneth turned to face the tiger when it reversed itself in midair and struck him across the side of the head.

Half his face missing and his jaw torn loose, Kenneth fell moaning onto the flight deck. The tiger leaped over Susan, following the engineer into the cockpit. Hansen turned, and the tiger sank its teeth into his right shoulder and tugged against the harness that strapped him to his seat.

Kenneth, blind with blood and pain, stumbled out of the flight cabin and collapsed in the aisle. Hansen groaned as the tiger's teeth tore through his flesh. He heard bones break. Unable to endure the pain, he unhooked his harness and allowed himself to be dragged out of his seat. He groped for help, and his hand found the fire extinguisher. He had been dragged almost off the flight deck when the extinguisher made its first hiss. He missed the tiger with the spray, but, startled, it released him and jumped back. Turning from the captain, the tiger lay down beside Kenneth and sank its teeth into his head. Kenneth screamed as a fang slipped into an eye socket.

Hailee was half inclined to go back to the station and wangle an assignment to the ship channel. Most of the reporters had called their desks and gone to the cargo hangar to await the arrival of the tigers. Instinct told Hailee to stay with the story until Morgan told her what the phone call was about.

"If I'm not back when they announce the flight landing, I'll meet you at the hangar," Hailee told Tony Garcia. She unbuttoned her jacket, mussed her sprayed, sculpted hair and slipped past the door through which Morgan had disappeared. She approached the first male World Air official she saw. "I'm Randolph Morgan's secretary, and I have a message for him."

"Supervisor's office. Down the hall and to the right."

Hailee walked down the hall until she heard Morgan's voice. Cautiously she approached the open door. "Loose in the passenger cabin? A tiger?" she heard Morgan ask. "They have no fear of man."

She left as quietly as she had come. She could confront Morgan to confirm the story and possibly alert the other members of the media, or she could go with what she had. She glanced at her watch. "Tony," she said, "pick a spot for a newsbreak. We've got a hell of a story."

She called the news director, who was not as excited as she expected. "You overheard part of a conversation, and you expect us to go on the air with that? Bullshit."

"I know what I heard," Hailee screamed. "I know who said it. We've got a story that will boost the ratings for this station, which, speaking of bullshit, is something you haven't done. Call the station manager."

The news director folded. "Okay. We'll say there are 'indications' that a tiger is loose in the passenger cabin. That's as far as I'll go. And it's your ass."

Tony picked a spot outside that showed the control tower through the fog. Hailee fixed her hair, took the mike, and stood waiting for a lead-in from the station. "Yes," she responded. "That is the story we are getting here. It is a Bengal tiger, the kind seen in old Tarzan movies. Yes, they are capable of injuring, perhaps killing a person. However, the tiger has spent most of its life in a zoo and should be comfortable around people. No one is saying whether they are going to offer it airline food. Hailee White at Houston Intercontinental Airport." The red light went off on the camera, and Tony gave her a smile and a thumbs-up.

Hansen's shoulder was crushed, but he was conscious. *Thank God, Darryl was at the controls.* Kenneth lay a few feet in front of him, half naked. The tiger had methodically stripped Kenneth's clothing with teeth and tongue and had torn a huge chunk of meat from his buttocks. Hansen knew he had to get to the flight deck. An emergency approach below minimums. Darryl couldn't do it by himself. Stifling a groan as pain shot through him, Hansen eased himself toward the cabin, dragging his shoulder and arm.

Careful, no sudden movements, he thought. *Keep eye on tiger. Move feet. Find door opening. Slowly ease body onto flight deck.* Everything before him turned to red. Hansen fought for consciousness, swam slowly upward toward the light, fought through the dark curtain, and he could see again. *Can't pass out. Can't. Help Darryl.*

He was on the flight deck. *Carefully close door.* "Darryl," he said softly. "Help me." Behind him he heard, "World Air 17.

Do you read me? You are off course. Repeat off course. Please state your intentions. World Air 17. Do you read me?" Through the flight deck he could feel the buffeting that preceded a stall.

Painfully Hansen turned his head. The flight deck was empty. *Where was Darryl? Jesus, where was the airplane?* I am the captain, he said, maybe aloud. *I am the captain.* Bracing himself against the pain, he half rose, paused until his vision cleared and moved into the left-hand seat. He blinked back the dark curtain and looked at the instruments before him. *Get the nose down.* The passengers had shifted the balance to the rear. He stabbed a finger at the trim tab. *Get help.*

With his right arm hanging uselessly, he slipped on the headset. "World Air 17, mayday, mayday. Request vector to nearest runway."

"Roger, Seventeen, Corpus Christi Naval Air Station has 8000 feet. Reporting 300 overcast and 1500 in heavy fog. Altimeter two niner—"

He could hardly hear through the dull buzzing in his head. And fog. The lights on the instruments panel fell like shooting stars into a sea of black. He fought back. "—teen, World Air 17, do you copy?"

"Negative."

"Contact approach control, 120.9. Do you copy?"

"Affirmative." With his left hand he dialed in the numbers. "Approach, World Air 17."

"We have you ninety miles out. Turn to a heading of two eight five for runway one three. Begin descent now."

"Roger." Hansen eased the controls forward. The throttles. Could he reach the throttles? Meant twisting into his broken shoulder. *Got to.* He could feel the broken bones shift. "Leaving—" Hansen blinked and tried to read the altimeter. "Houston, uh, Corpus Christi, I—"

2

During the confusion, Arina helped Susan scramble
to the rear of the first-class cabin, and with the help
of the other flight attendants, Susan had the passengers under control. She had convinced the bald man with
the orange-haired lady in his lap to remain where they were.
Any attempt to join the others would attract the attention of
the tiger. The woman who had fainted revived but was in
shock. She sat staring into space, her young son in her lap.
For the moment the tiger ignored them, intent on eating the
thighs of its naked victim.

Arina quickly established herself as the authority on the
behavior of the tiger. "You must be quiet," she said. "You
must not excite the tiger while it is eating. If you do not wish
to see, turn your head."

Arina wished she had a God so she could pray. She knew
that one of the pilots was dead. Another had crawled into the
cabin to die. Perhaps he was a brave man, but she knew what

a tiger could do. No matter how brave, he would lie down and die. *Perhaps there was another pilot?*

Susan stood beside her with her bleeding leg behind a seat so the tiger would not see, as though the tiger could not smell the blood. Without taking her eyes off the tiger, Arina spoke. "How many pilots?" she asked.

The first-class cabin was under control, and Susan felt pride that she had done her job. She did not want to cause more panic. *Should she answer this woman with the strange accent? Tell her the copilot and second officer were dead and the captain was injured?* Susan didn't know how badly he was injured, but she knew that if anyone could get them down alive, it was Robert Hansen.

Susan worked her way aft to the economy section. The other attendants had the crowded passengers calmed and strapped down. She tried to reach the flight deck by telephone but failed. Perhaps the circuits had burned out. Perhaps there was no one at the controls of the airplane that was hurtling through the sky at 300 knots.

Guardedly, she looked at the other flight attendants. They knew too; the plane was descending. A quick glance out the window offered no warm glow of lights beneath the fog. If they were landing, it wasn't Houston.

"Seventeen, can you read me?"

"Seventeen, roger." Hansen struggled for consciousness, fighting back the pain. *Got to. Organize. Set up for landing. Speed? Too fast. Get nose up. Flaps?* Had he lowered—

"Seventeen, you are high and off course to the right. Turn to heading nine five. Report when over outer marker."

Lose altitude. Correct course. Get outer marker on the needle. No go around. One chance. He tried to focus on the flight director. *Wings level. Pitch.* He blinked to clear his vision. He could see nothing. His eyes. *Got to open. . . .*

Hansen wanted to shut out the insistent voice in his ear. He wanted to slide away from the pain, slide into sweet oblivion. *No.* He was the captain.

" . . . repeat, high and off course. Seventeen, do you read me? You are above the glide path, off course. Seventeen, seventeen, abort. Do you read? Abort."

"All passengers," Susan said. She was afraid to use the PA system for fear of upsetting the tiger. She and the other attendants walked up and down the aisle checking the passengers, many of them sharing single seats. If this was it, she would go out like a pro. She could see it in the faces of the other attendants; they felt the same. "Be sure that your seat belt is securely fastened. We will be landing in a few minutes. The captain has declared an emergency and we will be coming in a little fast." She was guessing, but what else could she say?

The other attendants instructed the passengers in the proper brace position for an emergency landing. What should she tell them? She didn't know what was happening. The passengers knew any excitement would excite the tiger that might appear in the aisle at any moment. "Ladies and gentlemen," she began. "We have not been able to—"

A young sailor carefully beckoned her to him, and then motioned for her to lean across the other three passengers crowded into two seats to where he sat beside the window. "We're going to land in the ocean."

Susan looked out the window. The airplane was enveloped in gray. Through a brief break in the fog she saw water. She also saw the black skeleton of pilings and the flash of a beacon a few feet below the wing. She didn't know what it was, but she knew it didn't mark a runway. "At this time we are going to put on our life vests. Do not, repeat, do *not* inflate the vests until you are told to do so. Flight attendants, stand by for water landing."

. . .

Fog. He had to clear the fog from his brain. If only he could shake his head, but every time he moved his head bones grated in his shoulder. He saw sparkles before his eyes. *Stars? No, not stars, lights. They were blurred but they were there. Lights.* He was in the pattern, but where? *Where were the lights? No mistakes now. Too close.* He didn't remember the outer marker but the localizer was alive. The glideslope was alive. But the lights. *The lights were. . . .* The lights flickered and moved. Through the flickers he saw water. He was coming down in the water. *Nose up. Throttles. Got to reach the throttles. Reach across. Bones grating, tearing.*

"Seventeen, do you read me? Seventeen. Seventeen, you have overshot the approach. Turn to heading seven zero."

"We've lost him on the screen. Approximately twenty miles out. Contact Coast Guard. Vicinity Little Dagger Hill."

With his last remaining strength Hansen lunged across the seat to cut the throttles with his good arm. The 170-foot-long cylinder skipped on the surface like a flat rock and became airborne before hitting the water a second and final time. Hansen crashed into the control panel when the aircraft hit the water. He was still conscious when the airplane struck the bay again and was vaguely aware of the approaching light. He had brought his aircraft home. The light flashed before sweeping along the starboard side of the radome and cockpit, and Hansen allowed himself to abandon the flight as the aircraft spun violently to the right.

Morgan didn't want to call the director. Stuart Johnson didn't like bad news, especially about one of his pet projects, and he had handled this one from the beginning. Stuart had negotiated the loan of the tigers, flown to Moscow to make the arrangements, and would be on the West Coast to greet the Seattle tiger.

He was going to be furious that the airplane had crashed and the tigers killed. Unable to vent his wrath on anyone else, he would vent it on Morgan. Rand could visualize that smile curling his thick upper lip with the thin moustache. Stuart would be even angrier if television cameras showed up at his door before he had prepared a statement.

Morgan had been director of a zoo in the Midwest when he took the job as assistant director of NAZA. His wife, Peggy, wanted him to go into commercial business with more pay and less politics. Stuart had implied that the job was tantamount to heir to the throne, soon to be vacated when Stuart took early retirement. Peg's opposition vanished when Rand told her the director sometimes dined at the White House.

Rand was not told that he would be one of several assistants. He would have asked for his old job back if Peg hadn't told everyone that he was one step from the top. Now he feared he would end his career as assistant director or out of a job. There were rumors of cutbacks at NAZA—one of the assistant directors. The Houston assignment had provided him with an opportunity to establish himself as likely successor. He had done well at the press conference, but that would never be reported. His moment of success would be swallowed by headlines about the crash of the airliner and the death of the tigers.

Rand reached for the telephone in the World Air supervisor's office just as it rang. The supervisor, who was slumped in his chair, still reliving that last awful call, answered the telephone, then handed it to Morgan. "It's for you. Washington."

The director. *How in the hell*—Morgan's face flushed. "Hello, Rand here. Yes, Stuart, one of the tigers—Stuart, it's worse than you realize. The plane crashed. The Coast Guard has dispatched boats, but there have been no reports. Yes, sir, as soon as I hear. I think you might express regret to the Russians. Sir? Ms. Price? I can take care of—Okay. What flight will she be on? From New Orleans?" He dared not ask what Evelyn Price was doing in New Orleans.

"Damn bitch," Morgan said, hanging up. Rand, who tried to like everyone, did not like Evelyn Price. She had left her husband and son, had unusual travel arrangements and weekend plans, often coinciding with those of the director, and blamed men, particularly white men, for everything wrong in the world. "I hope her plane crashes."

Arina was underwater. She struggled to move but was pinned. She struggled again, and her face came out of the water. She gasped, choked, coughed, but it was air. She filled her lungs and struggled to raise her head a few more inches. The aircraft was in darkness. Already there were several inches of water on the floor, and she was pinned in the wreckage. How long before the airplane sank?

Even with one ear underwater she could hear people struggling to free themselves of the wreckage, making waves in their efforts to escape, waves that washed over her face. She could hear the muffled voices of the crew as they led people to the safety of the lifeboats. "Help," she cried and swallowed a mouthful of water. "Help."

Something heavy dropped beside her and water washed over her. Hands groped for her, tugged, then let go. It was the nasty American, and he was going to leave her. Her chest burned, but she dared not gasp for breath. The weight on her shifted a little and with her remaining strength she struggled for air. Strong arms helped her stand.

Susan stood in the hatch. "This way," she yelled. "Keep calm. Do not inflate your vest until you are in the raft. See that there are no injured or helpless people around you. Do not inflate—"

The training was paying off. There was water in the cabin but there was no panic, and as best she could tell in the darkness, the crew was doing its job. Susan said a prayer of thanks to Captain Hansen and that there was no fire. She dared not think what had happened to the tiger that was perhaps beside her, ready to catch her again with those claws that gripped just tightly enough.

In the first-class section, the mother clutched her son, not daring to move as water inched up her legs. Her son too was still, as though he knew instinctively that whatever the chaos behind them or the present terror, he must not move or make a sound. Even in the darkness she could see the yellow eyes of the tiger crouched a few feet in front of her.

"Please God, make it leave," she prayed. "God, I can't hold my son while he drowns. God, help me."

The woman heard the soft splashing of water, and the eyes were inches away. She could feel its breath tickling her cheek, its stiff whiskers against her face. The tiger ran a pink tongue over its teeth and was gone.

Leaving Janice in charge of the hatch, Susan stood on the port wing, making certain passengers had their life vests inflated, keeping them together until the rafts were inflated. "There are rafts for everyone," she said. "Keep together. Do not get into a raft until I tell you to do so. Be certain that your vest is securely fastened and inflated."

She felt a sickening lurch and almost lost her footing as the airplane slid forward and the water level rose. The tiger appeared in the open hatch. Susan and most of the passengers froze, but one man pushed past her and jumped feet first into the water. She watched in astonishment as his feet splashed into the water, hit something solid, and he pitched face forward into the sea. When she looked back the tiger was gone.

. . .

If World Air 17 had anything that could be called luck it was the place where the flight ended—the Laguna Madre that swept southward from Corpus Christi for almost 120 miles ending below Port Isabel near the Rio Grande. It was a lonely, remote stretch of water bounded on the east by the barrier island called Padre and on the west by the grass prairies and thorn-bush thickets of the King, Kenedy, and other large ranches.

The Laguna Madre ranged from a few inches to the twelve-foot depths of the Intracoastal Waterway that sliced through its middle. There were few natural but many man-made islands in the bay. Spoil islands, vegetated spits of sand, mud, and shell sucked by dredges from the canal and pumped to the edges of the waterway, flanked the channel in many areas. Fishing shacks occupied many of the islands, built by fishermen who ventured into the vast Laguna in search of red drum and spotted sea trout.

The plane struck hard, wheels up, and the belly of the air-craft gouged a deep furrow through the soft bottom of the shallow bay and pushed a miniature tidal wave before its black nose.

Pilings supporting the flashing beacon that marked a mile post on the Intracoastal Waterway ripped into the wing between the starboard engine and the fuselage. The swept-back wing was torn from the body, causing the aircraft to roll first to the right, then with the weight of the wing gone, to the left during the spin. The momentum carried the aircraft into the channel, and the port stabilizer dipped beneath the surface and dug into the mud bar at the edge of the canal.

The aircraft broke apart just aft of the wings. The forward section of the DC-10 settled into the mud bottom with the port wing sweeping up and back at an awkward angle. The tail section settled in four feet of water.

Rand knew that his scalp was red and that beads of perspiration clung to the roots of his thinning hair. He had met the airplane that brought Evelyn and had called the director to report the latest developments. "They're still searching for survivors. We think one of the tigers survived the crash," he told Stuart. "It was seen leaving the wreckage but it might have drowned—I know tigers are excellent swimmers, but no one knows the condition the tiger was in."

Morgan glanced at Evelyn Price who watched him with cold gray eyes. The first time he met her, Rand thought she was good-looking although her face was long and her teeth large. She was as tall as he, shapely, and she knew how to present herself—cool, confident, and never wrong. "Yes, do you wish to speak to her?" Morgan knew what "not now" meant. Stuart wanted to talk to her when he was not around.

"The people at Wildlife Conservation International said the best in this area is Jacob Trace in the western part of the state. He's doing puma translocation work for the Department of the Interior. He knows North American cats, but I'm not sure about tigers. The state wildlife cowboys are ready to run the tiger down and kill it, if it's still alive, but they aren't sure about capturing it. Yes, I'll send an airplane to pick up Trace."

Morgan stole another glance at Evelyn. "Yes, I'll tell Ms. Price she is to handle the state wildlife people. An international matter. We will do everything we can to protect it, if it's alive. Goodbye."

Morgan wondered what Stuart saw in Evelyn Price. Her tongue was sharper than her face. If he had made some of the remarks she had he would have been fired the next day. Of course, he wasn't sleeping with the director.

"Contact the state wildlife people and tell them how important the tiger is scientifically and politically," he said politely but emphatically. He had to establish that they were equals, working together. "Stuart is going to get the State Department's support with Interior. We are to go to Corpus Christi and to run the operation from there. We'll be stuck there until the tiger is confirmed dead or captured."

"Sure thing, Randy," she said, her eyebrows arched, her lips slightly upturned as she watched the red creep through his thin hair. Evelyn hoped they never captured it.

Evelyn Price didn't like seeing animals caged. Animals were not created for the pleasure of man. She had gone to work for NAZA because of its endangered species propagation program. Of the endangered species she had helped add to the survival plan—the Chinese alligator, Grevy's zebra—she liked the cats best, the Asian lion, snow leopard, cheetah, and the biggest of them all, the Siberian tiger.

Stuart had been her mentor, almost her father. He chided her sometimes for her strong views, but in a benevolent way. Stuart's wife had died a few years earlier, and he had never recovered from her death. Slowly, he had turned his dependency from her to Evelyn. Some of the others, like Randy, thought she was Stuart's mistress, but he had no sexual interest in her or any other woman.

Stuart put his arm around her sometimes in the presence of others. He winked at her and smiled at her in special ways. He wanted them to think he was strong and virile, but he was tired, depressed, and impotent. Evelyn allowed the others to think she had slept her way to her position. They didn't respect her or the job she did, but they feared her and didn't stand too close or say suggestive things the way most men did. It made her personal life seem more interesting than it was, it pleased Stuart, and she intended to be the first woman director of NAZA.

Pleasing Stuart was important to Evelyn because she had

never pleased anyone. "Get your big butt in here," her mother said, even when she wasn't angry. Evelyn exercised, she dieted, she lost weight everywhere but her ass. Her husband said that was the first thing he noticed and that helped, but that was when they were happy, before he got his degree and his job.

She never saw her father who died in Korea. She had had three stepfathers, all career military. One spent more time in Germany than he did at home, and her mother refused to accompany him, finding another husband who died in Vietnam. The last one never went anywhere. He was retired and mostly he watched television, drank beer, and brushed against her in the hall or accidentally walked in while she was in the shower.

Once he tried to get in bed with her. Her mother said he was drunk and thought he was in their bedroom. "Keep your big butt out of his way." Evelyn left home. The family of a high school friend took her in, and she attended classes and waited for her mother to come and get her. Her mother didn't come.

She worked as a waitress, took night classes, and was part of an anti-war group. She wanted everyone to love each other. Then Nixon started the draft lottery, and the group dissolved. She had intensified her protests and had been fired from her job. John, who had been a member of the group, took her in. She got another job, wrote anti-war pamphlets, and helped John complete his degree.

Then John accepted a job with a defense contractor. "Best pay, best fringe benefits, and best security," he told her while she stood speechless.

She should have left him then, but she was pregnant. They married, bought a house and a car. She gave up jeans, dressed like the wife of a man on his way to the top, talked about babies and recipes. She had done everything John asked her except give up her mind. She asked why there were no black executives. She didn't burn her bra, but she expressed sympathy with women who did. She didn't eat meat—not even at official dinners—she hadn't since junior high.

At a party the wife of one of John's superiors wore a leopard fur coat, and the other women sighed in envy. Evelyn tried to avoid her, but the woman had brushed the soft fur against Evelyn's cheek. "Doesn't that feel heavenly?" she asked.

"It feels like a dead animal," Evelyn said. It didn't seem like much; being married to John had sheathed her tongue. She might as well have said what she thought; John was furious. He said she envied his success, she wanted him to fail, she tried to hold him back because she couldn't compete with the other wives. "You stupid bitch, don't you understand they buy the bread you eat?"

"Maybe they bought your conscience, they didn't buy mine."

"You don't have a conscience, you have a cause. I'm tired of your self-righteous shit."

She had tried to make up, for Johnny's sake. She explained how she felt about animals. "For God's sake, Evelyn, we test weapons on animals," he exploded.

Evelyn was ashamed that she had stayed so long, that she had tried so hard to efface herself. Maybe no one wanted her, but endangered animals needed her. She would have to work at menial jobs and go to school part time to enter a profession in which few women succeeded, and she would have to leave Johnny behind. She had cried about it, prayed about it, she had talked to everyone she knew, but the answer was always the same. She could make it—alone.

She told Johnny. She hoped he understood. He sat stiffly, his hands at his side. He said nothing even though tears hung from the long eyelashes that were her gift to him. She had hugged him and kissed him and promised that she would come back for him, but he would not look at her, and when she left he would not say goodbye.

When she went to the bedroom to get her bags, John followed her. He threw her on the bed and held her down. She thought he was going to rape her, but he only wanted to humiliate her, holding her until, exhausted, she gave up the fight. He stood up. "Get out," he said.

Evelyn had gone back for her son as soon as she could. John had done a good job with him. He was a perfect gentleman, perfectly mannered, perfectly unfeeling, perfectly cruel. "Father and I have our life," he said, so stiffly she knew the words were memorized. "You are my mother, and I will always love you, but a boy needs a father to teach him manly things." She searched his eyes for feeling. "Father takes me to shoot doves. Sometimes we shoot pigeons. Real pigeons."

She had left the house in disgust as John had planned. He knew she could not stand deliberate cruelty. She could not shut out of her mind the soft doves with broken bodies and small dark eyes that blazed with pain. She thought of the pigeons, crowded into wire cages, frightened by the sounds of the guns, by the horny hands groping for them.

Johnny came for a holiday or a vacation, but he was hard, unfeeling, afraid she would destroy his masculinity. She cried in remorse. She should have stayed, she should have sacrificed herself for her son. No, that was the ultimate trap. John would have abased her until she had no dignity left, and then he would teach Johnny to do the same. She could see the fear in Johnny already, afraid to feel. He was a little boy trapped in the rigid posture of a soldier.

She looked at Randy Morgan. He too was a little boy. He hated her because he was afraid of her, because she was better at her job than he. Thank God for Stuart Johnson. He demanded the best from her, and she pleased him. She would see to it that the tiger was not killed.

It was dark when Jacob reached the truck, but the mule and dogs were as eager as he to get home. He loaded the cougar in its cage, and the mule jumped in the trailer and the dogs in the truck. He stopped in Fort Davis to pick up Reymundo Arredondo. For a week he had been in the field tracking the cougar. He was dirty, tired, and he needed help. Reymundo was young, strong, and a good companion. They would take care of the cougar, feed and put away the mule and dogs, drive to Fort Davis, have a couple of beers, steaks, and a few shots of bourbon while he listened to Reymundo talk. It was their ritual.

He liked being under the sun and stars with the mule, the dogs, the trail, but there were times he hungered for a human voice. He would laugh at Reymundo's stories of his wife and young children, and tell Reymundo about Red trying to get into his sleeping bag when it thundered, the eagle's nest he had discovered in the mountains, the moment he had seen the lion and known it was his.

He and Reymundo had finished the chores, and he had started to the house for a six-pack to help them on their way when he heard the telephone. There was a tiger loose in Texas. Rand Morgan explained that Texas Parks and Wildlife had recommended Jacob, and the Department of Interior had given NAZA permission to use him as long as needed.

It annoyed Jacob, that thrill of excitement that started somewhere below his navel. He had all the work he could handle, and they wanted him to track a tiger. That was the kind of challenge that had gotten him into trapping lions after he had failed to get a job as a biologist with the Feds. "I don't know anything about trapping tigers," he said.

"Neither does anyone else in this country. You're the most experienced cat trapper we have close by."

"It'll be a few days before I can get to it. I've got a cat that I've got to relocate." Cougars injured themselves if left for long in holding pens.

"Mr. Trace, you don't realize the urgency of the situation," Rand said. "According to the survivors, the tiger killed at least two people on the airplane. We have sent a chartered jet to pick you up at Marfa, the closest airport that can handle a Lear. We would like you to leave immediately, bringing only what is essential. We'll supply the rest when you get here. Can you leave now?"

Jacob disliked making decisions on the telephone, but he tingled with the excitement of the hunt and with more fear than he had ever known. Cougars were dangerous but not aggressive. Cornered, they would fight but preferred to run and when they fought, they usually attacked the dogs first. He wondered what his dogs would do if a tiger turned on them. Piss all over themselves and him too.

"I'm leaving now," he said, cursing himself for the fool he was.

Old Red had followed Jacob inside and flopped in his usual place before the couch. Red was the only companion Jacob had anymore, and he petted the dog while scanning the house for anything he needed to take with him. It was a small, two-bedroom, prefab house he had built four miles out of Fort Davis, too far for Pam. It remained much the way she left it, rugs on the floors, framed reproductions of impressionist paintings on the walls, a neat, efficient kitchen—she called it crowded—a small bedroom that was going to be a nursery and the master bedroom with the canopy bed and heirloom bedspread. The only changes he had made were the hat rack and gun case in the living room, the bootjack in the bedroom instead of the closet, the canopy off the bed, the gun magazines on the sofa, and the sex magazines in the bathroom.

Jacob grabbed his toothbrush, toothpaste, and razor, placed them in a bag, and checked his pockets. Keys to his house, which he locked only when he was gone for several days, keys to the truck, pocket knife, change, bandana, lock-blade knife in a sheath on his belt, waterproof Timex on his arm. He pulled out his billfold. Driver's license, hunting license, picture of Pam, telephone numbers of the regional office in Albuquerque and civilian contacts in Presidio, almost a hundred dollars, two national credit cards, two oil company credit cards, and a few large peso bills. Sometimes tracking cats required crossing the river. He carried telephone numbers of Mexican officials in Chihuahua and Durango, but sometimes *mordida* was faster.

His Ruger .44 magnum rifle and the tranquilizer gun were in the pickup. He took an extra box of bullets, extra darts, and bottles of tranquilizer from the bathroom closet, a six-pack from the refrigerator and led Red outside where Reymundo waited. "You're going to drive me to Marfa, and I want to pick up a bottle of bourbon on the way."

Jacob checked the lion and made sure the dogs were okay before he put Red in the kennel. Red shamed him with a look, and Jacob petted all the dogs again and promised, "I'll be back," before leaving.

In the truck, he outlined what he needed Reymundo to do—release the cat in the designated area and feed and water the dogs every day. "Keep the truck. I'll need you to pick me up when I get back. Need money?"

Reymundo shrugged. "Gas."

Jacob handed him the oil company cards and one of the national credit cards. "In case something breaks down," he said. "If you need cash, go to Mr. Williams at the bank. Tell him I'm out of town and you need a loan."

. . .

Jacob could see the Lear sitting at the deserted airport, the pilot standing beside it. He took the .44 magnum rifle and the CO2 Cap-Chur gun from the rack behind the seat, took a box of shells from the glove compartment and added it to the dirty duffel bag with his darts and drugs. "The only thing I know about tigers is that they eat people."

"Not if they get a sniff of you, they won't," Reymundo said.

Jacob laughed. He had bathed in the Rio Grande when the lion had led the dogs near it, but he couldn't remember how many days ago it had been, and he knew the smell of the trail was on him—sweat, smoke from campfires, the smell of the mule and dogs, the smell of the cat. It wasn't a bad smell, once he got used to it, but it took a couple of days.

Jacob walked to the airplane, Reymundo following with the bourbon and a large plastic cup of ice. Jacob stowed his gear, said goodbye to Reymundo, and poured himself a drink. The pilot dropped a packet in his lap. "Compliments of Rand Morgan." Jacob opened the packet and found a hasty collection of book and magazine articles on tigers.

One was a mystical book about the power of the tiger to look into a man's soul, to hypnotize one with fear, to stir primeval fears of nakedness and guilt before the savagery of nature. Never speak of a tiger by its name or it will appear, the book said. Jacob tossed the book aside. He needed information, not superstition. He didn't know what sights and sounds meant danger and which to ignore.

The other books and articles were more helpful. Tigers were unpredictable. Article after article pointed that out. They were solitary, individualistic, together only when mating. Some tigers were mean tempered, others not, some very aggressive. Some tigers were curious about humans and entered villages, even houses, without attacking. Jacob laughed, imagining some cowboy waking up with a tiger staring at him out of curiosity. But how did one know when they were aggressive? When they were breeding and when they were feeding, the books said.

The tiger was the most bloodthirsty predator, the best equipped for killing and the most feared by man. A tiger could sneak through cover as fast as it could trot. It could lie flat, seeming to sink into the ground. Tigers were very strong and with a forepaw could disable a buffalo with one stroke, often breaking its back. A tiger had jumped out of a cattle pen over a six-foot fence carrying a large calf. Single tigers had destroyed whole herds of cattle. With its short broad head and short jaws a tiger was able to crack the bones of a buffalo, even the strong bones of the pelvis.

Tigers had little sense of smell but keen eyesight. The eye of a tiger was particularly brilliant. A tiger averaged forty pounds of meat a day but might not feed every day. They hunted alone, easily traveling twenty miles a day. Jacob whistled. In a week the tiger could be in San Antonio, Laredo, Mexico. It could be anywhere except the Gulf of Mexico. One tiger had a range of two hundred square miles. *Damn!* Sometimes a tiger worked its territory back and forth although usually it encircled it. This was a zoo tiger without a hunting territory. It might travel across country or settle down to ravage a village.

In India, more than forty people were killed every year by tigers. In one area, a dozen villages were abandoned because of a tiger. *One tiger, twelve villages,* Jacob thought, picturing the panic if someone were killed in a suburb or one of the rural towns outside Corpus Christi. One tiger killed a cow, then the herdsman sent to look for the cow, then a second herdsman, then another cow in the same day.

The books said that hunting a man-eating tiger alone and

on foot was an unpleasant way to commit suicide. They described hunts from the backs of elephants or with dozens of beaters driving a tiger to hunters who waited out of reach of the tiger. He had no elephants, and he could think of no way he could hire beaters to walk through the brush whistling and banging pans to drive the tiger to him.

Nothing in Jacob's experience prepared him for this; the only way he knew to hunt cats was with dogs. And this was no ordinary hunt, trailing an animal until he could capture and cage it. He had to catch the tiger before it killed.

3

When they were certain Jacob Trace was on the way, Rand and Evelyn took a cab to Hooks airport where the weather was better and chartered a Cessna to Corpus Christi. There, Rand rented a car and dropped Evelyn at Sandy Shores Hotel. He wanted to charter a boat, but the Coast Guard had sealed the crash area. He drove to the Naval Air Station, showed credentials, and was sent to a huge hangar. He was surprised to see so many survivors. So many reporters. He was inquiring whether the Russian veterinarian survived when he saw Hailee. He told Hailee that a lion trapper would be arriving soon. "Corpus Christi International."

"I'll be there," she said.

When officials located Arina, he introduced himself and offered to take her to the hotel. On the way, he told her of Jacob Trace who was coming to locate and capture the tiger.

"I want to talk with Jacob Trace. But first, I must call Moscow. I must talk to the director."

"I'll call you before I leave for the airport, but I won't be able to wait." Rand did not intend to miss greeting Jacob before the camera.

"I have no clothes. My bags—"

Rand had hoped to meet Jacob Trace alone, just the two of them before the cameras. He knew Evelyn might have something Arina could wear, but if Arina went to the airport, Evelyn would also insist on going, and he didn't want Evelyn taking over. If he didn't get Arina clothes, she might complain to Moscow who might complain to Stuart who might put Evelyn in charge. "I'll see if Ms. Price has something you can wear."

Rand bathed, shaved, put on fresh clothes for the camera, and arranged a press conference with Trace in the hotel.

Arina sat on the bed waiting for Mikhail Kuzakov to return her call. Exhausted by the long, rough flight, she had used the last of her reserves facing the tiger, crashing into the sea, and being pinned in the wreckage. She and the others had waded away from the wrecked aircraft and huddled in shivering groups.

The Americans had surprised her; Americans were supposed to be egocentric. Like people everywhere some had panicked, some thought only of themselves, but the nasty American and the woman with orange hair had both acted bravely. The crew had been courageous, especially the captain who had crash-landed the airplane although mortally wounded.

Small boats had taken them to a huge hangar. She had been examined by doctors, then officials and the media—she could not always distinguish between them—who seemed more interested in details of the crash and the tiger than about her citizenship, although her documents and her luggage had been lost on the airplane.

"Where were you sitting when the plane crashed?" "How did you feel when you saw the tiger?" "Did you see the tiger eat the pilot?" "Is it true you rescued a passenger by kicking the tiger?" "What will the tiger do if it is alive?" "What will Moscow do if it is dead?" "What's it like being a woman veterinarian in Russia?" "What is your impression of America?"

So many trivial questions. Perhaps she would still be there if the orange-haired lady had not described in detail the killing of the copilot and how she had shielded a frightened man with her own body. An official from the zoo had taken Arina to a hotel. She had no luggage, but the hotel furnished soap, shampoo, and a bathrobe. She had to stay awake until she talked to Kuzakov. She thought of calling Andrei. She could tell him what she had endured, tell him about the media that had been as aggressive as the tiger. He would understand how tired and lonely she was.

She turned on both the radio and the television to keep awake but little of what she heard made sense. There were interviews with relatives of the dead who competed to exhibit the most grief and with survivors who vied to report the most horrifying and grisly story. Both television and radio interrupted the stories to sell frivolous items. Both reported that a tiger was believed to have escaped the crash. Both broadcast government announcements calling for calm, stating that the tiger was not believed to be dangerous. Both warned that a tiger was a good swimmer and could be outside the door at this moment. Lock your doors, lock your gates, lock up your pets. Don't go out unless necessary. Stay tuned for further reports.

A tiger had been seen downtown on Ocean Drive, near the pier at Port Aransas, outside the Lyndon Johnson space center, two hundred miles away. One person said the crash was deliberate so that Russians could steal space secrets. *How could such silly people become so rich? So powerful?*

Although Arina was certain there had been few deaths, reporters announced scores of dead and injured. One reporter identified her as a Russian diplomat and said she was dead. Another said a tiger would find its way to the zoo because that's what it knew best. One declared a tiger loose in Corpus Christi could kill more than a dozen people a night.

American reporters had a divine sense for the facile and imbecilic. What contempt they must have for those who read or heard them. They mistook their freedom to inform and to influence opinion as a license to report the trivial and to sell their worthless goods.

She jerked upright to see a man in war clothes on television. *Why had the Americans alerted the military? Such a paranoid country.* But no, he wasn't in the military, he was in the militia. He boasted of armed followers who were patrolling the streets to shoot the tiger on sight. The interviewer said the tiger was a protected animal and mentioned international relations, but the man—Bump Wilkerson, a ridiculous name—was not concerned about protected animals or international relations.

"The animal rights people and the Russians can go to hell," he said. "This is the reason our forefathers gave us the Second Amendment, to stop invasions such as this. And if the Russians think they can send a bunch of people over here to look for the tiger and snoop on the citizens of this country, they are dead wrong. And the same goes for the ATF and the FBI."

She wondered if the American tiger catcher, Jacob Trace, was similar to Bump. The peasants had more guns than the Russian army, and they were so eager to kill. No doubt they thought there was money to be made from killing the tiger.

Americans would kill for money, of that she was certain. She was a representative of the Moscow zoo, and the responsibility for the tiger was hers. She would insist that if Mr. Trace could not capture the tiger they bring in Russian tiger hunters.

What a chaotic country. Who could live here? She must remember to tell Andrei about the beautiful woman with the foolish name, Hailee. And the anarchist named Bump. *Why did Americans give their children ridiculous names? Why did they feel they must be armed against each other?* She would tell funny stories of America to cheer him.

Andrei loved to talk of the days when the Soviets defeated the Nazis. "We were united then. Our armies could have captured all of Europe, but Stalin trusted Roosevelt and Churchill. He allowed them to carve Europe, to divide Germany, even Berlin that we had taken. If only the Soviets had gotten the atomic bomb first. Imagine what the world would be like today. It would be the Americans who had to give concessions in Cuba, Korea, Vietnam."

Such an idealist. So passionate. It was that passion that attracted her to him, and frightened her away. That passion for his country, his work as a scientist. The telephone startled her. Moscow was on the line.

Mikhail Kuzakov reported that Adja Bayan's cat had been properly disposed of and waited to discover whether he had done the right thing. Even over the telephone the minister's agitation was apparent.

"We fear rogue scientists succeeded in developing feline carriers," the minister said, "including the tigers loaned to America."

"Feline carriers are harmless in zoos."

"The airplane carrying the tigers has crashed," the minister said. "There are reports that one of the tigers is alive."

Mikhail shuddered. If hooligan groups in America learned that Russia had sent tigers to their country to spread deadly diseases, nothing could prevent America from going to war.

"You will see to it that the tigers are properly disposed of." The minister rang off before Kuzakov could ask if Dr. Yeroskin had survived, and if so, how he could contact her.

While puzzling over how to proceed, Kuzakov was handed a message that Dr. Yeroskin had tried to contact him. He called the number she left. "Are the tigers dead?" he asked when he heard her voice.

"It is impossible to know anything here. There are news reporters everywhere, and they report everything—a tiger has escaped, Russia arranged the crash so we could steal their secrets, Russians are going to hunt the tiger so they can examine citizens' houses. Some ruffian group has organized to kill the tiger. Mikhail, you cannot believe—"

There was no one to ask what he should hear from this news. *Did the Americans know about the secret experiments? Did renegade scientists remain at the zoo?* "If the tigers are dead you must confirm their deaths and destroy their bodies. If a tiger is alive you must discover whether it is placed normally in a zoo or whether it is kept elsewhere—"

"You mean in a veterinary hospital?"

Fool, he wanted to shout, *don't you know how paranoid the FBI is? The CIA?* "You will insist that dead or alive the tigers must be returned to us. You will determine that they are dead and destroy their bodies, or you will discover whether any are alive and in what circumstances they are kept. You will remain in America until the disposition of the tigers is satisfactory to me."

"Please inform Dr. Velinsky that I will be in America longer than I had planned."

"I will be speaking to Dr. Velinsky shortly," the director said.

. . .

Dr. Velinsky was not pleased being called to the director's office.

Andrei Velinksy did not like Kuzakov, a bureaucrat who had no ideology, no commitment to anything other than his paycheck, like a dog that was loyal to whomever fed it. That was why Velinsky preferred cats. Feed a tiger as long as you like, if you were careless you could be its next meal. To preserve the sanctity of his paycheck the director did whatever he was told: eliminate the experiments, remove the scientists.

Andrei locked the lab, skirted the antelope compound, and entered the main building. The floor was bare, and his footsteps echoed although he tried to walk softly. Mikhail Kuzakov's office was large with two overstuffed chairs that faced a desk and a wall that had once held Lenin's picture. Now heads of animals, once residents of the zoo, flanked the windows that offered a view of the traffic on the Sadovaye Ring. A huge stuffed bear stood in the corner.

"You wished to see me?" he inquired. He watched Kuzakov lace his long, thin fingers together and wondered how a man could have that much black hair on the backs of his hands and so little on his head.

"Yes, about Adja Bayan."

"Ah, the Mongol." Velinsky did not like Adja because the old man flaunted rules and disobeyed orders, a loose thread in the fabric of the most efficient system the world had known. Such people should have been eliminated long ago so they did not mar the beauty of the pattern. Lazy workers lounging beside their tools while production goals collapsed. Their lassitude was incredible. He and Arina had argued about it many times. She said the desire for consumer goods made Americans more productive. He pointed out that their unending greed for worthless products made them victims of exploitation. As for their selfishness, putting themselves before the good of the state was abominable.

"Adja Bayan is dead," the director said. "He had a cat in his room. A coincidence is it not?"

A chill ran up Velinsky's back, but his face revealed nothing. He had been interrogated before. The fool Adja probably fed it with scraps from the tiger cages, had permitted the cat to bite him. "Cats were forbidden."

The director stared at him with icy silence. Velinsky stared back. Silence would not force him to talk. "There are no illegal experiments being conducted here?"

"None."

"The Afghanistan Alternative was terminated?"

"Of course." He almost said, "comrade," a fatal mistake. "The records and the animals were destroyed." He should have told Arina about the tigers, but they were caged. Now she was in Houston, and he did not know where.

"And since that time you have been working on—?"

"Health and propagation. Conditions have not been ideal since . . . democracy." The new vocabulary was awkward for him. "Conditions are worse in the republics. We have to conserve the animals we have."

"Have not the scientists caused enough trouble? Doing it on the left," Kuzakov said with all the contempt he felt for those who tweaked their noses at the rules and those who permitted such deviation.

The director was holding something back. Velinsky knew the power of secrecy and the fear when one recognized information was being withheld. "The tigers should be safely in American zoos by now. Have you heard from Arin—Dr. Yeroskin?"

"Do not attempt to contact Dr. Yeroskin. Do not accept any calls from her in your lab or anywhere else. That is all for now."

. . .

Hunting a tiger was thirsty work. Jimmy Guy Jameson and the four militiamen crowded into the Bronco began the search with beers in hand and rifles pointed at the floor. The search area Bump had given them was the deserted backroads around Laguna Larga. They had driven back into Corpus for two more six-packs, but Jimmy Guy was thirsty again.

Jimmy Guy Jameson had gone to Vietnam an alcoholic, and that country had done little to improve his habits. Jimmy Guy, who had supervised Vietnamese in a base laundry in Chu Lai, had learned two things in Vietnam—the government couldn't be trusted and the blacks planned a revolution. He had harbored those thoughts in the hard years after Vietnam. Hard because he couldn't keep a job. He was fired because he didn't come in some morning or came in so sick he couldn't work. It was malaria, he told them. Agent Orange. He sold used cars for a while, ran a swap shop, a flea market, sold guns, TVs of questionable ownership.

The only woman he had ever loved, Maureen, left soon after he returned from Vietnam. That other bitch, Betty Lou, stuck around as long as the sticking was easy, but when it got tough she split like everyone else he had ever cared for. Took the kids with her.

One Sunday morning he lay in bed smoking and listening to the radio preachers. Jimmy Guy wanted his kids to go to church, but he listened to radio and television preachers because they understood that the government was out of control, telling people they couldn't pray in school, couldn't put a Christmas tree in the courthouse, busing good kids to bad neighborhoods. Telling people they could kill unborn babies.

Jimmy Guy had a soft spot in his heart for kids. On Sunday morning he missed his kids more than any other time. Sometimes he thought of going to see them, but having to face their lumpy bitch mother was more than he could bear, the way he felt in the morning. But, by God, he'd kill the man who said his kids couldn't put up a Christmas tree.

One Sunday morning Bump Wilkerson knocked on the door of his rented trailer. "Mr. Jameson, I understand you were in Vietnam."

"Damn straight, and you can call me Jimmy Guy."

Bump was young, not big, but you could tell he was tough. Some said he was called Bump because he was a bow hunter and could sit motionless for hours as invisible as a bump on a tree. It was scary the way Bump knew the brush country and could walk through it without anyone seeing or hearing him, without leaving a track or getting a scratch. Sometimes he thought Bump had been born in a brush pile.

Others said he was called Bump because he walked directly in your face so that you had to step out of his way or be run into. Jimmy Guy also knew about the missing finger. Bump crushed his finger in a ranch accident. The finger required a tension splint, but that meant he couldn't play football. It wasn't his trigger finger, and he didn't use it for bow hunting, so Bump had the finger amputated so he could play football. He wasn't a star; he wasn't even a starter. He was committed.

Bump sat in the littered front room of the trailer and showed Jimmy Guy a thick notebook of proof that the United Nations had been created as a world government designed to take over the United States, turn it into a socialist country, and obliterate the white race. "Wetbacks crossing the border to get food stamps and vote for Communists. Blacks, browns, and yellows breeding with white people to mongrelize the race. They intend to destroy the Constitution and the Bill of Rights, beginning with the Second Amendment. Before they can completely take over, they have to disarm the citizens." For a kid, Bump made a lot of sense.

Bump was organizing militia to train in scouting, sniping, survival. They patrolled, looking for UN bases in Texas and intercepting wetbacks and scaring them back where they came from. That brought them to the attention of the authorities. Bump needed more members and firepower.

"I have fifteen members but none of them has ever killed a man. That's why I've come to you. I want you to be my executive officer."

Jimmy Guy had never killed a man either. He didn't own a gun, but if he had one he would sure as hell defend himself. White women, too. He had attended Klan meetings, but they were too theoretical. In Bump and the militia he saw friends who wouldn't run out on him when he was sick or things were tough. "You got your man, but I don't have a gun right now."

Bump looked at him, his mouth screwed a little to one side. When Bump looked like that, his eyes were steady and malevolent like a snake's eyes. Jimmy Guy looked away. "My ex-wife took it," he lied. "Bitch."

"I'll get you a gun. We practice on javelina, feral hogs, skunks. Skunks are carriers. Like liberals and them animal rights people."

Since that day Jimmy Guy had not felt alone. He was exec, and he had his own squad—the guys in the Bronco with him—guys who liked a few beers after training, a Mexican whore after maneuvers. "Hell, there's not any tiger out here," he said. "If there was you couldn't see it in the dark. Let's get back to Corpus before the bars close."

"Bump won't like it," Justin the Kid said, looking at Mike for support. Jimmy Guy looked at Mike too, but Mike said nothing.

"Bump won't know," Jimmy Guy said, looking at Hubert. The old man didn't want to get in wrong with Bump, but he liked a couple of beers himself. Mike wouldn't object unless Hubert did.

They drove back to Corpus to a bar at the edge of town. He should have known there would be trouble when they walked in. There was a Mexican flag over the bar, Tejano music on the jukebox, and Jimmy Guy was the whitest person in the room.

Hailee and her cameraman waited inside the GenAv hangar; she didn't want to alert other reporters that a tiger hunter was arriving on a chartered flight. She couldn't remember when she had slept last, but she was pumped up. Until Rand Morgan told her about Trace, she had no plan other than driving the backroads hoping to get the tiger on camera. She smiled thinking of traffic jams of reporters, photographers, hunters, and militiamen looking for the tiger and federal and state wildlife people trying to protect it. She hoped Jacob Trace wasn't an old fool. She needed a rugged, charismatic hero who made folksy but pithy statements. She wanted stories viewers could shout from car windows—exciting, real life stories of power and violence, good and evil.

She had gotten the jump on everyone about a tiger loose in the airplane, and the network had told her to stay on top of the story. She had made network spots with survivors and their horrifying stories and an announcement that a tiger was believed to be loose in Texas.

She hoped her parents had seen her doing a live report from Houston. She hoped everyone in Midlothian had seen her. She hoped that the tiger was loose and that it would stay that way for a few days so it could grow into a bigger story—interviews with terrified people who had encountered the tiger, footage of the tiger itself, and then a dramatic capture.

There was no power on earth that could get her off this story. It was big, it was hers, and it was taking her to the top.

Harriet Lee White had been Midlothian High School Homecoming Queen, Miss Midlothian, and runner-up for Miss Texas. Runner-up because her breasts weren't oversized. People asked, "Where's Midlothian?" "Just beneath Dallas," she answered.

Everything she knew was beneath Dallas. Even Houston. She had gone to SMU to be a teacher; her father and mother were teachers. Then she had met Judd Ashbel, a drama major. "Jerk," she muttered, loud enough for Tony Garcia to look at her. She became a drama major to please Judd Ashbel, and even the Dallas critics liked her, and they didn't like anyone.

She had been too good, overshadowing Judd, who lost confidence in himself, married a freshman ingénue who forgot to take her pill, and got a job selling cemetery plots. She had given Judd more than she had given any man. The Miss Texas contest was to show him what he had lost. When she didn't win the crown she knew she had something to prove—Hailee White was not runner-up to anyone.

She groaned at her last name. Black would have been better, but it was too obvious to change to that now. Hailee Morgan. Housewife. Hailee Trace. Stripper. It was a game she played when she met men, trying on their name. She needed something memorable. She would marry when the right man came along. Someone with money but not an entertainer—too frivolous. Not in the media—too competitive. A politician would be perfect. They could do favors for each other.

Hailee sighed. Until her politician came along she needed the tiger loose for a while. She needed Jacob Trace to be someone who could captivate the country for thirty seconds.

· · ·

Rand drove Evelyn and Arina to the airport. Even the sight of Hailee and Tony did not cheer him. He was the one who had called Jacob Trace, and if Trace failed, Evelyn would blame him.

Rand wished he were home with Peggy and the kids. They thought he was a success; they thought he would be the next director. That's what he had been led to believe. Peg would be devastated, humiliated after what she had told her family and friends. It wasn't the money or the title; it was travel, White House dinners with foreign dignitaries. Peg planned what she would wear, what she would say to the First Lady. But it wouldn't be Peg in the long gown that she had already mentally designed three times; it would be Ms. Price in a butchy tailored tux.

This tiger affair was going to end badly. He couldn't compete with Evelyn Price. He couldn't be that mean, that devious. She was a woman, and he had to be courteous to her. He was a man and had to take the blame even if it wasn't his fault. It wasn't fair.

Evelyn had hoped to be friends with the Russian; it couldn't be easy to be a woman veterinarian in Russia. The woman seemed grateful for the loan of her clothes but was more Russian than woman. When she met Hailee at the airport, Evelyn wanted to like her, but Hailee was too pretty, too willing to use her femininity to make her way.

Evelyn was tired, cross, and irritated by Randy being his officious self. He was an assistant director the same as she, but he thought being a man made him her superior. She had faced that attitude all her life. She had called him Randy once, a bit of irony because Morgan was not randy. To her amusement he had turned red with anger. She had never called him anything but Randy again.

She admired Jacob Trace because he did not kill cougars;

he transported them to an area where they could live wild and free. She hoped he could capture the tiger before some fool militiaman or frightened farmer killed it. She wished it did not have to be captured at all, locked away in a zoo. It would almost have been better if the tiger had died with the others in the airplane, rather than to have a taste of freedom and then be hunted down, captured, and locked behind bars. She would help capture the tiger, but she would not let it be tormented or harmed.

When Jacob Trace stepped off the airplane, carrying his rifle in one hand and the tranquilizer gun in the other, he was met by the blazing lights of the television camera. Hailee tried to question him about the rifle but was prevented by Rand who insisted she ask her questions at the press conference with the other reporters.

"Keep the camera going," Hailee yelled, catching a whiff of Jacob's whiskey breath. Tony took shots of Jacob staggering across the hangar until Evelyn led him through a door into a private office GenAv had arranged for them. Once the door had closed behind them, Rand introduced Jacob, who slumped into the nearest chair.

Jacob had been asleep when the airplane landed and, still groggy, had stumbled off the airplane into the blinding lights of the camera. Around the edges of the lights, he could see three women. When he was on the trail, Jacob didn't think of women until he crawled into his sleeping bag. If he were tired enough, he didn't think of them then. Only when he turned toward home, only when he opened the door knowing that Pam would not be waiting for him was he overcome with loneliness and turned to the bottle to help him sleep. He stayed home no longer than he had to.

The city, even a small one, brought him the sight, the

smell, the sounds of women talking, laughing. He found being close to them unbearable, he wanted them so desperately, but he could not share the tenderness he had known with Pam. He did not want to use them for his own pleasure, and the thought of prostitutes sickened him. He wanted fulfillment, not release.

Then he stumbled off the airplane into the presence of three women, all of them desirable in his loneliness and need, all of them repelled by his stench, his whiskey breath, his filthy clothes. He had seen the television reporter's look of disgust before he had escaped into the office.

"The rifle is not necessary," Evelyn said. "The tiger is not to be harmed."

Jacob did not get up or put aside the guns in his lap. With his eyes shielded by his hat, he studied her the way he studied sign on the trail. She was not as pretty as the television reporter, her lips flattened a little over her teeth, but she had striking features and soft hazel eyes, not domineering but determined. A woman who knew what she wanted. "I trap cougars for a living," he said. "Cougars are not normally dangerous, but I wouldn't go after one without a rifle. I don't know tigers, but I damn sure will not go after a tiger without a rifle."

Evelyn looked at Rand, but he said nothing. "Perhaps you should speak to Dr. Yeroskin about that. She's a Russian veterinarian. It's her tiger."

"Not until it's captured." He looked at the Russian. She was tired and without makeup, but prettier than Ms. Price. She had schoolteacher hair—neat, clean, but not stylish. Her mouth was almost too wide but turned up slightly at the corners. Her lips full, her dark eyes grave. Her fingers were long and tapered, and she chewed her nails. The Russian was tightly wound, and he was exhausted. "If you'll excuse me—"

"Mr. Trace," Rand said. "I have a press conference set up at the Sandy Shores Hotel in thirty minutes."

"The hell with it," Trace said. "I'm going to bed."

Arina watched him go with Rand trotting after him. *So American.* Dirty jeans, dirty boots, dirty denim shirt, dirty hair. *So arrogant.* No questions about the tiger. No time to learn. Only time to grab a gun.

The press conference had been a bust. Hailee knew the best footage she had was of Trace getting off the airplane carrying a rifle and Rand Morgan blocking her interview at the airport. Somehow Morgan had sobered Trace and convinced him to shave and bathe, but he still wore the filthy jeans. He was tan, muscular, good looking in a roughhewn way, but he had answered questions with a yes or no, letting Morgan do the talking.

Hailee didn't have much, but she was ahead of the pack, and she intended to stay that way. "Can you confirm that there is a tiger loose in Texas?" she asked.

"We have to presume the tiger is alive and on the mainland," Rand said.

"How about the other two tigers?" she asked.

"I'm afraid they're dead," Rand answered. "Divers will continue to search the wreckage, but the water is extremely murky. Visibility is zero. It will be some time before the Navy can remove the wreckage."

Rand announced that a media information office was being set up at the hotel, and reporters would receive information when there was something to report. Mr. Trace and Dr. Yeroskin would spend their time in the field and would communicate all information through him. Rand asked that members of the media refrain from interviewing them or interfering in their work. There would be a press conference and, if possible, an opportunity for pictures when the tiger was captured. "I want to thank all of you for your cooperation in this matter," Rand said.

Like hell, Hailee thought. It was almost morning and she was exhausted, but she waited in the lobby for a chance to talk to Jacob or Arina. They were escorted to their rooms by Rand Morgan. "Shoot some footage if you see either one," she told Tony. "I'm going to scout around."

The clerk refused to give her room numbers for Jacob or Arina, but for five dollars a bellboy was happy to oblige. On the third floor the elevators opened into a chamber that led to the restaurant. On either side of the chamber, steps led to doors that opened into wings of the hotel. Hailee opened the door to the south wing and was outside Jacob's room when she heard the door open again and she saw Evelyn Price enter the wing. Hailee walked down the corridor, pretending to fumble for a key. They would move Jacob if they discovered she knew his room.

Evelyn knocked on a door, but the voice that answered was not that of Trace. "My hand case," Arina said. "Thank you. All my money is here. But what of my luggage? I have no papers, no equipment."

"It wasn't easy getting this," Evelyn said. "Customs officials seem to think you are carrying some rather odd items."

"Not if you are working with tigers. Do you know if the vials are still intact?"

"All I know is there seems to be some problem with the . . . uh . . . gun."

"Blowgun," Arina said. "It is for tranquilizing tigers."

The two women said goodnight, and Hailee listened to Evelyn's footsteps fade down the hall, then followed. She caught up with Evelyn at the elevator. "Ms. Price," she said, pretending surprise. "What do you think of the tiger hunter? Just between us girls."

"He's never seen a tiger unless they have one in the Fort Davis zoo. I understand there is a lot of brush in South Texas and a lot for a tiger to eat. I don't think Mr. Trace or anyone else will see it again."

"You sound like you wouldn't mind if the tiger vanished."

"The problem is man and his incessant demand for reproduction. Between us girls, I almost wish for a virus that could painlessly wipe out a large portion of the population. I'd like to wake up one morning to discover that most of the people had vanished, and trees, whales, tigers, elephants had a chance to recover, maybe to survive another century."

Fifteen years earlier Bud Stebbins and Jim Lewis had laid claim to the forty-yard strip of grass-covered sand that rose no more than three feet above the Laguna Madre. They hauled scrap lumber twenty-five miles down the canal from the causeway to the narrow bar to build the two-room cabin. It had no electricity, plumbing, running water, screens on the doors or windows, and they had to haul gasoline lanterns, stove, and drinking water for their long weekends.

They did it for moments like this one when they stumbled out of the cabin to drink coffee and to watch dawn paint itself on the lagoon. In San Antonio, they supported homes, church, PTA, Little League, Boy Scouts, Indian Guides, piano lessons, riding lessons, and the boat. It took five hours to get the boat from home to the fishing shack. This was their reward for responsible if uneventful lives.

"Fire up the grill, and we'll have the last of the steaks for breakfast," Bud said. Fishing had been so good they had steak left over.

Jim poured charcoal into the barrel barbecue pit behind the shack and lighted it. Bud went into the shack, got a fresh cup of coffee, and brought the steaks outside. He removed the butcher paper from two huge sirloins and laid the meat on a small table beside the barbecue pit. Blood from the steaks ran across the uneven table and dripped into the sand.

Jim examined the steaks. "Aren't you going to eat anything?"

"Damned hog, if that won't fill you up you can eat some of that Vienna sausage we got left."

Jim laughed and went inside for more coffee. He had scarcely picked up the pot when he heard a gasp. Bud had either seen a huge school of redfish or a naked wader. He walked outside and followed Bud's gaze to see something gliding along the ribbon of gold on the surface of the lagoon, gliding toward them. "Don't move," he whispered.

"If I don't move, my bowels will," Bud said.

A tiger sprang out of the sea oats and cord grass, devoured the steaks, sniffed at Bud, and bounded away. Bud did not move. His bowels did.

4

Bud Stebbins and Jim Lewis hastily packed their gear and headed north along the Intracoastal Waterway. They saw lifejackets and other debris before they came upon the crash site guarded by the Coast Guard and had to detour across the flats. When they reached the marina they told what they had seen.

Their story spread quickly. Hailee White interviewed the two fishermen who said the tiger was as big as a cow and a woman who had seen the tiger headed north on a cattle truck. Hailee caught the nation's attention with her wrap-up, "Tigers come in two sizes here—Texas or Hollywood, over-sized or over-blown."

Russia offered experienced tiger hunters. Federal officials declined, fearing a meeting between Russian hunters and militia would provoke an international incident. Also, the hunters, like the dozens of American volunteers, were experienced in killing rather than capturing tigers. Federal and state officials debated whether one lion trapper was better than a dozen trappers. The governor called out select National Guard units to protect citizens from the tiger. "And keep the militia and headline hunters out of the area," he ordered the guard.

Federal officials announced that two fishermen had encountered the tiger but had not been harmed. However, they advised citizens to exercise caution. They warned that the tiger was an endangered animal, the property of a foreign government, and that anyone harming the tiger might be liable to civil and criminal penalty. Radio talk show hosts cited the announcements as an example of the government protecting animals instead of people and broadcast statements by angry citizens who declared their right to defend their lives and property.

Television reported that many Russians demanded the return of the tiger; however, the Russian government was silent. The media carried stories of big game hunters who wanted to help capture the tiger. Texas wildlife officials said their help was neither needed nor wanted but passed advice from the hunters to Jacob. The advice consisted of sitting thirty feet above a baited trap—there were few thirty-foot trees in South Texas—and using beaters to drive the tiger. Jacob shook his head at the notion of recruiting beaters who would bang on pans and drums while marching abreast through the near impenetrable South Texas brush.

A rancher said he was hiring hunters to protect his livestock. A woman declared, "If that tiger gets after my little dog, I'll kill it same as I would a coyote." Bump Wilkerson said it was a government plot to bring Russian scientists, ATF and FBI agents, and UN helicopters to Texas. He pledged his militiamen would hunt down the tiger and kill it.

. . .

Late that afternoon a National Park Service naturalist took Rand, Evelyn, Arina, and Jacob to Bud and Jim's cabin and then to the mainland. They were tired and spoke only as necessary. Arina wore new jeans and a cotton shirt. Jacob wore the same clothes, but the hotel had washed them. He carried his knives, waterproof kit, the Ruger, and Cap-Chur gun and darts. Arina carried the valise with her blowgun and vials.

"I use a solution of ketamine, an antibiotic, and xylazine, 5 mg per pound on a cougar," Jacob said to Arina.

"It was the bigger lioness that escaped, roughly"—Arina figured kilograms into pounds—"four hundred pounds."

Jacob wanted to like the Russian. He had met several female vets in his work. Most of them had been conscientious, intelligent, and efficient. Maybe it was the Russian part that bothered him. *Suspicious. Haughty.* He studied the soft curve of her neck.

When the water became too shallow for the engine, the men took turns poling the boat to shore. Cautioning Rand and the women to stay in the boat so as not to disturb sign, Jacob and the naturalist searched the shoreline in different directions looking for tracks. It was nearly dusk when Jacob found impressions in the mud beneath the surface of the clear water in the shallows. The heavy animal had left the water, crossed the narrow strip of sand and dead marine grass that lined the shore, then melted into the brush thicket.

Jacob called the others to him. "Cat tracks," he said. "Heading west. Bigger than any cougar I've ever seen."

He rose, dusted his jeans, and followed the tracks into the thicket. He heard a cry and turned to see Arina caught in catclaw. "You have to walk carefully in this part of the country," he said. "Everything wears thorns, even some of the people." He tried to help her extricate herself.

She pulled away from the thorns ripping her skin and snagging the threads of her new shirt. Jacob got out his water-proof kit and sterilized the scratches, then walked to the water's edge where Rand and Evelyn waited. "This has to be our tiger, but it's hurt and that's not good. Look here. And here." Jacob moved toward the thicket. "The tiger is putting little pressure on that foot. The left rear leg is injured, maybe broken. We could find the tiger dead in the brush. What's left of it when the coyotes, buzzards, and wild hogs get through."

"Oh, no," Evelyn said.

"Or it could slow it down so that it can't kill easily. There's a lot for a tiger to eat around here—cattle, goats, deer, horses, feral hogs—if it can catch them. It's already tasted human flesh, and a man is a lot easier to kill. We may not have time to capture it alive."

"No," Arina said. "The tiger belongs to—"

"The tiger must be taken alive," Rand interrupted. "There is a great deal at stake here, Mr. Trace. Under no circumstances can the tiger be killed. Unless you agree to that we'll have to get someone else."

"There are already people looking for this tiger," Jacob said.

"Militiamen," Evelyn said. "Hunters. Can't they be stopped?"

"Stuart Johnson is lobbying the government to protect the tiger, to pass a law if necessary," Rand said.

"It'll take the government if this tiger kills livestock. So make up your mind. We don't have a whole lot of time to waste trying, and I mean trying, to catch this tiger."

"He's right, Randy," Evelyn said. "Who knows how long it will take to get someone else. I don't want to see the tiger killed, and neither does Mr. Trace. I believe he will do his best to capture it alive."

"Are you willing to take the responsibility if something happens to the tiger?" Rand asked.

"Of course, Randy," Evelyn said.

"Very well, unless Dr. Yeroskin has an objection—"

They looked at Arina who scratched her ankle where she had brushed into cactus. "Perhaps we should capture the tiger and then decide who shall be the hero," she said.

Jacob pulled the lockblade knife from the sheath attached to his belt. "I can shave those off," he said. "That's the only way to get the little ones." Arina braced herself while he held her leg and shaved her ankle with his knife. He was so close he could smell the womanness of her and feel her warmth. He dropped her leg and turned away. "Do you have any idea which way the tiger will go?"

"It is a zoo tiger; perhaps its instincts are confused. Ordinarily a tiger will look for an area free of people and will stay close to water to keep cool. Also, the diet of raw meat gives it a tremendous thirst."

"There's a lot of area in South Texas free of people and the farther west, the freer it is. Rand, we need dogs to put us on the trail. As dry as it's been, they may not help, but they're better than my eyes. What we really need is a helicopter to determine which direction the tiger is moving. Can you get one?"

"Certainly," Evelyn answered before Morgan could. Rand's face flushed into his thin hair, but he said nothing.

"Tell them to begin here and sweep from the gulf to, say, forty miles north along a west line. Let's get back to Corpus and see if there are any more reports."

The Department of Public Safety had received reports of more than a hundred tiger sightings over a wide area, including a tiger seen in San Antonio that was headed for the zoo.

· · ·

The next day Jacob returned to the tracks with dogs, but the trail was cold. For the next three days, he, Arina, and Evelyn checked out promising sightings but found nothing. Rand vacillated between going with them so he was there for the capture and staying in the press office so he could meet with the media.

Rand took Arina and Jacob shopping for clothes. Evelyn went along to offer advice on sizes and fashions but followed Jacob's suggestion of sturdy boots and heavy denim pants for the brush and cotton shirts for the heat. They met at breakfast to go over reported sightings and plan their day, and over dinner they talked about the day's failures.

"How are things in Russia?" Evelyn asked Arina.

"It has become much like your country. Much disorder, anger, violence, lawlessness."

"What lawlessness?" Jacob said.

"Small towns have tanks—"

"National Guard."

"I saw a warplane hidden in the trees."

"It's a children's playground."

"There is an aircraft carrier and warplanes outside the hotel."

"It's a museum."

America had so many warplanes and ships that they used them for museums and playgrounds. "I love my country as you love yours," Arina said. "Russia has problems, but Russians admit their problems. Americans pretend their country is perfect. Some say that with better leadership the Soviet Union could have been the model of success. Even so, the Soviets defeated the Nazis. If there had not been the encirclement by NATO, the government could have improved the lot of the people, been first to the moon. But always the United States was there like a sword over our heads, arming, stealing Soviet secrets, infiltrating the government."

Jacob and Rand argued loudly that America had won the war, the Soviets made threats, stole secrets. The argument became so rancorous that they decided to change the subject and talk of personal things.

Evelyn said that at the time of the plane crash, she had been in New Orleans where her son attended a military academy, although she thought he had the soul of an artist. She did not say her son saw her only because school officials required a boy to write to his mother, to meet her in the visitors' reception center, and to escort her to the mess hall.

Arina said little except that she was not married. She permitted them to think Andrei Velinsky was her boyfriend. Rand showed pictures of his wife and children. Jacob answered their questions about his background—the ranch near Ozona, his father teaching him to hunt and fish before dying when Jacob was twelve. His mother teaching him to cook, wash, iron. He did not tell them she tried to keep him too close to the house, wanted his approval of her decisions, her dresses, the way she looked, wanted him to tell her about his girlfriends. She was always after something inside him that he did not want to give, so he was guarded toward her, making her feel distant.

He told them when he was a boy he had found a tortoise shell that had been cleaned by ants. He took it to his mother. He did not tell them that she put it outside or that she kept it in the barn with the fossils and arrowheads he gave her. Or that Pam had thrown them away.

He told them about college at Angelo State, then master's degree in biology at Texas Tech where he met an undergraduate from Tyler. He didn't show them Pam's picture or tell them that she was gorgeous, spoiled, and in love with him because he was a cowboy and like nothing she had ever seen. He didn't tell them that she had a manicure party for her bridesmaids where they all had their fingernails done. He told them that after the wedding in Tyler he took her to a catfish farm to feed the fish.

"Are catfish sacred?" Arina asked.

A vein throbbed in her throat, and Jacob watched it in fascination. "Not unless they're fried," he said. Evelyn explained the joke.

"Does she mind that you are away from home?" Arina asked.

He didn't tell her Pam was depressed when he was gone, and that he was gone much of the time. They fought, she cried, they made up, and he left again. Once she was sick, her parents were in Europe, and he was in the mountains. She said she couldn't take it anymore and left. Two years later he received divorce papers through the mail.

Arina waited for an answer. "She turned me out of the barn," he said.

Roy Pat Honnecut saw the tiger in his sleep. He was back in Vietnam where men lived like animals, eating without appetite, coupling without joy, killing without care, sleeping without repose, living without maintenance. Roy Pat was a Christian. He had kept himself clean, his marriage pure; he had kept hope and purpose alive by prayer and Bible reading. And faith had kept him unafraid.

Roy Pat walked point with God. He was careful but not so fearful that his eyes flickered over the foliage without seeing boobytraps or ambushes, confident that the Lord would preserve him but not so foolhardy as to test God. Those who got drunk, took drugs, and slept with whores listened when he preached to them. They trusted him when he walked point with God beside him.

Then he saw the tiger. They had been on the move since first light, expecting to be hit at any moment. Roy Pat moved slowly, silently, his mind praising God, his senses alert. Slowly he pushed through vines, thick leaves, the ill-begotten creepers that tangled his feet and exhausted his will, and came face to face with a tiger, as silent, sudden, mysterious as an evil thought. He had looked into its unblinking eyes, had breathed its fetid breath, and his bowels turned to water. The tiger bared its fangs, then disappeared as suddenly and silently as it came, leaving him empty. He sank to the ground, unable to move. The patrol leader tapped him on the helmet. "What's the matter?" he asked. "Move out." Roy Pat couldn't move. The others milled around him in confusion.

When they returned to the base camp, Roy Pat brooded about the tiger, able to move secretly through the blind, uncontrolled, mindless living and dying that was without knowledge or plan. He knew the tiger wasn't the devil, but he also knew that Satan took many forms. Satan had come to him before as doubt and loneliness, but Roy Pat had resisted Satan. Then Satan came to him as a tiger that he saw every time he closed his eyes. Roy Pat got drunk in order to sleep. He woke up with his buddies jeering him and saw that he was lying with a woman. He had committed adultery. God would punish him for that.

On the next patrol, he had taken the point and walked into an ambush. After that no one trusted him. Satan had come to him as a tiger, and lust, fear, doubt had overcome him. Roy Pat no longer walked point with God.

Roy Pat was not a city boy, but he hated the jungle—the disarray of plants growing out of ghastly decay. Grotesque vines, misshapen trees, disfigured rocks, entangled in a never-ending fight for survival. He hated the disorder and disuse, the desperate groping and grappling for rank, untended survival. He hated it but did not fear it. With a bulldozer, a flamethrower, a plow, he could tame the jungle, could return it to order and usefulness. That was before he saw the tiger, its blazing eyes, the infernal stripes and colors that identified yet concealed it, the lips that trembled over the terrible yellow fangs. The lord of derangement.

Roy Pat liked the neatness, the fittingness, the orderly intricacy of machines. He often thought of God as Designer of a Celestial Machine whose parts ran smoothly and efficiently until man's clumsiness, his need to tinker, his sin, had fouled, almost wrecked the scheme.

Awakened by the dream of the tiger, Roy Pat slipped out of bed so as not to disturb his wife and went into the attached garage that was his workroom and study. He turned on the light, moved a disassembled FAL rifle from the table, and opened his Bible. Mary Pat often found him here, praying, reading his Bible, or working on a gun.

He and Mary Pat hadn't planned to marry, but he had enlisted the day she had graduated from high school. They had gone to the same party, they had left together high with excitement, he had gotten carried away, and although Mary Pat said no, she didn't resist. Afterward, she cried, and he said, we got to get married. He didn't ask her. He didn't know if she would say yes when the preacher asked her.

She lived with her parents and went to college while he was in the army and for the year afterward when he hitchhiked around the country running from God. He had seen the blind fecundity, the rank, teeming, cesspools of cities, people without will or goal. When he went to Vietnam he sometimes confused God and country as though they were the same. After Vietnam he saw America as the jungle.

By the time he returned to Mary Pat and got a job, she was teaching school. She had saved enough money to make a down payment on a run-down house at the edge of town. He worked at a garage, fixed up the house, and reloaded ammunition for friends. He worked on a couple of guns, and soon he had so much business he had to turn his garage into a workroom.

Despite his sin, God had saved him in Vietnam, and Roy Pat promised God he would save Him in America. When the vacant house across the street went on sale, he bought the house, tore out the inside walls, put in folding chairs, opened a church, and went from door to door inviting people.

His hunting and fishing buddies came out of curiosity. Neighbors dropped in to hear what he had to say. Mary Pat's folks never came. He wasn't educated like the dry-lipped preachers in the high-steeple churches, but he could hear the voice of God as clear as any man. God said the country was in the grip of those who intended to make it part of the devil United Nations where all religion would be abolished. Roy Pat guarded the frontier between right and godly living and licentious, government-sanctioned moral chaos. He had fought to save America from godlessness once, and he would do it again.

He and Mary Pat couldn't have children because Satan had come to him as a whore and blighted his seed, but he had started a school in the church where he taught children about the conspiracy. He asked his followers to send their children to his school or to teach them at home. Public schools were trying to make their kids just like everybody else, something he would never permit.

The government that allowed people to kill unborn children but wouldn't let him pray at a football game was the enemy. He prayed for God to clean out the whole governmental, bureaucratic, Hollywood, and homosexual mess so that they could start over. Flood or fire but give him and his followers a chance to do it right. Until that time, Roy Pat would fight Satan wherever he saw him.

Some were repelled by Roy Pat's uneducated speech and his fiery mixture of biblical prophecy and political objectives. Some were attracted to his simple understanding of what God expected of him, of them, and of God's chosen nation. In some, Roy Pat's anger ignited their own rage that life had not lived up to its advertisements. His followers left church confirmed in their indignation and the virtue of their cause.

Although he didn't ask for it, they gave him money. Roy Pat bought the vacant land next to the church for a parking lot and ball field. Children played there. He played with them sometimes, and they showed their appreciation by inviting him to pray at a middle school football game. Then some lawyer said he couldn't pray at a public gathering.

They wouldn't let him use the public address system, but when the teams lined up for the kickoff, Roy Pat walked into the middle of the field and he prayed. Folks bowed their heads, too, both teams.

Tax collectors tried to make him pay taxes on the ball field because he rented it to Little League. They audited his personal records, asked how much money he made from weddings and funerals. That's God's business, not Caesar's, he yelled at them. His people gave what they wanted, and he used it how God wanted, and it was nobody's business.

Some people asked questions about his school as though God didn't have freedom of speech in his classes. Spies listened to his sermons, and he told them that if the government didn't leave God-fearing people alone the government would hear from him. Folks said he didn't have a degree from a seminary. He told them he had a degree from Vietnam. They said he hadn't been ordained. God ordained him, and he didn't know anyone else who would. He wasn't going to ask the church Mary Pat's folks attended to ordain him; they believed he should obey the law rather than God.

Bump Wilkerson came to hear him and stayed to talk. Bump was a kid, but Roy Pat had seen kids like him in Vietnam, not afraid to kill. Bump asked if he could make an M-15 fully automatic. He could and an M-1, too. Could he repair a machine gun? Yes. Metalife? Yes. Mag-na-port? Yes. Noise and flash suppressors? Yes, and laser sights too.

Bump wanted him to reload ammo and repair and modify their weapons, and Roy Pat was willing if he could turn Bump's army into God's army. He wanted them to make his church safe from tax collectors, his prayers safe from oppressors. He wanted to make unborn babies safe from abortionists.

Roy Pat wanted the brigade, in camouflage masks, to take over the tax office, destroy records, blindfold and put the fear of God in appraisers, while he was holding a wedding or funeral in front of witnesses. He, himself, led the raid on the abortion clinic. The building was vandalized and those inside warned. Some of the women were roughed up. Roy Pat didn't approve of that, and he feared he or Bump would die before they came to an understanding. Women were not to be molested.

The raid on the tax office had been planned when Bump heard the Russians were sending a tiger to Texas. Bump said the tiger was a Trojan horse for Russian scientists. The FBI would pretend to watch the Russians but would spy on Americans to discover what kind of weapons they had.

Bump planned to slip into the zoo, kill the tiger, and leave a sign, "Wake Up, America!" Roy Pat agreed to help if Bump added, "The devil, as a roaring tiger, walketh about, seeking whom he may devour. I Peter 5:8." The plane crash and escape of the tiger sent Bump into a frenzy. South Texas would be crawling with Feds. Bump called out the brigade.

Roy Pat saw the tiger as a sign. Satan had come to him as a tiger, and Roy Pat had bowed to him. Satan would come again, but this time Roy Pat would be ready. He would face the tiger alone and armed with his faith, by the power of God, destroy evil. Roy Pat picked up the FAL, reassembled it, and looked through its sights, seeking the heart of Satan.

. . .

Every day brought more tiger sightings. Every dead animal that had been chewed on by scavengers was a tiger victim. Rand attempted to restrain the media. Evelyn met with civic, environmental, and animal rights groups to reassure them and enlist their support. Jacob and Arina checked out the sightings and carcasses game wardens thought likely.

Citizens went armed, and several animals had been mistaken for the tiger and shot—three orange calves, a large yellow dog, and a VW Beetle. Stuart Johnson's lobbying efforts with Congress aroused a firestorm of hate mail so that Congress decided to debate rather than take action. The White House repeated that the tiger was an endangered animal, the property of a foreign government, and ordered Federal agents to arrest anyone who injured it. The president proposed the government pay for any livestock killed by the tiger. Congressmen declared the president put the rights of Russians above the safety and property rights of US citizens. Radio talk show hosts declared that US citizens had to pay taxes so that a Russian tiger could kill American cows.

Because of media-whipped paranoia and hate, the FBI and ATF kept a low profile. It was dove season in Texas, and hunters were in the field with shotguns. State game wardens were in the field also, checking licenses and looking for rifles. Small National Guard units patrolled back roads, ostensibly on maneuvers, but their presence made hunters wary and kept Bump and his militia off the roads. It was a temporary solution. Deer season opened in November, sending hunters in the field with rifles.

Most people who knew Sam Storey thought he lived off his inheritance. Sam snorted at that. There had been nothing to inherit except the small tract of land in the flood plain of the Nueces River. Sam caught and sold catfish for a living.

Sam washed the battered pie pan and cracked cup that were his breakfast dishes, lit a cigarette, and stepped out the door of the cabin onto the tiny stoop on a tree limb. He peered through the canopy of tall oaks and hackberries at the heavy clouds. *Frog strangler*, he thought, rubbing the stub at the end of his left arm. His left hand had been caught in a winch cable when he was a boy working on a shrimp boat. The captain had put a tourniquet on the mangled arm and headed the boat for Rockport, but he had lost the hand, and the stump advised him of weather changes. Cool front and thunderstorms.

When his father died, he quit his job in a fish market in Aransas Pass—one of the few jobs a one-handed man could find, his boss frequently reminded him. He retreated to the river, built a cabin suspended in the trees of the timbered bottom, and the river had supplied his needs.

Although the cabin was eight feet above the ground, it had washed away three times. Other floods had reached the floor of the cabin forcing him to climb into one of the oaks, but the cabin had withstood the force of the raging river. T.C. had urged him to move to higher ground after each flood, but Sam had refused.

"Too damn far to walk to the water," he had told T.C. "I only been wiped out three times in forty years. Hell, a man needs to replace things now and then. They'll just rot if you don't."

Sam stepped back inside the cabin and stuffed the coffeepot, his good fishing hooks, and knives into a flour sack he used as a pillow case. He tied the bag in a tree above the cabin and walked down the wooden steps at the front of the cabin to the river. It was rising slowly.

"I might oughta pull my lines in," he said aloud. Big rises on the river cost him throwlines even if the water didn't reach his cabin. "And I better do something about them fish." Sam had almost a hundred pounds of catfish in live boxes hidden beneath the surface of the murky waters. T.C., who black-marketed skinned catfish to select restaurants in Corpus Christi, was supposed to pick up the fish, but he wasn't always reliable. Sometimes the game wardens got him.

Sam stepped to the tree where a line was tied and pulled in the throwline by wrapping the nylon cord around his forearm just above the stump. He dragged a two-pound channel catfish to the muddy bank, pinned the flopping fish with a booted foot, removed the hook, and slipped the fish into a gunnysack. He was squatting on the edge of the river, untying the second line, when he heard a soft sound behind him. He stopped and listened. He could feel the skin crawl where eyes stared at the back of his neck. Sam never had visitors except for T.C. or some other buyer, and they always drove up in the yard. Only a game warden sneaked around trying to catch him doing something wrong.

Sam had sold catfish most of his life, and he didn't intend to quit because the state made the sale illegal. He had never been caught because he kept his live boxes hidden and never hauled fish away from the river to sell them. T.C., the middleman, took most of the risks.

Sam listened but didn't move. Nothing visible around camp but the lines. If it was the law, they had nothing on him. Minding his own business, doing a little fishing.

Without rising, Sam turned his head slowly to look over his right shoulder. A few feet away, almost hidden in the weeds, something furry had washed up on the bank. Sam saw oval, almost liquid eyes, fixed on him. For a moment he could not comprehend the message his brain received, could not move. He watched in fascinated horror as the eyes became slits and the orange fur wrinkled and curled back over long fangs.

With a scream that died in his throat, Sam attempted to launch himself into the water. The teeth of the tiger bit into his neck, forcing his head down. Feebly, he flailed at the striped body until bone cracked, and his body went limp.

The tigress backed away from the water without releasing her grip on Sam's neck. She dragged the limp body to a patch of grass near the cabin and began to worry the overalls with her teeth and claws. Once she had the soft flesh of the belly exposed, she settled down to feed.

T.C. Schumacher turned off the highway and stopped at the wire gap in the fence. He opened the gap, pulled the wire out of the way, got back in the blue Dodge pickup, drove through, then got out and closed the fence. He knew Sam didn't have any livestock, but old habits were hard to break, and T.C. had been taught to leave gates the way he found them. He drove down the rutted track toward Sam's camp.

T.C. bought from several fishermen along the river. Occasionally he encountered an outlaw saltwater netter who had redfish or spotted sea trout to sell, and T.C. bought those too when he was positive the netter wasn't an undercover agent for the state, but most of the fish he peddled through the back doors of restaurants were catfish.

The track crossed a field of sunflowers and Johnson grass, then wound for almost two hundred yards through a tangle of pecans, hackberries, and oaks hung with Spanish moss. Storey's International pickup that might have once been brown was parked beneath the cabin, and T.C. expected Sam to meet him, two wet beers in hand, as usual. Wet, not cold, because Sam had no refrigeration except the river.

Sam will be pleased, T.C. thought. Wardens had arrested several outlaw fishermen on Lake Mathis, putting them temporarily out of business, and the price of fish was up.

T.C. stopped the truck near the trees that supported Sam's house. Sam was nowhere in sight. He tooted the horn, then opened the door and got out. "Sam," he called. "Get your ass in gear." He started to the river to get himself a beer when a blur of motion caught his sight. "Jesus," he screamed and jumped back in the truck as it was hit by a weight that rocked it on the springs. He locked both doors before turning the key and pumping the accelerator. "Goddamn truck," he yelled.

With a screech like chalk on a blackboard, claws slid across the windshield and ripped across the top of the cab. The engine started, and T.C. popped the clutch. The truck lurched forward, and the left front slammed into one of the trees supporting Sam's cabin. The shack shuddered, but T.C. hardly noticed. He threw the truck into reverse, then forward again, and sent the truck careening through the timber and across the field, not slowing to open the gate.

He turned on the highway and pressed the accelerator to the floor trying to outrun something that hung just at the edge of his mind, nibbling at his imagination. Something that he had seen or thought he had seen. Something that looked like a giant, swollen, fly-covered fish belly. Something that might have been Sam's bloated stomach. To force the sight from his mind, T.C. opened his mouth as wide as he could without closing his eyes to the highway and screamed.

Jacob was angry when he stepped from the deputy's car and saw the crowd. Two deputies, a highway patrolman, the county medical examiner, and his assistant had joined the neighbors, obliterating sign near what was left of the body. The tiger had ripped the flesh from Sam's buttocks and thighs before it had been disturbed by T.C.'s truck.

Jacob asked everyone to remain where they were while he circled. He found the trail of the tiger fifty feet from the body, but the find did not relieve his frustration. He didn't know how a tiger would react in a situation, but he did know it was impossible to track a cat in a crowd.

"It's our cat," Jacob said when he returned to the NAZA group. "This timber is the best cover in this area, and the tiger probably will stick to the river. If the cat goes downstream, it will run out of cover when it nears the bay; if it goes upstream it should stay in the bottom and give—"

"You said the tiger was not dangerous, yet this man is dead," Hailee said, shoving her mike under Jacob's nose. "Will the tiger kill again?"

There were so many people that Jacob hadn't noticed Hailee and her cameraman. Her question rekindled his anger, and he turned to face her. "I didn't say—"

"Excuse me, Mr. Trace, may I speak to you for a moment?" said Game Warden Carl Weber. "Over here, if you don't mind."

Jacob allowed himself to be led away. "I just got a call from my warden in Jim Wells County," Weber said. "Arthur Blevins—he's a big rancher down there—was rounding up cattle this morning by helicopter, and the pilot found one of Blevins' top Santa Gertrudis bulls. Something killed it last night and ate on it. Mr. Blevins thinks it's the tiger, and—"

"A tiger isn't going to cover that much country on a full stomach, then kill and eat again. There have been tiger sightings all over South Texas. You and your wardens are going to run your asses off chasing every report. The tiger was here."

"That's what I told my warden, but Mr. Blevins is pretty excited about his bull, and he's willing to send the chopper to get you."

"Tell him I'll come if he'll loan me the helicopter for a while." The warden walked back to his car radio.

Jacob called his group to him and explained about the dead bull. Arina shook her head. "Not another kill so quickly."

"I'll take a look so we can get the helicopter," he said. "As soon as possible, I'll have the pilot bring me back for an aerial search. Arina, I'm going to need some answers about tigers."

Arina nodded. "I will help," she said.

"Rand, will you and Ms. Price return to town and charter a helicopter we can use until we find the tiger? And call the zoo in San Antonio to see how long it will take for their portable cage to get here."

"Right," Rand said.

Jacob took the Ruger and the Cap-Chur gun from the car of the deputy who had brought him to the scene. Evelyn frowned. She hated guns, and she had agreed to take responsibility if something happened to the tiger. "Mr. Trace, you are aware of the importance of the tiger."

"I have two guns. One shoots darts, one shoots bullets. If I see the tiger I will try to capture it. If I can't, I will try to kill it. If someone had killed it yesterday, that man over there would still be alive."

Evelyn didn't like to see the death of anything, but she knew the kind of man Sam Storey was. A man who thought of no one but himself, had no purpose other than to eat and get drunk whenever he had two bills to rub together. The world was crowded with men like that. Tigers were rare and beautiful creatures that might disappear forever if they were not protected. "I'm going with you," Evelyn said.

"Suit yourself," he said and turned to Rand. "Can you stall Hailee long enough for me to get out of here in a helicopter?" Rand hesitated. He wasn't sure he could stop her, and he didn't want to get on the wrong side of the media. "Let her see the body," Jacob said. "Maybe she'll faint."

Rand chuckled. "She probably will," he said. "I almost did."

Hailee was talking to the state trooper and a deputy sheriff when Rand approached. "Yes, Mr. Morgan?" she said coolly. She hadn't gotten a decent quote from him since Houston.

"If you and your cameraman would like, I can arrange for you to take some footage of the . . . uh . . . deceased. You might not be able to—"

"Lead the way," Hailee said, motioning for Tony to follow. Rand led them to the body, and both were engrossed in filming the death scene when a helicopter settled noisily in the field beyond the woods. Hailee looked toward the sound.

"A Department of Public Safety helicopter, I believe," Rand said, turning away from the grisly scene.

Hailee turned back to Tony. "That's too close, Tony. What we want is suggestion. Close-ups of the blood on the trees there, where he was dragged through the weeds, long shots of the body, several different angles, just enough so you know it's a body. We want them to shiver, not barf. Leave the stomach out. I don't have the stomach for that," she said, looking at Tony, who gave her a tight-lipped smile.

The three-place Hughes 300C lifted out of the field and skimmed the trees, heading southward.

A powerful animal had gripped the bull by the throat and choked it to death. Fang marks in the throat were large and deep, and the shoulders of the bull looked as though they had been raked with knives. The ground around the bull was torn by hooves and claws.

The battle must have been spectacular, Jacob thought. He picked up the trail of the animal that had done the killing and followed the tracks to a mesquite thicket where it had bedded down to digest its meal. Jacob walked back to Blevins, Game Warden Bill Peale, helicopter pilot Barry Windom, and Ms. Price. "It's the tiger," Evelyn said. "It has to be."

"A different tiger did this," Jacob said. "Bigger, maybe twice as big as the one that killed the man on the river."

Evelyn could not mask her elation. "Two tigers," she said.

"Two tigers to worry about," Jacob said. "There's nothing wrong with this tiger that I can detect. It ate last night and probably won't kill again right away. If it does it will probably be something bigger than a man. I hope. I've got to get back to the river after the first tiger. It's far more dangerous than this one."

"That depends on your point of view," Blevins said. "I'm going after this one. I don't intend to lose any more stock."

"You promised me the chopper," Jacob said. "That was the deal."

Blevins turned a cold eye on Jacob. He was a big man, and he was used to getting his way. "I don't like going back on my word," he began.

"Then don't," Jacob said.

For a moment the two men stared at each other, then Blevins looked at his watch. "You got the chopper for one hour, cowboy. That's all the time you give me, and that's all the time I'm giving you. Barry, pick me up here. I'm going to town to get a rifle and Farley's dogs. There's five hundred for him if he trees the tiger, and he can have the hide."

"You want to be careful, Mr. Blevins," the warden said. "The Feds want that tiger alive."

"Come on, Evelyn," Jacob said. "We've got an hour to find the tiger."

"Aw, hell, Bill, I'm just going to scare the tiger away from my cows. The rifle is to protect Farley's dogs."

"Mr. Blevins," Evelyn said. "I forbid you to kill the tiger."

"You don't forbid a damn thing on my place," Blevins said.

"The Federal government has issued warnings—"

"I'll take my chances with the Federal government and a local jury. And you got a whole lot more to worry about than me. You got that damn militia that shoots at whatever moves.

If I ever prove they shot my horse, I'm going to put Bump's ass in jail."

Evelyn turned to the game warden, who was climbing into the truck. "Mr. Peale." If she showed any emotion these men would dismiss her as a hysterical woman. "I was sent here by the North American Zoological Association to make certain that we get the tiger back alive. It belongs to Russia. The State Department, the Fish and Wildlife Service, the state wildlife agency, all are vitally interested in capturing the tiger. You must not let Mr. Blevins kill the tiger."

"Ma'am, this is Mr. Blevins' land. He thinks he has the right to shoot anything that comes on his land and kills his bull, and there are a lot of folks around here that agree. It don't make any difference if it's a Russian tiger or a Russian general or whether you or I like it, 'cause he ain't going to ask us. That's the way it is. Only, I'm not going to be a witness to it."

Jacob turned to Evelyn. "We've got an hour to find the tiger."

"I'm not going to let him kill the tiger," Evelyn said defiantly.

"I'm going back to the river," Jacob said. He climbed into the helicopter. "What's the litter for?" he asked the pilot.

"Pick up stray calves. It won't take long to take it off."

"Let's go." The chopper rose from the brush land in a cloud of dust.

Evelyn and the rancher turned their backs to the whirlwind and closed their eyes until the dust settled, then squared off again. "Mr. Blevins, I am not leaving until the tiger is safely captured."

"Fine. You can be tiger bait. Better you than one of my bulls." Blevins climbed into his Jeep and drove away, leaving Evelyn with the buzzards that had been held at bay by the crowd around the carcass.

When Sam's camp on the river was in sight, Jacob leaned toward Barry. "First, let's make a low sweep up the river."

Barry nodded and turned north at the river. Jacob got a glimpse of the cars and people before turning his attention to the brush and timber flanking the narrow waterway. He did not see Hailee and her cameraman run toward the KHTX helicopter at the edge of the field.

"We won't be able to go far," Barry said over the intercom, nodding toward anvil-shaped thunderheads rising over black, rolling clouds. Jacob was able to see beneath the canopy of the trees only occasionally. Twice he asked Barry to circle so he could check out movement below. White-tailed deer, terrorized by the noise of the helicopter, raced from the bottom and plunged through the low brush of the adjoining ranch lands. Once he asked Barry to hover over a motte to flush out what he was certain was the tiger. A brindle cow.

Windom punched Jacob on the arm and pointed at his watch. Jacob argued that he needed a few more minutes, a few more miles. Abruptly he leaned forward and stared at an opening in the cover ahead. *A flash of orange. Yes. Orange streaked with black.* "There it is," he yelled, pointing at the tiger dodging between the trees and through the underbrush.

Windom dropped just above the treetops. The injured tiger stopped in a thick clump of trees. Jacob opened his bag and removed an aluminum tube with a tuft of cloth at one end and a hypodermic needle at the other. "Get right over him," he shouted.

Jacob had loaded half a dozen large dart syringes. He knew that it would take more than one syringe. One dose should slow it enough to dart it again. Under ideal conditions he should be able to have the tiger off its feet in five, ten minutes, but these were not ideal conditions. It had been stressed by injury, and chasing it with a helicopter made matters worse. *I don't even have a cage to put it in,* he thought. *If I can get it down I can keep it down for at least an hour. After that? ¿Quién sabe?*

Jacob slipped the bolt out of the Cap-Chur gun, inserted the six-inch syringe, and locked the bolt in place behind it. He could see the tiger under the trees but did not have a clear shot for a dart. For a few minutes, Jacob and Barry looked at the snarling tiger. *God, it was big.*

Jacob tried to decide whether he should tell Barry to land so he could slip up on the tiger and dart it. If the tiger attacked there was no way he could get back to the helicopter or Barry could get the chopper off the ground quickly enough. He reached for the Ruger.

The tiger flushed from the sanctuary of the timber, ran through the brush and into a weed-choked field. Across the field a weathered, two-story house stood directly in the tiger's path. Jacob dropped the Ruger and grabbed the dart gun. "Thirty yards max," he yelled at Windom as the helicopter dropped toward the running cat. The tiger was a few yards from the house when Jacob leaned out the door. *Swing, shoot, and follow through,* he told himself. *Just like a crossing dove.*

The dart hit the tiger high in the hip as the cat reached the house, and Jacob saw it leap the steps to the wooden porch and smash through the screen door.

"Damn. Get us down. Away from the house."

Barry did not need to be told to put distance between the helicopter and the house. He settled the chopper into the weeds forty yards from the forlorn gray house. Jacob studied the house but saw no sign of life.

"Kill the engine," he said. Barry looked at him but did nothing. "I got to have it quiet." Reluctantly, Barry cut the switches.

The two men waited for the rotors to stop, for quiet to

come. Jacob yawned and pulled at his ears. The noise of the chopper had temporarily deafened him, and he wanted his hearing to be acute.

"You going in?" Barry asked.

"Not immediately," Jacob answered. "Got to give the drug time to work." He laid down the dart gun, picked up the semi-automatic Ruger and jacked a .44 magnum cartridge into its chamber.

"Good choice," Windom said.

"No choice," Jacob said. "There's a dart in the cat, but it looked high. Maybe bone. I'll dart it again if I get a chance, but I'm not going into the house armed with that pop gun. If the tiger's groggy and in a position to be darted again, I'll come back for the Cap-Chur gun."

"Mr. Trace." Barry hesitated before continuing. "I guess I could bring the dart gun, but I'm not going to. I flew dustoffs in Vietnam. Two tours. But I got a choice, and a man who doesn't use a choice is no better off than the man who doesn't have one."

"If I need you, it won't be to carry a dart gun. It'll be to get me to the closest hospital."

"You got it," Barry said with a thumbs-up.

A woman's high-pitched scream shattered the noontime stillness. "Oh, shit," Barry said as Jacob sprinted toward the house.

Jacob stopped at the bottom of four wooden steps leading to a veranda that stretched across the front of the house. *Maybe she just saw the tiger,* he thought. *Maybe the tiger is down. Maybe—*

Jacob heard a noise in the house and jerked the Ruger to his shoulder as a woman lunged through the broken door and fell on the porch. Jacob gulped; he had almost shot her. He stood braced, waiting for the tiger to roar through the door and pounce on its prey. One minute. Two minutes. Nothing. Not a sound.

Cautiously, Jacob turned his eyes from the doorway to look at the woman. She was pale, in shock; blood streaked her flimsy sun dress from shoulder to waist. With the rifle to his shoulder, Jacob slowly climbed the steps and knelt beside her. Keeping his eyes and the muzzle of the Ruger on the doorway, he slipped his left hand under the woman's arm and dragged her across the porch to the steps. She screamed again. Jacob stopped and stared into the dim interior of the house. Sweat ran down his forehead and stung his eyes. He wiped the moisture away with the sleeve of his left arm. "You're all right now," he said softly. "I'm going to drag you away from the house. Don't make any high-pitched sounds."

Jacob waited for his words to sink in and for his breathing to return to normal. "I've got you now," he said, grasping her slowly but firmly by the arm. He dragged her down the steps. She moaned softly as her head and feet bumped from step to step, but Jacob was worried more about the sound than her pain. If she survived the attack, she wouldn't ask about the bumps on her head and heels. He heard running steps behind him and whirled, the rifle at his shoulder.

"Don't shoot," Barry said. He helped Jacob carry the woman to the helicopter and laid her on the ground by the skids. Jacob slipped the woman's torn dress to her waist and saw deep fang punctures.

"Here, I'm a pro at this," Barry said, reaching into the chopper for the first aid kit. He glanced at Jacob to be certain that Jacob was watching for the tiger and went to work. "Compress bandages," he said, to reassure himself as much as the woman. "Front and back. Got to stop the bleeding. The bite is high. Missed your lungs. What's your name, honey?

Talk to me now. You aren't hurt bad, just scared. Don't go into shock, talk to me."

The woman's face was contorted with pain and fear and deathly pale, but she made an effort to focus her eyes on Barry. She moaned, more from fear than pain, and mumbled something.

"What?" Barry said, putting his ear close. The sound, when it came, was mostly a sob. "She's asking for help," he said to Jacob. "You're safe now. We've got you. We're going to have you in the hospital—"

He put his ear to the woman's mouth as she tried to speak. "I think she's saying the tiger is in the front room," he said. "She's in shock." He elevated the woman's feet and wrapped her tightly in his shirt. "We don't want to keep her here too long."

Jacob wiped his mouth with the back of his hand and looked at his watch. "If that tranquilizer is ever going to work, it will have worked by now." He stood up and weighed the Ruger with his hands. *Damn, it was light*. What he wanted was a bazooka. Thunder rumbled in the north; the storm was close. Jacob took a deep breath and started for the house.

He reached the steps and wiped the sweat from his eyes. There was not a breath of air. The heat was oppressive. *Or I'm scared to death,* he thought. He went up the steps and stopped to listen beside the door that hung from one hinge. Not a sound. With the rifle at his shoulder he stepped through the broken door and paused to let his eyes adjust to the dim light inside.

Jacob surveyed the interior. *Stairs straight ahead. Landing halfway up, then a turn to the right. Narrow hallway to the left of the stairs. Room at the back the kitchen, can see the refrigerator. Damn, two front rooms. One door open, the other closed.* He started toward the open door and stepped in something sticky. *Blood.*

Forcing himself, he walked to the open door and, poised to react to any sound or movement, looked in. *Nothing.* He took a deep breath to relax before psyching himself up for the closed door. He jumped at the sound. It was a soft, scraping sound, starting, stopping, then starting again. It didn't sound like anything he knew. It came from behind the closed door.

Stepping slowly to minimize the creaking of the wooden floor, Jacob crossed the room and stood beside the closed door. Scrape, stop, scrape, stop. With his left hand he turned the doorknob until it unlatched. The sound continued, but he also heard a soft gurgling. He gripped the doorknob with his left hand. He would open the door a few inches, and if the tiger was poised to spring, he would shoot and slam the door closed. *And then?* He'd think about that later.

Jacob opened the door a few inches but could see nothing. The sound continued. He opened the door a few inches more. Something moved. Another inch. Something plastic waved in the air. He shoved the door open and saw a child standing in a wooden playpen on the far side of the room. The boy, no more than a year old, was spinning plastic letters strung on a wire from the railing of the pen. He saw Jacob and smiled.

Jacob looked over his shoulder before stepping into the room. *That was why the woman said front room. Her baby. Her only child, if we're lucky,* Jacob thought. He stepped to the window, unlatched the screen, stuck his head out and waved at Barry. Barry said something to the woman, then trotted over, his eyes on the front door of the house.

Jacob took a quick look down the hall. No tiger. He picked up the child and handed him through the window to Windom.

"Oh, God," Barry said. "Are there any more?"

Jacob shrugged. He walked to the hall and listened. He heard nothing but the distant rumble of thunder. A door blew closed with a bang that stopped his heart. He leaned against the wall waiting to see if it would restart. A gust of wind swept down the hall. The wind felt good.

Jacob could hear nothing except the rush of blood through his ears. Then something else. The wap wap wap of a helicopter. He stepped to the front door and looked out. Barry kneeled beside the chopper, the baby in his arms, talking to the woman. A second helicopter skimmed the trees.

That's all I need, he thought, *the noise of Hailee's helicopter to drown out any sound the tiger makes.* He saw two, three drops of blood on the first step, another on the second. Drops, not splashes like the woman had left. The tiger was bleeding from the dart.

Jacob hoped that the stairs would not squeak, but they did. He went up slowly. He reached the landing and saw the dart, its barb stained with blood. The tiger was somewhere upstairs. He took another step and saw an ear. One unmoving ear at the top of the stairs. Even in the dim light he could make out the dark outline, the white tufts of hair.

The tiger was down, out, or groggy. Lying on its side, not crouched for attack. Jacob had his left foot on the next step when the KHTX helicopter passed over. He unconsciously glanced at the sound, then back at the tiger. Two ears.

Jacob's throat tightened as the tiger raised its head, and he was transfixed by the glaring yellow eyes, unable to move. The ears went back, the brows contracted, the tiger snarled and sprang down the stairs. Jacob pulled the trigger once, twice, three times. Three hundred pounds of maddened tiger crashed into him, driving him down the stairs and crushing him to the floor.

Jacob was stunned by the fall, the breath knocked from him. Pinned by the weight of the tiger across his chest, all he could do was suck air. He lay with his eyes closed and waited for the bite of the tiger.

And waited. He opened his eyes. Orange and black stripes filled his vision, and the sour cat smell filled his nostrils. *Orange and black. And red and white. Red blood and white bone.* The splintered end of a rib pointed awkwardly toward the ceiling. One of his bullets had ripped through the tiger's chest and lungs and exited through the top of the rib cage near the spine. He saw a second gaping wound where another expanding bullet had blasted into the tiger's throat and blown out the back of its neck, severing the spinal cord. He lay on the floor, too weak to roll the tiger off his chest. He suddenly felt the urge to urinate.

"Is it dead?"

Jacob saw Barry Windom's tall, slender frame outlined in the doorway. He was pale and shaking, but he had the useless Cap-Chur gun aimed at the tiger. "I think so," Jacob said hoarsely. "Get my rifle."

Barry made a wide circle around Jacob and the tiger to retrieve the rifle. "You okay?" he asked with the rifle between himself and the tiger.

"Get the son of a bitch off me."

Barry poked the tiger with the muzzle of the rifle to assure himself it was dead. Even then he was reluctant to touch the animal but pushed at it with the rifle until Jacob could slide from beneath it.

Jacob lay for a minute to regain his strength. Nothing appeared to be broken, and the blood that soaked his clothing belonged to the tiger. He would be sore for a few days, and he had knots on his head and elbows where he had hit the floor, but he was alive. Slowly he got to his feet.

"Didn't you know the Cap-Chur gun was useless if the tiger attacked?" he asked Barry.

"Yeah, but it's the only weapon I could find."

Jacob's astonishment at Barry's courage was lost in his awe at being alive.

Hailee tried to talk to the injured woman. The woman was incoherent, but Tony got good footage of her lying on the ground sobbing softly while her son played at her feet. She and Tony watched the house, the camera ready to tape whatever came out alive. They had taken shots of Barry going into the house, and when he did not come running out, they had inched closer. "Tony, start shooting and don't stop," she said, seeing Barry and Jacob in the doorway, and went to meet them, Tony at her heels. "The tiger?" she asked breathlessly. "Did you kill the tiger?"

"Either the Ruger killed it, or its time had come." Jacob's fear had been replaced by euphoria. Life had never felt so good. The sky was completely overcast, but he could see nothing but sun. "Never felt better," he said expansively. "The prognosis for the tiger is less positive." He smiled for the camera until Hailee led Tony into the house.

Lightning streaked the darkening sky and thunder followed almost immediately. "Come on," Barry said, strapping the woman on the litter. "We got to get this woman to a doctor. You'll have to hold the boy."

"Right," Jacob said. "We'll get her to the hospital. And then, we're going to celebrate."

5

Game wardens and National Guard activity sent Bump Wilkerson into hiding on his father's ranch. Bump raged about the government that had killed his father as surely as they had left POWs in Vietnam. Sometimes he wished his father had been a POW, but his father would never have surrendered.

Despite his fury, Bump had no plan of action until one of Roy Pat's followers, a gas station attendant, told Roy Pat that Blevins had seen the tiger and had hired Roy Farley's dogs to chase it. Bump wanted to hunt the tiger alone, to drape the tiger over the hood of his Jeep. Roy Pat insisted that Bump include him in any action against the tiger.

Bump put the men in paint and camouflage—only Roy Pat and Jimmy Guy's squad left jobs, wives, and sweethearts— and pretended the patrol was his idea. A deliveryman hid the militia in his truck and dropped them at Blevins' fence line.

They faded into the brush and marched forward, hoping the helicopter would lead them to the tiger.

Bump liked scouting the dangerous no-man's-land between freedom and government control. He liked carrying illegal weapons and moving stealthily through the country, spying unseen on those whose property he trespassed, terrifying those who illegally entered his country. He was not happy with the men who floundered through the brush with him. Roy Pat was quiet, alert, disciplined. The others whined at having to walk, to freeze every time an airplane went over, no matter how high. They had no discipline, no commitment. Sometimes he wondered why they joined, what they would do when the shooting started.

Mike Bentch had finished high school and gone to college, but he had been dismissed for painting swastikas on the doors of black athletes and harassing black women. He worked in the oil patch when he worked, and he was smart and strong. Roy Pat didn't like him because of his long hair and don't-care attitude, but when he was mad, the way he was when that wetback cursed him in Spanish, Mike was a good soldier. He respected Bump and took orders, but when Bump wasn't around, Mike followed Jimmy Guy, being irresponsible and getting drunk.

Kid, Justin Perry, was a friend of Mike's, although Mike pushed him around. His mother went to Roy Pat's church and thought Roy Pat was a good role model. When he was with Roy Pat, Kid was a good soldier. More often he goofed off with Mike and Jimmy Guy. But he could shoot. He shot Blevins' horse between the eyes at three hundred yards on a dare from Mike. Bump thought Roy Pat was going to quit over that.

Old Man, Hubert Slotsky, was a short, heavyset, bullshitter; life had been a disappointment to Hubert. His wife had gotten fat. His kids didn't respect him because he made them tend the hogs while he worked as a handyman. He pulled the girls in his lap and rubbed his chin whiskers against their necks and roughhoused with the boys, but they blamed him because they smelled like hogshit and weren't popular in school.

Old coot should have gone to Vietnam when he had the chance, Bump thought. Instead, Hubert had worked in the merchant marines, coming home with enough money to buy a pig farm. Hubert could make boobytraps and crude explosives with his short, stubby fingers, and he wanted to be considered dangerous, a soldier of fortune.

The Last Man Brigade was getting attention with radio talk shows, television, and newspaper interviews. It had been a long time coming. When wetbacks whined that they had been roughed up by the militia, bleeding heart liberals and their greaser attorneys had complained to the authorities who came out to Bump's ranch, poked into things that were none of their business, and told him he had been warned. Insulted was what he had been. They had threatened to take away his weapons. *By God, he'd like to see them try. By God, he'd defend the Constitution if they were too chicken-livered liberal to do it.*

Bump had two regrets—he wasn't six feet tall and the Soviet Union had collapsed. He had dreamed of killing Soviet spies or paratroopers in the thorny brush country of South Texas, hunting them down one by one. He was deterred from enlisting in the army by the thought that he might not get to fight. He didn't want to kill with a computer, and he didn't want to spend three years shining his boots and saying "Yes, sir" to some college boy who had never owned a gun, never shot so much as a rabies-carrying skunk.

He and his buddies talked about being mercenaries, but in some countries the United States supported terrorists called freedom fighters and in other countries, tyrants called friends. If Bump needed proof of perfidious government, that was it.

Although a loner, Bump organized a militia to protect himself from Federal or foreign dominion. "White men have always been able to organize and carry guns so that others don't get the upper hand," he told them. "A white man who can't use a gun is no better than a white man who doesn't have one."

He chose the motto "Don't Complain—Train" and called his group "The Texas Irregulars." When that led to jokes about bowel habits, he changed the name to "The Nueces Rangers," which was corrupted to "The Nuisance Rangers." Bump decided on "The Last Man Brigade" and required members to swear to fight to the last man.

No one had laughed when he said on television that the brigade was patrolling Corpus Christi to protect citizens from the tiger. He explained on talk radio how this proved again the need for every citizen to be armed. He warned that Russia and the United Nations would bring in spies disguised as scientists to set up bases in south Texas. The ATF would confiscate weapons and leave citizens at the mercy of the tiger and the United Nations. "This is an invasion of Texas."

Then that fool Jimmy Guy had taken his squad into a bar when he was supposed to be patrolling, and Mexicans had thrown them out. That made the brigade look foolish. Kid still had welts and bruises on his face; he had tried to placate everyone and suffered the most damage. Jimmy Guy threw a few punches but mostly kept Kid between him and the Mexicans. Hubert had covered their retreat with a broken bottle. When the Mexicans followed them outside, the militia grabbed their weapons, sent the Mexicans diving for cover, and shot up the bar, but Bump was not mollified. They had allowed themselves to be thrown out. When he walked into a place, he wanted bad men to crawl.

Bump had made Jimmy Guy exec because he had been to Vietnam and talked about smoking gooks, but Jimmy Guy hid in a laundry, terrified of being fragged by black soldiers who had to fight. That was why Jimmy Guy joined the brigade to "stop blacks from taking over the country." Bump wasn't going to let blacks take over, but the real threat was Washington. He had to keep Jimmy Guy and Roy Pat from using the brigade to fight their wars. As long as they had the same enemy, they could march together.

Bump wanted to replace Jimmy Guy as exec, but he needed him as leverage against Roy Pat. Roy Pat had been a real grunt. He never said much about it, just that when he walked that last klick to the Freedom Bird, he took a vow to save God in America, and he would keep that vow or die trying. He was Bump's best soldier, the brigade's armorer, but he would change the organization if he got control. Jimmy Guy was a banana peel that could make Bump look foolish. Roy Pat was a land mine.

Bump didn't know much about God except that God was angry with America for the same reasons he was. He didn't go to church because he didn't belong to anything he didn't control, but he knew the best recruits went to church—angry men, ready to take up arms against those who threatened white Christian supremacy. Roy Pat's church had an American flag on the front wall where most churches had a cross. He led the church in the pledge with everyone shouting "under God." Roy Pat said he would say the pledge whenever God wanted him to say the pledge. That's what he fought for in Vietnam, and the right to pray wherever he wanted.

Bump thought Roy Pat was a good preacher when Roy Pat preached about God-given rights and Goddamned wrongs. "God gave us the right to bear arms to stop wrongs like drugs, gays, and abortion," Roy Pat shouted. Folks whistled, stamped their feet, and clapped their hands at that.

But Roy Pat should keep it in church instead of preaching

at the guys for drinking after drill or using weekend bivouacs to slip off to Mexican whorehouses. He went ape-shit over the videos showing women—wearing nothing but ammo belts—firing automatic weapons, their breasts and asses jiggling. When Roy Pat smelled marijuana on Mike he got scary. He was even scarier when he preached to them about the tiger.

Bump thought Roy Pat would object to hunting the tiger, but nothing excited Roy Pat like the tiger. "The Lord stood with me, and strengthened me, that by me the preaching might be fully known, and that all the gentiles might hear: and I was delivered out of the mouth of the lion," Roy Pat said, "II Timothy 4:17."

"I thought this was a tiger," Jimmy Guy said.

Roy Pat's eyes blazed. "The devil can appear in whatever form he wishes," he said. "A tiger symbolizes seven kinds of devil—education that teaches secularism instead of the absolute values of our God-fearing founding fathers, sex education that leads to godless fertility, a legal system that allows mothers to kill their babies and favors a woman over a man, taxation that robs a man of the control of his money, a welfare system that robs the poor of usefulness and encourages blind fecundity, feminism that would replace man as head of the family, homosexuality that would destroy the family, the church, one nation under God.

"That tiger is devouring the heart of America, stalking your sons and daughters, lurking in the jungles of government, slinking through the courts of this land, snaring the godly, destroying the family, devouring the church, and perverting the American way of life. Our weapons are faith in God, faith in ourselves, faith in our arms, and the courage to do what's right. 'Resist the devil and he will flee from you.' James 4:7."

. . .

"I can't go no farther," Jimmy Guy said. "It's that damn malaria."

"You're the exec," Bump whispered, to remind Jimmy Guy to maintain silence and to keep the others from hearing. The ATF was looking for them, the FBI, game wardens, the National Guard. "Act like an exec."

The patrol got so noisy Bump had to give them a break. Hubert and Jimmy Guy collapsed on the ground, and Mike and Kid joined them in an undisciplined cluster. Only Roy Pat melted into cover. Bump knew he was on the verge of losing control. Then he heard an engine and the scrape of thorns against metal and slipped through the brush to investigate. Roy Farley and his dogs. *Hot damn, they were on the trail.*

He gathered his patrol and explained. "Be as quiet as you can. Stay within sight of each other. Listen for the dogs. They'll lead us to the tiger." He wanted to say the first shot was his but resisted.

Evelyn Price was close to panic. She was alone in the middle of nowhere in heavy brush that was too high for her to see over. Somewhere in that brush was the tiger, waiting to return to its kill. Quickly she looked over her shoulder. A buzzard coming to join the feast. *The heat, the smell.* She couldn't stay here. She looked down the dusty *sendero,* barely wide enough for the Jeep to pass. *Nothing.*

The tiger was out there, but it had no malice toward her. It had recently eaten. How could she help it escape? She didn't know much about tigers, but she knew men. They had gone for dogs and guns. They would come back to the carcass to pick up the trail, thinking she had left in fear. She would be waiting for them. Evelyn Price had taken on the Pentagon; she wasn't going to be intimidated by hunters.

She picked a spot close enough to see approaching vehicles but far enough not to smell the carcass. She checked the spot for thorns, burrs, and rattlesnakes, checked it again, then sat down to wait. It was hot and sultry and looked like it might rain at any minute. She wondered if rain would help the tiger evade the dogs. She hoped so.

While she waited, she thought of her son. She had called him, thinking he would be excited that she was involved in the tiger hunt. "A friend of mine says they're going to bring in UN troops to look for it and set up bases in Texas."

"Johnny, that's . . . unreasonable."

"You believe animals have rights the same as people, and you think I'm unreasonable?"

"Animals have a right to live."

"Until they end up on my plate."

Evelyn ended up crying as she always did. When she told him she might be the first woman director of NAZA he said, "I hope not." She told him it broke her heart when he talked like that. "Father says that whole bunch is an international group working to replace the Constitution with a world government."

"Your father thinks everything is a plot."

"He's damn near right too." As before, she wanted to tell him his patriotic father had protested Vietnam until he found he wouldn't be drafted. She had thought he was a war resister, but he was a coward. She wanted to tell her son but feared making him angrier at her.

Evelyn heard the truck before she saw it. A brown pickup came down the *sendero* and stopped near her. A cage containing dogs filled the bed of the truck. A rough, reedy man got out of the pickup. "Stop," she yelled. "We have to wait until Mr. Blevins returns."

"Mr. Blevins went to get the biggest rifle he has. He'll be back, and so will the helicopter."

"No. You can't shoot it from a helicopter."

Roy Farley squinted at Evelyn. "Ma'am, I ain't shooting

nothing," he said. "I just hope to get on its trail." He dropped the tailgate and the dogs jumped to the ground and milled, excited to be working. Farley had brought his best four Walker hounds, all broken to run only cats. He also brought five young Walkers and two catch dogs, glass-eyed Catahoula leopards that would worry a cat to keep it from running while the hounds bayed treed. They sniffed at the earth and nearby bushes, then urinated where they had sniffed.

Blevins drove up beside Farley and got out. He grabbed his hat as a gust of wind almost blew it from his head.

"Damn," Farley grumbled. "Dogs have hell following a trail in the wind." The dogs circled the dead bull and worked their way into and out of the thicket where the tiger had bedded down, and Farley paid more attention to his hounds. "By damn, they're cold trailing. Grab your gun and let's go," he said. Blevins looked at the sky. "The chopper can find us."

Blevins took a rifle from the Jeep and followed Farley and the dogs. Evelyn went after them, yelling for them to stop. The refreshing wind would make it harder for the dogs to follow the tiger, but there were more dogs than she had expected, almost a dozen.

Evelyn lost sight of the men; *how did they move through the brush so fast?* Her arms and legs were scratched, her shirt torn. She ran into a wall of whitebrush that was impenetrable. She tried to push her way, first forward, then backing into it. Falling into it, crawling over it, she made her way through and followed the sounds of the dogs.

Evelyn stopped to pick prickly pear thorns from her legs. She could not hear the dogs. "Mr. Blevins," she yelled. "Farley. Help." She turned and as she did, she saw a rattlesnake in the shade of a prickly pear. Looking carefully where she stepped, she backed away. She could no longer see it, but neither could she see her backtrack. Brush covered every landmark. She was lost, but the men would eventually return to the truck and look for her. Or would they think she had left? *Which way was the truck?*

The helicopter would see her. She would make sure it did if she had to take off her shirt; she wore no brassiere. But she didn't want the helicopter to return, not until the tiger escaped in darkness or rain.

She tried to reconstruct her path. She had followed the dogs and men into the brush, and they turned this way and then turned again and . . . they had led her in a circle. The tiger was headed back to its kill. Back to her. There was nothing to climb that was higher than a tiger could reach. She couldn't stay where she was. She had to find a clearing. Where she could be seen. Where she could see the tiger before—

She had taken a dozen steps into the brush when she heard rustling and rocks tumbling. She stopped, unable to breathe, and saw an armadillo rooting under a mesquite. She released her breath. A tiger would eat an armadillo before it would eat her. She was startled by a covey of quail that exploded around her, and then a single that flew up from under her foot. She found a small clearing. She also found a footprint. She had been there before. As she looked carefully for the rattlesnake, she heard the unmistakable sound of footsteps, soft, cautious steps of something stalking. She could detect nothing, but the corner of her eye told her she had seen movement. She placed one hand on her throat and the other on her mouth to stifle a scream.

Roy Farley cursed the conditions. His four Walkers were the best cat dogs in the state, but the wind and dust played havoc with the scent. They weren't magicians. One of the young dogs chased a deer as Farley and Blevins floundered through blackbrush. The going was tough enough without that kind of foolishness. He fought the brush and ran after the young hound. "Get back here, you son of a bitch."

The dog rejoined the pack. Farley worried that neither he nor the dogs knew anything about tigers. They had put plenty of bobcats up trees and a few cougars, but he didn't know about tigers. If the dogs bayed the tiger, would his 30-30 and Blevins' 270 stop it before it killed a dog? They were expensive, and he had a lot of time invested in them. *Where the hell was Blevins?* That's all he bargained for, pick up the trail and bay the tiger so Blevins could shoot it from the helicopter.

"Blevins, where the hell are you?" he yelled.

"Here." He was only a few yards away but completely hidden in the brush.

"Stay close," Farley said. "If the dogs flush that tiger I want you there fast."

Farley fought his way through catclaw and looked at the dark clouds scudding southward. They had blotted out the sun, and a few drops fell with a hiss on the hot ground. "Wind's switched," he yelled. "Might as well quit. They ain't bringing no helicopter in this weather. Besides, the wind's getting stronger."

He was raising the goat horn call to his mouth to signal the dogs in when he paused. "Listen. They ain't cold trailing no more. It's hot, and they're circling back toward the kill." Farley and Blevins plunged through whitebrush as the voices of the older hounds changed.

"Baying, by God they got him," Farley said. His yell of triumph faded as a spine-chilling roar drowned out the baying and barking pack. The roar died and when Farley heard his hounds again not all of them bayed. Some yelped in pain. Farley ran toward his dogs. He could tell by the sound of the fight that the tiger was not holding in the brush. It stopped, turned on the dogs, then ran again.

Farley found one of the older Walkers first. It was alive, but its stomach had been ripped open, its back broken. The hound dragged its entrails and rear legs over the ground. "Bess," Farley cried, stopping to kneel beside the hound. He looked up quickly when he heard the agonized yelp of another dog. "God damn him," he muttered. He cradled Bess' head on his knees, pulled a knife from its sheath, and cut her throat.

He ran again, Blevins beside him. They passed another dog, then another, another. They didn't stop; all were dead. Part of one hound's head was missing, and two had been bitten across the back of the neck. The tiger had bitten all the way through the bone on one dog, almost decapitating the young hound.

They were close. The tiger had taken a stand again in a thicket. The remaining hounds and the two catch dogs were still with the cat, trying to hold it in one spot until their owner arrived. Farley and Blevins slowed to a trot, then a walk, rifles at the ready, trying to see into the brush for a clear shot at the tiger. They saw bushes shaking and glimpses of the cat and the hounds and heard the growling of the tiger and the cry of another dog as it died.

"He's wiping me out," Farley said, in tears. Farley walked toward the thicket with his rifle to his shoulder. With a roar the tiger sprang from the brush. Before Farley could aim, the tiger drove him to the ground. Farley flailed futilely. The snarling cat closed its blood-stained jaws around the throat and lower half of Farley's face, drowning out his cry.

Blevins saw the tiger lift Farley from the ground and shake him once and knew that Farley was dead. He threw the rifle to his shoulder and fired, but the shot was high. The tiger lifted its great head and looked at him, its eyes blazing in fury. Blevins turned and ran as two glass-eyed dogs sank their teeth into the rear haunches of the cat. The tiger wheeled, crushed the skull of one and disemboweled the other. The cat sniffed briefly at its dead tormentors, then walked into the brush.

Evelyn heard it again, the rustle and soft scraping of something gliding through the brush. She could see something but could not make out its form. Then she saw eyes, eyes that stared at her without blinking. She gasped as a camouflaged figure slipped out of the brush. Even his face was camouflaged so that he was scarcely recognizable as a man. "Over here," he called. "I got a prisoner."

Camouflaged figures closed around her. One grabbed her shirt between her breasts. "Who are you and what are you doing here?" He was missing a finger and that made him more frightening and brutish.

"I . . . I'm with Mr. Blevins." It was the most powerful name she knew. "He and a man with some dogs are tracking the tiger."

"Which way did they go?"

"I don't know."

"You better find out damn quick," he said, shaking her so that the torn shirt ripped further. "You sound like a Yankee to me."

"I seen her before." The voice sounded young. "On TV. She's that animal rights woman."

"Is that right?" He tightened his grip. "You one of them skunk lovers? Out here to stop hunting? Maybe get our guns?"

Evelyn's courage failed her; these were not disciplined soldiers. Thank God Arina wasn't with her. One *nyet* and they'd both be dead. "I'm with Mr. Blevins."

"You done said that, but Mr. Blevins don't like skunk lovers. Who are you working for and what do they want to know?"

"Hey, Bump, when the wind's just right I can hear the dogs."

"You better talk and talk fast." He caught her by the nipple and squeezed so hard she gasped in pain. Despite herself she began to cry.

A larger figure stepped beside him. "No rough stuff," he said.

"She's lying."

"I can't let you hurt a woman," the other said. The two stared at each other. Evelyn feared they would fight. Then a gunshot snapped through the brush. "Lock and load," the larger one said.

"Damn it, I'm in command. Lock and load. Hold your formation and keep your eyes open."

They left as silently as they had appeared. Evelyn ran toward the shot. The militia was out there and the tiger. Everything around her was frightening, and Blevins offered the only safety. Thorns tore at her hands and face, but she scarcely felt them in her panic. She saw blood-streaked grass, blood splattered against mesquite trunks as high as her head. A dying dog whined, raised its head to stare helplessly at her, then lay back in a pool of its own blood. There was nothing she could do for it.

She stopped when she saw camouflaged figures. Farley lay on the ground on his back, his arms spread wide. His throat and lower jaw had been ripped away. One of the figures vomited down the front of his camouflage shirt. They jumped when they heard movement in the brush and opened fire with automatic weapons. Someone screamed.

"That's Blevins," one of them said. "Reassemble." They faded into the brush.

"Damn pissants." A shaken Blevins crawled out of the brush and looked at Evelyn. "We got to get back to the truck.

And hope the tiger goes after them instead of us. I hope next time I come this way I find their bones in a pear patch."

Evelyn looked over her shoulder, not at the thicket where Roy Farley and his dogs lay dead, but at the broad expanse of the brushlands. Her arms and legs stung from thorns, but she had saved the tiger.

Barry and Jacob delivered the woman and baby to the hospital, then flew to Blevins' ranch and landed next to the Jeep. The KHTX helicopter followed them. Blevins was furious. "Where the hell have you been?"

Barry told Blevins about the woman.

"Where's Farley?" Jacob asked. "Where's the dogs?"

"Dead," Blevins said, telling what happened while Tony Garcia filmed it. "Come on, Barry, I'm going to get that tiger," Blevins said.

"Not in this weather. I've got to get this chopper tied down."

"You've got to get Mr. Farley's body," Evelyn said.

"I need it for a lure," Jacob said. "If the tiger comes back to the body I can dart it."

"You can't," Evelyn said. "I saw Farley. You can't use him as bait."

"How are you going to take a stand?" Blevins asked. "There's not a tree out there that a tiger can't reach without jumping."

"I'll pick up Farley and then I'm heading for the hangar," Barry said.

"We're going too," Hailee said. "I want an overhead shot of the whole scene. The trail of dead dogs, the body—"

"I want your chopper off my place," Blevins said. "And I want Farley left with whatever dignity he has. The man didn't have a chance."

"Mr. Blevins, if we film the death scene and the pick-up of Farley's body, there's no story left here," Hailee said. "Otherwise you're going to have reporters running all over your place."

"Get the pictures and get out," Blevins said.

"Same as before," Hailee told Garcia. "Suggestion, shivers, no barf."

Blevins returned Evelyn to the hotel in a driving rain. She went to the media room where Rand and Arina waited alone. She was covered with dust, her hair tangled, her clothes torn, her face scratched and blood-streaked. She walked to the well-stocked bar that had been set up for the press, filled a tumbler with bourbon, and drank with a sigh. "There are two tigers," she said.

Rand and Arina looked at each other. "Jacob killed one of them," Arina said.

"The other escaped," Evelyn said. "I pray to God we never see it again." She took another drink that brought tears to her eyes. She leaned back and closed them tightly. "What do you know about Bump Wilkerson?" she asked Rand.

"From what I found Bump's father was in Vietnam. He came home badly crippled and in constant pain. People called him a junkie because he was glassy-eyed from medication. Bump's mother left when Bump was four, some say with a truck driver, but they never say that to Bump. His father shot himself when Bump was sixteen. He's been on his own since."

"The poor boy," Arina said.

"That poor boy almost killed me," Evelyn said. She didn't like being afraid, particularly of men, but his savage eyes, painted face, and single-minded purpose had terrified her. He was a guided missile waiting for a target. "I thought I was going to be gang-raped."

"That would have been worse than being killed," Rand said. "I'm sure my wife had rather be killed than gang raped by—"

"The National Radical Association? I'm not sure that she had," Evelyn said. "But I'm sure that you had rather she be killed than raped."

Red climbed Rand's face and into his hair. He twisted the ring on his little finger. "I think some things are more important than life."

"Next time you go, and I'll pose for the cameras."

"You wanted the responsibility," Rand said. "I've met the reporters, I've lined up press conferences and interviews, I've—"

Without a word, Evelyn refilled her glass and left the room, stopping at the door to make kissing sounds.

After Jacob and Barry secured the helicopter and caught a cab to the hotel, Jacob led Barry to the media room. The excitement of the chase had worn off, leaving him drained, and he wanted to collapse in a chair and have a drink. "Two tigers," he said. "One down, one to go."

"I told you the tiger was not to be harmed," Rand said. "I told you there would be consequences. Stuart Johnson was apoplectic. I had to close the press room because of angry calls. From all over the country. You killed a tiger and appeared on television, gloating, proud of it, like—"

"A little boy who has killed a rabbit," Arina said. *Cowboy hooligan,* she thought. *So eager to shoot, so reluctant to follow rules.*

"He saved a woman and child," Barry said.

"Those tigers have killed two people. Not counting the ones on the airplane they wrecked," Jacob said.

"You don't kill a zoo animal because someone foolishly enters its cage," Rand said.

"They're not in a cage," Jacob said.

"I can't let you carry the rifle again."

"Then get somebody else. I'm not facing a tiger bare-handed."

"The rain will make tracking easier, will it not?" Arina asked. "You must get more dogs."

"Nobody is going to use their dogs, and nobody is going to follow them when they hear what happened to Farley."

"What is your plan?" *More shooting,* she supposed.

Jacob shrugged. "We wait until the tiger kills again."

"Then shoot it?" Arina asked.

"If necessary." He didn't like the contempt he saw in her eyes. "I want the hide of the tiger I killed. And the fangs."

The American cowboy wanted a trophy of his triumph over authority. "The tiger belongs to my country. I have ordered it destroyed," she said.

"Come on, Barry, I promised you a drink," Jacob said.

"Here's to the way you handle women," Barry toasted Jacob. "And tigers." They had already toasted the dead tiger, the live tiger, the hunt, Farley, and most of his dogs.

"I think I've had better luck with tigers," Jacob said. The euphoria of being alive had changed to anger that Arina and Rand preferred that he had died rather than the tiger. Alcohol had made him morose. "Arina hasn't understood anything I've said or done."

"You can't always please women even when you know what they want. My wife didn't want me to go back to Vietnam. Said she couldn't take the strain. I knew she barely made it the first time. I went anyway."

"Why?"

"I don't know that I can say. I left buddies there, and I wanted to be part of what they were doing. I can't say I enjoyed Vietnam, but, damn, I was alive. Seemed like the lower I hit when somebody died, the higher I was when we made it back, and the closer we came to not making it, the bigger the thrill of walking away from that windmill. Chasing cows and counting deer is as close as I can get to the thrill. Like chasing a woman. You have new eyes that see the swell of her body, the curve of her ear. Your nostrils expand to follow her scent. You hear the sigh of her clothes, the movement of her hair, the parting of her lips. Anticipation pumps your whole body."

Jacob nodded. "When I see a fresh track or dogs pick up the trail, I'm focused. My eyes see everything. I can read the voices of the dogs—how hot the trail is, how close they are to the cat, which dogs are competing for the lead. When I see the cougar and know it's mine there's a moment . . . I'm like a kid at Christmas before he opens his present. I can't wait and yet I want the anticipation to last forever. The end of the hunt is quick, but I savor it for a long time—the skill and determination of the dogs, the courage and endurance of the cat, my own part. I enjoy wrapping up the job, leashing the dogs, loading the cougar, breaking camp. It's over but there's pleasure in doing it right. I even enjoy the blunders if no one is hurt."

"That's how hunting differs from women," Barry said. "Someone is always hurt, and there's no neat wrap-up, no walking into the hangar and getting a high five. No laughing at things that could have been disasters but weren't. My wife left like she said she would, but it wasn't neat."

"I haven't been able to wrap mine up either although she remarried and has kids," Jacob said, ordering another round.

"That TV gal looks like she's been to the barn," Barry said. "Good looking woman if you don't mind being on a short leash."

"She'll make a couple more trips to the barn before she saddles a horse," Jacob said, "But it won't be from West Texas."

"South Texas either. More likely east-side New York. But I'd like to give her a ride before she leaves the cow pasture."

"Until she finds the thoroughbred that can win her the roses, she might bareback a bronc or two," Jacob said.

"Evelyn's okay if you like a big-butted woman, and I do."

"It's not her ass that bothers me, it's her aspirations. I hope she gets the brass ring, but I don't want to be the pony she's riding."

"I know, you have your sights screwed down for Ms. Red."

Jacob was embarrassed to be so transparent. "Pam was a looker. That helplessness appealed to me, but it's a good thing my mother taught me to cook, iron, and sew, because hers didn't teach her anything except how to stop conversation when she entered a room."

"I hope you like Eskimos. Ms. Red'd freeze the olives in a martini."

"I'd like to be there when she thaws out."

"Jacob, me boy, I think you may be."

Jacob returned to his room surprised at how happy it made him to talk about Arina. When he lay down, he tried to picture the way she looked—the frankness of her eyes, her mouth on the edge of a smile, because when he closed his eyes, he saw the tiger's fangs reaching for his throat. As drunk as he was, each time he dozed, he awakened with a start, reliving the moment he had almost died.

If he had died he would have been an oddity in a newspaper account and a tasteful but terrifying picture on the television screen. He could think of no one who would miss him. Old Red. Reymundo. Perhaps the woman in the farmhouse.

Pam wouldn't know he was dead until after he was buried. He wondered if she would cry when she heard the news. He wondered if she would remember the times they drank coffee and watched the sun rise on the mountains, or if she would remember that the supplies, the guns, the dogs were always already in the truck.

For a long time he waited for Pam to come back. Sometimes he still caught himself believing she might be there when he returned. Even after she had remarried. Maybe she would discover she had made a mistake, maybe her husband would die. He had daydreams where he adopted her children. He could not accept that she was out of his life forever.

When he learned she had remarried, he had taken Red, the tent, a sleeping bag, some food and a lot of alcohol and gone to the mountains to die. Not because she had remarried but because he had failed her, failed himself. He was angry at God for not giving him a higher I.Q., greater ambition so he could have been a biologist, home every night for dinner.

Damn, every time he drank he became sentimental. He had never been able to read stories about dogs or horses without crying. He feared sentimentality, but he carried Pam's photograph. "Pam's not coming back," he said. He got out of bed, tore up her photograph, and flushed it.

He was awakened by Rand's telephone call. Demonstrators outside the hotel demanded government officials be punished for the deaths of Roy Farley and Sam Storey. Others condemned Jacob for killing an endangered animal and demanded that the other tiger be protected. "I have a roomful of reporters who can make you a killer or hero," Rand said.

Jacob looked at his watch. Seven o'clock. "I have no comment," he said and hung up. He took a hot shower to relieve the soreness of his back and turned on the television while he dressed. His chest hurt from the weight of the tiger falling on him, and he had noticeable bumps on his elbows and the back of his head.

Television reported a furor over the deaths of Storey and Farley. The government said the tiger wasn't dangerous; the government would pay for livestock killed by the tiger. How much would they pay for Sam Storey? For Roy Farley? "Where would taxpayers find the money to pay for someone's life?" angry citizens asked. What was the government going to do about the remaining tiger? Animal rightists demanded that Jacob be replaced with someone more competent and less gun-crazy. "People have nothing to fear from animals that are left alone," one protester said.

An anchorman said people were prisoners in their homes, afraid to go outside. Landowners and sporting stores reported dove hunting was down because hunters were afraid to go into the field. Those who did go into the field were harassed by game wardens, National Guardsmen, and animal protectionists. Hunting brought a lot of money to South Texas and many motel, restaurant, liquor store owners, and landowners feared the entire hunting season would be ruined.

A likely presidential candidate offered to come to Texas and kill the tiger if the president didn't do something. A Mexican official complained that the United States was driving the tiger into Mexico. The newscaster predicted the tiger would cause additional problems between the two countries. "I wish they would drive it to Mexico," said Jacob, who wished he knew as much about the location of the tiger and its intentions as reporters did.

He left by the stairs to avoid reporters waiting in the lobby. In the parking lot he saw signs protesting the killing of the tiger and the deaths of Storey and Farley. "American dogs are as valuable as Russian tigers." "The earth belongs to all living things." One showed a tiger, a hammer and sickle, and an

ATF badge with a slash drawn across them. Another said, "Where have all the flowers, whales, seals, eagles, tigers gone?" Jacob avoided the demonstrators, walked across the street to a cafe, and called a taxi. The cab took him to the hospital to see the woman he had saved. Her name was Jonelle Parker, and she was in stable condition. Her child was unharmed. She promised to name her next child after him. Her husband, who worked on an offshore oil rig, embraced him. Jacob was embarrassed by their gratitude but also pleased.

When he returned to the operations room, he had a message from warden Peale, and Arina waited. "I am glad you were not injured," she said.

"I'm sorry I got angry," Jacob said. "I had a rough day."

"Now, we must disarm the militia who are trying to kill the remaining tiger."

He had explained it to Rand, he had explained it to Evelyn—"Arina, this is a free country. Any adult can own a gun. The militia have been warned not to shoot the tiger, but until they do—"

Arina shook her head. Americans frightened themselves by seeing silly movies and reading foolish books about imaginary terrors and then they bought guns to protect themselves against their terrors, killing instead the boy next door. Andrei would be amused to hear that the citizens of the richest and most powerful country in the history of the world were terrified of everything—bad breath, body odor, taxes, poverty, loss of respect, loss of privilege—and the solution was to buy bigger guns. The more guns they bought the more terrified they were of their helplessness. The country had become addicted not only to violence but to guns to protect themselves from that violence. Officials sanctioned their fear, condoned the slaughter of the innocent in order to protect themselves from the imaginary. "What you have described is not a free country but a lawless country. Americans are so proud of their freedom and all they do with it is shoot each other."

Damn, why did it always have to be a fight? Jacob thought. "Peale said the rain washed out the sign, so unless the tiger comes back to its kill there's not much I can do until there's a sighting. I want to be close to the scene, and I want to look the country over. You're welcome to come."

"Yes. I must not be left behind again. If necessary, my government will appeal to your government."

"Not necessary. Be prepared for hiking through the brush. Hat, boots, long sleeves."

Each morning, Jacob and Arina left before sunrise to avoid reporters. Jacob stopped at a 7-11 and bought coffee and sweet rolls. If she found the breakfast peculiar, she said nothing. Jacob headed generally west, taking back roads. Game wardens, highway patrol, and local officers checked reported sightings. Jacob and Arina checked the uncertain ones.

One morning as dawn came over the rolling brushy terrain, Arina said, "Before I came here, I thought America was cities, factories, crowded highways."

"This is the real America," Jacob said. "People in the city are shaped by the city. Noise, crowds, bargains, jobs. Getting ahead of someone else, then trying to find space where you can enjoy it by yourself. People in the country are shaped by the country. Space and distance have more to do with who you are than your job or how many cars you own. The most important news is the weather report, and weather controls more of your life than the government does."

"So much news," Arina said. "You can't escape it, and you can learn nothing from it. What starlet sleeps with what rock singer."

"Why are you so interested in the news? Every time I see

you, you're reading a newspaper or watching TV. Are you sure you're not a spy?" He intended it as a joke.

"What could I learn? It is all—" She turned her face to the window.

They checked the carcass of a deer that had been run down. "No," Arina said. "Tigers are hard to see, stealthy. They attack from ambush. They drag the kill to a shady or secluded spot to eat it."

They checked a report by citizens of Seven Sisters who had heard a lion roaring and had been afraid to venture out of their houses. By the time they got there, a highway patrolman had discovered the sounds were made by a junior high student learning to play the tuba.

Arina laughed. It was the first time he had seen her laugh. "A deputy patrolled the area all night in his squad car," Jacob told her. "He heard a noise behind one building and couldn't get to it by car. When he walked around the corner, a cat screeched and jumped out of a garbage can. He shot the garbage can twice. Walking back to his squad car he shot at an orange colored chow that ran out of the alley." They laughed together. *God, it felt good to laugh with someone.* He wanted to squeeze her hand.

"Would you like to go to a movie sometime?" he asked abruptly.

"I have seen American movies," she said. "They blow up cars because cars represent the things they most value— power, money, speed, illusion."

"This is a century, a country, where the smallest action may have consequences beyond your imagination," Jacob said. "You slight someone at work, and eight people are shot to death. You refuse to move to the back of the bus, and you begin a revolution that saves your country's soul. In those movies, you shoot someone, make love to someone, wreck a car, blow up a building—no consequences. It's the perfect escape."

"You don't like such movies?"

"I like movies about real people, real consequences."

"Yes, I would like to see such a movie with you."

When they returned to the hotel a soft, gray-haired woman behind the desk told Arina she had a message. Dr. Andrei Velinsky. *How did he find her,* she wondered. *He knew only that she was going to Houston.* "What did he say?"

"Something about . . . here, I wrote it down. Afghanistan alternative."

"Yes? What?"

"That's all he said. He said to tell you 'Afghanistan alternative.' He was still speaking, but the phone went dead."

"I must know exactly what he said," Arina said, aware that people had turned to look at her, including Jacob. "Please."

"Don't worry, honey," the woman said, patting her arm. "He'll call you back."

"How about that movie after we get cleaned up?" Jacob asked.

"No," she said. "I must call Andrei." Abruptly she walked away.

From his room, Jacob watched Arina walk across the sand to the surf and stand looking at the lights of hotels sparkling on the choppy waters of Corpus Christi Bay. He wanted to hold her, to walk along the shore beside her, but the mention of Andrei's name had driven him from her thoughts.

Arina stared at the lights reflected in the waters of the bay, pondering Andrei's message. "Afghanistan alternative." *What did it mean? How did he find her? Why did he call?* At best it was difficult calling from Russia. *Had the connection been lost or had Andrei been cut off?*

When she called Andrei's apartment there was no answer. When she called his lab, a strange voice answered. She called the zoo director, Mikhail Kuzakov, told him that a tiger had been killed, she had overseen the destruction of its body, and that another tiger had escaped the crash. Kuzakov seemed surprised but said nothing. "Please inform Dr. Velinsky that I may be in America longer than I had planned."

"Dr. Velinsky is no longer associated with the zoo," the director said, hanging up.

Rand Morgan sat at his desk in the media room. He was hounded by reporters who wanted interviews with Jacob Trace, who didn't want to talk to anyone, animal rights activists who demanded guarantees that the remaining tiger would not be killed, and farmers and ranchers who demanded that US Army helicopters kill the tiger to protect them and their livestock. There was a soft tap on the door, and Hailee White stuck her head in. "Got a minute, Rand?" she asked.

"Come in," he said. Hailee had been the star of the tiger story. She had made live reports on the network news, and newspaper and magazine reporters had done more stories on her than on Jacob Trace. But he hadn't had a story for her since the portable cage had arrived. It was three feet wide and seven feet long. The inside of the box was lined with sheet metal, and holes had been drilled to provide passage of air. He thought its arrival would make a good story, but Hailee had made her disappointment clear. Rand wanted Hailee on his side. He wanted to stand close enough to catch his share of the glare that reflected from her.

"I wanted to say thanks," Hailee said. "I'm going to write a letter to the president of the network telling him you're doing a fine job. I wonder if you'd like me to send a copy to anyone else?"

Rand was no fool. He knew such a favor had a price. "You could send a copy to the director of NAZA," he said, pretending nonchalance.

"Stuart Johnson, right? How old is he now?"

"He's still very active."

"You've done a fine job," Hailee said. "Which can't be said of all NAZA assistant directors." She smiled at Rand. He had never been unfaithful to his wife, but Rand had fantasies about Hailee—she network anchorwoman, he director of NAZA, together at White House dinners and on cruises.

He was pleased she was unhappy with Evelyn, but he couldn't attack Evelyn through the media. He decided to offer a weak defense. "Ms. Price is a very capable assistant. She faces extraordinary difficulties." He twisted the ring on his finger and took a chance. "She is an independent . . . spirit." He avoided "woman."

"Two men were eaten, a woman injured, a child threatened. A tiger was killed, another tiger found, shot at, lost. Maybe it wasn't her fault, but she was not in control. In a man's world, a woman who can't control the situation had better turn it over to a man who can."

Rand knew that what she said might or might not be her opinion, but his statement would be the only one the public would ever hear. "I'm sure Ms. Price acted as she believed appropriate to the situation. She isn't experienced in that kind of work," he added.

"I have arranged an interview with Bump Wilkerson," Hailee said. "He wanted money, and the network has agreed to pay it. I wanted you to know so that you aren't caught off-guard by the other reporters."

"Thank you," Rand said. A second favor. "I have something you might be interested in. A flight attendant, Susan somebody, survived the air crash and died at home. I can get the name for you."

Hailee mentally wrote the newscast. "There has been a tragic footnote to the fatal crash of World Air 17. One of the heroic"—over stale pictures of the wrecked plane. "Thanks, but I don't think it would make the air. What will make the air is an exclusive interview with the man you hired to capture the tiger. You're his direct supervisor. Or is it Evelyn?"

If he said he was in charge, she would insist that Jacob submit to an interview. If he said Evelyn was in charge, he no longer would be the subject of her camera. "I'll see that you get an interview," he said.

"Thanks, Rand." She leaned across the desk and kissed him on the cheek. "I want an exclusive."

Damn. How would he get Jacob to agree? Jacob had no interest in being a celebrity. He could have Jacob in his office, and Hailee and her cameraman could walk in unannounced. Jacob might walk out, and that would leave Rand looking foolish. He could ask Jacob as a favor. Jacob hadn't wanted the job and could walk away any time he wanted. Until he killed the tiger he could have walked away. Now he couldn't quit without appearing a coward. Let Jacob show the world that he was still trying to capture the tiger and then insist he do an interview with Hailee.

"The lab has been sealed, the records destroyed, Dr. Velinski put under arrest," Mikhail Kuzakov told the minister. "One tiger has been destroyed, but there is a second tiger." Even if he had been so bold as to take a seat without being told, the only chair in the room was behind the desk, and it was occupied.

"Alive? A second tiger?" The minister was little more than five feet tall and so thin he could not buy clothing that fit properly, and his suit hung on him like an empty sack. His face was long and thin and scarred by acne. Despite his appearance he radiated power. "You oversaw the crating and loading of the tigers for America?"

"Yes," Kuzakov said. "The tigers could not have escaped."

"Then they were set free in the airplane," the minister said. "Fools, they would destroy everything in the name of order."

"But who?"

"Who?" the minister asked. "Mad men who sent tigers carrying diseases to America and arranged their escape."

"But why?"

"There is a plot—a plot worthy of the devil—to destroy Russian democracy, perhaps Russia itself. But who are the devils? Dr. Yeroskin was on the airplane when the tigers escaped. She can be trusted?"

"Yes, of course."

"See to it that the zoo's felines are destroyed."

"All felines?" Kuzakov asked. "Endangered species?"

"Immediately. The order did not originate with me."

"Higher than the minister? How will I explain the death of the felines? Rare disease?"

"There must be no mention of disease."

"And the tiger in America?" Kuzakov asked.

"Our embassies in Washington and Mexico City will arrange to have the tiger destroyed. It is hard to overestimate the consequences if they fail. Did you know the Chinese use tiger bones in wine as a cure for rheumatism, the fat to cure impotency and the blood as an aphrodisiac? The heart of the tiger imparts to the one who eats it the courage and strength of the animal itself. And now the tiger has the power to destroy a nation. Perhaps the world. Is that not ironic?"

Between the wings of the third floor of Sandy Shores was a chamber that extended from the elevators to the bar and restaurant. Jacob and Arina met there each morning. One morning he found her reading a newspaper. "The flight attendant who was licked by the tiger died," Arina said. "They do not tell how she died."

"She was caught by a tiger, survived a plane crash, and died at home," Jacob said. "That's the story. No one cares how she died."

They rode down the elevator in silence. In the lobby, the receptionist handed Arina a telegram. Jacob watched as she read it. "Bad news?" he asked.

She crumpled the telegram and thrust it into her pocket. "It is nothing," she said, waving her hand. "Something about my passport," she said. "My papers were never recovered."

"Don't worry about a passport here. No one will ask for it."

In the truck they rode in silence for a while with coffee and doughnuts. Arina did worry about her passport. She dared not tell Jacob her government had canceled it.

"Why hasn't the tiger been seen?" Jacob asked.

"Undisturbed, a tiger eats most of its kill; there is little to see."

"It could be in Mexico by now. It could live for years in thickets. It could lie down and die. I predict we'll never see or hear of it again."

"We will hear of it," Arina said.

"Arina, I've enjoyed having these breakfasts with you." He was rewarded with a wan smile. "I hope that we are friends."

"Yes."

"Then tell me what is bothering you. You are eating your fingers."

"Something is wrong," she said. "Something is terribly wrong. I think Andrei has been arrested."

"Why?"

"Andrei was a dreamer, a Communist."

"What has this got to do with you?"

"Nothing. I don't know. Andrei loved the Soviet Union. He believed that the Soviet Union would be restored but that first Russia would have to be destroyed. The Nazis destroyed much of Russia, but the Soviet Union became stronger than ever. Risk all to gain all, he said. We argued many times."

"Why didn't you marry him?"

"Andrei? No. Andrei is a brilliant scientist. He is amusing, surprising, but a husband? No."

"Why not?"

"Too dedicated."

Yeah, so had he been. That's why Pam left.

"Let's not talk about him anymore. We are not . . . we have not been lovers for a long time. We are too different. Andrei thinks in absolutes."

"Black and white."

"Yes, black and white."

"And you see gray?"

"I see people," Arina said.

"Am I one of them?"

"Yes. I know I am not stylish. I do not know how to dress like an American."

"Come here," he said. He reached out to her, and she slid into his embrace.

"Will you tell me about the woman you love?" she asked.

"Yes," he sighed, "but it'll take all afternoon and a six-pack of beer."

Jacob drove to Freer, stopping at Muy Grande Village Grocery and Sporting Goods. Arina stiffened as a pickup stopped beside them. Two men in camouflage stepped out of the truck. Two other men dressed in camouflage waited in the bed of the truck, guns in their hands.

"Hunters," Jacob said. "Come on. We're going to get lunch." He asked what she wanted, but she shrugged and watched the men in camouflage who bought shotgun shells.

Jacob bought Shiner beer, bread, mustard, and bologna. He bought a camouflage cap and placed it on Arina's head. "Souvenir," he said. She did not laugh.

Jacob parked in a shady spot beside the road, made sandwiches, and opened beers. While he ate he told her that after he married Pam he had applied for a job as biologist for the Federal government. There were no openings. He was given a contract in a Federal program to relocate mountain lions from areas where they were destroying bighorn sheep. It meant a move to Fort Davis.

He didn't tell her that he didn't mind his mother teaching him to cook and sew. He didn't mind learning embroidery; working beside his mother was pleasurable to him. He didn't want to fill his mother's emotional needs. He became more private; she demanded more of his thoughts and feelings; he left in anger. It was a pattern he had repeated in marriage. "You don't always love the right person," he said. "She needed someone to show her off. I needed someone to keep supper warm until I got home."

"There have been no other women?"

When he came home, Pam was waiting for him, like a bride, shy, vulnerable, eager. The love they made was the truest thing he had known. "It would have been a fraud. At first I couldn't do that to Pam, then I couldn't do it to myself. Now I couldn't do it to someone else."

It was a wonderful afternoon, the happiest Jacob had known in a long time. But when he drove up outside the hotel he didn't know how to prolong the closeness he felt. "Arina—"

"Jacob, I must be alone," she said. "I must think." When she turned on the TV for news of the flight attendant she saw stories of rogue cowboys and rogue policemen who exacted vengeance, not justice.

. . .

Bump Wilkerson received two important telephone calls. The first was from Hailee White who offered to give him a voice on network TV. It was so exactly his dream that he was slow to seize it. Thinking the pause was hesitation, she had offered him money, enough to buy an Uzi.

Bump was suspicious of the second call, coming so soon after the first, from a caller who would not identify himself. "I am a property owner," the caller said. "And gun collector. The fewer who know my name, the smaller my chances of being robbed." *Or investigated,* Bump thought. "I want to protect my rights, and I want Federal agents out of my hair. I will pay cash to assure that the tiger is killed quickly. The FAA has restricted airspace around the area, so that means killed from the ground and that means you. Ten thousand now, ten more when the newspapers say the tiger is dead, an additional ten for the tiger's ashes."

"Ashes?" Not ears or tail as proof of kill?

"Ashes and I want all of them. Ten thousand."

"How do I know you're not a Fed?"

"If I was, this would be entrapment, and you could kill the tiger and go free. I want the tiger dead. Not captured. Dead. I want ashes."

"Thirty men at a hundred dollars a day—"

"You don't have thirty good men. Good men," the caller reiterated when Bump tried to interrupt.

"We know this country."

"So do I. I know who is in the brush, and what they're doing. If I see you breaking your ass, I'll send more. Both you and I will be happier when the Feds have no excuse for prowling the country."

Bump wondered who he could count on. Roy Pat for sure; he wouldn't have to pay him. Jimmy Guy would go for the money and so would his team. If they could kill the tiger there'd be enough money for Uzis, MAC-10s, maybe an M-60. "You won't see or hear us in the brush."

"I'll know. And when I have the ashes, I'll know who killed it."

Bump didn't like the way the caller was so sure of himself, like a Fed. He could be walking into a trap but nothing they couldn't shoot themselves out of.

6

Rand insisted that Jacob submit to an interview with Hailee White. "She thinks you're just waiting for the tiger to kill again. There's a lot of pressure to capture the tiger quickly. From Stuart Johnson, from Congress, animal rights activists, the public, the media. If that tiger kills another person, we can lose control of the situation. She thinks you and Arina are more interested in each other than in the tiger."

Jacob glared at Rand, who shrugged apologetically. "Hailee will have a story—you and the tiger, you and Arina, or you the mystery man."

"No questions about my personal life, past or present," Jacob said.

Hailee had seized the attention of the country with her newsbreak about a tiger in the passenger section of an airliner. She had held their attention with news of the crash and interviews with survivors who had witnessed a tiger attack. When interest waned, Tony had gotten spectacular footage of blood-splattered trees, dead dogs, and the tasteful but identifiable corpses of two men.

She had interviewed a woman who was unable to hang out clothes because a tiger hid in her back yard, a rancher who had seen Russian hunters in his pasture, a teenager who had seen UN bases along the border, a man who had discovered a plot to breed tigers in Texas. So had every other reporter. Fear, anger, and suspicion gripped South Texas, but there was nothing that demanded a camera on the scene. She needed a network story. Hailee liked Jacob Trace, but this wasn't about him. This was about news, and she needed him to provide it.

She wanted to interview him outdoors pointing at tiger sign, or walking cautiously through the brush with his rifle before him. Jacob insisted that he be interviewed in the media room. He refused to pose with his rifle, and he was dressed for the outdoors, looking like a man taken away from his duties by the camera.

"Mr. Trace, why have your efforts to capture the tigers been unsuccessful?"

"I got a dart in the tiger, enough to slow it but not enough to stop it."

"You have been accused of being a Lone Ranger."

"I work alone, with my dogs, but I'm under contract—"

Hailee cut him off. No one wanted to hear about puma relocation. "You were the lone ranger when you followed a tiger into a house. You took your rifle, not the tranquilizer gun, and you killed the tiger."

"A woman had been attacked by the tiger, there was a baby in the house, there was no one to go with me, and the tiger could have eaten a good part of me before the tranquilizer took effect."

This sparring was going nowhere. She began again. "Why are you the only one capable of capturing the tiger."

"I'm not. I'm the one who has been hired. If we locate the tiger only one person is needed to put a dart in it. The important thing is locating it. There's a lot of country and a lot of cover and a lot for a tiger to eat. Something is driving it westward. The more people looking for it, the farther the tiger will be driven.

"Since this method hasn't worked, why haven't you tried other methods?"

"We are trying other methods. The Fish and Wildlife boys have baited traps and have caught everything from coons to cougars but no tiger. To bait the tiger, we have to know where it is, and it has to remain long enough for the bait to attract it."

"Couldn't you use the militia to help you locate the tiger?"

"There is a difference between a hunter and a shooter. I am trying to capture the tiger. I carry a rifle in case I am attacked. I don't carry a gun when I'm not trailing a dangerous animal. I'm not that frightened."

"Are you saying that people who carry guns are cowards? Bump Wilkerson, for example?"

"I'm saying you need a reason to carry a gun, and fear is the usual reason. Fear of not looking macho or fear of not being macho."

"Some people say that you are more interested in protecting the property of Russia than the lives and property of US citizens."

"I don't think you should quote such stupid statements without identifying the source."

"You didn't answer my question."

"You didn't identify your source. It wasn't you, was it?"

"Mr. Trace, there is a tiger loose in Texas. People want to

know why the tiger has not been captured. Why aren't more people looking for it?"

"Every game warden and police officer in the state is looking for the tiger. Pilots, truck drivers, motorists, citizens have reported seeing the tiger. We check out every sighting."

She fired more shots, but she knew she had missed the heart. The only use she could find for this was as an intro to the interview with Bump. She looked at Tony Garcia. He signaled a chop, and she ended the interview. She would settle with Mr. Trace later.

Tony Garcia drove Hailee down the unmarked, unnamed caliche road, following the directions he had gotten over the telephone. He stopped the car when a figure dressed entirely in camouflage stepped into the road. "Put these over your head," the militiaman said, handing hoods to Tony and Hailee. "I'll drive." Tony smelled beer on the man's breath. Tony knew the brush country, and this was smack in the middle of it, not a house, store, or gas station for miles.

The car drove down the road for an indeterminate time, then bumped and wound around what was clearly not a road. Tony heard brush scraping the sides of the car and wondered what the car rental agency and the station manager were going to say about that.

"Why would a man such as yourself look for a tiger?" Hailee asked.

"Because Federal agents are going to snoop around until we find it. They want to know who we are, what kind of guns we have. They want to regulate us out of business the way they do everything else. Maybe replace us with UN troops or spic militia."

"And for that you would kill an endangered animal?"

"This is not about endangered animals. It's about control. They can't control immigration, they can't control drugs or crime or the budget, so they try to control guns. If they can put us out of business, they have put the Constitution out of business. The only rights we have are the ones guaranteed by the right to bear arms."

"Isn't the militia violating the rights of landowners by hunting the tiger on private property?"

"I'm not supposed to talk to you. No more questions."

When the car stopped and the blindfolds were removed, Tony saw Bump Wilkerson. His face was painted, and over cammies, he wore a web belt with a Colt .45 on one side and a K-Bar jungle knife on the other.

Tony had grown up in Robstown and knew Bump was named after his mother, Irma Diego, but anyone who called him Diego was looking for a fight. Bump had once deliberately walked into Tony. Tony could whip Bump, but Bump would shoot up his car, maybe shoot him.

"No pictures of our weapons, just me," Bump said, putting a hand on the camera. Although Bump and the driver were the only ones visible, Tony knew others were out of sight.

Hailee signaled to Tony that she was ready. The first take had to be scrubbed because the mike picked up a jet, and Hailee wanted nothing to spoil the sense of wilderness isolation.

"We are in the brush country of South Texas with a group of hardy men who have pledged their lives to defend their country in the event of a takeover by left-wing forces, either foreign or domestic. Here with us is the leader of this army, Bump Wilkerson. Mr. Wilkerson, is this secrecy necessary or is it game playing?" Hailee asked.

"We don't bother anybody—except those who want to regulate us and take our weapons. Federal agents spy on us, they violate our privacy rights, they try to track us down in the brush. We have a few surprises for them."

Tony had heard stories about hunters and game wardens

stepping into snares, dead falls, pit falls, animal traps, treble hooks hanging in trails.

"There are rumors that the militia recently got into a brawl over a racist remark by one of your men and were thrown out of a bar."

"I don't know how stories like that get started, but I know how to stop them. We will not be intimidated, and we will not be ridiculed."

Bump described his men as ordinary citizens who walked an extra mile for their country. When Hailee asked why they weren't in the military service or National Guard, Bump answered that some of the men were veterans, some were too young, too old, had too many dependents, or had jobs that were important for the community. "We cost the taxpayer nothing," Bump said. "Not even for arms, uniforms, or training. My men are rangers, trained to move about unseen, to live off the land if they have to. Folks around here don't have no idea how many of us there are. If there is a war we can't be betrayed because no one knows who or where we are."

Tony only half-listened. He knew Hailee would never use any of this. This was to start Bump talking, to make the important questions seem less pointed. His ears perked when he heard Hailee mention the tiger. That was Hailee's beat.

"How do you know where to look for the tiger?"

"We have our methods, our intelligence. And we're doing better than the Feds who have helicopters and airplanes."

"How do you account for that?"

"They aren't looking for the tiger. They're looking for us."

"But you want to kill the tiger."

"The Russians sent tigers over here to gain access to the country and spy on us. The plane crash was no accident. People who were buckled down were killed, but two tigers walked out of the wreckage? State and Federal agents look for the tiger, but only one man can capture it; not kill it, but capture it. Why? Because as long as the tiger is loose, Russians and Feds will run around and pretend to look for the tiger and spy on citizens. And they're going to keep looking until that tiger is dead."

"Or captured."

"Dead. Because if it's captured it will escape again, maybe in another part of the country, and the spying will start all over again. Who's looking? Jacob Trace, a Federal agent, and a woman who represents Russia or the United Nations or both."

"Mr. Trace says the tiger could be dead or in Mexico."

"If the tiger is dead, the government will never admit it so they can keep looking. It's up to us to find it, dead or alive. If it's in Mexico, we'll go to Mexico to get it."

"Mr. Trace said your efforts to kill the tiger were driving it westward."

"Our efforts to keep the tiger out of Corpus Christi and other cities have been successful. I'm happy to see he gave us credit for that."

"Mr. Trace says people want guns because they're afraid."

"Yeah, I'm afraid," Bump sneered. "I'm afraid the government doesn't want America to be different from other countries, doesn't want America to be armed so that Americans are safe to do business anywhere in the world, doesn't want law-abiding citizens to carry guns so they can sleep, live, work without fear of robbers, murderers, rapists. Oh yeah, I'm afraid Mr. Trace won't be armed when I run into him in the brush."

"Mr. Wilkerson, are you religious?"

"I know God is on my side. I know that in the beginning America belonged to God and now it doesn't anymore, and that's why all these horrible things happen—blacks rioting, looting, raping, living off welfare. Mexicans coming across the border and taking jobs from white people, and bringing drugs and diseases with them. The godless UN is trying to take over America, and our government is helping them. What you see here is a very small part of the picture."

Hailee looked at Tony, Tony signed okay, and Hailee ended the interview. Tony was impressed. A loco army was running around in South Texas, and nobody did anything about it.

Jacob and Arina checked out a site where several sheep had been killed. Coyotes. They stopped for lunch in a small town with a single cafe, Chance and Chaos Chili. When they walked in, Arina caught his arm. "Everyone is looking," she said.

"Look back and nod. Smile if you want to." Jacob nodded, and the diners returned to their food. He decided to let Arina discover small towns for herself.

"Sit anywhere, honey," the waitress said. She was thin, wrinkled, and cigarette smoke curled past her lip, past her colorless eyebrows and through her bright red hair.

"No smoking section," Arina said.

"No one's smoking at that booth over there."

Arina looked at Jacob; he shrugged and followed the waitress to the booth. "May I see a menu?" Arina asked.

"Hamburger, Mexican plate, or chili."

"Bowl of red," Jacob said.

"I wish to see a menu," Arina said.

The waitress made a smacking noise with her mouth and left. It took her a while to find a menu, but she was cheerful about it. "Here you go," she said triumphantly, handing Arina a stained and yellowed menu.

"I would like a fruit plate."

"Let me see that menu," the waitress said, jerking it from her hand. "We've never had a fruit plate. Let me see if Spud used all the nanners in the pudding." She returned in triumph. "I can slice two nanners on a plate for you. You want crackers and peanut butter with that?"

"You should have tried the chili," Jacob said, trying not to laugh at Arina's confusion as she stared at two sliced bananas on her plate.

When they left, the waitress stopped them. "Where did you get your accent, honey?"

"Russia," Arina said defiantly.

"Spud, come here. We got a visitor from Russia. This is my husband, Spud. We own this place."

"Where you from?" Spud asked Jacob.

"Fort Davis. Know where that is?"

"I think I do, but I think I'm wrong."

"Here, I want to give you something," the waitress said, handing Arina an ashtray in the shape of Texas. "To remember us."

Arina left the cafe in tears. "What's the matter?" Jacob asked.

"There is no menu, no fruit plate, no non-smoking area, and they give me an ashtray," Arina said, laughing and crying at the same time.

"What did you want? Another nanner?" he asked as he drove away.

"They were so . . . trusting."

"The kind of people it's easy to fool. But when they figure it out, watch out. Those are the people who forced Nixon out of office."

"They seem so content with themselves."

"They're married. Didn't you ever want to get married?"

Arina stared out the window of the truck. Stepan Pagodev, her fiance, had introduced her to love. After he died she was filled with longing for what she had felt with him but believed it would never happen again. "He was a scientist. We met in school; we planned to get married. He was sent to Tobolsk.

141

It is a very old, very beautiful city in Siberia. Oil was discovered nearby. Many scientists were sent there. There was an accident."

"What kind of accident?"

Arina shrugged. "Officials said there was an accident. He was dead. Since then—for a long time I was lonely. For a woman it is not easy. Men want to be companions for a few minutes or for a lifetime. There were no men with whom I wanted to spend a lifetime or a few minutes. Then I met Andrei. He was lonely too. Sometimes we spent our loneliness together. He is a brilliant man, but he does not fill my heart. Do you understand?"

"Yes." Until he met Arina, Jacob did not know he was lonely. He thought what he felt was grief. "I don't get lonely when I'm alone." On the trail of a cat in the mountains, going to sleep looking at the stars, listening to a fire, he was not lonely. He looked into Arina's eyes and believed he saw a longing as intense as his own. Arina dropped her eyes.

"No," she said, touching his arm. "It cannot be. No matter how much we both desire it. Things are happening in my country, your country that we do not understand, that we hardly know about. But we are a part of it."

"Part of what?"

"Things we don't know about. The airplane crash, the death of the flight attendant, the—" She almost said, the telegram.

"I don't know what you are talking about."

She tried to form words then made a gesture with her hands. "In movies Americans meet, they make love, they say goodbye. Making love is everything. Ideas, promises, duties mean nothing. I am not like that. I am . . . I am out of date."

Jacob nodded. He didn't make love to Pam until they were married. After the engagement, Pam was willing, but it was important to him to prove that he wasn't controlled by his body or its demands. Just as he could keep trailing when his body screamed stop, he could stop when his body screamed forget consequences. He wanted to be better than that, and he had been. He wanted to tell Arina that he was out of date also, but he didn't know where to begin. "People think we are in love, perhaps lovers."

"In America everything is a movie," she said. "I need you to be real."

Arina lay on her bed, tired but too agitated to sleep. She loved her country with its glorious and painful history. How many times she and Andrei had argued how to make the country better. He was so brilliant, so impatient. Then democracy had come—democrazy—Andrei had called it. What had happened to her country? *Why had she been ordered home?*

Jacob had introduced her to fajitas, margaritas. He taught her to dance to "La Bamba," "Whiskey River," "Cotton-Eyed Joe." He had introduced her to Americans who criticized their country but loved it, who had little but gave much. She loved Jacob, but he was an American. How could he escape the values of his country? The violence, arrogance, greed, individualism to the point of paranoia, worship of private property above the common good? She dreamed of marrying Jacob, giving him the happiness that a woman could give a man. It was a lovely dream, but only a dream.

She did not want to believe that Andrei had been involved in biological warfare research. The project had been canceled, the labs closed, the scientists arrested. *But why had Russia canceled her passport and ordered her to return unless Andrei had clandestinely continued the experiments? Had he implicated her?*

Every day she expected the Americans to deport her at Russia's request. She would have no opportunity to explain to Jacob. He, Evelyn, Rand, would believe that she and Andrei were co-conspirators. She had to tell Jacob she had been ordered home. She knocked on his door. But if she told him he would have to report her or be in trouble with his government. He appeared, tucking in his shirt.

She looked at him in confusion. "I must talk to you," she said. "Would you come to my room?"

South of the junction of Highway 359 and a caliche road that wound westward through the chaparral to the Conoco Driscoll oil field in Duval County was an oasis of twisted mesquites and battered pickup trucks. Its primary feature was an unpainted, one-room structure on short juniper pilings with exterior walls of weathered boards and a peaked roof covered with cracked asphalt shingles. "Tortuga's" was painted above the single front door, but only the center of the word was lighted by the glow of a dust-encrusted sixty-watt bulb above the wooden stoop and entrance.

Tortuga's was a landmark, especially to employees of the Texas Mexican Railway that sliced south out of Benavides, through brush country, and curved eastward to parallel the highway near a dry prong of Concepción Creek. The line passed within fifty yards of the rear of the cantina, and freights blew their whistle and slowed to a crawl so that Tortuga could hurry out the back door and pass bottles of cold beer to occupants of the locomotive and the caboose. The railroad men discarded the bottles down the line. *El Tonto* returned the bottles to Tortuga.

Emiliano "Tortuga" Martinez was five-feet-two but weighed 220 pounds. His nickname had been hand-tooled across the back of a wide leather belt, but it, and the gold and silver western buckle, were hidden by his overhanging belly. He had inherited his hooked nose from his Aztec ancestors and his lumbering walk from his years as a cook aboard a destroyer. There was a hint of gray in his dark, oiled hair, and he moved slowly and deliberately, even when breaking up fights between patrons.

Tortuga's was open seven days a week, but Saturdays were the busiest. Every Saturday morning, Tortuga barbecued young goats over a pit behind the cantina and sold cabrito tacos, beans, beer, and soft drinks to ranch and oil-field hands and their families on Saturday afternoon, while the men and their sons played baseball on the grassless diamond that was flanked by the highway, the railroad tracks, and the dry arroyo. Tortuga baked the heads of the goats in a hole beside the pit and saved the succulent meat for his family's Sunday breakfast. What was left over he gave to *El Tonto* for returning bottles.

At night Tortuga's was a man's place. Tortuga ignored fighting as long as it took place outside his cantina. When his property was threatened he plodded from behind the bar with a taped grubbing hoe handle in his pudgy hands. Rowdy patrons learned to respect the hoe handle after more than a few had gone to Sunday morning Mass with fresh stitches in their scalps.

The jukebox beside the back door blared *conjunto* songs from the 1920s and 1930s. Tortuga refused to change records even after they became so scratched the lyrics to *"Tenia Una Negra,"* sung by Los Hermanos Chavarria, backed by guitar and accordion, were no longer discernible. He and his customers knew the songs by heart and often sang along.

> I had a dark skinned lady whom I loved
> and never, never was I to forget her,

> but the ungrateful one was disloyal,
> she was untrue and did me wrong.

Two oil-field workers, Enrique Vara and Reynaldo Lopez, came in. There was room for four tables and sixteen chairs between the bar and the five windows in the wall opposite the bar. The bar was lined with patrons, and all but one chair was filled. Vara sat in the empty chair. Lopez grabbed the back of *El Tonto's* chair and motioned him to move.

Tortuga did not like Vara or Lopez. He knew they would drink enough beer to get high, then go to bars in Benavides and Freer frequented by women. He liked *El Tonto;* he did not like to see him pushed around, but if the boy did nothing to defend himself—Tortuga shrugged.

Felipe Serna, called *El Tonto,* or the Dunce, was born on the JT Ranch and still lived there with his parents. He was slight, of medium height, and able to gentle and train horses faster and better than any hand on the ranch. The JT paid him enough to drink at Tortuga's on Saturday nights. Twice a year he bought himself a bright western shirt with pearl-colored snaps instead of buttons.

El Tonto tried to find a place at the stained, wooden bar, scarred by countless cigarettes. Patrons in scuffed boots caked with cow dung, jeans and shirts streaked with oil-field grime or blood from castrating and ear-marking calves stood shoulder-to-shoulder. The rubbing of shoulders was a frequent source of friction as the men jostled one another.

> I loved her, I adored her
> and she fell in love with another man.
> Oh! What an unfortunate fate of mine;
> how impassioned I find myself.

Tortuga watched his customers through puffy eyelids and listened to their conversations. The patrons switched from Spanish to English to a Tex-Mex mixture of the two. Most of the talk was about women, and women were trouble. The name of the wrong woman, spoken by the wrong man, in the wrong tone of voice was certain and sudden violence.

Enrique Vara headed for the back door to relieve himself. Two wooden outhouses were located twenty yards behind the bar, but at night no one walked that far. Some didn't even walk down the steps outside the door. *"¡Hijuela chingada!"* The cry was loud and prolonged, and Vara was still finishing it when he burst through the back door, his eyes wide, his fly open. He ran through the cantina and out the front door. The patrons stared, stunned by the sudden entrance and exit, as if expecting Vara to race through the cantina again. Los Hermanos Chavarria sang:

> Now the locks are all shut
> because one man did not know how to live.
> Oh! Love don't leave me,
> I want to die in your embrace.

The music did not drown out the snarl, and every head in the cantina turned to see the back door filled with Siberian tiger. Outside they could hear Vara trying to start the engine of his pickup. The tiger took two hesitant steps inside the door as the patrons froze. Vara's pickup roared to life. There was the crunch of gravel, a crash as he hit a parked car, the squealing of tires on the pavement as he sped away.

Lopez jumped from his chair, screamed *"Vamonos, cabrones"* and dived head first through a window. Others followed, some diving through windows, others through the front door. A few, unable to escape, remained where they stood, crossing themselves, and whispering prayers to the Virgin Mother.

> I still remember that afternoon
> when I slept in your arms
> never thinking you were another's.
> I only thought you were mine.

El Tonto whipped his leather belt from his waist, picked up a chair and held it in front of him as he advanced toward the tiger. "Ha." *El Tonto* shoved the chair toward the massive head of the tiger and tried to use his belt like a bullwhip. It wasn't long enough to make a loud pop. "Ha."

"*Cuidado, hombre,*" Tortuga said hoarsely.

> My love, I bid farewell,
> we'll never talk again.
> You left me, rejected me,
> you didn't want me, let it be God's will.

The words of caution seemed to spur *El Tonto*. He spoke softly in Spanish to the tiger, then shoved the chair toward its face again and slapped the belt against the floor. "Ha, *tigre.* Ha."

The tiger's ears and lips trembled. It plucked at the floor with its claws, lashed its tail from side to side but retreated a step. Spectators peering in the door and windows cheered, "*¡Ole!*" The cry drew the cat's attention, and *El Tonto* took advantage of the distraction. "Ha." He thrust the stool at the tiger and slapped the belt sharply against the floor again.

The tiger snarled at Felipe, baring its long fangs. It clawed at the legs of the stool, peeling splinters of wood, but it retreated another step. Felipe pressed his advantage. The tiger snarled again, turned, and walked out the door. *El Tonto* closed the back door.

The patrons dived back through the windows and jammed the front door, trying to get inside. They slammed shut the door and braced tables against the windows. Once the cantina was secured, Tortuga stepped behind the bar and opened a longneck. *"El Tigre,"* he said handing it to Felipe. "I drink to *El Tigre."*

"El Tigre," the others shouted, crowding around, slapping him on the back. *El Tigre* smiled. No one went home that night, no one ventured outside. Tortuga broke the liquor laws and sold beer until daylight. Except to *El Tigre*. For *El Tigre* the beer was free. And no one in Duval County ever called Felipe Serna *El Tonto* again.

Jacob was awake, pissed off, and in love. He had followed Arina to her room, but before she could speak he had crushed her against the door, pressing his body to hers. "No," she said. His mouth was on her mouth. His hands were in her hair. "I must tell you something," she said.

"And I have to tell you. I love you."

"Russia is finding its way in a new world. Some prefer the old way, some would destroy the government, perhaps the country, to restore the old way."

"We'll find our own way," Jacob said, licking her ear.

"There were Russians who were committed to the Soviet Union, even if that meant war with the West. They did not change overnight. The government knows who they are. Mostly, they are powerless."

"I'm powerless around you," he said, kissing her neck, the hollow of her shoulder.

"Andrei spoke of experiments . . . ."

"Forget Andrei. We'll have our own experiments." His hands caressed her arms, her belly.

" . . . biological warfare . . . the old regime."

"This is the new regime."

"Jacob, please."

His hands, his mouth found her breasts. "He worked on these experiments?"

"No. He said . . . he did not. He knew some who . . . did. Jacob . . . Jacob . . . I must . . . Jacob, I want you." Slowly they slid to the floor.

Later, he carried her to the bed and made love to her again, this time thoroughly, less urgently. He had been awake most of the night, but he did not move because Arina's head was on his shoulder. For a long time, after their bodies had lost their urgency, they had held each other and talked. She told him about childhood in a small town on the Dneiper. "My mother and father were very poor," she said. "Times were hard, but people worked together. And together they were the first to put a man in orbit."

Every morning the cowherd came down the street blowing his horn. Her father led their cow out of its stall to join the others that the cowherd took to pasture. Then he hobbled to school where he was a teacher. As a schoolboy, he had been injured in the bombing. Her mother, the train master of the village, died of cancer. Arina had excelled in school, and her father had wanted her to be a doctor. She did not want patients who suffered the way her parents did. She became a veterinarian.

"I want to show you Moscow," she said. "The ballet, of course, and Red Square when the soft snow is falling. Gorky Park. The zoo is not so nice. But I want you to see the people. I want to drink coffee with you in a small, crowded cafe, ride the subway, and walk the streets."

Jacob told her of his beloved Davis Mountains. He wanted to ride the hills with her, to lie with her under the stars, to sleep with her between a campfire and a stream, to watch the sunrise and sunset.

His talk of Texas seemed to calm her, but she persisted.

"Will you live in Moscow with me?" she asked. His look revealed his answer. "You see. It is beautiful but impossible."

For a while they held each other, the silence making their togetherness complete. "Jacob, why have they not reported how the stewardess died?"

"They reported her death because it's weird that she survived a tiger and a plane crash. No one is interested in how she died."

"Your media grow rich by creating interest in soap, cigarettes, rock singers, athletes. But they don't create an interest in important news."

"Why do you care? You're not even an American," he joked.

She did not move, but he knew she had retreated into the secret self he did not understand. "You don't care to know why the stewardess died?"

"I'm sorry she died. Sam Storey and Roy Farley died. Jonelle Parker would have died if I hadn't killed the tiger."

"When you shot the tiger—"

"I was scared out of my wits."

"It was necessary to save the woman, was it not?"

"I had gotten her and the child out of the house. I was trying to save myself."

"But you shot the tiger for no other reason but to save yourself?"

He was puzzled by her question. "I don't have anything personal against tigers, if that's what you mean."

"Why did you want the hide? The fangs?"

Jacob shrugged. "Souvenir. If I kill this one—" She jumped, and he held her tight. "If it is necessary to kill this one, I'll have you a necklace made of tiger fangs and claws."

She had quietly drifted to sleep. Jacob had not. He tried to picture himself in Moscow, some job where it was not necessary that he speak or read Russian. After work he would meet

Arina to drink coffee in a small crowded cafe. They would ride the subway to their home and make love every night. Desperately he tried to hold that picture in his mind, but always the dream shattered.

While he had been worrying about the tiger, this woman had attached herself to him. Slipped inside him and taught him that loneliness was being without her. But being with her was impossible. He lay awake wondering if love was worth the pain. He had disappointed his mother. He had disappointed Pam. He would disappoint Arina by loving her and refusing to go with her. He wondered if he could endure again the reproach he had seen in Pam's eyes. "I loved you. I gave you everything, but you preferred your mountains, your dogs."

His thoughts were interrupted by knocking. Forgetting he was in Arina's room, he opened the door and saw Evelyn.

"Jacob," she said. "I have been calling your room for an hour. The tiger has been seen. You'd better bring her too."

Arina quickly dressed while Jacob returned to his room for fresh clothes. When they entered the media room Evelyn looked at Arina, her eyebrows arched, her mouth droll. Arina knew what she thought—Russian woman seduced by handsome, rugged American. Everything was a movie.

"I hope you two slept well," Evelyn said.

Rand unfolded a state highway map on his desk. He, Jacob, and Evelyn closed around it. Arina had to look over Evelyn's head. "This is where the tiger was last seen," Rand said. "Near Realitos. It walked into a bar and walked out without attacking anyone. This one isn't a man-eater."

"Not necessarily," Jacob said. "I read about a tiger in India that picked up a woodcutter in its jaws, then dropped him and walked away."

"Zoo tigers are even more unpredictable," Arina said, "and very intelligent. Some think tigers actually reason."

"Still heading generally westward," Jacob said. "I think we should move our operations to Laredo."

"Right," Evelyn said. "Randy, tell Stuart from now on we're working out of Laredo."

"I have no authority—" Rand began, then stopped. "I don't think it's necessary. Besides it will take days to get reorganized."

Arina did not believe that the petty bickering that preceded every decision, the reluctance to take responsibility, was usual for Americans. If rogue scientists had succeeded in developing tiger carriers of deadly diseases, as she suspected, it was necessary to capture the tiger quickly. "Jacob, we must use your dogs to locate the tiger."

"Not my dogs."

"The tiger must be located quickly or more people will die."

"Including whoever follows the dogs."

"Perhaps NAZA will buy your dogs," Arina said.

"I trained my dogs. They do what I ask them. We trust each other. If a cougar turns on me, those dogs will risk their lives to help me. I'm not putting them up against something they can't handle. Not for any money."

"Then how will we find the tiger?"

"Helicopter. We know the general direction the tiger is going. We start where it was last seen, near Realitos." He looked at Arina. She looked away. "We need a helicopter, Rand."

"Barry Windom said he would work with you again. I need confirmation from the director. I expect him to call."

"For God's sake, I'll call," Evelyn said, grabbing a telephone.

"Tell him we're moving to Laredo," Jacob said.

Rand assumed no authority, Evelyn assumed too much authority, and Jacob acted as though there was no authority, Arina thought. If Jacob was not working for NAZA, then who was he working for?

"We're moving to La Posada in Laredo," Evelyn said. "Stuart is making reservations. And you've got a helicopter," she said to Jacob as though personally granting his request. *How could she accomplish so much so fast?* "How do we proceed?" Evelyn asked Jacob as though he were in control.

"I'll ride in the helicopter and watch for buzzards. When the tiger kills again, I'll set up a stand, wait for the tiger to return, and dart it."

"I must be there when the tiger is captured," Arina said. "I must see that it is properly caged."

"It's too dangerous," Jacob said. "You and Evelyn take the pickup and get things set up in Laredo. Rand, try to get the media to hold the tiger sighting. We should be miles ahead of the militia on this."

7

Curiosity seekers who came to hear the story of *El Tigre* had obliterated all sign around Tortuga's. Jacob walked in ever larger circles looking for tracks but found nothing. Then he and Barry looked for the tiger while Barry flew low S-patterns working generally westward. They landed twice to check buzzard feasts but found no sign.

When they returned to Laredo, Jacob waited for Arina to knock on his door but she did not. Desperate to talk to her, he walked down the hall to her room.

"Jacob," Evelyn said, coming out of her room. "I was coming to get you and Arina to have a drink with me."

"I'll take a rain check," he said. "I'm going to bed." All the way to his room he cursed himself. *He wasn't married, he didn't care what Evelyn thought, why didn't he tell her he wanted to talk to Arina alone.*

. . .

Life in Laredo followed the same pattern as that in Corpus Christi except that the search was aerial and, to keep their eyes fresh, observers rotated at regular intervals, even Rand taking a turn. Jacob and Evelyn spent a hot, dusty afternoon in the helicopter. Twice they landed to check out carcasses. Twice they refueled the helicopter before Windom set it down for the night at Laredo International Airport. Jacob offered to buy everyone a beer to cut the dust, but Barry wanted to prepare the helicopter for an early morning start.

"I guess it's the two of us," Evelyn said. "You're a native, where do you want to go?"

"A nice, quiet place," he told the cabbie. His ears still rang from the noise of the helicopter.

The driver left them at a bar that was cool, dim, and deserted. Even the jukebox was silent. They sat in a booth away from the bar and talked.

"I insist," Evelyn said, pressing her money on the waitress but smiling at Jacob. "I'm a liberated gal. I pay my own way."

"Tell me about your son."

Her eyes misted, and she looked away. It happened every time; two beers and mention of her child reduced her to tears. "Bright. Tough, but that's all right, I'm tough. Hard, and that's not all right. That comes from his father. That's what attracted me to him, I guess, only I thought it was strength. I thought he had values. He went to work for a defense contractor. I could accept that if he believed in defending the weak."

Thought of her ex-husband turned tears to anger. She knew it was not healthy to have such violent thoughts. "I used to think love was so rare and wonderful that it could work out anything." She smiled, tried to change her mood. "What if you threw pride to the wind and went to your ex-wife?"

"She has a husband and two children."

156

"I'm sorry," Evelyn said. To feel hatred, love, grief, anything, for someone who was dead was painful but there was a limit; that was dead pain. But to hate, or love, or grieve someone who was alive but beyond reach was live pain, pain without limitation, without surcease. "I try to understand people, but deliberate cruelty—" She shook her head. "I can't understand people like John, or Bump Wilkerson."

"Bump fears a world government will take over the country."

"He's right to fear globalization, but it won't be the UN. It will be control by multinational companies that have no allegiances to countries or constitutions, to peace, people, or the environment, that know no laws except profit. And the poor of this country will furnish the armies that defend them from competition and regulation."

Jacob signaled to the waitress, and this time he paid for the drinks. "I'm an unliberated man," he said.

Evelyn laughed. She needed to laugh. "You look pretty liberated to me," she said, bumping him with her elbow. "You know what you want. That's rare in men. Women too. We're two rare birds, almost extinct." She laughed again. She wanted a man who was reliable and straightforward or dashing and dangerous. John was reliably dull and cruel. Rand was bookish. Barry was self-sufficient. Jacob resisted labels. "You risked your life to save that woman and baby from the tiger. I know you didn't want to kill the tiger."

"Have you ever looked a tiger in the eye?"

"Yes," Evelyn said, thinking of the soft orange fur, rounded ears, the pale, almost liquid eyes. "Yes, I have."

"Through bars," Jacob said. "What I saw was blind ferocity, totally devoid of empathy. I was meat. Killing me meant no more than tearing into a loaf of bread. When I saw that tiger at the top of the stairs, I wanted it dead more than I've ever wanted anything."

"Because you were scared."

"Damn right I was scared. Did you look at Sam Storey's body? There is no mercy in a tiger. One of the stories I read was about a tiger that grabbed a boy out of his mother's arms and ate it. The mother fled to a rock ledge, and the tiger came after her. She jumped to her death rather than be eaten alive." Jacob shook his head.

"Do you ever wish the world was the way it used to be? Bears, wolves, buffalo on the prairies, beavers in the creeks?"

"I thought you were a liberal, and you're a conservative."

"Conservatives want to plunder the earth for their profit. The only thing they want to conserve is their right to do so. We can't turn the world back to the way it was, but we can preserve a bit of it for our children. I don't like putting animals in cages, but sometimes zoos seem the only way to save them."

"Maybe that's why I like the mountains," Jacob said. "There's not a lot you can do to a mountain. About the only thing we have to fear is developers turning it into ranchettes."

Evelyn took him lightly by the arm. "You do understand," she said.

"Come to Fort Davis some time. I'll show you around."

"I'd like that," Evelyn said. "Miles and miles without cars or houses, animals living the way God intended."

"None of them likes to be petted and some, like snakes, skunks, scorpions, can be unpleasant."

"I'd feel safe with you," she said. "Jacob, I'm sorry if I embarrassed you when I came to Arina's room."

Jacob shrugged but didn't say anything. She admired that. So many men would boast about screwing a Russian, as though they'd defeated the Soviet Union. He was lonely, away from home. So was Arina. It was understandable. "Jacob, do you ever wonder what Arina is doing here? She was sent to oversee the tigers until they were safe in zoos.

What's her job now? There are plenty of Russian officials here."

Jacob had asked himself that question but didn't like the answer. Thus far her only official acts were to see that he didn't get the tiger's hide and that her government intruded into everything.

"I can see how a woman away from home could be attracted to you, especially a Russian who is used to men who are drunk, smelly, and dressed in fur. I'll bet you've left a string of broken hearts along the border."

Jacob looked away, as though embarrassed. She was surprised he didn't want to brag about cherries he had popped. And pleased. Maybe they didn't believe in the same things, but they were both believers.

"Jacob, if I got some quarters for the jukebox would you teach me to dance like a Texan? It may be a long time before I get to Texas again."

Jacob got to his feet. "The first lesson will be a Mexican polka. And I'll feed the jukebox."

Arina lay on her bed puzzling over Jacob, so in control, telling others what to do, even Rand and Evelyn who were his superiors. *What did it mean? And why had he not come to her room?* Angry at herself for waiting for Jacob to come to her, to explain himself, she called his room, but he did not answer. She went to the lobby. "I wish to return this," she said, handing a bottle of shampoo to the young woman behind the counter of the La Posada gift shop. "I was not satisfied with it."

"Throw it away and buy something else."

"The box says satisfaction guaranteed."

"They always say that. It don't mean nothing."

Americans. Their guarantees were no better than East German cars. She wanted Jacob to be different, to be who he said he was, a biologist hired to trap the tiger. Perhaps it was best he had not come to her room; he was a dangerous dream. Still she wished he would tell her that in America anything was possible.

As she left the gift shop, she saw Jacob and Evelyn enter La Posada laughing, arm in arm. They were tipsy, and Evelyn stumbled on the steps. Jacob caught her. "Did you find the tiger?" Arina asked.

"Did I ever," Evelyn said, lightly slapping Jacob on the cheek.

Evelyn followed Jacob through the door into the patio, past the swimming pool and into the rear building. She caught him at the elevator and followed him to his room. "Do you have a drink, Jacob? The buzz is wearing off, and I feel awful." Jacob poured bourbon for each of them. "It was fun being with you tonight, and when I saw Arina—I'm sorry."

"It's okay," he said.

"You're a hunter, and I tried to hate you. You killed the tiger, and I told myself you were cold and unfeeling. When I found you with Arina, I was so jealous I knew I was in love with you."

Evelyn looked at Jacob and then returned her attention to her drink. "You couldn't have been any more surprised than I. It was hard to admit to myself, and it's harder to admit to you. I'm in love with you, Jacob."

"You're a fine person, Evelyn, but I love someone else."

"I'm not asking for commitment. I have a job in Washington, you have a job here."

"Making love to you would mean more to the one I love than it does to either of us."

"Don't call it love, call it sex. What could that hurt?"

"Sex doesn't always hurt. Love does."

160

"You'll never again see me play that silly female game you saw downstairs." She handed him her glass. "Thanks for the drink."

Jacob watched her walk to the door. "Evelyn." He didn't understand Arina—since their night together she had treated him like a stranger—and now Evelyn. He admired her guts. He wasn't sure he could do what she had just done. "I'll fix us another drink." He handed her a drink and sat on the bed. "I love Arina. I'm not happy about it. But I do."

"Would you like me to explain to Arina that I was showing off? I try to do what I believe is right, no matter who it hurts."

"It's best to leave things as they are. It's doomed anyway." He spread his hands. "I've loved two women, and I've lost them both."

"Oh, Jacob." Evelyn sat on the bed beside him. "I'm sorry." She put her fingertips over his lips. "Shh. Lie back and let Evelyn rub your temples. Relax, I'm not going to do anything. Does that feel good? I'm going to caress your eyes and smooth all the lines out of your forehead."

"You're going to put me to sleep."

"It's okay. Whatever you want is okay. I just want you to feel loved. I know you don't feel about me the way that I do about you. That's the way it is sometimes. It doesn't change the way I feel. I want whatever part of you I can have. Whatever—" She was interrupted by a knock on the door.

"Jacob, may I speak to you, please?" It was Arina.

Jacob looked at the door, uncertain what to do.

Evelyn had hurt him again, without intending it. She had to make it right. She might not always be a winner, but she always played by the rules. "Arina," she said, hurrying to the door. "It's not what you think. Let me explain." When she opened the door, Arina was gone.

. . .

One morning Evelyn and Rand were in the helicopter, and Jacob found Arina alone in the hotel restaurant. As he approached her table, he saw that she was immersed in a San Antonio newspaper with Houston and Dallas newspapers beside her. It amazed him, the amount of time she spent with newspapers and magazines. *What was she looking for?*

"Arina, I want to explain—"

"No. I must tell you something. The woman you saved, died. Of complications."

"Jonelle Parker?" He took the paper from Arina and read the story. *If he had acted faster, gotten her to the hospital sooner instead of—* He threw down the paper. "Damn lot of good it did me to save her."

"Jacob, I must tell you what I fear."

"What I fear is I caused that woman's death posing for the camera," he said. "I've got to talk to her doctor." He turned and left the restaurant.

Little newsworthy copy on the tiger had been generated for days, and Hailee was back in Houston. Tony was pleased to be back home. He feared reprisal from Bump after Hailee's interview. She had cut his remarks about God and patriotism, making his individual sovereignty look like the babbling of a spoiled and egomaniacal child.

Hailee was angry at being jerked back to the station. She had interviewed businessmen who were upset that beer and bullet sales were down, an FBI agent who threatened to confiscate any aircraft the militia used to hunt the tiger, a professor who researched the ATF's use of unmarked helicopters, a hunter who had been confronted by masked men in military uniforms, and a militiaman who claimed ATF agents invaded private property and intimidated legitimate sportsmen.

The tiger was her beat. Everyone wanted to talk to her

about the tiger, but what stories did they give her? "Ribbon-cutting crap," she snapped at the assignments director.

The director said nothing, not in the middle of a rating period when the station had increased its share of the audience. He knew it was because of Hailee and the tiger. He also knew that he had given Hailee every top assignment available. An explosion at a chemical plant. A blowout on an oil rig in the gulf. Not a single ribbon cutting.

Hailee called Rand Morgan every day. She still got beat on the story when the tiger appeared near Realitos. Hailee was furious; she wanted to take the helicopter and interview *El Tigre* at Tortuga's. She raged at the news director who refused. "It's my story," she screamed.

She also raged at Rand for not telling her of the tiger's appearance before San Antonio stations reported it. Rand told her of the death of Jonelle Parker. The director refused to let her take the helicopter to interview the bereaved husband. She reported the story rerunning tapes of her interview with Jacob before the farmhouse. The story was bland, and the humiliation after being so near the top drove her to fury.

When Jacob called the hospital where Jonelle Parker had died, everyone he talked to told him he would have to talk to someone else until Rand interceded. He eventually reached a doctor who said she died of complications. "What kind of complications?"

"Severe anemia. She was a young woman with a baby. It's rare but not unusual. She also had a high fever, probably caused by decaying matter beneath the tiger's claws. There was nothing you or we could have done."

White flashes of sheet lightning radiated across the horizon. The storm rolling across South Texas toward Mexico was still a long way to the north, and the following thunder was little more than a growl, but something had awakened Ramiro Perez. He sat up and listened. He heard only the heavy breathing of his wife, Rafaela, and the soft, quavering call of a screech owl in the mesquites in front of the house.

Ramiro stroked his wife's body. Unlike Ramiro, who had shriveled and dried, she had added weight over the years. Too many tortillas and frijoles. And children. All boys. *Gracias, Rafaela,* he thought, running his hand lightly over her broad hip.

Ramiro, Jr., and his brother, Hector, were in the Air Force. Jaime was in college at Kingsville. He was going to be a teacher of English. Jaime was the first member of the Perez family to go to college, but Lalito, who was twelve, would follow. "Lalo," Ramiro corrected himself. The boy had asked to be called Lalo. Rafaela had pulled the boy to her ample bosom and told him that he would always be her Lalito. Ramiro knew what it was to be a man, and he tried to remember to say Lalo.

The small oscillating fan on the floor near the foot of the bed stirred the warm, humid air in the bedroom. Mr. Cogden promised to air-condition Ramiro's house and install a telephone, but the air-conditioning would wait until spring, and Ramiro was in no hurry for the telephone. It made it too easy for Mr. Cogden to call him. Ramiro went to the hunting lodge once a week and called Mr. Cogden for instructions.

The Cogden ranch bordered the Rio Grande south of El Indio. Cogden, an investment banker in San Antonio, did not mind spending money on the ranch. He had built a hunting lodge on a hill overlooking the river and the Mexico border. He wanted the roads graded after heavy rains, the fences, equipment, and vehicles kept up and the livestock in good shape. Ramiro never caught up with the chores.

Lightning flashed, and Ramiro was waiting for the roll of

thunder when he heard the horses. He leaned forward to stare though the window screen. Lightning flashed again, and he saw the white barn and the black outline of the corrals a hundred yards to the south. The corrals had been built by sinking two parallel rows of mesquite posts in the ground and stacking logs between them. The fences were almost a foot thick and sturdy enough to stop the wildest bull. A horse whinnied and kicked the side of the barn, and Ramiro heard the goats bleating and the tinkling of the bell on the lead nanny.

Ramiro had put nineteen Spanish nannies and their nursing kids in one of the pens. Mr. Cogden served cabrito to his hunting guests, and he wanted the milk-fed kids ready. Ramiro heard the horses running inside the corral. Robert the Bruce, Jaime's border collie, ran barking back and forth along the chain-link fence around the house.

"Damn it to hell," Ramiro muttered, reaching for his trousers.

"*¿Que es?*" Rafaela asked drowsily.

"Something is bothering the goats. Go back to sleep."

Ramiro eased off the bed and slipped into his jeans and boots. He walked through the kitchen, picked up a two-cell flashlight and stepped out the back door. "Quiet, *perro*," he ordered the dog, but Bruce paid no attention. Ramiro was a dozen steps from the house when he heard the door open and close.

"Papa?"

"A coyote is after the *cabras*, Lalito," Ramiro said without waiting for his son. "Go back to sleep." He continued toward the corral where the horses snorted and whinnied. The bleating goats ran in circles.

"*Oye,*" Lalo said. "What's that?"

Ramiro heard the snarl and the strangled cry of one of the nannies. A streak of lightning turned night to day, and he saw

165

something long and lithe leap over the corral with a goat in its jaws. *"Dios mio. Chupacabra."* All his life he had heard of the horrible goat sucker that ripped the entrails out of goats and sucked their blood, but Jaime called it superstition. "Lalo, get my rifle. Run, *muchacho.*"

Ramiro raced for the corner of the corral and flashed the light toward the chaparral that began a few yards beyond. The beast had bounded over the six-foot fence and was gone. *"Dios mio,"* Ramiro repeated, turning to the house, impatiently awaiting Lalo with the .25-35 Winchester. "Lalo, in the bedroom closet," he yelled.

The back door opened. "Ramiro, what's the matter?" Rafaela called.

"I don't know," he answered, unwilling to pronounce the dreadful name. "Tell Lalo to hurry with the gun. And tell that damn dog to shut up."

"Hush, *perro,*" Rafaela shouted. "Lalito came with you."

"I sent him for my gun," Ramiro yelled in exasperation. "Hurry."

Lights in the house came on as Rafaela went from room to room. "He's not in the house." Through the open windows, Ramiro could hear her crying before she reappeared. She screamed again, "Ramiro, he is not in the house. Lalito. Lalito."

"Quiet, woman. He is here somewhere." He picked up a rock and threw it at the barking dog. "Lalo, where the hell are you? Bring me the gun."

Ramiro flashed the beam of the flashlight toward the brush, then the barn and back to the brush. He swept the light toward the brush again when he saw something glinting on the ground. He kept the light on the spot and walked to it.

"What is it?" Rafaela asked, wringing her hands and moaning as she trotted toward him.

"Blood," he said.

"Lalito," she screamed.

"Shut up, woman," he said. "It's a *chupacabra*. With a goat."

"Madre de dios," Rafaela wailed, crossing herself.

Drops of blood trickled toward the east. Ramiro flashed the light along the blood trail and saw tracks like the tracks of a giant cat. He tried to cover one of the pug marks with his hand. "Jesus, Mary, and Joseph," he said, crossing himself.

The *chupacabra* had carried something that dragged the ground. The vision of the beast that had leaped the fence with the goat in its mouth flashed in his mind. *Chupacabras* sucked the blood of goats, not children. Still on his knees, Ramiro threw his arms around Rafaela's trembling thighs. "Lalito," he called. *"Mi hijo."*

"Llevame con el," Rafaela screamed toward the heavens. "Take me with him."

Ramiro jumped to his feet and ran into the brush with the flashlight. He ran until he regained his senses, then retraced his steps, frightened but calmer. He found Rafaela in the house, praying. While he loaded the rifle, he talked to her. "Rafaela, take the truck and go to the lodge. Call the sheriff. Tell them Lalito is gone and there is a huge *chupacabra.*"

Rafaela collapsed in tears.

"Woman, you must be calm. If you cry, they will not listen. They will think you are drunk. Tell them a big *chupacabra*. Big." He tried to think of a way to convince them. "Tell them its foot is bigger than a man's hand." Still it did not sound convincing. "Call Mr. Cogden. Tell him what has happened. Tell him I said for you to ask for help. Mr. Cogden will believe you. Hurry, I must go."

Ramiro tied a short rope around Robert the Bruce's neck and took the dog with him. Bruce strained at the leash but stopped barking and trailed silently. The dog was able to stay on the trail even after the blood had stopped. Ramiro looked at the last drops of blood, trying to decide if it was a good sign. *Did it mean the wound had stopped bleeding or that there was no more blood?*

The beast left no tracks on the flinty hills, but the dog was able to follow. Ramiro stopped on one of the hills and tried to unravel the twisting trail. The *chupacabra* had led them north, then west, then in a wide circle southward. The blood-sucker searched for something.

Ramiro and Bruce stumbled through the brush for three hours before the trail led them into the big timber and thickets near the river. Dense underbrush clutched at Ramiro's face and clothing. At times he was forced to crawl along game trails that tunneled beneath the brush. With the rope and flashlight in one hand and the rifle in the other, he was unable to push aside the thorn-covered branches, and blood streaked his face and neck.

Ramiro was on his hands and knees, close enough to the river to smell it, when Bruce stopped and stared in the darkness, hackles bristling. Ramiro gripped the rifle tightly. The dog growled, and an answering growl rumbled in the bottom, seeming to shake the leaves of the trees. Through the night, the brush, Ramiro had been driven by rage, a grief that was deeper than rage, a hope that fed the other two. In an instant they were gone, and he knew only fear. His heart swelled until he could not breathe. His legs turned to sand. He shined his feeble light ahead of him and saw eyes glowing in the underbrush. Bigger than the eyes of any buck he had ever seen. Two, then four, then two again.

Bruce whimpered and tried to crawl under Ramiro as the brilliant eyes floated upward like giant fireflies. Ramiro shook the flashlight, trying to get more power from it. The weakening light flashed brightly outlining a cat-like form. Jaime would never believe him. The animal raised its head, and its white chin was stained pink. Ramiro watched as the animal rose to its feet, and his mind almost failed him, refusing to accept what his eyes saw. The *chupacabra* was a hellcat, and he could hear the moans of the damned.

The beast ran its broad, pink tongue over its upper lip and nose, then lowered its head to sink its teeth into something it held between its front paws. The animal raised its head, tearing the red flesh. *"Cabra,"* Ramiro said aloud. "Please God, let it be the goat."

Ramiro heard the rustle of leaves to his right and swung the light in that direction. *Eyes again.* The *chupacabra* had moved without moving, in two places at the same time. It turned its head toward Ramiro. Its upper lip curled over yellow fangs, and it crouched low to the ground, its whole body quivering, ears cocked and devil's tail thrashing the brush.

Ramiro thumbed the hammer on the Winchester to half-cock, then on his knees, tried to back down the game trail, hoping to put something solid at his back. He was hampered by Bruce as the dog tried to bury its head between Ramiro's knees.

It wasn't a big tree, but it was the only one close. Ramiro stood, slowly raised the rifle to his shoulder and tried to brace the flashlight against the stock so he could see the front and rear sights in the fading beam of the light. The flashlight rattled against the wooden forearm of the rifle, and he forced himself to steady it.

He pulled the hammer to full cock and tried to align the sights on the goat sucker as it glided silently through the bottom. The shadows thrown by the dim light shimmered and swayed, and the specter disappeared before his eyes. Ramiro prayed while his eyes sought the prince of darkness. And found it.

He wrapped a trembling finger around the trigger and followed the wraith, hoping it was going away. He knew the

117-grain soft-point bullet would not knock the creature off its feet even if it were flesh and blood. He shifted his aim until the sights settled on a yellow patch between streaked white spots above the animal's eyes.

With a roar, it sprang at Ramiro. Bruce yelped and ran in a circle, wetting Ramiro's feet. Ramiro pulled the trigger and in the muzzle flash saw a fury of eyes and teeth. A stinging blow knocked his legs from under him, and he hit the ground hard, landing on his face. The rifle flew from his hands and he kicked out wildly. Jaws closed over his foot, and fangs penetrated leather, flesh, and bone.

Ramiro screamed, lashed out with his other foot and felt it strike solidly against the head of the beast, but it tightened its grip on his foot, and he screamed again. He heard Bruce growl, felt the dog brush past him, knew Bruce was attacking. The cat snarled, and Ramiro's foot was free. He scrambled to his feet and tried to run, but his right ankle folded under him, and he fell heavily. Behind him he heard yelping, snarling, the snapping and thrashing of the underbrush as Bruce tried to escape the hellcat.

Ramiro got to his feet again, hobbling, stumbling, tripping on logs, falling. In his panic, he forgot that his ankle was broken, the bones of his foot crushed. "Rafaela," he called as he crashed through the brush. "Rafaela."

8

Arina was kept awake by her thoughts. Jacob was hired by NAZA, but he gave orders to Evelyn and Rand. He was hired to capture the tiger, but he had killed it. When he discovered there was another tiger he refused to use dogs to locate it. He said he loved her, but he was quick to sleep with Evelyn. When she told him about the death of the stewardess, he had dismissed her fears. When she tried to tell him why she thought she had been ordered home, he was interested only in the death of Jonelle Parker.

More than jealous, she was perplexed. Perhaps he was a Federal agent sent to watch her. Perhaps he was a renegade American trying to confirm for renegades in Russia whether their scheme worked. Perhaps he was an adventurer working for no one but himself, heedless of the rest of the world.

She was alone in a strange and sometimes frightening country, yet to return home was to face arrest. She wanted to trust Jacob, but she remembered tales of American duplicity.

She had discovered for herself their worthless guarantees. She was startled from her thoughts by a knock at her door.

Cautiously, she opened the door. "Jacob. I want to talk—"

"There is a man in Memorial Hospital in Eagle Pass who says he was attacked by a *chupacabra* on a ranch near El Indio. Whatever it was bit clear through his foot, boot and all. His son is missing, his wife is hysterical. I'm going to talk to him."

"Wait, I must go too," she said.

"Barry is on his way to the airport to preflight the helicopter. I'll meet you in the coffee shop for breakfast."

By the time she had dressed, Rand and Evelyn had joined Jacob in the coffee shop and were discussing the *chupacabra*, a mythical cat-like beast with an almost human face that eviscerated goats and sucked their blood.

Barry was waiting for them at the airport. Arina carried a shoulder bag containing her blowgun and darts. Jacob carried the Ruger and the Cap-Chur gun. Evelyn had the duffel bag containing ammunition for Jacob's two guns. "We're all going," Evelyn said.

"No, you're not," Barry said. "This is a three-seater at best."

"I'll stay at the hotel and brief the press," Rand said.

"I am the field director of NAZA who is paying for this helicopter," Evelyn said. "I want to see that the tiger is not harmed."

Arina waited for Jacob to choose her, but he looked away. She was confused about many things, but she knew her duty. "I am going."

"We don't even know that it is the tiger," Jacob said.

"Well, hell, how long will it take to put the litter back on?"

"Five minutes, including the time it takes me to get it."

"Get it and I'll ride in it."

Barry attached the litter and strapped Jacob in it, then bolted the counterweight on the opposite side. "It'll be nice and cool out here, Jacob, and I got to be in that stuffy cabin with two good-looking women."

Jacob didn't laugh. "A game warden is meeting us at the ranch, but I want to talk to the man in the hospital first."

Windom nodded, climbed into the helicopter, wound up the engine and lifted off. He headed northwest beneath the clouds that shadowed southern Texas and northern Mexico.

Ramiro Perez was in the intensive care unit of the hospital. The attending physician said a powerful animal caused the injuries and that he had never seen anything like it. Evelyn and Arina talked to the weeping Rafaela in the waiting room while Jacob talked to Ramiro.

Although he was sedated, reliving his terror brought a chill to Ramiro, and Jacob tucked the sheet around him. "Its eyes floated in the dark. Sometimes it was in two places at once. It appeared and disappeared like a devil. When I could not see it, I could smell it. I could smell the pit of hell, *señor*, and hear the moans of the dead. The dog saved me. He will save my boy."

A nurse approached the bed, but Ramiro spoke again. "Lalito is a good boy. The devil cannot take a good boy. You will find my son, *señor*. You will bring him to me, *por favor*. Go with God, *señor*."

"Well?" Evelyn asked when Jacob entered the waiting room.

"He's worse than Rand thought."

"I mean the tiger. Was it the tiger?"

"Maybe," he said. He looked at Arina. "How is the woman?"

"She is frightened for her son. Can we offer any hope?" Arina asked.

"I don't think we'd better," Jacob said. "Ramiro will be okay."

"The fever is a complication," Arina said.

"Cat scratch fever, only worse. We need to get to the ranch and check the tracks before it rains."

Game Warden Herbert Telford led Jacob to the dark spot on the earth where pooled blood turned black in the sultry heat of the morning. Jacob stabbed a forefinger through the congealed crust and withdrew it. His finger was tipped in red. He wiped his finger on his boots and followed the trail of blood and tracks toward the brush, then stopped to kneel and spread his hand on the ground beside one of the pug marks. "It's the tiger," Jacob said. "Not much doubt about that."

"And the boy?" Arina asked.

"If this is the boy's blood, the tiger must have dropped the goat and circled back to attack him. I'm going to track the tiger to the kill before rain wipes out the trail. I'm hoping the cat will return to it. If not, maybe Barry and I can flush it from the air."

"I am going with you," Arina said.

"So am I," said Evelyn.

"Like hell. I need someone with a backup gun."

"I'm going," Evelyn said. "I'll carry your gear. But no more guns."

"I agree, Jacob," Arina said.

Jacob turned to appeal to Telford but saw that he was in his truck talking on the radio. "All right. One of you can carry the Cap-Chur gun, but I don't want a dose of tranquilizer in my butt."

"I have used such a gun," Arina said, reaching for it.

"Fine," Jacob said. "Evelyn, you get the bag of darts. I'm

carrying the Ruger. And stay behind me. Several feet behind me. I don't want you messing up the tracks."

Jacob yelled at Barry, "Get the portable cage out here," then turned to the two women. "Okay, let's go, Frankie Bucks." He started toward the brush so briskly that Evelyn and Arina had to trot to keep up with him.

"What is 'Frankie Bucks'?" Arina asked.

"Frank Buck trapped animals for zoos. Jacob's being a chauvinistic ass."

It was the middle of the afternoon before Jacob and the women neared the river bottom. The tracking had been easy in the sandy areas, but he lost the trail several times where Ramiro had crossed rocky hills. Twice he left the women on one side of a hill and circled until he found tracks on the other side. The clouds were lower, the smell of rain in the air.

Jacob worked his way slowly through the underbrush. Like Ramiro, he had to crawl on his hands and knees in places, and he knew he was more vulnerable then than any other time. The women stayed so close they stepped on his heels. He cursed himself for not waiting for Telford so they could cover each other.

Jacob entered an opening in the brush, rose to his feet and saw what was left of the border collie. Only hair and part of the dog's head remained. Jacob looked beyond the dog and saw a hand. The small, brown hand protruded, palm up, from a pile of sticks and leaves on the far side of the glade. Arina and Evelyn bumped into him. Arina started to speak, but Jacob motioned for her to be quiet.

"Listen," he whispered. He had heard only the buzzing of blowflies, but he knew the command would keep the women quiet and alert. He tried to see through the thicket around them, but the wall of brush was impenetrable, even to his experienced eyes.

"Wait here," he said hoarsely and walked quietly to the kill.

Arina saw the hand before Evelyn did. She turned her head. "The little boy," she whispered. Evelyn started forward, but Jacob motioned her back.

"The tiger covered the kill," he said. "It's probably coming back to finish it. It might be watching us right now."

Evelyn paled but could not take her eyes from the hand, the size of her son's hand, that seemed to reach for her. Flies crawled on it. She wiped at tears and streaked mascara and dust across her cheek.

Jacob saw a second mound of debris behind the first. Something round and white glinted dully through the sticks. An eye. He walked forward until he could identify hair around the eye of a goat. Two kills.

He eased forward, cautiously examining the ground. The stench was stronger than the smell of death. It was the smell of tiger. The scent evoked the terror he had felt in the farmhouse when he saw two erect ears, flattening in fury. He retreated, keeping his eyes and the muzzle of the rifle on the brush until he reached the women.

Evelyn bent down to brush flies from the small, cold hand. She wanted to draw it to her breast, but it was stiff and when she moved it she saw the shoulder bones and part of the head of what had been a curly haired child. "No," she said.

Jacob pulled her to her feet. "Let's get out of here," he said. "Now."

"The boy," Evelyn said. "We can't leave—"

"Move," Jacob said, pushing Arina ahead of him, dragging Evelyn. "Now. Back the way we came." He heard Evelyn sobbing as he fought the brush and his rising panic.

Evelyn stumbled from the brush into the clearing around the barn and corrals near the ranch house. She wrenched her arm free of Jacob and wiped at her eyes, oblivious of the hair that hung wet and stringy in her face, the cut on her forehead and the scratches on her arms. Oblivious of the camera and Hailee White who stood beside it.

"What did you find?" Hailee asked.

Evelyn brushed past her and sat heavily on an oil drum lying on its side. Behind her, Hailee fired questions. "Ms. Price, did you find the tiger?" The voice seemed to come from a distance. "Tony, get a closeup of her face. This is going to be great. Did you see the tiger?"

The tiger was a rare and magnificent animal. She must save it.

"What about the boy? Did you see Lalo Perez?"

Evelyn stared at a tire swing hanging from a mesquite. "His hand," she mumbled. "I touched his little hand." A boy not much younger than her son. She had wanted to pick the boy up, carry him to his mother. She wished nature were not so raw, that animals could live in peace. Some animals had to kill to live, but she despised photographers who took pictures of predators dragging down and devouring prey, writers who gloried in violent death. She identified with prey, their terror, their futile attempts to escape fangs and claws, their bleating cries of pain. She shuddered as she thought of the boy crying for his mother, flailing futilely at the unfeeling maw that had him in its grip, trying to awake from a horror where monsters devoured the innocent.

The tiger was not a monster. Designed to kill, yes, but not to kill a child. Man had disrupted nature's concord and created havoc. The tiger in the farmhouse and this one, the one that killed the boy, had been hounded until they turned on their tormentors.

"Was the little boy all right? Did you rescue him?" Hailee asked.

Evelyn looked at Hailee in astonishment. *Hailee was going to film the boy's hand, his ruined head, his pathetic grave, use the boy's death to sell the news, to sell hate and fear until the tiger, already driven to desperation, was forced to kill and kill until it too was killed.*

"Leave him alone," she screamed. "Leave him alone." Evelyn wasn't sure when she had gotten up, but she was standing. "You're perverting nature, you're corrupting creation, destroying harmony—" Evelyn attacked, with her hands, her nails, screaming, flailing.

Jacob stepped in front of her and took her firmly by both arms. "Evelyn. Stop it. That's enough. Stop."

She collapsed sobbing in his arms. Tony rolled tape. Jacob looked at Hailee, who rubbed the welt on her cheek. "Stop the camera," he said.

"Like hell," Hailee said. "Nobody slaps me."

"She's had a bad shock. We all have. Ask me anything you want, just don't use those pictures."

"On one condition," Hailee said. "You tell me, on camera, what happened out there. Then you tell me how you plan to capture the tiger. And you tell no one else. Later, tomorrow, maybe the next day I want an exclusive interview, and this time you're going to bare your ass."

"I got a message for you on the radio," Telford said. "Mr. Cogden, who owns this place, offered the use of his hunting lodge to NAZA. There's food and drink there, but nothing fresh. You could do the interview there."

"I want it here with the house and the corral for background," Hailee said. "I want Jacob standing over that dried blood." Tony nodded.

"Arina, why don't you and Evelyn go to the lodge?" Jacob said.

"No." Evelyn pushed away from Jacob and wiped at her eyes with her bloodied hands. "I represent the tiger."

"Okay," he said. He told Hailee how they had followed the tracks of the tiger to the river bottom and discovered the bodies of the goat and Lalo Perez covered with debris. "The dog was eaten. Parts of the boy and the goat are still there. There are two tigers."

Everyone stared at him. Arina recovered first. "Are you certain?"

"I saw their tracks," Jacob said. "Two tigers."

"That's wonderful," Evelyn said.

"It's a hell of a story, that's for sure," Hailee said to Tony.

"There is a big tiger, probably the one we've been following across south Texas, and a smaller one that has got to be the other female. That's what Ramiro Perez saw, two cats, the eyes of two tigers, but in the darkness he wasn't sure what he saw."

"Damn," Telford said. "I don't know how we're going to protect people from two tigers."

"You must keep people from provoking the tigers," Evelyn said.

Telford ignored her. "Two tigers and deer season just around the corner. Ranchers down here ain't gonna like it."

"What are your plans for capturing the tigers, now that there are two?" Hailee asked, pushing the mike toward Jacob.

"I'll tell you, but no camera and no mike."

Hailee thought for a moment, then signaled for Tony to stop taping. "Let's hear it, then we may want to hear it again on camera."

"If we're lucky the tigers will return to finish the boy and the goat. I'm going to get in the biggest tree that overlooks the kills and wait for them. I should be able to dart one, maybe both. Telford, I need someone to cover me until I get into a tree."

"Sure," the warden said.

"Jacob," Arina said, shocked. "You can't." *Who was this person she had allowed inside her?*

"No," Evelyn said. "You can't let the tigers eat the boy.

I'm going to bring him home. I'll go after him by myself if I have to. I'm not leaving him to be eaten." She shuddered remembering his exposed teeth and skull.

She started for the brush, and Telford had to restrain her. "Hold up a minute. Nothing's been decided yet," he said with misgiving.

Arina put her arm around Evelyn. "I will go with you, if necessary. Jacob, you cannot do this dreadful thing. You saw the boy's mother, his father. How will you tell them what you have done?"

"I'm trying to catch the tigers," Jacob said. "They will either eat here or they will eat something or someone else."

"There is only one reason the tigers are together," Arina said. "The female is in estrus. She marked her trail as she crossed the country. The male followed her."

"That's got to be it," Jacob said. "I've lured cougars into traps with female urine; we could try it with tigers. Evelyn, tell Stuart to contact every zoo with tigers and get us urine from a female tiger in estrus. ASAP." Hearing the beating of helicopter blades, he turned to see Barry returning with the cage. "Until we get the urine, we continue the air search. We know they're close. If we have a choice, we dart the female first and use her to trap the male. How long do we have, Arina?"

"They will mate for about three days. If conception occurs, they will go their separate ways. If it does not she will come back into estrus in about twenty-five days. Perhaps he will stay near her until then, perhaps not."

"Let's get in the air," Jacob said.

"Two helicopters are better than one," Hailee said. "We'll help. Maybe we can get some footage of a tiger." She started toward the KHTX helicopter but stopped to speak to Jacob. "I almost wish you'd used the kid as tiger-bait. It would have been a screamer on network TV."

Jacob was glad the women had protested the plan. He had no stomach for using a child for bait or for sitting in a tree in the vicinity of two man-eaters. "Help me catch the tiger, and I'll give you two interviews."

"Let's get moving." She pointed at a cloud of dust on the road between the house and the highway. "That looks like the competition."

"Telford, we'll sweep the bottoms and flush the tigers if they're there; then we can get the boy out. How about taking Arina and Evelyn to the lodge? I don't think they're up to being interviewed right now. Ask the press to hold the news of the boy's death until his folks are notified."

"I'll get Cogden to break the news to them, entertain them until then. I got lots of stories those boys ain't ever heard."

Jacob and Barry conferred, and Jacob trotted to the KHTX helicopter as the rotors turned. "When we reach the kill site, we'll split," he said. "You head down the river; we'll go up. Switch to 117.2 so we can talk."

Both helicopters lifted off as three cars and a van carrying a TV crew pulled up at Ramiro's house. Jacob saw NAZA's rented pickup. "Rand leading his troops into battle," he said.

Barry grinned and banked the helicopter toward the river. Jacob could not pinpoint the spot from the air, but it was vivid in his mind. He was relieved not to have to go back into that dark thicket. Even with two guns. Even if the boy's body hadn't been there.

Barry and Jacob were a couple of minutes from the area of the kill when they saw the tiger lying in shallow water at the edge of the river. It looked over its shoulder at the approaching aircraft. "Same as before," Jacob said, slipping a dart into the Cap-Chur gun. "Get close."

The tiger got to its feet, looked back again and ran through the shallows toward the Mexican side of the river. They were three hundred yards away when they saw a much larger tiger bound from the dense stands of cane flanking the Rio Grande. The smaller cat was near the middle of the river, swimming steadily.

"Hurry," Jacob yelled. "The female first. Don't let it get away."

"We're not going to make it," Windom said.

The first tiger rushed from the water on the Mexican side and melted into the cane. The larger, stronger tiger was only a few feet behind her. Windom pulled the helicopter up and away from the river before Jacob could use the dart gun. The KHTX helicopter followed the tigers.

"What the hell are you doing?" Jacob demanded.

"Wrong side of the river."

"I can still see it. We can get them before they kill someone else."

"Do you know how much smuggling goes on across this river? Authorities can show up at any time."

"I don't believe it," Jacob said. "That's the closest we've come, and you let them both get away."

Barry put the helicopter down near Ramiro's house. "I can't risk it," he said. "Not in broad daylight. I know how close we came and how much it means to you, but I didn't have a choice. The only skill I have is flying prop-tops. Every dollar I own, every dollar I can borrow is invested in the chopper. I can't afford to lose it or my license. I can't afford to spend a few days in jail or to have the helicopter impounded while someone explains to the authorities."

"You're a good pilot," Jacob apologized. "If the tigers come back over here, I want to be riding in your chopper. But as long as they're in Mexico, it looks like you're out of the picture."

"They might get *turista* and come right back," Barry said. "I'll fly to Eagle Pass and see if anyone needs a cowpuncher or deer counter. And when I'm in the air, I'll keep a sharp eye for tigers."

"Thanks," Jacob said.

"I'll give you a call when I know where I'm staying."

It was late afternoon when the reporters finished interviewing Jacob. He and Rand followed Telford to Cogden's single-story, hilltop hunting lodge. Rand parked the pickup in a metal garage large enough to hold four vehicles. It contained a Jeep and a Chevrolet Blazer. "Mr. Cogden said you're welcome to use the vehicles in the shed," Telford said. "The keys are on hooks inside one of the cupboard doors in the kitchen."

Evelyn and Arina waited in the big room that served as both a living and dining area. Both were still shaken by the discovery of the boy's body. "Stuart said getting urine from tigers in estrus was a long shot, but he's trying," Evelyn said.

Jacob turned to Rand. "You probably don't want to move your headquarters again, but Mr. Cogden said we could use this lodge, and I'm going to use it. I have a friend across the river who can help me catch up with the tigers."

"I'm going back to Laredo," Evelyn said. "I'll run the press office for a few days. Please don't argue, Rand. I've cleared it with Stuart."

Rand had never seen her so defeated. "Fine. You deal with the media and their incessant demands for favors. I'm glad to be in the field for a change," he said, looking at the utilitarian lodge. "I'll have to call my wife and tell her where I am. I don't want her to worry." He did want her to worry a little.

"Phone's in the hall," Telford said.

"I'll rent a car and drive back to Laredo," Evelyn said.

"I'll give you a lift to Eagle Pass," Telford said. "That's the closest place you can rent a car."

"Thank you, Mr. Telford. I'm ready to go if you are," Evelyn said.

"Stuart is going to go through the roof when he sees what we're paying for the helicopter, food and lodging, an open bar for the media, rental cars," Rand grumbled as he went to the telephone. "I know who he's going to blame, and it isn't Evelyn Price."

Jacob sat down beside Arina to tell her about running the tigers into Mexico, but before he could begin, Arina said, "You should have said something to Evelyn." He looked at her without understanding. "She is upset about the boy's death. I think she may go to her son."

"Arina, nothing happened between Evelyn and me. She was showing off in front of you and came to my room to apologize."

"Jacob, I want to believe what you say, but your actions—"

"We have a bigger problem," Jacob said. "The tigers are in Mexico, and everyone who listens to the news knows it." Jacob doubted Mexican officials could keep Mexican ranchers and cowboys from killing the tigers, and it would take both countries to keep Americans from crossing the river and shooting them from airplanes or helicopters.

"Evelyn said that Mr. Johnson has been in contact with Mexican authorities in case the tiger should cross the river," Arina said. "He said Mexico and Russia will cooperate to capture the tigers. Evelyn wouldn't leave without such assurance."

The unexpected death of Jonelle Parker had been a shock. The sight of Lalo's body had been a bigger one, although he thought he had prepared himself for it. There was Sam Storey, and the stewardess who had escaped the crash, and everyone who had died on the airplane. Jacob wanted the tigers. He wanted to drop them with a clean shot and watch their blood spread over the earth and dry as black as the blood of Lalo Perez. They were killers. Capturing them was cold satisfaction.

Arina was so light she could almost fly now that her fear was gone. *The tigers were no longer her problem, no longer Jacob's problem. Perhaps she and Jacob had a chance. The Russians could capture the tigers, and no one in America would know anything.* "Russians know Russian tigers best and how to capture them," she said.

"Peg said for me not to go outside alone," Rand said, returning to the room. "I told her I had two tiger hunters to protect me."

"Rand, you report to Stuart," said Jacob. "Who does he report to?"

"He is liaison between US and Russian officials."

"He tells the Russians everything we know about the tigers? The Russians know where the tigers are?"

"As well as we know."

"Moscow can have Russian hunters on the border in two or three days," Jacob said.

Arina did not like the look in Jacob's eyes. He did not want her government to capture the tigers. *But why?* "Jacob, the tigers are no longer your concern. Mexico, Russia will capture them."

"The tigers are mine," he said.

That night the moisture-laden clouds that had teased the border country for two days poured their contents on the thirsty land, and arroyos ran bank full on both sides of the Rio Grande. Arina was awakened by the violent storm outside her window and at first did not recognize the tapping at her door. Then Jacob stood beside her bed. He spoke her name softly. "Jacob," she said, "there is much between us." He kissed her until there was nothing between them.

He made love to her so slowly she buried her face in his shoulder lest Rand should hear. He told her he loved her, that he wanted to spend the rest of his life with her. In their nakedness she believed he would tell her who he was. Instead, he slipped into sleep.

When she awoke he was gone. When she saw Jacob again, he was that other person, the day person, whose mind was closed against her.

Jacob was up early. He needed to think, and he could not think with Arina beside him. He slipped out of bed and went outside. The sky was clear, and the air, cleaned of dust, was sweet. He made coffee and took a cup to a long veranda that overlooked a bend in the river. He gazed toward the timbered bottom where Lalito had died, then across the rough draws and bluffs along the river to the endless brushy flats of northern Mexico.

Somewhere in those thickets the tigers waited. Before Russian hunters or dogs reached the border, Mexican ranchers, American sportsmen, or the militia would kill the tigers. If the tigers were to be captured, it was up to him to do it. He wondered if the professional satisfaction of a capture would be enough. He still remembered the euphoria when the first tiger lay dead, and he walked into the sunlight alive. Arina wanted the tiger alive, and if that was what she wanted, that was what he would do.

He went inside and was dialing the telephone when Arina came down the hall. She looked sleepy and so sexy he wanted to take her back to bed, but the phone was ringing. He nodded to Arina, then spoke into the phone in Spanish. Arina took coffee outside after giving him that look he never understood. *What did she want?* He told her he loved her, that he wanted to be with her when the job was done.

Arina did not look up when he joined her. "I called

186

Santana Zavala, my friend on the other side of the border," Jacob said. "I caught a lion for him once that had killed two of his horses. He lives in Piedras Negras, but he went to his ranch yesterday. It's up the river, not more than six or seven miles as the crow flies but more than fifty by road. His wife said he's due back this morning. Can you wait a while to eat?"

Arina nodded. "Good," Jacob said. "We'll eat lunch, or breakfast if you like, at the Moderno across the river. I'll call him again from there."

"Jacob, why must you be the one who catches the tigers?"

He started to explain, but it could wait. "That's what I was hired to do," he said.

"We must tell Rand what we are doing."

"No, this is something I'm doing on my own."

"Without permission or knowledge of the authorities?"

"Rand tells too much to the wrong people."

Either he worked for someone other than NAZA or he was a cowboy acting on no authority but his own. There were men like him in Russia, men who did whatever they had to do to get what they wanted. She feared Andrei Velinski was one of them. "I cannot cross the border." She wanted to tell him she had been ordered home but hesitated.

"Why not?"

"I lost my papers in the crash. They have not been replaced."

"You won't have to show any papers," Jacob said. "They'll ask us a couple of questions, that's all. You probably won't have to say anything, but if you do, don't worry, half the people in this part of the state have some kind of accent."

"I cannot take that chance."

"Thousands of people cross this border every day without showing any papers. Thousands more cross by wading the river. You can come back that way if you want to." Jacob grinned, but Arina flushed at the remark.

"You Americans are so . . . so . . . flippant."

"I'll get you back. If we want the tigers, we have to go over there and get them. That's what I was hired to do."

By whom, she wondered. "You are a tiger. You see what you want, and you go after it heedless of others."

"We're all tigers sometimes. We all hear the dogs baying, and we'd like to turn and destroy them. But the dogs can't harm us, just annoy us. It's only when we give them our attention that the hunter has a chance to kill us. A smart tiger will keep the dogs at a distance without allowing itself to be run up a tree. Once it's treed, it doesn't have a chance."

Jacob Trace is not going to be treed, she thought.

Bump and two carloads of his warriors pulled up in front of an Eagle Pass motel that advertised "clean rooms, affordable prices, long boy beds." Only Bump got out. He asked for three rooms, one at either end of the front, one at the back of the motel. He didn't intend to be pinned down. He assigned the rooms, four men to each room, and watched while they whisked their weapons inside unseen. "Clean up, weapons first. One man on watch at all times. And get some rest. We're crossing the border before daylight. Leaders in my room in fifteen minutes. No outside calls and no calls between rooms except emergency."

Bump pulled off the soiled fatigues he had worn for a week while he and his men scouted Webb County for the tiger. There had been a run-in with a rancher who wanted to arrest them for trespassing, but Bump had fired a burst over his head and, while the rancher dived for cover, he and his men had faded into the brush. They had interrogated wetbacks, ranch hands, roughnecks, pumpers, hunters. None had seen tiger sign. Then they heard on the radio that two tigers had killed a boy near El Indio and had escaped into Mexico.

"Three tigers," Bump had said. "And two of them still

loose. Hell, the tigers weren't even on that damn airplane. There's no way all three of them could have escaped the crash. I know it, you know it, when I get through, the world is going to know it. We're going to Eagle Pass tonight."

The men brightened at that. Bump enjoyed the heat, the solitude, the hunt, but only the pay kept most of them in the field. Talk of Russian spies and Federal agents no longer inspired them, and the occasional airplane that flew over filled them with alarm. Except for Roy Pat. Roy Pat was on a mission that only he understood. Bump wanted to be the one to kill the tigers, but he didn't want to get between the tigers and Roy Pat.

They drove to Eagle Pass and learned the location of Cogden's ranch. Crossing the river would be no problem, although they'd have to leave two drivers with the vehicles and a radio to arrange a pickup. The Mexican side was even more sparsely populated than the Texas side, and Bump had no qualms about killing any greaser who might interfere. Finding the tigers would be difficult. Bump was disappointed that he had not located the tigers, and he had no confidence in the tracking skills of his men.

When Roy Pat and Jimmy Guy reported to his room, he told them their men were not to leave the room for any reason.

"Aw, Bump," Jimmy Guy protested. "One six-pack per room won't hurt nothing. We've been in the brush for a week. Hotter than hell. You can't tell me the Feds aren't manipulating the weather."

"I'm not worried about the weather, I'm worried about those helicopters," Roy Pat said. "They knew where we were the whole time."

When the telephone rang, they froze. No one should be calling the room. Roy Pat, on watch, shook his head; he had seen nothing. Bump signaled the others to take weapons and defensive positions, then picked up the phone without speaking.

The same mysterious voice that had called him at home was on the other end of the line. "Patrol the north side of the river to prevent anyone from crossing, including the Russian woman and the trapper. Do not cross the border. Repeat, do not cross the border. We have friends on the other side who will drive the tigers to you. Treat anyone who crosses the river, either way, as a spy. When the tigers are dead, everyone will receive a full share regardless of who kills them." The telephone went dead.

Bump replaced the receiver, too stunned to speak.

"Who was it?" asked Jimmy Guy.

"Our sponsor. Wants us to patrol the Texas side of the river. Kill anything that tries to cross either way."

"It's the Feds trying to set us up," Jimmy Guy said.

"If it was the Feds, why didn't they tell us to cross and have the Mexicans grab us on the other side?" Roy Pat asked.

"Because we'd blow their asses away," Jimmy Guy said.

"And when we tried to cross back, we'd be sitting ducks for the Feds," Roy Pat said. "It can't be them."

"Then who is it?" Jimmy Guy asked.

"Get back to your rooms and get your gear cleaned up. We leave in two hours. Friends across the river are going to drive the tigers to us," Bump said. Giving orders made him feel better but did not quiet his misgivings. *How could anyone know they were in the motel?*

"If one of the friends puts a foot in the river, he's a dead friend," Jimmy Guy said. "We should have done this a long time ago—stop them before they outnumber us and bring drugs and diseases with them."

9

Arina walked outside to find Jacob waiting in Cogden's Blazer. "We can't take the truck, not with that animal cage in the back," he said.

"We have no papers for the car."

"We don't need papers. No one cares about the car."

Arina could not believe what she heard; *Americans valued personal property above the life of another.* "I do not want to come to the attention of the authorities."

"Cogden is letting us use it because he wants the tigers captured."

Again, his actions confused her. "So his ranch, his vehicles are communal property for a common good? Yet you defended ranchers who would kill a valuable tiger to save an ordinary bull."

"It's more complicated than that, Arina. Everyone can do with their property as they wish. Some want to help us. For others, we have to have legal permission to set foot on their land, even to capture the tiger."

That wasn't freedom; that was anarchy. If individuals did not recognize a common good greater than their own desires there was no civilization. Reluctantly she got in the Blazer.

They drove in silence to Eagle Pass "Where Yee Haw meets *Olé*." Jacob was explaining the meaning of the sign when the international bridge came into view. "Stop," she demanded. "My government has not replaced my passport," she said.

"They won't ask for passports or papers," Jacob said impatiently.

Arina considered. In America she could be deported at any time. Across the border she could be detained by Mexican officials or encounter Russian officials sent to expedite the capture of the tigers. She wasn't safe anywhere, but across the border she would discover who Jacob was.

"I have to cross the bridge," Jacob said. "Are you coming or not?"

"Jacob, if I am arrested, I will never see you again."

"You won't be arrested," he said, driving to the bridge. Jacob handed money to the uniformed man at the tollbooth and drove across the bridge. Mexican officials took a cursory look at them and waved them through. "You can relax now," Jacob said.

"Is that all they will do?"

"You can't get into the interior without papers, but as long as you stay on this side of the checkpoints you don't need anything. They're glad to see you."

Jacob drove to the market in downtown Piedras Negras. An urchin waved him into an empty parking place, opened the car door for him, and pledged to guard the car with his life. Jacob gave the boy money, and he vigorously washed the car windows with a dirty rag.

"The Moderno's around the corner," Jacob said.

It was her first view of Mexico, and she thought it little different from the town across the river. The streets were narrower, more crowded, a little dirtier, the pedestrians a little poorer, the dogs unleashed and half-starved. But what caught her eye were the brilliant colors—purples, yellows, turquoise in shirts, dresses, flowers; greens in parakeets and parrots that were sold on the street.

Jacob led her across the narrow street, around the corner, and into the restaurant through double wooden doors. A waiter in a white jacket led them to a table near the entrance to the bar.

"How about a Bloody Mary before lunch?" he asked.

"Today you are my guide. I will trust you."

Jacob laughed. "In that case we'll have two Bloody Marys."

Arina looked around the dining room. A small dance floor extended from the bandstand at one end of the room half way to the other, and floor-to-ceiling mirrors lined the walls on either side. The mirrors were in wide panels, each bordered with drapes and tiebacks to give the appearance of openness. She looked around the room again. It was not as large as she had thought. She sat with her back to the front entrance, facing a mirrored wall and the reflections made the room appear to be a multitude of identical rooms. The restaurant, like the customs house, made a brave but futile attempt at grandeur.

It was a little before noon, and most of the tables were empty. Two American couples sat at a nearby table drinking beer, and a woman and young boy sat at another eating ice cream.

"I called the hospital before we left," Arina said. "Mr. Perez has been moved to San Antonio Medical Center because of complications."

"He'll be okay," Jacob said as the waiter brought their drinks. "He ran three miles on a crushed foot and a broken ankle."

Arina lifted her drink to her lips and looked over the rim of the glass, searching Jacob's face. "The stewardess and the woman in the farmhouse died in the hospital. Now Mr. Perez has been moved to a medical center." *He seemed to accept the news without question.* Arina lowered her glass and opened a menu. "Everyone the tiger has bitten has died. Doesn't that trouble you?"

"Those people suffered shock, trauma, their immune systems were already stressed. How do you like your drink?"

"I don't know."

"You took a drink."

Arina picked up the Bloody Mary and tasted it. "Very good. Cold but hot. You are a trustworthy guide. What do you recommend I eat?"

"Cabrito, same as the tiger." She looked at him with troubled eyes. "It's good. Trust me."

"Order me something to give me strength," she said. "I'll need it to cross the border again."

Jacob nodded. "Two orders of cabrito, and I'll call Santana again," he said, getting up and walking into the bar that was separated from the dining room by an archway in the mirrored wall.

Arina took another sip of her drink, trying to decide whether she liked it. She looked into the mirror in front of her and saw the reflection of two men at a table near the front door. They looked away, not like American men who openly ogled her. They did not want her to know she was being watched.

"Santana's back," Jacob said, startling her. "He'll meet us here." He sat down blocking her view of the mirror. When she looked again the two men were gone.

The waiter set steaming plates before them, and Jacob ordered another round of Bloody Marys. He watched her as she tried the food. "Well?" he asked.

"The meat is very tender. The rice is unusual," she said. "This—" She poked at a thick brown substance with her fork.

"Frijoles."

"This frijoles is the only bland thing on the plate, and you have added spicy sauce to yours."

"When I bite into Mexican food I want it to bite back," he said. "Maybe you aren't used to highly seasoned food."

"I am accustomed to fish," she said, and when he laughed she said, "Fish is good, and it is good for you."

"I don't want my fish to bite back," he said.

"Jacob, it is possible that someone saw me at the checkpoint and followed us here."

"Not a chance," he said. "You lived in a communist country too long."

"I am not accustomed to informal border crossings."

"I am your border guide," Jacob said. "Let me do the worrying."

They had finished lunch and were having coffee when Jacob stood. Arina glanced in the mirror and saw a curly haired man striding confidently toward their table. He was Jacob's height but heftier and better looking with finely chiseled features.

"Jacob," he said, stretching his arms wide.

"*Compadre,*" Jacob said. The two men embraced and patted each other on the back.

"Arina, I want you to meet Santana Zavala. An untrustworthy Mexican if there ever was one. Santana, Arina Yeroskin."

"*Con mucho gusto, señorita,*" Santana said, smiling broadly.

"Jacob, you tell lies as usual, but you have excellent taste in women. I have always said so."

"Thank you, Mr. Zavala," Arina said.

"Please. Santana."

"And I am Arina." She liked him instantly. He was not so guarded as Jacob. His openness and enthusiasm swept away all opposition.

"Bueno," Santana said, sitting down and grasping Jacob's shoulder. "So, you have been chasing tigers across Texas. Now you have driven them to Mexico. What are you trying to do, pay us back for all the *mojados* we send across the river? It is an unequal exchange, *amigo.* Hungry tigers for hungry Mexicans. Your tigers will eat more."

Jacob grinned. "They've been eating cattle, deer, and people all the way across south Texas. I don't expect them to starve on this side."

"So, we must capture them, just as you did the big lion on my ranch."

"We hope, *compadre.* They belong to Russia, and I've already killed one. We want to keep the other two alive."

"We will," Santana said. "I will get dogs—"

"I don't think there's a pack of cat hounds in Texas capable of stopping a tiger."

"We will use Mexican dogs," Santana said. "We will overwhelm the tigers with numbers, just like at the Alamo."

Jacob shook his head. "There's no—"

"Hear my plan," Santana said. "My neighbors and I will have our *vaqueros* comb the country for tracks of the tigers. The earth is soft because of the rain, and we have good trackers. I have seen Jorge Chapa, my foreman, follow a buck across rock. Jorge has a dog that will take the track of whatever Jorge puts it on. And there are other dogs like it in the area. We will use these dogs to follow the tigers where a man cannot. I will hire men to gather all the stray dogs in Piedras

Negras, and we will take them to the tiger tracks. When we know we are close to the tigers, we will turn all the dogs loose. We will overwhelm the tigers, *compadre*. Many of the strays may be killed, but they have no purpose in life except to dig through the garbage and spread disease. This way they will have a glorious purpose. We will have so many *perros* that the tigers will tire of killing them, and when they make a stand, we will have them."

Santana stopped talking, leaned back in his chair triumphantly and waved for a waiter. *"Tres cervezas,"* he said. "We will toast our victory."

Santana was so confident and enthusiastic that Arina couldn't help but share his optimism. "It's worth a try," Jacob said, raising his glass of beer. "Remember the Alamo."

"Remember Montezuma," Santana responded. "I will start our campaign immediately by rounding up recruits for our canine corps. Where can I reach you when it is time to launch the attack?"

Jacob gave him the telephone number for Cogden's lodge and started to pay the check, but Santana had already taken care of it. Jacob drove the few blocks to the bridge. Without realizing it, Arina chewed her nails. "Relax," Jacob said. "If you look guilty, they may get suspicious. If you are relaxed, they won't take a second look."

Jacob paid the toll on the Mexican side and drove across the two-lane bridge. He stopped under the large shed on the American side and greeted a uniformed official. The officer glanced at Arina, then spoke to Jacob. "Where have you folks been in Mexico?"

"Piedras Negras for lunch," Jacob answered.

"You bringing anything back? Any fruits, plants, liquor?"

"No fruits or plants and only the liquor in our stomachs."

The guard demonstrated his disgust at the tired joke. "You both US citizens?"

"Born and bred," Jacob said. Arina nodded.

He stepped away from the vehicle and waved them forward. "Okay, folks. Thanks," he said.

Unbidden, Arina's nails leapt to her mouth again. Jacob grinned. "Told you," he said.

"Is it always like that?" she asked.

"Unless they think you're smuggling drugs. Then they'll search you and the car. Crossing the bridge is easy. Getting into the countryside is more difficult."

The tigress lay on her stomach in the weeds near the edge of the stock pond and looked over her shoulder into the thorny retama and granjeno bushes behind her. The dry arroyo that funneled flood waters into the pond wound through the thicket, and she was able to see less than forty feet along the draw before it turned to the right. The tigress moaned softly and lashed her tail in the tall weeds. The day had dawned clear and cool, but the temperature rose with the sun and by noon was in the eighties. Flies buzzed around the remains of a buck she had killed during the night and shared with her mate.

The tigress ignored the flies and moaned again, then got to her feet to stare up the arroyo as the tiger appeared at the turn in the draw. He walked quietly in the soft, moist earth, entered the clearing around the water hole, and flopped heavily to the ground. The female watched the male for several minutes, stretched and moved slowly toward him. She sniffed at the huge male, then lay on her belly in front of him with her head stretched out on the earth. The tiger got to his feet, straddled the tigress and mated with her. At the moment of climax he bit her neck and snarled, then leapt from her back as she turned her head to roar at him.

The male walked away from the tigress and stared toward the east. The female rose to join him, and both listened intently. Dogs. Yapping, yelping, barking. The pounding of hooves. The grinding of gears as a vehicle strained to keep pace with the horses and hounds.

The tigress trotted up the arroyo and disappeared around the bend. The tiger stared in the direction of the sounds. His lips curled back over long, yellow fangs, and he snarled and twisted his head to the side as if ripping the throats of his enemies. He turned and with a growl rumbling deep in his belly followed the tigress up the creek.

Vaqueros had spotted the tigers' trail the previous evening and had followed it until it was too dark to see. They returned to the ranch with the news, and Santana had called Jacob at the lodge. "We have a dozen dogs that will take a trail, and a barn full of strays," he laughed. "Daylight, *compadre*. Come earlier for breakfast, yes?"

Jacob was glad he had not revealed his plan to Rand. It took heated words before Rand agreed to return to Laredo, check out of La Posada, and tell Stuart they were bringing a tiger across the border. "Tell him to get whatever clearances are necessary, pay whatever or whomever he has to. We can straighten out the legalities when the tiger is on this side."

Arina watched him, *a cowboy again. Shoot first and worry about the consequences later.*

"If you go, you may have to swim back," Jacob told her. "The Mexicans will ask questions about that crate going over but probably none a few dollars won't answer. If we bring back a tiger, there'll be a lot of questions on this side until Stuart clears things with the government."

There would be questions about her passport, her work for the zoo, what she knew about the tiger. Perhaps there would be questions about Andrei, his work for the zoo, his friends. She did not want to face the questions, but they would come regardless of whether or not they captured the tigers, whether she was on this side of the border or the other. She would be as eager as anyone to discover the truth about the tigers, about Jacob. "I will take my blowgun," she said.

"We may need it. I can't take my rifle across, but I can borrow one from Santana."

Jacob left the Blazer for Rand and took the pickup with the cage in the back. "Follow my instructions when we cross the border. If we get in a bind just say what I say. Follow my lead, okay?"

"Yes," Arina said. "I will follow your lead." She seemed to mean more than her words, and Jacob looked at her, but her face revealed nothing.

The yapping of the dogs was music to Jorge Chapa's ears. His brown, calloused hand gripped the reins lightly for the roan needed little guidance in following the dogs as they puzzled out the trail of the tigers. Jorge normally was a happy man. On the trail of game or a stray cow, he was ebullient. Jorge watched the dogs pick up their pace and was pleased that his dog was in the lead. He reined the roan toward the pickup as Santana steered it through the brush and over a dead mesquite limb.

"They have the trail, *patrón*," Jorge said, grinning broadly. "It is getting warm."

"*Ahora*, then, Jorge?" Santana asked, braking the truck to a stop.

"I think so, yes, *patrón*."

Santana shifted the transmission to neutral, honked the horn loudly, and stepped to the ground. He cupped his hands over his mouth and, facing the woods behind him, yelled, "*Adelante.*"

A bobtail truck headed toward Santana. Before daylight, ranch hands had tacked chicken wire around the stake bed of a bobtail truck and packed dogs from the barn into the wire enclosure.

A few of the dogs had been injured fighting during the night and had been left behind. Others had snapped at the cowboys and scooted between their legs to escape in the predawn darkness. Still the hands had more dogs than the enclosure would hold, and some of the men from El Cruce had tied ropes around the necks of the dogs that could not be stuffed aboard the truck and now led or followed the dogs on foot and broke up fights between the snarling canines.

Santana pulled a revolver from the holster on his belt, pointed the muzzle skyward, and squeezed the trigger. The bobtail stopped, and the dogs were released. The men following on foot released the dogs they led. Santana reholstered his revolver and scrambled into the pickup. "They're coming," he said to Arina and Jacob, who were riding in the cab with him, then turned to peer through the rear window at the two men in the bed of the pickup. "*¿Listo?*"

"*Sí, patrón,*" they replied.

Dogs passed the truck, following those on the trail ahead. Brown dogs, black dogs, red dogs, spotted dogs, most with ribs protruding, raced through the bottom. Two or three trailed leashes.

Jorge's roan pranced impatiently, and the pickup lurched forward as Santana released the clutch and pressed on the accelerator. Jacob heard the pounding of hooves and the yelling of men behind him.

"*Vámonos,* Jorge," Santana yelled. "Hold on," he said to Arina and Jacob. Limbs slapped the windshield, and Arina and Jacob covered their faces with their arms in case the glass shattered. The pickup swerved to miss a dog chasing a jackrabbit, and Santana dismissed the rabbit chaser with a wave of his hand. "We have thousands of dogs, thousands. Maybe even a hundred. We will overwhelm the tigers."

Arina was caught up in Santana's enthusiasm, but Jacob envisioned chaos, and thus far that's what he had seen. If he had the helicopter they could get both tigers. He was sure of it. If Stuart had gotten permission. This way—He shook his head. The tigers would run until exhausted. They would bay and kill however many dogs were in the chase before the horsemen caught up. If the *vaqueros* got there before the tigers could run again either the *vaqueros* would die or they would kill the tigers.

Santana swerved the truck around an ancient mesquite and over a dip hidden by the tall grass. Jacob braced his knees against the dash and held Arina with his left arm, try-ing to protect her. He glanced back and saw one of the men in the bed of the pickup fly into the air, legs and arms wav-ing wildly. The truck shot out from under him, and the man fell to the ground but bounced to his feet immediately. Santana did not stop.

Arina looked at Jacob. He shrugged. The man wasn't hurt and stopping would take valuable time. The other *vaquero* screamed and pounded on the cab. *"El tigre,"* he yelled, pointing back through the trees. *"El tigre."*

"We're ahead of the dogs," Jacob yelled at Santana. "Hell, we're ahead of the tigers."

"The cowboy," Arina said. "He is on the ground with the tigers."

"I must get him," Santana said.

"Let us out," Jacob said. "We'll get in a tree and try to dart them." The pickup skidded to a stop. "After you pick up the *vaquero*, try to run the tigers through here. Maybe we can get a shot at one of them."

Jacob and Arina grabbed their dart guns and bags of darts

and jumped out of the pickup. Jacob slung the borrowed 30-30 over his shoulder. Santana sped away. "Find a tree," Jacob said to Arina. "I'll pick one near you. Maybe one of us will get a shot."

Jacob jogged through the brush until he found what he was looking for. The mesquite had a straight trunk and a fork about fifteen feet above the ground. It wasn't high enough, but it was the best he could find. He hoped the dogs would be close enough behind the tigers to keep them moving. Fifteen feet was no protection from a tiger with time to spring.

Arina ran to the tallest tree in sight. The incline made it easier for her to climb with the clumsy blowgun. Positioning herself, she readied a dart. She did not have long to wait. She saw movement out of the corner of her eye. It was a blur, but she was certain it was the tiger and out of range. She wondered if she should call to Jacob. *What could he do?* The tiger was beyond his range too and appeared to be moving away from them.

She was trying to catch another glimpse of the tiger when something caused her to look down. The tigress, directly below her, had stopped to pant and look back in the direction of the dogs and horsemen. Arina was so startled she almost dropped her blowgun. Her hands shook as she pointed the tube toward the cat. She blew hard into the blowgun and saw the dart strike the tiger in the muscle of the shoulder near the spine. The cat wheeled and bit at the dart. Unable to reach it, the tiger tore at the grass and raked the tree with its claws.

Arina was loading another dart when the cat, attracted by the movement, looked up at her. Its lips pulled back from the fangs, pushing up ridges beneath its eyes. Masses of muscle quivered with rage. Arina was not high enough to escape the tigress' attack. The cat could spring up, catch her in its claws, and drag her from the tree. A scream tried to escape her constricted throat.

The tigress snarled and tensed, measuring the distance it must jump to pull her from the tree, when a thin, long-legged, long-eared dog burst from the brush. The dog was in mid-bound when it saw the cat and tried to stop, skidding and pawing furiously to reverse direction, yelping and wetting as it knew the effort was futile. The tigress roared and pounced on the dog, biting through its back and hurling it fifteen feet through the air. The cat turned on two more dogs, disemboweling one and breaking the back of the other before running again. Suddenly there were dogs everywhere. Some of them stopped to sniff or bite the dying dogs; others pursued the tiger.

"Jacob," Arina screamed. "Jacob."

Suddenly Jacob was on the ground below her. "You all right?"

She clung tightly to the tree, trying to catch her breath. "Jacob."

"Come on," he said, glancing around nervously. "We have to find Santana and the truck."

"Jacob." She realized she was not making sense, but she could not release her grip on the tree. She did not want to be on the ground.

"Let me help you," Jacob said, reaching as high as he could.

Slowly she relaxed her grip on the tree and inched down until Jacob caught her and helped her the last few feet. She did not stop when her feet touched the ground but slid until she sat beside the tree. "Jacob."

"What is it?"

"I darted the female."

"Get a move on. The dogs will kill it if we don't get there

in time," he said. "Besides, the male is around here some-
place."

"Wait," she said, looking at the crippled dogs that were
whining and pawing, pulling themselves over the rough
ground. "They saved my life."

Jacob took the knife from the sheath on his belt and
quickly dispatched both of them. He wiped the blade on his
boot, replaced it, and caught Arina's hand, pulling her over
the rough ground.

They had run only a few yards when Jorge and three other
cowboys overtook them, followed by Santana in the pickup.
Arina and Jacob jumped in the cab, and Santana bounced the
truck over the rough terrain, no longer trying to avoid small
trees and shrubs that he could knock down or run over. A
trail of dead and injured dogs led them to the tigress, its back
to a tree. The drug was working; the tiger staggered but was
still on its feet. It snarled and lashed out at the braver dogs
that worried it.

Jacob moved in close with the Cap-Chur gun and darted it
again. The tiger went down on its haunches and slowly collapsed. Jacob, Jorge, Santana, and the two *vaqueros* beat and
pulled off the dogs that tried to close in for the kill. The dogs
milled about, getting underfoot, snarling, snapping, and
barking at the tiger.

Jorge examined his chase dog. It was okay. He backed the
truck as close to the cat as possible. Lifting the cage out of the
truck was no problem. It weighed slightly more than a hundred pounds, but when they put the tigress in the cage they
added four hundred pounds. Two cowboys tied their lariats
to the cage, threw the ropes over a stout limb and took a turn
around the saddle horns. The horses, straining against the
weight, were able to raise the cage enough to slide it into the
bed of the pickup.

Jacob turned from the caged tiger and blew out his breath.

He looked at Arina. "I'm going to have to teach you to high five," he said, giving Santana and Jorge an *embrazo*.

"That is good enough for me," she said, and he embraced her as well.

Santana put his arms around both of them. "The other tiger got away," he said. "The dogs—" he gestured with his hands.

"We got the female, we can catch the male," Jacob said.

"*Bueno,*" Santana said. "At the *hacienda* there will be *cerveza* for everyone."

With a shout, the *vaqueros* coiled their ropes, jumped in the saddles, and galloped toward the headquarters. The dogs followed.

Santana turned to the man who had fallen out of the truck. His clothes were torn, his elbows skinned, but only his pride was injured. "I will ride in back with you," Santana said. "Jacob, you drive." Jacob said there was room for three in the cab. "No, my friend. I will ride in the back with the animals," he said, laughing with his men.

Jacob parked the truck in the shade. Arina feared that the tigress, overheated from the chase, might die of heatstroke since the drug slowed its heartbeat and respiration. They opened the cage, and Arina checked the condition of the cat. She dressed the wounds left by the darts and by the chase through the brush and gave it antibiotics.

"I am going to keep it sedated until we can get it in a large pen where it will not hurt itself," she said. "It will be able to move as much as the cage will allow, but it will be quiet."

"How long can we keep it like this?" Jacob asked.

"Long enough to catch as much urine as we need."

"*Bueno,*" Jacob said.

"Now we celebrate," Santana said, leading them to the house.

. . .

The tiger had run until it could run no more. Strings of spittle flew from its mouth as it was brought to bay by a pack of curs. The tiger wheeled on the dogs, forcing them to scramble out of reach. Even exhausted, the huge male was more than a match for the dogs. Three of the curs, unable to contain their enthusiasm, darted within its reach and died quickly as the cat used fang and claw to rip the howling dogs apart. The others kept a distance, bawling and yapping at the infuriated cat.

The tiger whirled, snarling and spitting at its tormentors, then stood panting, its dripping tongue lolling over its lower lip. It turned its head, watching the dogs through narrowed, amber eyes filled with hate. Sinewy muscles in its legs and shoulders rippled beneath the pale orange hide as it crouched. The dogs made so much racket they did not hear the rumbling begin deep in the tiger's belly and rise toward its throat. It was the sound of molten lava breaking through the thin crust of a sleeping volcano, and it erupted in a terrifying roar.

The dogs, stumbling backward over each other, did not anticipate the swiftness of the attack, and the tiger was on them before they were able to evade. Its massive jaws snapped over the spine and rib cage of a brindle dog. The dog howled in pain as splintered ribs pierced its lungs, and frothy blood shot from its nose and mouth. The dog pawed the air with its front legs, as the tiger's claws ripped into its body cavity. The remaining dogs turned tail and ran, and the tiger trotted after them, the dog's legs and head flopping, entrails dragging, as the cat continued the pursuit. The tiger's head was held high, and its long tail whipped furiously in the air above its back.

The tiger stopped and watched the dogs disappear in the underbrush. It lay down in the shade of a mesquite, dropped the dead dog between its front legs and cleaned itself, licking the blood from its fur. When it had finished, it cleaned the dog with its broad, rough tongue from head to tail and then placed a front leg over the upper part of the dog's body to hold it down, sank its teeth in the haunches of the animal, and ripped at the flesh, pulling, twisting, and chewing until a leg was torn free.

The tiger ate everything but the entrails and stomach before rising and walking ponderously to another dead dog. It sniffed it, then raised its head in the direction it had last seen the tigress, emitted a low, grunting moan and glided through the bottom, tail held low, retracing the route it had taken through the twisted mesquites and underbrush while pursued by the dogs. Occasionally it lifted its head to sniff the wind and was rewarded with the faint scent of its mate. It followed the scent to where the tigress had fallen. The smell of men, dogs, and horses mingled with hers, confusing the tiger, and again it raised its head and moaned.

It continued on the back trail, up the river to where the dogs had jumped it and its mate that morning, and beyond, toward the repugnant smell of man.

Humberto Barboza, commandant of the *Sección de Seguridad Administrativo* of the northern district of the state of Coahuila, sat in the shade of Santana's porch. Two of his men lounged nearby. Four more stood beside a two-ton truck. None was in uniform, but all were armed. "Ah, it is my host," Barboza said, waving his glass at Santana but not getting up. "Your man was kind enough to fix me a rum and Coke."

Barboza was sixty-two years old, graying and short of stature. He had a grandfatherly appearance. Except for his eyes. They were black and emotionless. When men looked into his eyes, they quickly looked away. Some men found it difficult to talk when Barboza stared at them. Some women found such power attractive.

Barboza had served his country as an officer in the army for more than twenty years and had retired at the rank of general almost as poor as when he began soldiering. Before he retired, while he still had power, he spoke to certain people in certain positions and stepped from the army into the SSA, where he had even more power. There were debts to be paid, and Barboza was a prudent man. He paid his debts and then began to accumulate personal wealth, much of it invested in a ranch of 20,000 hectares on the Mexican side of the border.

"*Buenos tardes,*" Santana said. "To what do I owe the honor of your presence?"

"We are neighbors, are we not?" Barboza said, waving his hand toward the west where the boundary of his ranch met that of Santana's. "But this is not a neighborly visit. No, this is official business. We have had reports of dangerous animals invading our state. As the one most personally responsible for the safety and security of our people, I have come with some of my men to catch the tiger." He paused to take a sip of his rum and Coke. When he raised his arm to drink, Jacob saw a 9 mm Beretta in his waistband beneath his *guayabera*. The pistol had silver grips. His initials, H.B., were inlaid in gold. "It is to my deep regret that I come too late to assist you in the capture."

"There's another tiger," Jacob said. "Headed west."

Barboza smiled. It was a smile of understanding, not of warmth. "Toward my ranch," Barboza said. "That will be convenient. I will not have to trouble you in order to catch it. But first, we must celebrate the capture of the one, must we not?"

"Of course, general," Santana said. It was a title Barboza liked. "Drinks for everyone while I see that the cook is busy."

Rounds of drinks were followed by courses of food

through the long afternoon. Barboza's men did not drink but ate the food passed to them.

After everyone had eaten and drunk all they wanted, Barboza stood. "Santana, *mi amigo,* I have brought a truck. Do you have a hoist? Please ask your men to load the tiger in my truck."

"Not so fast," Jacob said.

Barboza's eyes did not waver. "You will be given credit for the capture of the tiger," he said, "but only I can guarantee its safety."

"If you can help us get it across the border, I can handle it from there," Jacob said.

"I wish it were so simple," Barboza said. "But there is your government, my government, red tape. No, it is impossible."

"The tiger belongs to the Russians," Jacob said, reminding himself to be calm and courteous. "This woman was sent by her government to see to the security of the animals. She is a veterinarian and has orders to be with the animals at all times."

"Ah, three governments," Barboza said with a shrug of his shoulders. "You see, impossible."

"I represent the North American Zoological Association," Jacob said, hoping to impress Barboza with the title. "They, along with the Russian government and the US government, are vitally concerned with the well-being of the tigers. If you accompany me to the border, you will be handsomely rewarded for the tiger's safe delivery."

Barboza shrugged again. "I am an old man," he said. "The safety of the tiger and the safety of the people is all the reward I wish." His face became hard. "Santana, if you will speak to your men," he said.

"General, I regret that I do not have a hoist," Santana said. "Jorge, take the pickup with the tiger to the general's ranch. See to it that the tiger is placed wherever the general wishes the tiger to be placed. You are to assist the general in any way he requires. Do not return until he dismisses you."

Jorge nodded and went to the pickup. He signaled two *vaqueros* to join him.

"Thank you, Santana," the general said. He turned to the two men lounging nearby. "Bring the car," he said.

Jacob watched the general get in the car and drive away, followed by the pickup carrying the caged tiger and the general's truck. An armed man stood on either running board of the truck. Jacob turned to Santana. "What the hell?" he asked.

Santana shrugged. "You must understand, my friend, the general is commandant of security."

"You didn't have to let him take my tiger."

"Jacob," Arina said, "the general will return the tiger to Russia."

Jacob looked at Santana. Santana shrugged. *"¿Quién sabe?"*

"Call Moscow, tell them the Mexican authorities have the tiger," Jacob told her. "Ask them to request the tiger be released to us."

"Jacob, I—" Arina began and faltered. She could not call Moscow. *Was he testing her? And why must the tiger be returned to him?*

"Tell them to hurry because we don't have much time before the tigress is out of estrus."

"There is not enough time," Arina said.

"We trailed that damn tiger from the Gulf of Mexico. I didn't come all this way to give it up to the first guy who flashes a badge. I'm going after that tiger, Santana."

Santana held up a hand. "Do not be so impatient, my friend. The rooster does not always chase the hen. Sometimes he crows. Sometimes he sits in a tree and watches the sunset, eh? Miguel," he called to a servant. "Coffee for my guests," he said, smiling at Jacob and Arina. "Let us contemplate the sunset and enjoy our success."

"I'm not crowing until I get the tiger back," Jacob said.

"Jacob, you are so quick to act, so slow to think. Did not Jorge go with the general? Will not Jorge return here? Will not Jorge tell us what the general has done with the tiger?"

"You're not a rooster, you're a fox," Jacob said in admiration.

"You are going to steal the tiger from the general?" Arina asked.

"Not I," Santana said. "The general is a representative of my government. He is a neighbor, a friend. I do not defy the general."

"I'll steal the tiger," Jacob said.

Arina looked at him in disbelief. "But what if you get caught?"

"Do not get caught," Santana said.

"The jails down here are not very hospitable," Jacob said.

Santana sighed and extended his arms. "The general was once a good man, but life has made him hard. He is not a cruel man, but he has a cruel job, and he employs men who do cruel things. It is not jail you must fear. I speak to you plainly. Do not get caught by the general or his men."

With the confidence that came of power, Barboza eschewed pretension. His home in Piedras Negras was large and comfortable but not stylish. His ranch house was utilitarian, his office on the second floor bare except for the wooden desk, manual typewriter, telephone, and four wooden chairs. His only luxury was the air conditioner. Barboza sat in the large chair behind the desk and spoke into the telephone.

"General Humberto Barboza, commandant of the *Sección de Seguridad Administrativo* of the northern district of

Coahuila," he said into the telephone. "I have a tiger that I believe belongs to you. The female is alive and will lead the male into a trap. I have plans for such a trap."

"You will deliver the tigers to us?"

"But of course," the general said. "To you or to the Americans. There is the matter of expenses."

"Your expenses will be paid."

"Not my expenses, *señor*, but the expenses of the SSA. America is rich. Mexico is poor, and capturing the tiger has been very expensive."

"We will pay the expenses."

"Why bother if you are going to return the tigers to the Americans? Let them pay."

"They are our tigers, and we will pay for them. Perhaps the Americans have not been responsible, permitting the tigers to escape. Perhaps my government does not wish the Americans to have the tigers."

"That is nothing to me, but the Americans have agreed to pay five thousand dollars, not pesos, for the expenses in capturing the first tiger. The second may be even more expensive."

"My government is prepared to pay more—"

"As an initial payment," Barboza interrupted. "You may seek the assistance of the Federal or state police, but I feel I should inform you that my agency has jurisdiction in these matters."

"Of course. Your permission and cooperation is necessary. My government will pay when the tigers are captured or dead, provided it is both tigers. My government is not pleased that an American cowboy is free to pursue the tigers in Mexico. He has already killed one tiger."

"I believe there is a Russian woman assisting him."

"She does not act under our authority or protection."

"*Bueno.* I will see that they are unwelcome in my district."

"It is a pleasure to deal with a man of authority, General Barboza. I hope to hear soon that both tigers are in your possession, dead or alive."

Humberto replaced the telephone. It was a pleasure dealing with men who were anxious.

Jorge returned to announce, "The tiger is in the general's truck. The truck is parked between the houses of the *vaqueros* and the *hacienda*."

"The headquarters is on a hill," Santana said, drawing a map. "The *hacienda* is here. There are sheds over this way. There are two houses for the *vaqueros*, here and here, perhaps a hundred and fifty yards from the *hacienda*. And the truck is here?" he asked, pointing a finger between the two houses.

"Here," Jorge said, pointing a little beyond the second house.

"At least the tiger is where it will catch the breeze," Arina said.

"*Sí*. The truck is open. The cage sits here."

"No sideboards on the truck?" Jacob asked.

"*Sí*," Jorge said. "Sideboards, but no—" He searched for the word.

"No tailgate."

"*Sí*. No tailgate."

"Did he have any men besides the six here with the truck?" Jacob asked.

"*Dos*."

"Were they armed?" Jorge mimed holding a gun that shook his body. "Machine guns?"

"*Sí*."

Jacob looked at Santana. "Do Barboza's men have machine guns?"

Santana shrugged. "The general is involved in many things."

214

"Where are the two men?"

"Here and here," Jorge said, indicating the front and back of the truck. "The others are in the *casas*."

"If I could distract these two guys, maybe I could drive off with the truck," Jacob said.

"You would never reach the border," Santana said.

"If I got enough of a head start, I could hide the truck in the brush—"

"One of my men could accidentally block the road, and you could hide the truck on my ranch," Santana volunteered.

"Too risky," Jacob said. "We can't involve you if we can help it. We need the helicopter. I hate to put Barry on the spot, but there's no other way. I'll drive in to Piedras Negras and call him. I don't want them to trace anything back to you. It's better if I'm seen in town."

"And I will be seen in El Cruce," Santana said. "Almost every family there has someone who works for the general. I regret I cannot go with you, but when you return, Jorge will be waiting on the road to guide you to the general's ranch. Once you are inside the ranch, he will return here."

"Good," Jacob said. He solemnly shook hands with Santana and Jorge.

Jacob took Arina back to the Moderno, loudly ordered drinks and dinner and went to the telephone. He hated to ask Barry to do something Barry might not want to do. Barry answered on the first ring.

"Hey, Jacob," he said. "I've been going nuts waiting for this damn telephone to ring. I need a job."

"I've got one. I'd better tell you about it first," Jacob said, relating the capture of the tiger and the general's appropriation of it. "I've considered every possibility, and the only chance is to pick it up by helicopter. The general has men with guns, but I hope to surprise him."

"You're asking me to fly illegally into Mexico, dodge gunfire, and steal a tiger from the most dangerous man on the border?"

"That's the size of it," Jacob admitted.

"What's the damn thing weigh? This chopper is supposed to lift 850 pounds on a sling, but it depends on how much fuel I'm carrying, ground effect, wind, temperature, and how far I've got to drag it."

"I don't understand all that," Jacob said. "Just tell me if you're interested."

"As long as it's dark and I can lift it."

"The tiger weighs roughly 400 pounds, the cage 100. It'll be a short trip; the *hacienda* is close to the river. I'll sneak up to the ranch and be in the truck when you come in with the hook. I'll attach it, you head for home, and in the confusion I'll slip back to the pickup and run for the border."

"What time?"

"We want to be sure they're asleep. How about two?"

"How will I find you in the dark?"

"How about a flashlight?"

"Good enough. Just be sure I see it. I'll leave here shortly before two and stay over the river until I see your light. I'll stay high enough that I have good visibility and can come in hot."

"Call Rand at the lodge and tell him you're bringing the tiger."

"I'll need him to find a sitdown for me and to mark it so I can see it. I'll rig the chopper for a sling. What am I going to hook on to?"

"Will nylon rope do?"

"Strap is better. Just be sure it can handle the load. If it breaks we splatter tiger all over the countryside."

"Right."

"Jacob, I don't want to spend a lot of time hovering over

the truck. Fast blink twice for lower. Full on for stop. Then off for go. The line is going to be short and I'm going to be low. Don't let the blades hit you and don't take a lot of time hooking it up."

"Anything else?"

"It's my ass and my helicopter. There's an emergency release in the cabin, and if I can't make it, I'm cutting the damn tiger loose."

"Understood," Jacob said. "Barry, I want you to know I appreciate what you're doing. I'm sorry I had to ask you."

"You're the one on the ground with the bad guys."

The spicy *chile relleno* stuck in Arina's throat when Jacob told her he was going to place a strap around the tiger crate and Barry was going to lift it with the helicopter. "I'll take you back across the border," he said.

He had refused to risk his dogs, but he was willing to use a boy's body to capture the tiger. Now he was willing to risk his life, Barry's life. "The general has the tigress; he can trap the male. Why must you do this?"

"There are people who will pay Barboza big money to shoot it. That's if Barboza can keep someone from shooting it while it's sitting in his front yard. Arina, neither country does a good job of controlling the border. Besides, I didn't like his arrogance."

He did it again. Just as she was ready to believe he valued the tiger, he suggested he was acting out of pique. "For this you will risk your life? Barry's life? There are at least eight men. Will you kill them?"

"I won't kill anybody for a tiger, and if we do it right there won't be much risk. They'll be drowsy, won't know what's going on. Barry will pick up the crate and I'll be out of there before they know what happened."

"Who will signal while you are attaching the hook?"

Jacob shrugged.

She could not return to Russia without arrest, she could not return to Texas without the risk of deportation and arrest, she could not be jailed in Mexico or captured by Barboza's men. *Could she believe Jacob was risking his life to take the tigress to safety?* "Jacob, you must tell me. Do you work for anyone other than NAZA?"

"I told you, I'm on loan from a cougar relocation project. When the tigers are in NAZA's possession I'm going home. I want you to go with me."

"I am going with you," she said, "to Barboza's."

"I can't ask you to do that." She said nothing. "It's going to be scary."

"I am properly frightened." If she were captured, no one would come to her assistance.

10

Jacob eased the truck off the road, cut the lights, and turned off the ignition. For a few minutes he and Arina sat in the darkness, hearing only the ticking of the cooling engine. Then they smelled the pungent odors of human and horse sweat, and Jorge appeared at the door. Arina slid next to Jacob, and Jorge climbed into the truck.

Jacob started the engine and pulled onto the highway again. They rode several minutes in silence, then Jorge said, *"Despacio."*

Jacob slipped the truck out of gear so that it rolled on its own momentum. *"Derecha,"* Jorge said, and Jacob pulled off onto a dirt track almost hidden in the chaparral. He put the truck in gear, steered through a thicket and stopped before a heavy gate with a sign. *"Privado."*

Jacob and Jorge got out to inspect the gate. Arina followed. The gateposts were set in concrete, the gate secured with a heavy chain and lock. Jorge produced a pistol from his pocket and pointed it at the lock. Jacob caught his arm. "How far to the *hacienda?*" he asked.

"Over a hill and another hill. Maybe six miles. Many shots at night on the river. Poachers. Smugglers. *¿Quién sabe?*"

"Okay," Jacob said. He led Arina behind the truck.

Jorge pointed the pistol at the lock and pulled the trigger. The lock jerked but did not break. He shot it again. And again. Jacob walked around the truck to inspect the lock under the headlights. The bullets had nicked it and dented one side. "Very good lock," Jorge said.

"What now?" Jacob asked.

Jorge motioned for Jacob to work the truck between the brush and the fence. He walked ahead, looking for a clearing. When he found one he hammered the wires with the pistol until he knocked loose the staples from two posts, then stood on the top wire, stretching it. Jacob stood on the wire beside the other post. Between them they forced the wires to the ground until Arina was able to drive the truck over the fence.

They got back in the truck, and Jacob drove slowly along the road, steering by the light of the moon. The night was clear, and the visibility good. That would help Barry find them in the dark and help Jacob locate the hook and attach it to the cage, but it would also make it easier for Barboza's men to see them.

At the bottom of the second hill Jorge signaled for him to stop and got out of the pickup. "I go this way," he said pointing through the chaparral. "I leave no tracks. *Vaya con Dios.*" He shook hands with Arina and Jacob and disappeared into the brush.

"I think this is as far as we'd better go," Jacob said. He backed the truck into the brush so that it was partially hidden but pointed in the direction they would leave. He took the key out of the ignition and held it up. "I'm putting this under the left front tire. If you should get back here ahead of me, don't wait. If I see I can't make it, I'll head for the river or take off through the brush like Jorge. If I get back first, I'll come looking for you. Try to stay close to the road but not on it. If you see me, jump in front of the truck but don't yell. I won't be able to hear you, but they will." Arina nodded.

"Let's be sure we have everything we need." In Piedras Negras he had put the Cap-Chur gun, Arina's blowgun, and the darts in a box and had them delivered to Cogden's ranch. He wanted to cross the border in a hurry without being slowed by curiosity about the guns. He had bought an axe handle, a flashlight and batteries, a heavy strap to place around the crate, and duct tape. He had taped a can with both ends cut out over the front of the flashlight to prevent the light from being seen from the side. "Put the flashlight on the floor and see if it works." It did.

Should he warn her about snakes? Rattlesnakes hunted for food during the cooler hours of dusk until dawn. He decided against it. She had enough to worry about. "Try to think of the darkness and brush as a friend. They will protect you. Don't worry about getting lost. Head in the opposite direction of the helicopter and look for the road."

She nodded. "The male tiger is out there, perhaps has detected the scent of the female and is nearby," she said.

"After that chase today, it's probably hidden in a thicket." Jacob looked at his watch. "We have plenty of time. Let's make it slow and silent." He waited until Arina got out, then slipped out of the truck, pushed the door closed until the light went off, and, motioning her to watch, placed the key under the front left tire. It was out of sight but could be found in the darkness and in a hurry.

Jacob slung the heavy strap over his shoulder, leaving both hands free to use the axe handle. He carried the duct tape in his pocket. Leading Arina he started up the hill, keeping to the side of the road. He had no idea what he was going to do. The plan that seemed simple when he had explained it to Barry now seemed complex and foolhardy. He and Arina had to overcome six, perhaps eight men, wait patiently for Barry to come, hook up the crate with the tiger, then outrun the general's men back to the truck and across the river. This time there would be no one to open a hole in the fence or show the way, and if the general alerted the border, they might have trouble crossing the river.

He dared not express his fear to Arina. He had allowed her to come, had asked Barry to bring his helicopter, knowing that it was dangerous and illegal and that being shot might not be the worst that could happen to them. Whatever happened to him or the tiger, he had to do all he could to see that Arina and Barry got back all right.

The thrill of the hunt was gone. *Why were they doing this?* Because the tigers were rare and valuable creatures, because they were man-eaters, because he needed the tigress to lure the male into a trap, because he had accepted the job. Because he had promised Arina, Evelyn, Rand, and everyone watching television that he would do everything he could to capture the tigers. "That's why," he muttered to himself. "Dumbass."

They followed the road until they could see the *hacienda* on the hill silhouetted against the sky. Jacob studied the layout, wanting to get his bearings straight so that he and Arina wouldn't stumble into something unexpected or run in the wrong direction. When he was sure he could find his way around in the dark he looked at Arina. She nodded. He left the road and picked his way through the brush, wanting to approach the truck from the side of the last *vaqueros'* house. *Surprise was in their favor. If they don't have a dog,* he thought.

Damn! Why didn't he ask Jorge? If there was a dog, they were dead. A dog would wake up the entire country. And lead the general right to them. He stood for a moment worrying about the dog when it occurred to him that if there was a dog, it would have barked at the tiger all night. For the first time since leaving the pickup, he took a deep breath.

The brush was thick to the back of the *vaqueros'* house. Jacob dropped to his hands and knees and crawled under the open window. It was unlikely anyone was awake in the house, but there was no reason to take chances. When he looked back he saw that Arina followed him. He motioned for her to stay at the house.

At the corner of the house where he could see the truck, Jacob stopped and listened. He could not see guards. *Was the truck unguarded?* A snore came from inside the house. He looked back at Arina; she smiled. Jacob slowly rose to his feet. When he did he saw that a guard was asleep in the bed of the truck, lying beside the cage.

Jacob crossed silently to the truck. The sleeping man did not move. Jacob listened for a moment to his heavy breathing, then walked along the side of the truck looking for the other guard. The man stood at the front of the truck, leaning against the fender. He seemed to be looking at the stars. Then his head fell forward, caught, fell again. For a moment his chin was on his chest, then he jerked alert, glanced from side to side and, again looked at the stars. Jacob readied the axe handle, and when the man nodded again, he swung the handle, hitting the man in the back of the head.

Jacob froze. The sound was louder than he had expected, both the thump of the handle against the head and the thud of the body on the ground. Jacob heard no one moving and again slipped to the back of the truck. He readied the handle in one hand and shook the sleeping man by the foot. When the man raised up on his elbows, Jacob hit him. He waved at Arina to signal with the flashlight and went back to the front of the truck. He taped the man's hands and mouth and searched him for a weapon. He found a bulky machine pistol of a type he had never seen before. Taking it with him, he got in the bed of the truck.

Arina climbed on top of the cab and turned on the flashlight. Jacob examined the cage to decide how best to attach the hook. The sling used to hoist the cage was still in place. He placed the strap around the crate anyway. He looked at the luminous dial of his watch. He hoped Barry was punctual; things had gone too smoothly to screw up now. He watched the sky, looking for the position lights.

Suddenly he heard the popping of the helicopter coming in low and fast. He was trying to locate it when he heard cursing and the doors of the houses slamming open. Men tumbled outside, yelled, then ran back inside. They had not seen him or Arina. He looked again for the helicopter and spotted its outline against the sky. Barry was running without lights. Already he was past the *hacienda*. "Watch out for the hook," Jacob hissed. The helicopter was almost over the truck when gunfire erupted from the two houses.

Bump's men dived under the brush and buried their faces in the ground as the helicopter passed overhead for the third time. They didn't look up until it was almost out of hearing. Hearing was their only knowledge of it. Although it had passed directly overhead three times, they had not seen it because it showed no lights. "We've got to get out of here," Roy Pat said. "They spotted us."

"They couldn't have seen us in all this brush," said Kid.

"They have infrared, night vision, and heat detection capability," Bump said.

"They had that in Vietnam," Roy Pat said. "No telling what they got now. They know exactly where we are and probably who we are."

"I say we fire a few shots across their bow. That'll get rid of them," Jimmy Guy said.

"They got more fire power than we got," Roy Pat said. "We don't shoot at them until we know what capability they got."

"Get down," Bump ordered, hearing the helicopter coming back. His anger at Roy Pat for making every statement sound like an order evaporated in the face of his fear. *The damn helicopter had their position fixed and could shoot at any time.* Suddenly, the helicopter veered across the river and flew into Mexico. His men crowded around him.

"That was a UN helicopter," Jimmy Guy said. "They can cross the border any time they want to, and we can't do a damn thing about it."

"The hell we can't," Bump said.

"They could be smugglers," Roy Pat said.

"Wouldn't it be a good thing to shoot them down?" Jimmy Guy asked. Does 'not letting anyone cross the border' include anyone in a helicopter?"

Bump knew he had to come up with an answer before Roy Pat did. He also knew he had to be right. "If it tries to come back across the river we blow it out of the sky. Now, spread out and dig in. We don't know what kind of fire power they got."

Barry flew a teardrop pattern along the north side of the river. He had covered the aircraft numbers with tape and kept his lights off, but he stayed on the Texas side of the border until he saw the light. He headed for the light, losing altitude and trying to penetrate the darkness. The moonlight was good, but the shadows were tricky. Neither he nor Jacob knew if there were power lines, poles, or antenna. A high windmill was dangerous as low as he was. "Guide me in," he muttered.

He could see the roofs of the *hacienda* and the houses and shadows that appeared to be trees along the brow of the hill. "Drop inside the trees and there'll be no target at all," he encouraged himself. He saw the truck and maneuvered the hook over it. Suddenly he saw flashes of light from the houses, like the glitter of an electric bug light. He knew what that was, and the excitement that had sent his pulse racing was replaced with a cold hand that grabbed his gut. He knew what that was too.

With a loud clunk, something hit the helicopter and the canopy filled with smoke. Barry could not see, could not breathe. He coughed and, in a panic, tried to read the instruments, tried to retain control. He pawed at the instruments and found them covered with dust.

Instantly he knew what had happened. A bullet had come through the open door and hit the fire extinguisher, filling the canopy with a greasy, chemical powder. Barry dropped the helicopter off the side of the hill, putting the trees between him and the guns.

Arina had dropped into the bed of the truck to escape the helicopter blades, and both she and Jacob lay beside the cage. Arina tightly squeezed his arm, and he looked at her, not sure what to do. He didn't know if the helicopter had been hit or not. He didn't know if Barry would come back. If so, he had to stop the guns or draw their fire. Barry had no chance against them. If not, he and Arina had to get away quickly. From inside the houses he could hear the men calling the names of the two guards.

Barry checked the controls and the instrument panel. Nothing seemed to be damaged except the fire extinguisher, and he could fly without that. Using his handkerchief he wiped at the film on the canopy, wondering what to do.

226

Whoever shot at him must also have been shooting at Jacob. He was almost certainly dead. Or wounded. The best he could hope for was that Jacob had fled in the confusion. Best to fly back to Eagle Pass, gas up, and head for Corpus Christi. Pretend he knew nothing.

That was the best thing to do, but he couldn't leave not knowing what had happened to Jacob. There was no way to get the tiger now. And no way to get Jacob if he were wounded. Barry swore. As in Nam he had no choice. He had to go back, and this time they would be waiting. *Okay, he would come in behind them.* "If you're alive, Jacob, give me a light," he shouted into the roar of the helicopter. "One pass is all I've got in me."

Jacob gripped Arina's shoulder. "He's coming back," he said. Arina nodded. "Get the truck between you and the guns," he whispered.

Arina waited until the sound of the helicopter was so loud everyone would be looking for it, then slipped over the side of the truck next to the cab. She did not want to put her feet on the ground. Standing on the running board she pointed the flashlight around the cab and flashed.

Jacob crouched behind the sideboards, wishing he could tell Barry to leave. Then he and Arina could make a run for it in the darkness. They'd lose the tiger, but it was their only chance. He could hear the helicopter, but he wasn't sure where it was. Barry seemed to be circling. *Was he looking for them on the ground?* Then he knew. Barry was creating confusion before he made his run. He would come in on their blind side.

Barboza's men heard the chopper coming and ran outside to shoot at it. Jacob pulled the trigger on his weapon but nothing happened. He fumbled around for a safety, cocked it, and sprayed the roof of the *hacienda,* driving the men back inside. A shot from the *hacienda* shattered the windshield of the truck. The general had entered the fight.

Arina ducked behind the cab and dropped the flashlight as a bullet ripped through the hood. She climbed into the back of the truck and saw a man running toward them. She called, but Jacob could not hear her above the noise of the helicopter that was almost on them. She tried to reach Jacob but found the axe handle instead. When the man rose above the side of the truck she looked at him in surprise, then swung the handle.

When the helicopter came over the house, the men inside fired through the windows. Jacob aimed at the gun flashes and fired. Then fired again. "Arina," he yelled even though he knew she could not hear him above the roar and wash of the helicopter. "Arina."

The hook was over him. He fired at the windows again, grabbed the hook, and attached it to the sling, but he had no way to signal that the hook was attached. He looked up, his eyes blinking in the mini-tornado the helicopter blades stirred up, but he could see nothing through the blur of the canopy.

"Arina," he yelled and saw her looking over the side of the truck. The crate lurched and banged into the sideboard of the truck. It lurched again, this time hitting the opposite wall before careening toward them. "Get on," he yelled. "Get on the cage." He wrapped his gun arm around the cable and grabbed Arina with his other hand as she tried to climb onto the cage without being crushed against the sides of the truck.

Jacob emptied the gun at the houses and dropped it in order to grab the cable with both hands. The cage came free of the truck, swung, hit the ground almost dislodging both of them, and bounced into the air again.

Barry knew he was in trouble when he tried to lift off with

the cage. He pulled collective and advanced the throttle to pick up the drop in RPM. The load did not clear the sideboards of the truck, and the cage caught and pulled. When he tried to slide it off the back of the truck he discovered it was heavier than Jacob told him. Even in ground effect he was not going to be able to lift it above the trees. He reached for the manual release then jerked his hand away. *Not yet. Give it one one more shot.* He over-torqued the maximum power limitations and dragged the cage along the ground toward the edge of the hill.

Barry knew that once he was off the hill he was going to lose ground effect and maybe the load and helicopter as well. It was lucky that he had not made it on the first run and had burned off fuel coming back for a second try. Any more fuel aboard and he wouldn't have made it at all.

Suddenly the cage dropped off the hill and the helicopter sank and Barry's stomach with it, but he gained airspeed. The increased airspeed put him through translation lift, and he was flying. The helicopter staggered into the night.

Shots still came from the ground, and he saw headlights. They were trying to cut him off from the river. With the weight he was carrying and maneuvering around tall trees, they could beat him there. But he remembered something they hadn't counted on; he had seen an arroyo on his way to the ranch. He could drop into the arroyo and follow it to the river using the trees for a screen. They wouldn't know where the helicopter was. Barry watched the lights as the car bounced across the ground trying to head him off.

Jacob wrapped his arm around one of the nylon straps attached to the cage and held Arina's arm with the other as tree limbs whipped his face and tore at his clothes. A branch caught Arina's hair, jerking her head back, and for a moment he thought he was going to lose her. He pulled her higher on the cage. Beneath him he could feel the tiger moving, clawing at the thin metal beneath the wooden shell.

Barry watched the headlights of the car closing on him. He lost precious time skirting trees that loomed suddenly through the smeared canopy. He dared not make sudden moves that would cause the crate to swing more than it was already. A sudden shift of weight would send the helicopter out of control.

From the corner of his eye, Barry saw gun flashes as the car turned sideways to afford the gunmen a better target. They were too close. *Where was the damn arroyo?* Then he saw the dark outline of trees along its edge and looked for an opening. He could not get the cage over or through the trees. He almost wished the general's men were shooting tracers. At least he would know how accurate they were. One bullet in the engine and it was goodnight.

Then Barry got his wish. Tracers flashed in front and below the helicopter, and he was struck with the irony that if he survived he might get back to the ranch to discover the tiger had been killed. He didn't think about it long. The automatic weapon was in the car, and they were getting the range. He reached for the emergency release to drop the load. It was his only chance to escape with his life. As his fingers closed over the release, he saw the car lights drop, lift, then drop again. The car had fallen into a small creek that ran into the arroyo, the shots had gone wild, and there were answering shots from across the river. *What the hell?* The creek was below him, giving him a small opening through the trees. Barry took a deep breath. *Down the creek, right into the arroyo, and head for the river.* He was going to make it.

The wind whipped tears from Arina's eyes, but even through the tears she saw the tracers. It looked as if Barry were flying into them, but she had no time to think of that. Jacob was pulling her arm from the socket. Her shirt caught the wind, choking her so that she could hardly breathe. Suddenly the helicopter turned, swinging the cage. The cage hit the top of a tree, bounced and spun, slinging her loose, breaking her grip, and she slid down the cage. She screamed but could not hear her own screams. Jacob pulled and she could feel her muscles tear, but she did not care. He was pulling her back on the cage. Then something struck the cage. The wood splintered before her eyes, boards ripped away. In one corner the sheet metal liner had been rolled back by the force of the blow, and she could feel the hot breath of the tiger in her face.

The general stood on the veranda of the *hacienda* in his underpants, the monogrammed pistol in his hand. "Damn," he said, turning away in disgust. He went upstairs and picked up the telephone. "The tiger has been taken by helicopter," he said when the proper party was awakened. "Probably by the American cowboy. There was much shooting, but the helicopter has escaped. With so much shooting, the tiger may be dead."

"We will pay dead or alive if the body is delivered to us."

The general went back outside. He stood on the porch watching the night. Every car on the ranch carried armed men. A car drove to the veranda, and the driver reported. They had found a truck and had disabled the engine. Whoever had entered the ranch was now on foot.

"*Bueno,*" the general said. "I want everyone looking for the *gringos* who did this. Set up a patrol along the river. Then drive to El Cruce and awaken every man. I want them on horseback at first light. No one makes a fool of Barboza. Someone will pay if I have to cross the river myself."

. . .

The arroyo was not as deep as Barry had thought, nor as wide. Gnarled mesquites and hackberries grew along its sides. In places, branches from either side almost met in the center. Barry tried to steer a middle course down the arroyo, guiding the cage through the branches. He wondered what Jacob would say if the cage came apart, but he knew he had the tiger, dead or alive, because of the weight, and he had burned off a lot of fuel. The weight was more manageable now and ahead of him he could see the gleam of the river.

Arina screamed as claws appeared in front of her eyes. She knew the metal liner prevented them from reaching her face, but how long before that too was ripped away? Jacob's arm seemed to be tiring, his grip weakening. She kicked her feet trying to work her way back atop the cage, but she could not. Below her she saw water.

Bump had his men digging in when he heard gunshots across the river. Automatic fire. Then he heard the helicopter returning. The helicopter seemed to fly an evasive pattern. He could see gun flashes and flashes of light from a moving vehicle. A bullet hit nearby, and his men opened fire before he could give the order. Above the noise he heard the helicopter and fired a long burst.

Rand Morgan stood in the Jeep on the barren hilltop east of the lodge listening to what sounded like war between smugglers and drug agents when he heard the approaching helicopter. He turned on the lights of the Jeep, then turned on the lights of the Blazer. He had placed them some fifty yards apart to mark what he thought was the best spot to land. He had driven a pole into the ground in front of the lights and tied a shirt to it to indicate the direction of the wind.

Rand took the two flashlights he had found in the house and waved them in the air. He was so intent on watching the helicopter that he was almost struck by the cage. He dropped the lights to unhook the cage and was startled to see Jacob and Arina clinging to it. Neither made a move as Rand reached up and pulled the release. Jacob and Arina slid to the ground.

Rand picked up the lights and waved them in crossing patterns to indicate to Barry that the cage had been released. Still the helicopter did not move. Rand ran a few yards to one side and waved again, indicating a safe place to land. He held his fingers in his ears until Barry cut the switches and the rotors stopped.

Barry climbed out of the helicopter. "Is the tiger all right?" he asked. "I have to go back and look for Jacob." He started to the cage and saw Jacob and Arina slumped beside it. "What the—When—?" He sat heavily on the ground. "Jesus," he said. "I was going to drop the cage. You dumb son of a bitch, I was going to drop the cage."

Jacob's arms were so tired he could not lift them, and they stung as the blood returned. His legs burned from the scrapes and scratches. He slumped against the cage, too weary to sit erect. He looked at Arina. Tears dripped from her cheek. Blood ran from her scalp and down her forehead. "You okay?" he asked. Softly she retched.

Rand went to the lodge and returned with water and brandy. He washed the blood off their faces, gave them a sip of brandy, and inspected their wounds. "No deep puncture wounds," he said. "Any broken bones?"

"I can't open my hand," Jacob said. "I think it's muscle cramp."

"Here, have another shot of brandy," Rand said. "It'll relax you. You feeling better, Arina?" Arina nodded, too tired to open her eyes. "Rest a minute. A bath and brandy and you'll be as good as new. We're going to have to burn those clothes though. Then I want to hear what happened."

"Barry came in under fire and lifted us out," Jacob said. "And the tiger. They shot at us all the way to the river."

"They shot at us from both sides of the river," Barry said.

"Are you sure?" Jacob asked.

"I can't hear gunfire, but I can see it."

"The tiger," Arina said. "Is the tiger okay?"

"A little excited," Rand said. "You may have to give it some more tranquilizer." He looked at the tiger and then at Barry who was still sitting on the ground. "I'm sorry, Barry, how about some brandy."

"No thanks," Barry said, getting to his feet. "I'm going to rip the tape off my numbers and get back to Eagle Pass, maybe Corpus. In case somebody files a complaint."

"I need you to give the tiger one more lift, and I'll need a few minutes to get ready," Jacob said.

"I'm ready to celebrate," Rand said. "I want to call Stuart and Evelyn and give them the news. Those are two calls I'm going to enjoy."

"Fine," Jacob said. "But the tiger is going to need water and food, and we don't have much time, maybe twenty-four hours, before we have to take her to the zoo in San Antonio. Before we take her I want to collect urine."

"I'd like to celebrate with you guys, but I think I'd better make it some other time," Barry said. "Where do you want the tiger?"

"In that trailer made of the back of a pickup," Jacob said. "I've got to spread some plastic in the bed. Rand, there's a roll in the garage. Bring some boards too. I want to put them on top of the plastic to cushion the cage. I need something to block up the front of the trailer. And look for something to catch urine in."

"And rags to wash the canopy with," Barry said.

"Barry, set the cage in the trailer so we don't tear the plastic."

"You guys want to hang on for the ride? I don't know if I can fly this thing under gross without somebody shooting at me."

"Do the best you can. We have to get some urine and fast. Barboza probably is so mad by now that he will go after the male himself."

"Are you going back over there?" Barry asked.

"I have to lure the male back to this side."

"If they catch you—Well, if they catch you listen for the sounds of a helicopter. I guess I can fly in and bust you out of jail."

"I hope that won't be necessary, Barry. But if the general offers you a job rounding up cattle, I think I'd decline."

"That's affirm," Barry said.

Rand brought back a roll of plastic, boards, bricks, and buckets and prepared the trailer under Jacob's direction. Jacob could hardly move his arms. Rand parked the Blazer and the Jeep on either side of the trailer and turned on the headlights to illuminate the target for Barry. Barry wound up the helicopter, picked up the crate, and, with Rand guiding, set it in the trailer. Rand turned off the car lights to signal to Barry that he could release the cable.

Barry lifted off, circled once with his lights on, then headed for Eagle Pass. Rand hitched the trailer to the Jeep, backed it into the garage, and blocked up the tongue. Jacob arranged the plastic to channel urine into a bucket he set under the tailgate. Arina checked the tiger as best she could by shining a flashlight through the air holes in the crate, and Rand hammered the metal liner back in place.

The tiger, still affected by the tranquilizer used to capture it, clawed at the inside of the cage. "I will have to anesthetize her again before I can make a thorough examination," Arina said, "but as far as I can tell, she is in better condition than either of us."

"I can't do anything about the flight," Jacob said, putting his arm around her, "but I'll buy you a drink. Rand, too, for bringing our bags from Laredo."

"How can we guard the tiger?" Arina asked. "The general—"

"He doesn't know exactly where it is, and it's dangerous for him to look for it."

"But we crossed the river."

"That's different."

"You can go there, but they can't come here?"

"It's more complicated than that, but yes. Relax and have a drink." Jacob was less confident than he pretended. *If Barry was right about gunshots from this side of the river, who shot at them? No one could have known the helicopter carried a tiger.*

"First, a bath," Arina said, "proper clothes. I am almost indecent."

"You look great," Jacob said. "Doesn't she look great, Rand?"

"Both of you could use a bath," Rand said. "I'll mix the drinks while you shower. Then I'll call Stuart and Evelyn, and then I'll see if I can find something to eat. I'll bet you're hungry."

"I could eat a tiger," Jacob said. "But first, let's drink to madam tiger and hope she empties her bladder tonight."

The tigress did. While Arina, Rand, and Jacob slept, the tigress backed to the end of the cage, lifted her tail and sprayed. The hot urine ran down the side of the crate, dripped onto the plastic and streamed to the back of the trailer, cascading over the edge into the plastic bucket.

. . .

Bump and his men watched the river all night, expecting to be attacked. By dawn they were exhausted. Nevertheless, Jimmy Guy was expansive. "We had our baptism of fire," he said and caught himself. "I mean, as a group. And nobody ran."

"Do you think we killed anybody?" Kid asked.

"All the shooting we did," Jimmy Guy said, "we're bound to have hit something."

"We didn't hit the helicopter," Bump said.

"I heard them damn things taking off and landing all night," Jimmy Guy said.

"There's a UN base real close," Bump said. Although he had said so for years, the confirmation came as a shock.

"Are we going to attack it?" Kid asked.

"How are we going to attack a military base?" Roy Pat said. "We scout it out, find its exact location, what they got—"

"I give the orders here," Bump said. "Everybody shut up until I figure this out." He wished he could call their mysterious sponsor, but he couldn't go back to the motel and wait to hear without losing control. He wished he knew what the hell was going on, but that meant reconnoitering the UN camp. He could send some of the men back to the motel to wait, but he'd have to send a leader with them. If he ran into trouble on the patrol, he wanted Roy Pat with him, but couldn't send Jimmy Guy back to the motel for fear he'd get drunk and screw up everything.

"Here's the plan," he said. "Roy Pat is going to take the vehicles, half the troops, and a radio back to the motel. Three rooms same as before. Two men in each room, one on watch at all times. The rest of us are going to fade into the brush and rest until dark. Then we'll see what we can find out. Roy Pat, at midnight, I want a man in a vehicle on the radio. That should give us time to locate the camp. We'll send back information as long as we can. We'll hole up after daylight but keep somebody on the radio in case they discover us or we need a pickup. Tomorrow night we'll switch places if we can. This is what we trained for. This is what we came for. Let's do it right."

Bump took Roy Pat aside. "You may get a phone call. Be sure it's not somebody leading us into a trap. If you're sure it's the sponsor tell him right now the UN base is our objective."

Evelyn's return to Laredo had not been a happy one. She had called her son and told him she wanted to see him, but he insisted that she not come. They knew what she did and made fun of him. When he caught a grass snake they said his mother would make him wear a dress and sit in a corner if he hurt it. He had popped its head off to show them, and he had strangled a visitor's dog with his bare hands and put it under a tormentor's bed.

Evelyn refused to believe he did such things, but she was horrified that he invented such stories to hurt her. She had lost her son. He had become as cruel as the other boys, as cruel as his father. She thought of calling Stuart again and asking to return to Washington. He would view it as weakness, as failure, and not recommend her as his replacement, but she couldn't endure any more cruelty.

When at last she fell into a troubled sleep she was awakened by the telephone. Rand called to boast about the capture of the tiger. She called Stuart although she knew Rand had reported the capture. Stuart told her the Russians wanted the two remaining tigers returned to them. When they learned Trace had recklessly endangered another tiger to gain headlines and vindicate himself, there would be a storm of protest not only from Russia but from both sides of the Mexican border.

"Evelyn, Rand has lost control of the situation. I want you

to restrain Trace until I can find a replacement. I'll facilitate the return of the tigers to the Russians."

Stuart virtually promised that she would be the next head of NAZA if she brought order to the chaos Rand had permitted Jacob to create. As head of NAZA, school authorities would listen to her complaints about cruelty at her son's school. Still, Evelyn regretted that Jacob had captured the female and was using it to lure the male. When the tigers crossed the river she had hoped they could evade capture in the mountains and brush of Mexico and live their lives in peace. The thought that both tigers would be returned to cages in Russia made her melancholy.

It was still before dawn, but Evelyn had packed to rejoin Rand and the others when the telephone rang. A foreign but cultured voice explained that a wealthy Mexican landowner wanted to talk to her about the welfare of the tigers. She agreed to meet him for brunch at a restaurant in Piedras Negras.

In Piedras Negras she was surprised at the shabby appearance of the restaurant. She had expected something grand from a wealthy Mexican landowner. However, the restaurant belied its appearance. The tables and linen were immaculate, the waiters wore white jackets and dark trousers, and the Mexican awaited her with flowers.

"Call me Beto," he said, bowing and kissing her hand. "I took the liberty of ordering for us a Tequila Sunrise."

Humberto was stately despite his short stature, a safe man, grandfatherly, almost like Stuart Johnson. When she looked into his eyes she felt something she hadn't felt in a long time—the attraction of a powerful man. She prepared her guard against his authority, his assumption, but he spoke so simply, so emotionally, she listened.

Dishes appeared almost without her being aware of it.

Juices, fruits, delicious concoctions. None of the dishes contained meat. "What is this, Beto?" she asked.

"Do you like it?" When she stated her pleasure, he called for the chef. "From this day, this will be called 'Evelyn's Delight,'" he said.

"*Sí, señor,*" the chef said, bowing. "You have been greatly honored," he told Evelyn.

Despite the excellence of the restaurant, no one was seated in their alcove. As she sampled pleasure after pleasure, Humberto explained he had learned of her feelings for animals through the media stories. He too hated the confinement of animals. He owned a huge ranch, more than 250,000 hectares, in the mountains of southern Coahuila. There were valleys, springs, a river. On his ranch he had released animals from around the world, animals that were doomed to extinction in their native lands.

There were, he confessed, men in the United States who did the same. Evelyn nodded. She knew of these men, but the intentions of many were not honorable. They released the animals to be hunted for money.

Yes, he said, it was very sad. He refused to sell animals to zoos, to hunters. He did not sell to anyone. He set the animals free. Free to live as their creator had intended. His ranch was so vast few animals found reason to wander onto the lands of others. He would like to set the tiger free; it had suffered so at the hands of those who wanted to cage it.

"I wish there was a way," Evelyn said.

"I am a very rich man," Humberto said, looking directly at her. He held up a hand to stop her protest. "I do not wish to insult you by offering money to you. I have for a long time wished to establish an international foundation for the liberation of animals. I have waited because such a foundation must have as its director a person who not only loves animals but has the courage to act for their benefit. A person who would—out of love—buy animals and discover the best place to set them free wherever that might be in the world. I think I have found that person."

Evelyn's pleasure was greater than her surprise. She would have a position equal to, perhaps greater than that of Stuart. But she would not be caging endangered animals but setting them free. She had not dreamed such a possibility. Despite the exquisite food, she could not eat. "If we could also capture the male tiger, we could begin species propagation."

"That is my dream," Humberto said. "And my plan."

"Please, tell me how, Beto," she said.

As tired as he was and despite the celebration, Jacob was unable to sleep well because he was stiff and cramped. Nevertheless, he stayed in bed until Rand tempted him up with coffee, bacon, and eggs. He took another shower, hot as he could stand it, and stretched his sore muscles. Before accepting breakfast or coffee he checked the tiger. He found Arina in the shed. "The tiger is fine," she said.

"How are you?" he asked.

"I can hardly move my arms."

"Rand had muscle relaxant. I should have given you this last night," he apologized. "I think I had all the muscle relaxant I could handle last night. Today I'll stick with aspirin. I need a clear head."

After breakfast he stretched some more. "I'm glad I don't have to do any close work with these hands," he said. "We don't have nets or traps and not enough time to dig a pit that would hold a tiger. I'll have to find a stand and dart it." He left to search the garage for useful items.

Jacob removed the straps from the crate and added an axe, pruning saw, and bottle of skunk scent left by a hunter, probably a bow hunter, who had used it to mask his own scent. He returned to the house, got coffee, and sat on the veranda to plan. Before he finished the coffee he heard the crunch of tires on gravel at the back of the lodge. Fearing it was Hailee and her camera, he tried to think how to hide the tiger.

He heard Evelyn's call with relief. "Jacob?"

"Out here."

Evelyn burst through the door, hurried to Jacob, who slowly stood and stretched. She kissed him on the cheek. "Congratulations," she said. He had never seen her so animated. "It's wonderful. We are going to save—we have saved one of the most magnificent animals on earth. Now, we must save the male. We must collect urine to lure it to a trap. When—"

"Whoa," Jacob said. "We're already collecting it."

The telephone rang, and Jacob walked inside to answer it. Evelyn followed and poured herself coffee.

"Santana," Jacob said. "You okay? Good. I'll tell you the next time I see you . . . on this side of the river. Yeah, well, uncles come in handy, but I hope you don't have to use him." Jacob relaxed; Santana was safe. "Are you sure? Jorge is certain? Not old tracks of the female? Sure I'll meet him. Where? Okay, the cantina. Not the cantina? You're joking. Okay. Tell Jorge I'll be there tonight. Two knocks. Tell—"

"No," Arina said.

Jacob hadn't seen her enter the room. He ignored her. "If there's some way to get that truck back—if not, it's a rental. Okay. *Adios.*"

"You cannot go back," Arina said.

"After last night they're probably out of bullets. That was Santana. He's okay. He has money, and his uncle has a straight line to the president. Barboza won't push him too hard. Jorge tracked the male tiger and got close enough to see it. I'm going to meet Jorge at El Cruce, not more than three miles from here. Jorge will take me to the tiger, and I'll lure him across the river."

Jacob poured himself another cup of coffee. "Jorge thinks we can dart it from the truck, but I don't want to be over there in the daytime, it's too hard to dart it at night, and we don't have any way of getting the tiger across the border; Barboza will see to that. So I'll have to lure it."

"We could have both tigers by morning," Evelyn said.

"Santana said there's an old ford near El Cruce. I'll mark a trail with scent from where Jorge found the tracks to the crossing and hope the tiger will get the message. I need to lure it far enough on this side that it can't cross back after I dart it."

"The general and his men will be looking for you," Arina argued.

"I'm not going far, and I'm not going to be over there long."

The phone rang again, and Jacob answered it. "Hello. Hello, Hailee," he said for the benefit of the others. "Nothing yet. Windom? I don't know where he is. Maybe he had a charter." He turned to Arina and showed her his crossed fingers. Evelyn smiled and explained to her.

"Not today. I know I promised, but I can't give you an interview today. No, don't come here. Wait, Hailee. Tell you what I'll do. Give us your telephone number, and we'll call in the morning and tell you where to meet us. We'll have an exclusive. Bring Tony, we'll have some shots for you. We'll have a blockbuster tomorrow. Guaranteed."

Arina looked at him so strangely that Jacob tried to explain. "She was going to come here, but we can't let her know we have the tigress. Tomorrow one of you has to take it to Houston. I'd like to take it now, but I want more urine. Meet Hailee, show her the tiger, but don't tell her how we caught it or that we did it in Mexico. And don't tell her that you're bringing back the cage for the second one. By the time she reports it, the female will be in the zoo, and we'll have the male. Arina, how long can I keep the tiger sedated if I get it tonight? I won't have a cage."

"Jacob, it's too dangerous," Arina said.

"It's the only way," he said. "Once the cage is back we can get help to load it. I need you to bottle the urine for me while I look for a place for a stand. Evelyn, how about rousting Rand out of his nap? Be gentle with him. He dipped his nose in the jug last night."

"I know," Evelyn said. "He was giggling when he called me. I hope he was giggling when he called Stuart."

Jacob studied Evelyn. She was different, but he had no time to think of that now.

Arina found two mayonnaise jars under the kitchen sink. She washed them, took them to the garage, and poured the urine into the bottles. She stuck the end of a garden hose through one of the air holes in the crate to provide water for the tiger. The tiger jerked it and bit it in two. Arina turned the water on, waited until it spurted through the hose, and stuck it back in the air hole. The tiger snarled and backed away. Arina left the hose dripping water in the crate and rearranged the plastic under the crate to funnel most of the water away from the urine.

Jacob led Evelyn and Rand along the bluff above the river looking for a tree he could use as a stand. Within an hour he found an ancient oak that had lost its lower branches to fire or flood standing alone with nothing but small brush around it. It was not as tall as he wanted, but it would have to do.

He climbed into the tree, selected a spot twenty feet from the ground where two branches forked from the trunk and gave him a good view in every direction except directly behind him. He pointed out brush and limbs that he wanted Rand and Evelyn to cut, and while they did so he wound the strap around and between the forked branches to form a web that he could sit on with his back against the trunk. He tested his position, turning from side to side, imagining the shots he might have. He hoped that if the tiger came at night he would have enough light to shoot it. He pointed out more brush and limbs for them to clear, and when he was satisfied, he tied knots at intervals in the strap and dropped it to the ground. He would need it to climb in the darkness.

Jacob led them back to the lodge, making certain that Rand could find his way back to the tree. He went to the garage, put the skunk scent in the bag with the darts, and got two gallon plastic jugs, one for drinking water, one for urination. He added the Cap-Chur gun to the pile and paused to puzzle over the Ruger.

When Jorge led him to the tiger's lair and he began leaving tiger scent, he would be the object of the tiger's desire until he had encircled the tree with the scent and safely climbed to his haven. If he bumped into Barboza's men, he would like to keep them at bay. On the other hand, the Ruger would be heavy to carry and awkward to climb with.

Taking the Ruger, he returned to the tree and secured the bag, Cap-Chur gun, Ruger, and bottles to the tree. He uncapped the essence of skunk, left it upwind to cover his scent, and walked to the river. He wanted to be certain he could find both the ford and the tree in the dark. And maybe in a hurry. He stood under a tree at the top of a bluff observing El Cruce.

Jacob could see where the town got its name. A rutted track ran from the river and up the cut bank to become the main street of town, bordering the plaza with its shade trees, benches, and inevitable statue, and faded into the asphalt ribbon of Highway 2. Over the centuries so many wagons had crossed the river that the wheels had cut six-inch-deep ruts in the exposed sandstone at the edge of the river. The crossing was on a gradual curve in the channel, and floods had deposited tons of silt to obliterate all traces of the wagon ruts on the Texas side.

The village of perhaps three hundred residents had three streets running east and west and at least three, possibly four, running north and south. None was paved. A couple of hundred yards beyond the village on the west side was a large white barn, set back from the road and, except for the church, the most impressive building in town. Social center, Jacob decided, along with the church and the cantina.

He studied the town until he was certain he could find his way in the dark, returned to the lodge and announced he was going to rest. He wanted to eat about an hour before dusk. He stretched again, hoping his energy level would build before he crossed the river. When he closed his eyes, he remembered Barry saying they had been shot at from this side of the river. The thought agitated him so he couldn't sleep. *Who had shot at them from Texas soil? Smugglers thinking they were narcotics agents? Narcotic agents thinking they were smugglers?*

Bump had led his men into deep cover, formed a close circle, and ordered them to rest, partly because they had been up all night but mainly to keep them quiet. He dozed some, but mostly he thought about the task ahead. *How cleverly was the base concealed and how heavily was it guarded?* Despite all the stories, he would be the first to discover a UN base on US soil. If he could collect evidence—and get back alive—he could alert the world on national television.

At dusk he ordered Mike Bentch to make radio contact with Roy Pat's team. Roy Pat was waiting. "Got a call," Roy Pat said. "The tiger is your first priority. It's at the camp. Proceed with caution, avoid detection, and kill the tiger. If the tiger is dead, destroy its body."

"We'll kill the tiger after we find the UN base," said Bump, who grabbed the radio when Roy Pat responded. "We'll turn the tiger's ashes over when we're paid in full. Did you tell the sponsor we took fire from Mexico?"

"Hung up before I could."

Bump didn't like puzzles. There had been shooting on the other side of the river and a shot landed near him. *Was it a stray round fired by compadres shooting at the UN helicopter or was there a Mexican flank of the UN base?* Bump almost asked what Roy Pat thought, then caught himself. "We'll report every hour. If we don't report, lay chilly tomorrow and look for us tomorrow night. Out."

If they didn't report, they would be dead or captured. If the latter, UN forces would have all day to interrogate and maybe torture them, but Roy Pat's team had no chance in daylight. He gathered his team around him and assigned two-man teams. "Put on fresh paint," he told them and applied cammo paint to his face. "We know the helicopter pad is north of us. We'll move inland, and I'll drop off teams as we go. Head northwest until you run into opposition or discover the base. Scout it as best you can. Hole up near the river before dawn, and we'll link up there. Don't be seen. If you're seen, don't be captured. If you're captured, don't talk. Don't mention Roy Pat's team. They're our hope for rescue."

"If we're seen, do we run or fight?" Jimmy Guy asked.

Bump looked at each of them to demonstrate determination. "Evade if you can. Fight if you have to."

He wished he felt as confident as he sounded. The next time they reported he would tell Roy Pat to alert other militia units if they failed to respond. He and his team might not be rescued, but enough people would know about the base that someone would discover it. And warn Roy Pat that the United Nations might have a base on the other side of the river.

He paused to decide the makeup of the teams. He should

take Jimmy Guy to keep him from doping off, but Jimmy Guy was supposed to be a leader, and Jimmy Guy would want to hold his hand the whole time. He'd take Mike. Mike wasn't afraid to be alone. Jimmy Guy and Old Man. Both goof-offs, so he'd keep them closest to the river where they were least likely to run into anything. That left Kid and Leonard Jukam. Kid was a follower; Leonard was an ox, physically and mentally. But they were shooters. With Roy Pat leading them they'd attack Quantico, but alone they weren't likely to discover anything unless they blundered into it. He put them between him and Jimmy Guy. If they stumbled into something, maybe Jimmy Guy and Old Man would come to their rescue and he and Mike could report whatever they discovered. He dropped the teams a mile apart with orders to work northwest. He and Mike walked the last mile.

At dusk, Jacob got up, stretched, had a sandwich, glass of milk, and more aspirin. The others joined him. "I brought some news," Evelyn said. "Ramiro Perez died in San Antonio. Complications."

"What kind of complications?" Arina demanded.

"I don't know. Complications. What difference—"

"Excuse me, ladies, but I don't have much time, and we need to work out signals. If I dart the tiger tonight, I'll fire three shots in rapid succession. Rand, you bring wire. I hate to use it but we have to keep the cat immobile until Evelyn delivers the tigress and gets back with the cage, and it can bite through the strap. I'll keep it sedated until we have the cage and some help to load it. Arina, I'd like you here to keep an eye on the tigress to be sure it doesn't injure itself."

"Do not risk being bitten by the tiger," Arina said. "It is better to kill it than to be bitten."

"No," Evelyn said. "Our job is to save the tiger."

"I'm not going to take any chances," Jacob said. "If I can

dart it, we can get it to the zoo. I need something to wrap around the bottles of urine so they don't break. Can you give me a hand, Arina?"

Arina nodded and followed him into the kitchen, away from the others. "Jacob, the scent will lead the tiger to you."

"If I see the tiger, I'll drop the bottles and run like hell."

"You must be careful not to get the urine on your clothing."

"I promise," Jacob said, kissing her. "I have a lot to say to you when this is over, and with luck it could be over tonight. Until then, don't make any plans without talking to me. Think about becoming American."

"I will think about you," she said. "Jacob, you must come back."

"This is not a war," he said, trying to lighten the mood.

"Here," she said, tying a cobbler's apron around his waist. The apron had smoke and barbecue stains. "Like for pistols." She pushed the bottles into the side pockets.

"I'll need a couple of hand towels, too," he said, wrapping them around the bottles for a closer fit.

"Jacob, there was a Russian hunter at the general's house."

"They couldn't get a Russian hunter there that fast, even if he didn't have to go through immigration."

"I saw him. I hit him with the axe handle."

"If there was a Russian, he was from the embassy."

"Andrei told me of experiments in biological warfare under the old regime."

"You told me that."

"When the Soviet Union collapsed, the biological warfare labs were closed, the records were destroyed, the experiments outlawed, and the scientists removed. Most labs at the zoo were closed and the scientists removed. Andrei stayed because he was not involved in such experiments."

"What's the point?" Jacob asked impatiently.

"Perhaps he was involved in the experiments. Perhaps they think I collaborated with him."

"It's okay, Arina. I don't think that."

"My passport has been canceled. I have been ordered home."

"I don't have time for this now. We'll talk about it when I get back. Don't go anywhere without talking to me."

"I will be here," Arina said. "I have no place to go."

11

The moon was well above the horizon when Jacob unwrapped a jar of urine, poured urine on the towel, and dragged it down the bluff and through the dense stand of cane on the Texas side of the river. The moon had risen round and full before sundown, and there was not a cloud in the sky. The night would be bright.

Jacob squatted behind a screen of cane at the water's edge and waited until there was no sign of life along the Mexican shore, hung the towel in the cane, then removed his boots and socks. He pulled a bandana out of his pocket, dropped it on the bank at the edge of the water, poured urine on it, replaced the jar lid, and waded into the river.

The bed of the river was wide at the crossing, the water was low, confined to a shallow channel near the Texas side. When the water reached his waist, he placed the bottles of urine in his boots and held them over his head as he stepped gingerly along the bottom. The current was strong, and Jacob leaned into it to maintain his balance. A line of boulders stretched from the sandstone flat on the Mexican side three-quarters of the way across the river. The water became shallower as he neared them, and when he reached the water-worn rocks, he tucked his boots under one arm and dribbled urine on the larger stones. In Mexico, he slipped into his boots and twice marked the trail between the river and the line of brush below the village, then melted into the thickets.

Kid moved slowly through the brush, coming upon a wide trail, almost a road. He and Leonard looked carefully in both directions but could see little as it wound through the brush. They knelt to look for truck or tank tracks but found nothing. Nevertheless, they followed it as best they could, losing it several times before finding it again.

They stopped, seeing moonlight reflected from a weathered metal roof. Signaling to each other, they agreed to circle it. Kid saw a structure he believed was a bunker, but closer inspection showed it to be a corral made by driving two rows of mesquite posts into the ground and filling the space between with smaller posts. What he thought was a radar disk turned out to be a basketball goal with a basket made of a trailer tire rim. He made his way around a picnic table, oil drums, and a barbecue pit and was startled by something jumping from under the brush. A bell tinkled, and he waited for his heart and the goats to settle down.

He saw movement he thought was Leonard but waited until he was certain. *Damn, someone in camouflage could walk up and cut his throat.* The thought so unnerved him that he waited until Leonard was almost on top of him before revealing himself. Leonard jumped. They lay down under cover and conferred in whispers. A ranch house. They had read stories of bamboo huts concealing entrances to tunnels and bunkers.

Leonard entered first, Kid behind him. They moved carefully but tried to get close enough to objects to identify them in the dark. They were in a large family room that was kitchen, dining room, living room, and den. They moved down the hall and stepped into another room. There was a single window, and the moonlight streamed on a bed. There was someone in the bed. Leonard moved slowly to minimize the creaking of the floorboards, placed the muzzle of his rifle to the sleeper's head, and whispered, "Don't move or make a sound."

"Aiee!" Rafaela screamed. "Jesus, Mary, and Joseph. *Sabadao me, Dios.*"

"Shut up or I'll shoot," Leonard said, causing her to scream louder. He put his hand over her mouth, but she fought him off and continued screaming. *"Chupacabra, chupacabra."*

He caught her by the throat, silencing her. "We're going. If you make a sound, we'll come back and kill you." When he released her throat, she screamed again. He grabbed her throat, silencing her. "I'm going to have to kill her to shut her up," he said, pulling his knife.

Kid turned and ran. Leonard squeezed her throat again and followed, jumping the fence and tripping over bedsprings leaning against it. He got up, jumped over a woodpile, and ran through the brush a couple of hundred yards before falling to the ground and crawling under cover beside Kid. They could hear the woman screaming but saw no movement and looked at each other, puzzled. They ran until they could no longer hear her prayers.

Jacob stayed in the trees and skirted the northern edge of El Cruce, stopping occasionally to leave scent. If his rendezvous with Jorge Chapa failed, he intended to leave a trail in case the tiger accidentally crossed it. He wanted to have one bottle of urine when Jorge led him to the cat and half of the other to lead the cat from the river to the tree. When he held the jar to the moonlight he saw less than half of it left.

He eased his way through the mesquite toward the village, approached from the north, and slipped between two small houses. A light shown from the windows of one, and Jacob could see a woman moving inside. He approached the north-west corner of the plaza, staying in the shadows of the closed general store.

The plaza was empty, not even a burro or stray dog. He could see a light in a building on the south side across the street from the plaza. A man in uniform walked from the door to the middle of the street, stared up the road toward the highway, then returned to the building. Police station. Jacob flattened himself against a concrete block wall and listened. The sound of music drifted through the night from the west.

Santana said there was only one cantina in town; that had to be where the music came from. He pulled his hat low over his face, stepped into the center of the street, and, hoping the cobbler's apron aided his appearance as a resident, walked casually toward the sound of the music. He turned left at the first corner and saw the cantina a block away, on the east side of the street. Keeping to the opposite side of the street, he strolled by the open door. He did not see Jorge. Perhaps he was late.

The building was rectangular and detached with a short bar near the front. At least four customers, maybe more. He turned the corner and saw another door opening to the main street. He slipped into the dark, narrow opening between the cantina and the adjacent building and saw the wooden out-house where Jorge would meet him.

He crouched in the shadow the lean-to provided and waited, listening to the music from the jukebox. Twice patrons visited the toilet. He was so close he could hear them urinate, but neither knocked. He waited for more than an hour and was considering leaving when he heard boots scraping the wooden floor of the cantina and someone caution, *"Cuidado,* Jorge."

Jacob heard the man walk from the bar into the toilet and waited for Jorge to knock on the wall. He heard a knock. Santana had told him there would be two knocks, and he was to respond with two knocks. Maybe he misunderstood. Jacob knocked twice and was relieved when he heard two knocks in response. "Jorge," he whispered.

"Sí."

Jacob was puzzled. Why didn't Jorge come out and join him? He tried again, a little louder this time. "Jorge?"

"Sí, me llamo Jorge. ¿Como se llama?"

Jorge Mendiola was drunk. He had returned from El Norte with money in his pocket. He had avoided both Border Patrol and coyotes who, for exorbitant fees, provided transportation in the trunks of cars and in hidden compartments in the backs of trucks. He had earned gringo pay and returned without being robbed on either side of the border. He had enough money to take care of his wife and three children for six months, maybe longer, enough money to get drunk and bet on the cockfights.

He had staggered from the bar, half-filled beer bottle in hand, and stumbled into the toilet. He fumbled with his zipper, lost his balance, and reached for the back wall to steady himself. The bottle rattled against the plywood, and when something knocked sharply against the wall in front of him, he stepped back, puzzled. He stopped trying to unzip his fly and knocked on the wall. Answering knocks came immediately. Jorge stared drunkenly at the wall.

"Jorge," the wall said.

"*Sí,*" he answered, looking over his shoulder to see if anyone watched.

"Jorge?" the wall said, louder this time.

"*Sí, me llamo Jorge. ¿Como se llama?*"

Mendiola returned to the cantina and focused his eyes on the bartender's face. "*Wicho,*" he said. "Your toilet spoke to me."

Two men sitting at a small table at the end of the room laughed. "Did it speak to your ass?" one of the men called. Both men laughed.

Mendiola turned slowly so as not to make his head spin. "The wall knocked, and then it spoke my name. 'Jorge,' it said."

The two men looked at each other, jumped to their feet, and pulled handguns from their waistbands. One raced for the toilet, the other out the side street door and around the back of the building.

As soon as Bump was out of sight, Old Man stopped and turned to Jimmy Guy. "You as tired of this crap as I am?" He had been off work for more than a week. His wife was going to be pissed, and this wasn't fun like getting drunk with the boys or running to Mexico for poontang. He was flat-ass tired and achy from sleeping on the ground.

"We're close," Jimmy Guy said. "Real close."

Old Man liked Jimmy Guy—he was always ready for a break, a beer, or a broad—but he didn't respect him. He was a scrounge who never had an honest job for more than a month. Jimmy Guy might be exec, but he didn't give Old Man orders. "We didn't hear a damn thing all day."

"'Cause you was asleep all day. I heard something, maybe thumping."

"You heard thumping. Jesus. We're breaking our asses because you heard thumping."

"We're not going to be relieved until we link up with Bump at the river so we might as well hump it and hope we ain't in Indian country."

Jimmy Guy. Using all that Vietnam lingo. *Hell, that war was over years ago.* He was right about linking up with Bump though. At least he and Jimmy Guy had the shortest distance to walk. He wasn't scouting for no UN base though. First sign of trouble he was headed for Eagle Pass.

He stopped when he saw the caliche road. Good road and there had been traffic on it. Jimmy Guy sidled up and told him to cross to the other side. "Stay in the brush with the road in sight. Let's see where it leads."

If it was a road that led to the camp, it was patrolled. You didn't have to be a veteran to know that. Anyone crossing the road would be outlined against the caliche. "You take the other side," he said.

Jimmy Guy sighed. "Cover me," he said.

Old Man lay down under cover at the edge of the road where he could fire in either direction. One burst, and he was out of there. He saw Jimmy Guy cross and waited until he knew Jimmy Guy was moving again. He intended to be back a little, not the first to blunder into a trap.

He stopped when he saw lights. *Close enough.* He would wait and see what was going on. A good soldier was patient. He saw Jimmy Guy step into a little clearing and wave him forward. *To hell with it.* He was observing. He heard the crunch of boots as Jimmy Guy crossed the road.

"Looks like a house. Let's check it out. I'll go first. You cover me."

"Watch for dogs," Old Man said. *It was stupid to check a house with the lights on. Someone was awake.* He waited until he could no longer see or hear Jimmy Guy, then crept forward. He was in no hurry.

Jacob realized his mistake when the man in the toilet asked his name. He slipped through the narrow passage between the two buildings to the main street and turned toward the plaza, walking as casually as his nerves would allow. There was no reason to panic. The man was drunk; no one would pay attention to him. Jorge Chapa had been delayed or wasn't coming. Jacob was not waiting; he would work his way around the village, use the remainder of the urine, cross the river again, and hope for the best.

A light-colored pickup was parked in front of the police station, and three men walked awkwardly from the truck toward the front door of the building. Two of the men supported between them the third man who resembled Jorge Chapa. Jacob was trying to get a better look when he heard a sharp command behind him.

"Stop."

Jacob glanced over his shoulder at the man running toward him. Moonlight glinted off the pistol in his hand. Even though he had to pass in front of the police station, the shortest route to the river was down the main street. Jacob ran toward the three men to discourage gunfire, ducking around them and behind the pickup at the last moment. The first shot was high. The second was close enough for Jacob to hear the bullet, like cloth being ripped. He ducked and zig-zagged down the street.

"Es el gringo," someone yelled. The pickup door slammed, and the engine started. He had reached the intersection, still more than a block from the cut bank that could protect him, but he couldn't outrun the pickup. He dodged right at the intersection and down an unlighted side street.

The pickup stopped at the intersection. "It's the gringo

tiger hunter. You and you, cut him off at the river," Jacob heard someone shout, then the pickup turned onto his street. He darted between two houses and ran west, away from the river, to confuse pursuers. A cur came from beneath one of the houses, yapping hysterically and snapping at his heels. Jacob whirled and kicked at the dog, raking the side of its head.

The dog yelped and backed away. A light came on in the house. Jacob ran across another street, staying between houses. He heard the dog bark, a solid thump, and the dog yelped in pain. *He can kick straighter than he can shoot,* Jacob thought. He crossed the third and last side street and was in the low scrub brush that bordered the western side of the village.

Ahead of him loomed the large, white barn he had seen from the bluff. He was close enough to make out a sign on the side of the building. *Asociación Ganadera del Cruce.* Cattlemen's Association. He stopped to catch his breath and saw the headlights of the pickup coming slowly along the road. Several men in straw hats approached the barn from the road. Behind him he heard pounding footsteps on loose rocks. The only chance was to disappear in a crowd.

Jacob walked toward the barn and emerged from the brush as the knot of men neared the side door of the barn. He increased his pace to catch up with them at the door, hoping to hide in what was probably the only crowd between Nuevo Laredo and Piedras Negras.

The barn was packed with a hundred men, and all eyes were on the well-lighted fighting pit constructed of used corrugated metal. The sheets were fastened with baling wire to form an irregular enclosure two dozen feet in diameter. In the center, two gamecocks wearing razor-sharp metal spurs slashed at each other. The spectators yelled encouragement as the birds flew into the air, collided briefly as each tried to sink a spur in the heart of the other, then dropped to the dirt floor.

Jimmy Guy studied the situation. *Looked like a hunting lodge but could be a command post.* He circled the house, then eased up to a window. *The animal lover they had seen in the brush.* Someone else was in the room. He ducked below the window and looked from the other corner. *The commie broad. He was in the middle of the enemy camp. Where the hell was Old Man?*

He retreated from the window and waited to catch sight or sound of Old Man. *Nothing.* Old Man would move in, capture them himself, be the hero. Jimmy Guy circled to the front door and tried it. Unlocked. Carefully he pushed the door open with the barrel of his rifle then stepped inside. "Evening, ladies," he said.

Both women jumped and turned to face him. Totally camouflaged with paint on his face, he knew he was a sight to put fear in their hearts. He moved into the room.

"Bump . . . er . . . Mr. Wilkerson, please don't make trouble," the bunny lover said. Her face was ashen. He had an almost irresistible impulse to show her his cock, watch her eyes get big, hear her gasp.

"I ain't Mr. Wilkerson," he said. "You two alone or do you have some comrades hiding under the bed?"

"We're . . . we're alone," the bunny lover said. *The commie was too stunned to say anything, or maybe she didn't understand English.*

"Where's the tiger?" he asked.

"It's gone."

"Where's the tiger hunter?"

"He's gone, too."

"And left you all this booze." Jimmy Guy moved to the

side bar and poured himself a generous slug of bourbon. *Damn, that tasted good.* "Where did he go?"

"Who?" the bunny hugger said, getting her breath back.

"I guess I'll have to wait," Jimmy Guy said, pouring himself another drink and slipping the bottle into the side pocket of his cammies. "While we're waiting, you can entertain me and my friends. We ain't seen naked women for a while. Every time I have to ask you a question, this lady takes something off. Let's see how long it takes us to get to the bare facts."

"I'll tell you," Evelyn said. "Whatever you ask, just don't hurt us."

Jimmy Guy put down his glass. "This goes first," he said, grabbing Arina's blouse and jerking it so that buttons popped off. Her eyes widened, and she paled. "You got a right to be scared of me," he said. "I hate commies. Me and my buddies want to show you what we do to Russkies. Take it off." The Russian opened her mouth but made no sound.

"He went to Mexico," the bunny hugger said in a wavering voice. "A village not far from here. The tiger's there. The Mexicans have it. Jacob and some men who are going to bring it back. A lot of men." The words came in a rush.

The two handlers picked up their roosters. One handler, a well-dressed man in a tan suit, alligator boots, and felt hat with a gamecock plume in the band, cooed to his bird, then took the rooster's beak in his mouth and blew gently into the bird's lungs.

The other handler, dressed in dirty jeans, scuffed working boots, and sweat-stained shirt, nestled his red-and-black bird in his left hand with the legs of the cock held firmly between his fingers and caressed the head, neck, and back of the rooster with his right hand. He was bareheaded and young, and his curly hair fell over his forehead. He and his rooster were favorites with the crowd.

The young handler picked up a bottle of tequila, tipped it to his mouth, raised the tail feathers of his rooster, and spat the tequila on the bird's anus. Jacob stood at the back of the crowd in the shadows and watched the ritualistic restoration of the gamecocks. He didn't know how effective such efforts were, but he had seen them before.

The handlers grasped their gamecocks with their hands over the wings of the birds and thrust the roosters at each other, letting them peck at each other's necks to stir the adrenaline and bloodlust within them, before putting them on the floor of the pit again.

Jacob glanced at the white, slender hands of the well-dressed handler, saw the pressure applied by the man's thumbs, and knew that the rooster would soon be dead. He wasn't certain what effect the pressure on either side of the backbone had, but he suspected ribs were splintered and lungs punctured, the rooster drowning in its own blood. He had seen it done at other fights, and he knew why. Jacob also knew if he were caught cheating, the handler's blood would join that of the gamecock's.

As the handlers let their roosters peck each other, the cries of the crowd grew louder, and only a few spectators standing near the side door turned their heads when the door burst open and three of Barboza's SSA agents stepped inside. All were armed. Two carried revolvers, the third a machine pistol. Jacob, on the far side of the pit opposite the door, saw the commotion as the spectators stepped aside to allow the three men to approach the pit and ducked behind the man in front of him.

The handlers put their roosters on the floor as the spectators yelled for blood. Each rooster sprang into the air, attempting to bury a spur into its opponent's body, but both roosters died in mid-air without touching and fell in separate heaps of feathers. Each handler had bet on the other's bird, and the crowd realized it.

The man in front of Jacob lunged for the pit, leaving Jacob exposed, and the agent with the machine pistol saw him and raised the weapon to fire. A fight, one of many that erupted, broke out between two men standing beside the agent, falling into him as he pulled the trigger. Bullets cut holes in the side of the barn above Jacob's head, climbed the wall, and continued across the corrugated tin roof. Chunks and splinters of wooden rafters rained down.

The well-dressed handler bent over, gasping for breath and clutching his stomach where a knife had entered. Blood dripped between his fingers. The young handler was curled on the floor, blood dribbling from his nose, trying to protect his head from the vicious kicks of two maddened *vaqueros.*

Jacob dropped to the floor and crawled to the sheet metal wall around the pit. Most of the fights had ended by the time the agent had emptied the machine pistol. Some of the spectators rushed for the side door, pushing the two pistol-carrying agents ahead of them. Others struggled to open the sliding front doors of the barn that were secured by a padlock. A rancher jerked a revolver from his pocket, stuck the muzzle against the lock, and blasted it open, releasing a tidal wave of frightened men. Jacob tried to be in the center of the wave.

One of Barboza's men spotted him, and even though the agent was pinned against the wall by spectators trying to get out the side door, he reached over the shoulder of the man in front of him and fired. A farmer beside Jacob fell to the floor with a bullet in his back. Before he could fire again, Jacob was in the open and running. He sprinted to the road, crossed it, and was vaulting over the barbed-wire fence when the pickup slid to a stop near him, spotlighting him with the headlights. Two agents leaped from the back of the truck and ran after him.

Rand was shaving when he heard a male voice. He thought Jacob had returned and almost called out to ask if he had forgotten something when he realized it wasn't Jacob. *Barboza's people,* he thought. *After the tiger.*

He shook so that the razor clattered when he put it down. *A weapon.* He needed a weapon. He slipped down the hall to check the bedrooms. *Arina's blowgun.* He assembled it, put a dart in the mouthpiece, and took another one in his hand. He laid the blowgun on the bed and wiped the palms of his hands on his undershirt, then picked it up again and moved cautiously toward the sounds of the voices. The blood racing through his veins was so loud in his ears he could not tell what was being said.

He peeked around the corner. A camouflaged figure drank bourbon from a glass but held a rifle in his other hand. "Drop the rifle," he croaked, stepping around the corner and placing his mouth to the blowgun.

The man dropped the rifle and slowly turned to face him, seeing the blowgun. "What the hell," he said and reached to pick up the rifle.

"It's loaded with deadly curare," Arina said.

Shaving cream covered Rand's face, and he panted around the mouthpiece, but he spoke again. "Put your hands in the air. I don't want to hurt you."

"You said no one else was here," the man said, accusing Evelyn. He turned back to Rand. "I can't believe you'd kill an American like yourself to help the communists."

"Don't nobody move," said a camouflaged figure from the doorway. He jerked the blowgun from Rand's hands and struck him with the butt of his rifle. Rand fell heavily to the floor, clutching the side of his face.

"Rand," Evelyn screamed. She knelt beside Rand and lifted his head. Blood streamed from his mouth and turned the shaving cream red.

"I said get back," the second figure said, grabbing her by the hair and dragging her to her feet. "What the hell is going on here?"

"A party now," said the first. "With babes and booze." He picked up his glass and reached for his rifle, but Arina beat him to it. "Get out. Both of you," she said.

"Commie bitch knows how to handle guns," said the second man. He had lowered his rifle when he grabbed Evelyn, and he slowly raised it. "Spies gotta know things like that."

The shot was deafening in the room. The bullet cut a small, black hole in the wall behind the second man's head, and sheet rock fell to the floor in the adjacent room. The rifle from the camouflaged hand clattered to the floor.

"Get out," Arina said.

"Okay. We're going." He pushed the first man through the door, then turned back. "Give us our guns back. There's a tiger out there. Besides, those guns are expensive."

Arina fired a shot past his ear. The two men ran down the road. Arina raised the rifle to her shoulder and fired again. They ducked and dodged into the bushes. Rand picked up the second rifle and followed Arina to the door. Evelyn led him to a chair and cleaned the blood from his mouth. His lip was split open and swelling, the flesh covering the cheekbone was already discolored, and the side of his head was swollen.

"We must take Rand to a doctor," Arina said.

Rand shook his head. "No," he said, trying to talk without moving his lips or jaw. "We have to protect the tiger."

"Rand," Evelyn said, putting her hand on his uninjured

cheek, "you were magnificent. Let me get you a drink and an ice pack." When she turned to get a glass she saw that the bourbon was gone.

Jacob ran for the river, no longer trying to outsmart his pursuers. He skirted the northern side of El Cruce and reached the timbered area near the river where he ducked through the trees and stopped to catch his breath and locate his pursuers. He heard gunshots, but they were across the river and too far to concern him. He was so winded that he was bent over, gasping and wheezing, when he heard another sound. It began slowly, increased in intensity, reached a crescendo and held it. *Rattlesnake.*

It was too close for him to move without knowing where the snake was. A coiled rattlesnake could strike half the distance of its length, but he did not know the location of the snake or its length. *Three feet? Four? Six?* There was moonlight enough for Jacob to see dim outlines of dead mesquite limbs on the ground. All were sticks but one. He heard agents moving through the bottom, calling to each other. They probably guessed he was unarmed. He was close to the river, too close to fail now.

The buzzing dropped in intensity, hesitated, then stopped altogether. Jacob felt the hair on the back of his neck stand on end. He didn't know which was harder on his nerves, knowing a rattler was near but still or knowing a rattler was near but moving, slithering silently over the ground, its forked tongue darting in and out, its heat-seeking nostrils locked in on the warmth of his leg.

Bump was tired. Only his patriotism and the need to exhibit leadership had kept him going. Then he had heard a muffled gunshot, like from a bunker. He had stopped to listen and heard two more shots. Not automatic fire but spaced

266

shots. *Two of the team had been caught and executed? Shot at as they evaded?* Bump flicked his rifle off safety and then back on, trying to decide what to do. They had not walked far enough yet, but he decided to pinch toward the river in case he was needed.

He and Mike moved quietly but faster for half an hour until they heard more shooting. They stopped again to listen. The night was quiet, then shooting broke out again, including automatic rifle fire. It sounded far off, probably too far for Kid. Jimmy Guy and Old Man had been shot at from a bunker, evaded a couple of more shots, been discovered again, and returned fire. Bump didn't know how else to interpret what he had heard. Indecision tore at him. But he was no longer tired.

"Tell Roy Pat one team has come under fire. Results unknown. We are going to check it out. Then follow me, but keep your distance. They could be anywhere, and we don't want to both be pinned down."

Jacob considered reaching down and picking up whatever he could find to pitch in front of him to make the snake rattle again, but his hand was unwilling. His feet and legs were partially protected by boots and jeans. If the rattler struck him low, the fangs might not penetrate deeply and less venom would be injected. His arm and hand were unprotected. Movement or the heat of his hand might provoke a strike. He couldn't do it.

He slipped his hand into the pocket of his jeans and found the waterproof case with matches. Cupping his hands, he struck a match. It flared, and he dropped it ahead of him, but the fire went out halfway to the ground. He struck another that flared briefly and went out. He struck another, held it until it was in full flame, and tossed it ahead of him. The match went out when it touched the ground. He struck another, but the match broke in his shaking hands. Then a match stayed lighted on the ground, inches in front of a coiled rattler, a big one, at least five feet in length, as big around as Jacob's forearm, coiled within striking distance.

Jacob swallowed hard and jumped backward, landed awkwardly, and sprawled on his back. Bullets thudded into the mesquite over his head and ripped foliage from limbs. He slithered away as fast as he could, from the snake, from the flaring matches that had given away his position. The agents closed around him.

"We found the enemy camp," Jimmy Guy said. They had run for what seemed miles, heedless of the noise they made, not stopping until they reached the high bank of the river. There they had melted into cover, and Jimmy Guy had produced the bottle. "Could be the headquarters with the rest of it underground. Could be an outpost to stop people from going any farther."

"We're supposed to kill the tiger," Old Man said as Jimmy Guy took another slug of whiskey.

"Did you see a tiger? And we ain't got no weapons," Jimmy Guy said. "We wait till sunup, walk along the river till we find Bump, and tell him we found the headquarters. They took our weapons, but we got away."

"What's he going to think when all he finds is those pussies?"

"He's not going in there before tomorrow night. By then they could have moved out a whole army." He eyed the bottle against the moon, gulped his share, and handed it to Old Man who finished the bottle and threw it at the river. The bottle shattered against rocks. Instantly they heard bodies hitting the ground close by.

"Don't shoot. We're not armed," Jimmy Guy said.

"Jimmy Guy, that you?" a voice whispered. "It's me, Kid. Holy shit, man, we almost shot you. What are you doing here?"

Jimmy Guy and Old Man crawled through the brush to the other team. "We found their headquarters," he said. "They got our weapons, but we got away. What did you see?"

"We're not sure," Kid said. "We been hearing shots from across the river. Like they have their own fight going on."

"We're not supposed to let them cross," Jimmy Guy said, "but we ain't got any weapons."

"Here," Kid said. He handed a .45 to Jimmy Guy who passed it to Old Man. "We need a password."

"Look," Old Man said, pointing at a flare of light across the river. "They're signaling." There was another brief flare.

"Get ready to shoot," Jimmy Guy said, burying his head in the ground.

Bump heard gunshots again as he neared the river. He scrambled into cover and waited, intending to answer the next shot. *Fire and move.* They wouldn't know how many men he had if he fired and rolled. And if they set one foot in the water, they were dead. He saw a flash, a flicker, a flare. *Signals.* They were preparing to cross. Gunshots rang out as they prepped the river for crossing. Bump scooted low and aimed at the gunflashes.

Jacob ran for the river. He was closer than he thought and caught a tree to stop himself from plummeting over the thirty-foot bluff. The bank did not slope gently to the water here as it did below El Cruce. He paused at the edge of the bluff, wondering whether to go up or downstream when he heard a scream, a cry of *"Cascabel"* and gunshots as an agent sprayed the ground around his feet. There were more gunshots, these from across the river, quickly answered. Then screams. *"Ayuda."* "Help me." "I have been bitten." "I have been shot."

Someone was providing covering fire. Rand? Holding the bottles with one hand, he stretched out at the edge of the bluff, dangled his legs over, and wriggled backward until he slid, face down, off the bluff and into the cane. He protected his face with his arms, but the exposed roots of trees and shrubs lacerated his legs and chest. He checked the urine. One jar had shattered. He plunged through the cane and into the river.

Bump ducked as bullets whizzed past. He moved to another position, aware that someone else on his side of the river was shooting. He hoped his men were aware of his position and didn't shoot at him. In moving he almost didn't see something moving in the cane on the other side. *The tiger? Too far to tell. Maybe that was what all the shooting was about. Or they were creating confusion to slip a spy across the river. Maybe a man, maybe a tiger. No matter. Once it was in the water, it was dead.*

Whatever it was scurried across the clearing at the edge of the water and plunged in. He aimed, then raised his head, and removed his finger from the trigger. Let it get halfway across so there was no choice of turning back. He took a breath, released half of it, and focused on what was in the water. The moonlight shimmered pale and white like winter ice on the surface of the river and outlined the movement in the water.

He jumped at the sound of gunfire behind him. He scrambled around, keeping low. "Bump," he heard a loud whisper from above and behind him. *Mike.* He looked back at the river but could see nothing. *Damn, why hadn't he worked out a password?* He heard more shooting on his side. It had to be

his men. He wondered what they saw. "What are you shooting at?"

"I don't know," Mike said.

"Someone just crossed the river," Bump said. "I'm going
after him. Hold your position and don't shoot me."

He had taken only a few steps when bullets passed over his
head, and he heard Mike scream.

Jacob pulled himself from the water and flattened himself
in the dense cane, grateful for whoever had provided covering fire. He poured urine on the ground, splashed it on the
cane, then poured some on the second towel and the apron
and threw them high in the cane.

He made his way up the bank, pausing to pour urine.
He would leave the jar open near the tree. He wondered if
he should forget the hunt and get back to the lodge. He
wanted to know what the shooting was about, but he would
feel foolish if he found everyone asleep. His job was to capture the tiger. He worked his way toward the tree, marking
the trail.

Kid, Leonard, and Old Man had opened fire when they
saw gun flashes across the river. They were stunned by return
fire. They had no cover except brush and darkness. Leonard
died with a bullet in his brain. Cursing and crying under his
breath, Kid fired back. Old Man passed the .45 to Jimmy Guy
and took Leonard's AK47. A bullet hit between Kid and Old
Man. Jimmy Guy kept his head down but raised the pistol
and fired.

"We gotta get out of here," Old Man said.

When they heard gunfire from farther up the river, Kid
said, "It's Bump. We oughta link up with him." He jumped
up and ran toward Bump, then dropped with a bullet in his
stomach.

"It's not Bump, it's the ATF," Old Man said, thinking the bullet had come from the Texas side. He fired a long burst the next time he saw a gun flash from his side of the river. He heard no more shots from America.

Jacob was still splashing urine when he heard a low moan close by. He froze. The tiger was already across the river; had gotten there before he had. The tree held his rifle and his safety. He threw the bottle as far as he could, hoping the tiger would go for it. Then as quietly as he could he hurried toward the tree.

Bump dropped to the ground when he heard something in the brush nearby. He was still on the ground when something hit a rock, splattering him with glass and liquid. Afraid it was acid or poison, he wanted to run to the river to wash it off but feared being shot. Maybe by his own men. *Damn, they needed radios so they could locate each other. Probably it was Jimmy Guy and Old Man shooting, but where was Kid's team? Had Mike been hit? Maybe Mike was stalking the spy too. Damn. He'd have to be careful or they'd shoot each other.* Silently he rose from the ground and moved toward a rustle like someone moving through the brush.

Jacob could still hear gunfire from the right, the left, and behind him. *What the hell was going on?* He moved when there was shooting and listened when it stopped. He felt as much as heard the soft footfall of the tiger. He was so close to the tree he almost ran for it. Thought of exposing his back to the tiger while climbing the tree held him in place. He would never make it to safety in time. The tiger was too close. He turned to face it and in the moonlight saw a glimpse of moving stripes.

. . .

Bump stopped and breathed silently through his mouth. The moonlight helped, but shifting shadows made it difficult to see. He felt secure in his camouflage. He wouldn't be seen unless he did something stupid like rolling a pebble under his boot or firing at the wrong target, exposing himself with the muzzle flash. He saw movement, like someone turning to look at him. Slowly he raised the M-15 to his shoulder. He had to be certain. *One move,* he thought. *Make one move and you're dead.*

Something soft touched his leg, something stiff brushed his trousers. He looked down to see the tiger sniffing him. Then the tiger looked at him, its cold eyes glinting in the moonlight. Bump jumped and pulled the trigger.

. . .

Gun flashes split the night, and by their light Jacob saw the tiger, heard it snarl. Unable to control himself, he ran for the tree, fumbled for the strap, and pulled himself up, expecting the tiger to claw him from the tree at any instant. He scrambled into his nest, grabbed the Ruger and levered a shell into the chamber, aware that he made a lot of noise. He tried to take a deep breath but couldn't; his heart beat too fast.

Rand was awakened by his throbbing cheek and stinging lip. He had medicated them with scotch and aspirin—more scotch than aspirin—and had gone to bed with an ice pack. The aspirin had worn off; the ice pack had melted. He endured the pain, trying to put himself to sleep by thinking of what he would tell Peggy, how he had confronted a man with a gun. He didn't care if he had a scar. His face was too smooth anyway, too boyish. A scar would give him character as director of NAZA.

One rifle stood at the foot of his bed; Arina had taken the other. They had heard distant shots and feared the militia would return. Rand wondered if he could have shot those goons had they returned. He'd like to see them cower, but he didn't think he could shoot them. He didn't even know how to use a gun. With a moan, he got up, and stumbled down the hall to the kitchen. In the darkness he found the aspirin on the table where he left it, but it was difficult to drink with his cut and swollen lip. He refilled the ice pack and looked out the window.

He saw a dim yellow light around the closed door of the garage where the trailer was parked with the tiger. He should turn it off; the creeps that attacked them had not seen the tiger, but the lighted garage could attract attention. He started outside when he remembered the tigress was to lure the tiger that might be lurking near the garage. *Should he go to his room and get the rifle?* His swollen face forbade him to smile as he thought of how he would explain to Stuart Johnson that he had killed the tiger after luring it to the cage. He opened the door and looked out. Seeing nothing, he walked to the garage. Inside he saw the outline of someone with a flashlight beside the tiger's cage. "Arina?" he said.

The beam of a flashlight blinded him, and he lifted his hands to shade his eyes. "What's wrong?" The light held steady on his face. *Militia.* He turned to run when the dart hit him in the right shoulder. He felt only a stinging sensation at first, then a sharp pain.

As he ran for the garage door, Rand reached for the dart with his left hand and tried to pull it out. He screamed from pain as the barb tugged sharply at his flesh. He passed the garage door and was running across the gravel when he fell. The dart wobbled, sending a piercing pain down his arm. He reached for the dart again, clenched his teeth and jerked. The barb tore free.

He struggled to his feet and staggered toward the house. His legs were asleep. He had to reach the lodge, had to warn the others. He reeled, the lodge dancing before him. He steadied himself on both legs, then crumpled slowly to the ground. The dart clenched tightly in his hand, he tried to crawl to the lodge, but his arms collapsed under him.

He tried to raise himself but couldn't. The muscles in his throat cramped, saliva dribbled over his split lip and down his cheek. His eyes were open, but he couldn't see. He tried to close his eyes but couldn't. Attempts to breathe resulted in a hollow rattling. He stopped trying.

Jacob sat in his nest in the tree, kept awake by knowledge that the tiger was nearby. The gunfire had stopped. He listened intently, hearing nothing but the trilling of a nighthawk and the distant murmur of the river. Then he heard a violent, moaning roar that ended in a series of explosive grunts that set every dog in El Cruce to barking. A pack of coyotes west of the village joined them. Jacob shivered, but not because of his wet clothes or the cool of the night air.

He gripped the Ruger in stiff hands and tried to figure out what had happened. *Barboza's men had Jorge Chapa and would have had him, too, if it hadn't been for the distraction from this side of the river. Who could it have been except Rand, and maybe Arina, because more than one person had been shooting. But where did they get weapons? Automatic weapons? Had they been hurt?* He had heard return fire, screams.

He had seen the tiger in flashes from an automatic weapon, fired by someone but who? For much of the night he considered taking the Ruger and making a run for the lodge. The uncertainty of the dark, the heavy brush, and the growing stiffness in his joints that was going to make it hard for him to get out of the tree and limp to the lodge kept him in his nest until it was light enough to see.

He moved one painful limb at a time, stretching, then tested his hands on the knotted strap. Hanging on to the crate beneath the helicopter and climbing the strap into the

tree had sapped his hands of their strength, and he fell the last
eight feet, sliding down the tree and landing in a heap. He
unshouldered the Ruger and slipped off the safety, ready to
fire at anything that moved. All was quiet. He got slowly to
his feet and, acutely aware of the scrapes and bruises from the
night, hobbled to the lodge.

It was sunrise when Jacob saw the lodge, and something
on the ground between the lodge and the garage. He kept to
cover until he was close enough to see what it was. *A man.*
Even more cautiously, he approached until he recognized
Rand. *Maybe Rand was drunk,* he hoped, as he thought of
Arina. He left his cover and ducked under a window looking
inside. Arina was making coffee.

Shaking his head at the fool he had been, he went to Rand.
Even before he reached for Morgan's neck to feel for a pulse
he knew Rand was dead. He went inside. "What happened?"
he asked.

"Two men came with guns," Arina said. "They asked
where you were. Rand tried to defend us. I have not slept
wondering where you were."

"Barboza's men?" he asked. "They killed Rand?"

"They were militia," Evelyn said, coming into the room.
"They didn't kill Rand, they beat him. You should have seen
him, Jacob. He was so frightened and so brave. Be sure and
say something to him."

"He's dead." Both women looked at him in disbelief.
Evelyn looked toward Rand's room. "Outside."

"No," Evelyn said. "He can't be dead. He's . . . asleep."

Jacob took a blanket from the lodge, covered Rand, and
called the Maverick County Sheriff's Department. "No, I
don't think it was his heart," he said into the telephone.
"There's blood, and he's got a dart in his—a hypodermic

dart, the kind I use. He's holding it in his hand. Yes, I'll hold." He turned to the women. "They're shorthanded this morning. Last night was a high crime night." He turned his attention back to the telephone. "I think they may have been here, two of them. Men in camouflage. The women ran them off. No, I haven't moved him. We'll be here."

He turned back to the women. "We have to take a number. There are bodies on both sides of the river."

"Did you check the tigress?" Arina asked.

"My God, the tiger," Evelyn said. "Not the tiger too."

Jacob hurried to the garage, trying not to look at Rand when he passed. He wouldn't have wanted to share a camp with Rand, but he was a good man and in an emergency he had been a brave one. He had liked Jonelle Parker; she had been brave too. Hell, he had liked Sam Storey and Lalo Perez and he didn't even know them. *I've liked everyone those damn tigers have killed, and I haven't stopped a single death. Not one.*

Jacob flipped the switch to the overhead lights in the garage, saw the blowgun on the floor beside the trailer. He flashed a light through one of the air holes in the crate and saw the tigress lying with its mouth and eyes wide, just as Rand's were. Saliva drooled from the side of its mouth. The beam of the light flashed on a shiny object in the tiger's shoulder, an aluminum dart embedded in an animal he had risked his life to save.

He picked up the blowgun. *Why? Why go through what we went through to kill the damned thing once we saved it?* Her words came back to him. *She had seen a Russian across the river. But if she was working for whatever replaced the KGB why would she tell him she had seen a Russian? Had she killed the tigress so he would take no more risks? So that she could say there was nothing more she could do and go back to Russia? Why kill Rand?* He walked back to the lodge, placed the blowgun on the bar that separated the kitchen from the living area and turned to Arina. "Why?" he asked. She stared at him but did not answer.

"The tiger?" Evelyn asked.

"Dead." He turned back to Arina. "I want to know why."

"Perhaps there are those in Russia—"

"Forget people in Russia. Rand is dead with one of your Russian darts in his fist. The tiger's dead with a Russian dart in it. Your blowgun was lying beside the cage. Why, Arina?"

Arina left the room. "You're not going anywhere," Jacob called after her. "I've already notified the police." She returned almost immediately with her shoulder bag. She opened the bag and thrust it at Jacob. He stared at the blowgun not knowing what to say.

"I did not kill Rand. Or the tiger. I do not know who used a 'Russian' blowgun to kill him, if that is how he died. I am sorry you do not trust me," she said. "When the authorities come, I will be in my room."

"I killed the tiger," Evelyn said in a voice gone dead.

Arina stopped. Jacob sat down on a stool.

"I was trying to save it. Rand startled me. I just wanted to knock him out for a little while. They said it was a tranquilizing drug, the same as you and Arina use. They said—" She covered her face and cried.

"Who said?"

A rich Mexican knew how she hated caging and killing animals. He had a huge ranch in Mexico where he freed animals from around the world. He had given her a package and told her to sedate the tiger. His men would take the sleeping tiger and let it awaken in freedom. "The darts were already prepared," Evelyn said. "I don't know what went wrong."

"What was his name?"

"Beto"

"Humberto? Barboza? He's the one who took the tiger after we caught it."

"No. He wanted to save the tiger. I was going to be . . . I didn't know. I swear to God I didn't know," Evelyn said, breaking into tears. "I've been such a fool." She fled to her room.

Arina watched her, not certain whether to follow. "What will the authorities do to her? She intended no harm."

In spite of his anger, Jacob felt sorry for her. Evelyn was committed to a cause, and in her zeal she had not only destroyed the thing she tried to save but herself as well. "It depends on how much Stuart pays for lawyers and how big a stake the media has in it. There is a public attitude about these things, and the media has a big part in shaping it. She may be a martyr who sacrifices her freedom to save that of animals. She may be a foolish woman who was duped by scheming men. She may be a romantic figure who risked her life for love. I don't know how they will play it, but she will be someone neither of us will recognize."

"Poor Rand. Those men were so insolent, so brazen." She did not tell him about their threats or her torn shirt.

"When the authorities get here, go to your room and stay there unless they call you. Do not answer any questions. Tell them you won't talk without a lawyer. Whatever you do, don't tell the police about your conspiracy theories. They'll put you in the loony bin."

The telephone rang. Jacob picked it up with dread. It was Hailee White. "I'm sorry, I had a story for you, Hailee. Now, things are so confused—What kind of police reports? Yes, Rand is dead. No, he was not shot. That is correct; we have the tiger. We wanted you to film it—There's no need for you to come here. We can come to Eagle Pass. Wait—"

He put down the receiver and turned to Arina. "Hailee is

on her way. She heard police reports of a border war out here last night. She knows Rand is dead. She'll be here when the police question Evelyn. I think we should prepare Evelyn. If Hailee puts her on the air, we want her to look as sympathetic as possible," Jacob said, wondering if he believed that. Rand was dead, leaving a wife and children. Jacob would like to leave it to a judge and jury to balance mercy and justice, but lawyers figured in the equation, and money and Hailee.

Heaving a sigh of both weariness and vexation, he led Arina to Evelyn's room. Evelyn was gone.

Evelyn could not endure the room. Jacob and Rand had shared a room so that she and Arina could have privacy, but it was a man's room, and except for two bunk beds and a closet it was as bare as the day it was built. She heard Arina's and Jacob's voices. Although she could not hear their words, she knew what they said—she was a killer, a fool, a hypocrite.

She walked outside, but seeing the blanket covering Rand's body, she quickly put the lodge behind her where she could not see Rand or the garage. She had been a fool. *Why had she trusted Beto? Because she wanted it to be true. She wanted to believe that somewhere there was someone who cared about life, all life. Someone who was not a . . . killer.* The word almost drove her mad. *Johnny could boast to his friends that his mother was a killer. She had killed a tiger. She had killed a man.*

What would she tell Rand's wife? She . . . liked Rand. *Yes.* She hadn't respected him because he was a bureaucrat, so . . . but that was before last night. She would tell Peggy that Rand had saved her and Arina from terrorists. When he saw her darting the tiger, she had to knock him out until Beto's men rescued the tiger. When he woke up, what he saw wouldn't matter. He would be the next director of NAZA, but she would be director of an international foundation. Now neither of them would—she would go to jail. She would be caged like a zoo animal, no longer real but a semblance of what was real. She had rather be dead.

She would kill herself. She hated violence; how could she make her life, her love for life, a lie by killing herself? She had already made it a lie by killing Rand. But she hadn't intended to kill Rand; she intended to save the tiger. Now, only one tiger remained. If she could save it, then she would go to jail. She would die knowing that she hadn't failed at everything. *But how? How could she save the tiger?*

Idly, she stared at a strap hanging from a tree. Jacob's tree. There was the brush she had cut. Up in the branches was the nest Jacob had made for himself. She saw the Cap-Chur gun hanging from a limb, the bag of darts, and shuddered. Quickly she walked away from the tree with its reminders of death.

She would save the tiger. There were rich men in America, in Mexico, who would help her if she could reach them. The media. The media would cover her trial, but she would not defend herself; she would plead for the tiger. *Do with me what you will. I unintentionally did harm to save that tiger, and I will give my life to save this tiger. I am not afraid to die. I do not choose to live in a world that condemns animals to die for man's pleasure. If I live, I will live for life, and if I die, I will die for life.*

So enraptured was she by her speech to the jury, to the world, that she wanted to return to the lodge and write it down before she forgot. She looked about her. This time she couldn't get lost. Over there was Jacob's tree; behind her she could hear the river. The emptiness and silence made her nervous. She was a city girl; she loved wild animals, but she didn't care for wild spaces. She looked behind her, but there was nothing. Brush and a few big trees. Noises. Rustling. *Probably the leaves.* Scurrying. Mice. She shuddered involuntarily, and backed away.

At first she did not identify the pile of leaves and brush. Then she saw camouflage cloth. She had blundered upon the tiger's kill, and somewhere it watched her. "I didn't mean to interrupt your meal," she said softly. "I want to save you. I am going to the lodge now to write a speech to save you." She saw the glaring yellow eyes of the tiger, almost crossed in the intensity of their focus upon her, the hairs on its neck as stiff and erect as bristles. A low growl emerged from the tiger's throat.

She turned and ran, the brush ripping her skin and tearing her hair. A huge weight landed on her back and fangs ripped loose her scalp and lanced into her neck. She saw her ear dangling below her eye, heard gristle part and bone break. She clawed at the ground, crushed by the weight on her back. Then she was picked up and tossed like a doll. She tried to scream but had no breath. She landed in the brush, heedless of the thorns that tore at her hands and face. She tried to crawl, but her arms and legs refused to move. A shadow moved over her and darkness covered her head.

12

ailee and Tony reached the lodge minutes ahead of the sheriff, but Jacob would not let her remove the blanket from Rand or open the crate so Tony could get shots of the dead tiger. "Nothing is to be disturbed until the sheriff gets here," he said.

Tony contented himself taping Rand's covered body and the lodge. Jacob refused to say anything except that Evelyn and Arina had intended to give Hailee an exclusive about the capture of the tiger before taking it to the Houston zoo. She was not mollified. The sheriff arrived and went into the lodge with Jacob, telling Hailee to wait outside.

"You take one side, I'll take the other," she told Tony. "See if you can hear anything."

"Okay," Tony said. He pulled the blanket off Rand, recorded the body from several angles, took a close-up of the dart clenched in Rand's hand, and replaced the blanket.

. . .

"Seems like we had a border war here last night, and two governments are upset about it," the sheriff said. "Some people over here started shooting across the river and then started shooting at each other. Border Patrol picked up two guys in tree suits, one of them gut-shot who said he was militia. The other one, who wouldn't identify himself, said he was out for a walk when he saw the wounded man. Before he went into surgery, the wounded one said there were twelve of them, six still in a motel. His squad was supposed to find a UN base and kill the tiger. Two of the militia were killed, and he was shot. Border Patrol found another one who was shot. He carried a radio. We found five heavily armed men at the motel and got all of them without a fight. None of them had an ID, but we'll get one. The sixth was in a vehicle with a two-way radio. We haven't found him yet.

"I know what you are doing here. What I want to know is what you were doing in Mexico. Give it to me straight so we don't have to go through this but once. I got a lot to do this morning."

"I'm not answering any questions without a lawyer," Jacob said, "but I will offer a hypothesis. Suppose the female tiger was in heat, and both tigers crossed into Mexico. Suppose someone went over there and caught the female to lure the male into a trap. Suppose someone like Humberto Barboza took the tiger, but the tiger escaped and ended up in a cage back over here."

"The tiger swam the river with the cage on its back?"

Jacob shrugged. "Bump Wilkerson and his militia group vowed to kill the tiger. Maybe somehow they bumped into Barboza's men who were trying to kidnap the tiger and got to shooting at each other."

"There are a lot of holes in that hypothesis, but I don't have time to fill them now. And we haven't found Bump Wilkerson. One of the militia said they had a 'sponsor' but

284

that not even Bump knew who he was, just someone who sent money and told them what to do. So what about the man out there in the driveway? Who killed him?"

"I think Evelyn Price, who was here last night, has a statement to make," Jacob said. "But she seems to have disappeared. We do have a couple of rifles the militia left last night."

"We're going to have to sweep this whole damn pasture looking for evidence and maybe bodies," the sheriff said. "We'll find her. You got a lot more questions to answer so don't go wandering off. Anybody else here besides you and Price?"

"Arina Yeroskin, a Russian citizen. Her embassy will want a lawyer and a Russian official at any interrogation."

"I don't want any of you wandering off. But if I were you, I'd move to Eagle Pass for a while, some place where there's a lot of witnesses."

Neither Tony nor Hailee overheard anything of consequence before the arrival of deputies and Border Patrol forced them to give up the effort. Tony rolled tape as detectives collected evidence around the garage, and then he and Hailie followed deputies and Border Patrol who searched the brush for more evidence. She didn't have a story until deputies came upon the body of Evelyn and the remains of someone dressed in camouflage.

"They found Evelyn," Jacob told Arina. "The tiger killed her and ate most of someone who was missing a finger. I'm taking Evelyn's car to Eagle Pass. I don't think we want to be out here by ourselves."

"I will get my things."

While Jacob was packing, Santana called. Jacob reported the call to Arina. "I wasn't able to meet Jorge last night because Barboza's men had him. Santana is bringing him to a hospital on this side. He'll be okay, but Santana wants him to work over here until things calm down. Some of Barboza's men were shot last night."

"By you?"

"I tried not to hit anyone."

Jacob was sore and exhausted and could hardly drive. "I'm sorry I accused you," he said. "I should have trusted—"

"I have not trusted you either," she said. "When you killed the first tiger I didn't know who you were. You were so American, so . . . lawless, telling superiors what to do, willing to use Lalo's body as bait. When the tigers crossed into Mexico, I thought our problems were over. The Mexicans would capture the tigers and return them to Russia. You were willing to steal the tiger from Mexico, to risk lives, to shoot at people—"

"It was ego, a lot of it," Jacob admitted. "Anger, pride— Barboza had no right to take a tiger we had captured. It was also wanting to do a job right."

"I believe Russia has been trying to kill the tigers. They feared the United States would discover the tigers were carriers and believe the tigers' escape was intentional. There would be—who knows what horrors—if your government believed Russia was engaged in bacterial warfare."

"I'm having a hard time following this."

"I do not know how they discovered the tigers were infected," Arina said. "but when they knew, they knew the tigers must be destroyed. They hired Bump to kill the tiger. They hired Barboza. Barboza used Evelyn."

Jacob shook his head. "Not Bump. Not if he knew they were Russian."

"How would he know? They tricked Evelyn into killing the tigress. We must do an autopsy on the tigress. We will need an American vet and his laboratory."

Jacob stopped at the first motel because he didn't have the energy to look elsewhere. After he and Arina checked in, he called the sheriff's office and got permission for the autopsy, promising the hide would not be damaged. The sheriff wanted the hide for his office and recommended a veterinarian, Dr. McMullan. While Arina and Dr. McMullan collected samples from the tiger, Jacob lay down, too exhausted to sleep well.

Roy Pat had been parked off the highway on a brush-covered hill when he received a call. "We're under attack, both sides of the river." When he did not receive another call by dawn, he took off his cammies and slipped into jeans and a T-shirt. He hid the cammies and the radio in the brush, drove back to town, and called the motel rooms from a pay phone. No one answered. He spent the rest of the day slowly driving county roads looking for survivors, encountering county, state, and Federal agents.

Sooner or later the vehicle would be traced. He disassembled his rifle, put it into his bag, and went back to town. He drove through a car wash, wiped the steering wheel and surfaces clean, and abandoned the vehicle near the motel. He walked until he found a white clapboard church with no sign designating the name. He went inside where a handful of people had gathered, said he was on a mission for God, and asked for their prayers. The pastor invited him to spend the night and kept him for several days. He repaired the cars and weapons of the church members, prayed, read the Bible, went to church, and listened to the news.

Bump was dead, and the others were dead or under arrest. No one had found a UN base, but that did not concern him. His war was with the tiger. He did odd jobs for cash and slept on the pastor's screened-in porch. He wanted to let his wife know he was okay but did not know how without alerting the authorities to his whereabouts. He saved his money waiting for news of the tiger, confident God would deliver the tiger into his hands.

He heard others laugh at Bump for emptying the magazine of an automatic weapon without hitting the tiger, but Roy Pat did not laugh. Roy Pat understood. He too had known that fear. Not of losing his life—that could happen any time in Vietnam. If he did not have dominion over the earth, he was no different from an ape, witless beneath the stars, struggling in an unformed, undifferentiated swamp, without purpose.

Roy Pat had gone to Vietnam on a mission to save America. He shot when shot at, sweated the boonies, humped the hills, but he was sure of himself and his right to do what he was doing. His friends were killed; his unit was sent into combat and told when and where they could shoot. He was tempted with sex, drugs, futility by those he tried to serve, with rage, confusion, despair by those who did not want to serve but who applauded the death of his buddies, the death of Vietnamese, the death of the Republic of Vietnam.

He had been dispirited by what happened to him, to his buddies, what happened back in the world, but he did not realize his apostasy until he had faced the tiger. Fear had erased faith leaving him a body without soul. He had to face that fear and, armed with faith, master it. Then he would rise again as the untroubled, undoubting, single-minded lifer he had been.

It was the next morning before Jacob awakened, roused from a deep sleep by Arina who had brought coffee. "We should have done this with the first tiger," Arina said quietly. "The tiger carried a virulent form of a common bacteria, a rickettsia. Strains are found in several species—felines, rodents, canines. The bacteria is transmitted through saliva, causing anemia, parasitemia, pneumonia, often death. The feline strain can be especially lethal. The virulent strain even deadlier. Soviet scientists succeeded in developing feline carriers."

Jacob shook his head. "For what purpose?"

"Before he was arrested Andrei sent me a warning, 'Afghanistan Alternative.' Every day I am thinking, what could it mean? The Soviets desired warm-water ports on the Indian Ocean to keep NATO and China at bay. That meant the allegiance or conquest of India, and the British proved there were too many people to feed, to control. The Soviet invasion of Afghanistan was a disaster. Perhaps scientists attempted to use animals as carriers of deadly disease. Particularly cattle. All suspect cattle would have to be killed. In India the government wouldn't dare destroy sacred cattle. Millions would die. The country would dissolve in chaos. The Soviets could step in, restore order, bring hospitals and tanks, and have ports on the Indian Ocean."

"Every country has contingency plans," Jacob said, "wild scenarios like that. No one takes them seriously."

"The Soviet Union failed, and the experiments were stopped. Perhaps hooligans viewed the dismantling of the Soviet Union, of nuclear weapons as the end of everything they had lived for and continued the experiments in secret. Then the democratic government agreed to loan infected tigers to America."

"If Americans found out about it—"

"What would prevent America from bombing Russia now that Russia is weak and divided? Even a subnuclear war would create chaos, anarchy in Russia. People would demand order, regimen, a strong central government. The Soviet Union would rise again."

"That's pretty wild," Jacob said.

"There are people who would risk all to gain all. It

wouldn't be the Soviet Union that was destroyed but the rebellious Muslim states. Out of the chaos the party could arise stronger than ever because no other force could unite and control the people."

"If there was such a plan, they had to have a way for their people to survive in the infected areas."

"Inoculation perhaps. Tetracycline. Transfusions."

"I'll check with people I know," Jacob said. "I don't want any more Jonelle Parkers."

Jacob took a long hot shower to relax his stiff muscles and walked to the sheriff's office to limber up. The sheriff introduced him to a Texas Ranger and a Border Patrol officer. They had identified the bodies of Hubert Slotsky, Mike Bentch, Leonard Jukam, Bump Wilkerson, and Evelyn Price. Jimmy Guy Jameson and Justin Perry were in custody.

"We found one excited woman, Rafaela Perez, who says *chupacabras* came to her. Sometimes there was one of them, sometimes two. One of them grabbed her by the throat. The doctor who examined her said the *chupacabra* that choked her wore gloves. Cogden is ready to go to war with uninvited people on his property bothering his help."

The sheriff hunched his chair closer to Jacob. "Some gringo was across the river causing trouble last night, and Barboza's men shot at him. Some of the shots landed on this side of the river, and the militia shot back. You don't know what a gringo would be doing over there, do you?"

"He might have been trying to lure the tiger back to this side."

"He sure as hell succeeded because the tiger killed two people over here and is still out there somewhere."

"Any new information on Rand Morgan?"

"The Bexar County medical examiner in San Antonio is conducting the autopsy. It'll take a while, but we know what was in the darts." He pronounced the word a syllable at a time. "Tetrodotoxin. Common name, blowfish poison. Toxic as hell. Paralysis within a minute, doesn't take much to cause death."

"Where would you go to get it?"

"We don't know yet. And I'm not going to get a new rug. The Russians want the tiger back, hide and all. Already picked it up."

Leaving Arina out of the story, he told what Arina suspected. The sheriff looked at the Ranger. "Does this have anything to do with the UN base that everybody knows where it is but can't find it?" the Ranger asked.

"Some talk-show idiot said the militia had found a UN base," the sheriff said. "He was signing up militia volunteers from as far as Michigan and California."

Jacob realized Arina's story had no chance competing with conspiracy theories as entertainment. "The tiger carried a rickettsia that can be transmitted through water. You might warn authorities."

"Well, the tigers have been all over South Texas, and there hasn't been a report of it yet. If I were you, I wouldn't look for the tiger outside the city limits and probably outside your motel room. Your chances of finding the militia are a lot better than your chances of finding the tiger. If they don't kill the tiger, they'll push it into Mexico or move it west out of my county. And the farther west you go, the sparser the population gets. If you leave the county, be sure you let me know where to reach you. And right now might be a good time to leave."

Jacob believed Arina was right—Soviet scientists had developed a virulent disease in felines but had been unable to transmit it to other carriers. The Afghanistan Alternative had come to nothing. However, democratic leaders in Russia feared the experiments had been continued successfully by renegade scientists, and when they learned the tigers were loose in the States, they had panicked. Andrei had been arrested while trying to warn Arina. Officials had ordered Arina home and made frantic efforts to recover the tigers, dead or alive. *They can have the last one,* Jacob thought. He gave the sheriff his telephone number in Fort Davis.

When Jacob got back to the motel he had a message from Hailee. She wanted an interview, and she didn't know who to call with both Rand and Evelyn dead. He didn't either. He was sure he didn't want to be spokesman. If he went home, the militia would ignore him, the media forget him. He called NAZA headquarters and asked for Johnson.

"Jacob," Stuart said. "My God, man, I'm in shock over Evelyn and Rand. It's a serious setback, but the tiger must still be captured."

"Not by me," Jacob said. "I'm quitting."

He hung up the telephone and looked around the room. He hadn't unpacked from Cogden's lodge. Leaving would be easy except for one thing. He loved Arina, but was that enough to surmount their differences? When he was younger, he had said yes and he had been wrong.

He went to Arina's room and told her he had gone to the sheriff. "I told him what you . . . what we suspected. He didn't believe me. There have been no reported incidents of infections."

"Perhaps it takes direct contact, a bite, for the infection to work."

"Go home with me. There are two bedrooms and no conditions. We can talk. You can look at what I have to offer, then make up your mind."

"The authorities will look for me. I will cause you trouble."

"Once I make the announcement that I'm quitting, we'll be instantly anonymous."

292

"Moscow may demand my return."

"If we're married, you'll be a US citizen."

She put her hand over his lips. "It is a sweet thought, Jacob. One I have thought many times. I want to make you happy, I want to give you children, but I am afraid I will cause you difficulty."

"Arina, we could go to Mexico and get married today, but I'm afraid to cross the border. That's why I'm asking you to go to Fort Davis with me. See what my life is like. Then you can decide."

"I want to be with you the rest of my life no matter what your life is like. I don't like coming to you with nothing to offer but desperation."

"I'm as desperate for you as you are for me."

With a chuckle that turned to tears, she buried her face in his neck.

Hailee's report on the killing of the tiger and the murder of Randolph Morgan was supported by Tony's video of Rand's body with a close-up of the dart in his hand, the mound that held Bump Wilkerson, and the blood-splattered brush where Evelyn had died. The story made the network, and Hailee was once again on top of the heap.

Hailee interviewed Humberto Barboza, whose men had repelled an invasion by militiamen, residents of El Cruce who had been wounded or widowed in the battle, militia who had come to Eagle Pass to search for the UN base, the sheriff, and politicians who were eager to discuss the border, illegal immigration, smuggling, protection of endangered species, the rights of landowners, and crime. None of the stories had made the network. She was packing to return to Houston when Jacob called.

Hailee turned to Tony Garcia. "Jacob Trace is quitting. Walking out. We'll run this and then 'Where is the tiger now?

And who is looking for it?' stories until NAZA sends someone else. People were getting tired of Jacob Trace anyway. He
lacked authenticity." That's what separated her from the pack:
she was learning authenticity.

"Did he have anything to say?"

"Yeah, we're to warn people about a disease, richetts or
something."

Jacob called Reymundo in Fort Davis. "Everything okay?
Good. I need Alta Marie to clean the house. I need you to get
a church and a preacher; I'm getting married. We want you
and Alta Marie to be best man and best woman. Nothing formal. A suit's fine, and if she wants to wear her high school
formal that's fine. Can she still get in it? That's great. Can you
come and get us? Bring my truck."

Jacob met Reymundo in the motel lobby. "Drove kind of
fast, didn't you?"

"I wanted to see this woman you are marrying. Alta Marie
said she must resemble Old Red if you want to marry her."

They went to Jacob's room, bumping shoulders, pushing
with elbows, shoving, wrestling each other through the door.
"I'll teach you to smart off to your *patrón*," Jacob said,
pulling Reymundo's cap over his eyes.

"Why you breathing so hard, *jefe*? Woman make you
weak?"

"You're bigger than you were the last time I saw you,"
Jacob said.

"You spend too much time in motels. When I told the
dogs I was bringing a woman to take their place, they tried to
bite me."

Reymundo carried their bags to the truck, and Jacob and
Arina walked down the street empty-handed, without checking
out. They would keep the rooms for a while. Jacob wanted no

one besides the sheriff to know they were leaving or where they were going.

"You going to introduce me to the lady?" Reymundo asked when he picked them up a couple of blocks from the motel.

"Arina, this is Reymundo. He's at that insufferable stage of employment—indispensable."

"Jacob is a lucky man," Reymundo said. "With both of us."

"I'm starting to worry," Jacob said, and they all laughed.

"So you are giving up the chase?" Reymundo said.

"It was getting too crowded; someone was sure to get shot. We'll hear from the tiger, either that it's dead or alive. If it's alive, I'm going after it the way I always have, with the best dogs I've got, minus the media, the politics, the show. This time it'll be me and the tiger."

13

They were married in a utilitarian but comfortable church. Jacob's friends and church members who came with gifts and well-wishes held a reception in the church's Sunday-school center. Jacob had planned to take Arina to Indian Lodge for a honeymoon, but Arina wanted to be in her new home. Jacob carried her over the threshold and showed her the house.

Arina had been overwhelmed by small-town openness. "They're friendly," Jacob agreed, "but you'll find out it takes a while to be accepted. You have to show you're one of them."

"How do I do that?" she asked, coyly backing into the bedroom.

"Accept their faults. Forgive their narrow-minded meanness. Don't pretend you're better because you're from some place else or have a better education or because you're beautiful and smart, and I can't believe you're mine." He held her tightly as he led her to the bed they would share.

"They are so kind; how could I not like them?"

"They are good people, Arina, but they would have been willing to drop a bomb on you and fifty million other Russians to convince you communism was evil."

Although they were married, Arina still feared deportation. She was bewildered rather than frightened at her new circumstances because of the steadfastness of Jacob's love. Other women had left the safe and familiar because of love for a man; she could do it too. Jacob would help her become one of them. "The wedding ceremony was simple but—"

"Effective," he said, lying down beside her.

"Yes, but I mean to say that it was not a formality like official weddings or a ritual like religious weddings. The preacher explained our duties to each other, to our children, and to the community."

"They have expectations of us—to take care of each other and our children and to contribute to the community."

"It was as though he wanted us to be members of the party."

"Except this party is not supposed to rule but to lead by example."

"Your people will be my people and your God my God," she said. "I have read the Bible in the hotel rooms. Jacob, if I displease you—"

"We'll have an argument, and then we'll kiss and make up. You will displease me, Arina, and I'll disappoint you. The important thing is that we get together like this—"

"Like this?"

"Exactly like this. Memorize this position. We'll get together like this, and we'll work it out. I don't want to lose you, Arina."

"You cannot lose me, Jacob, not even if you go to Russia."

He looked at her so sharply that she hastened to explain. "It is a joke, Jacob. I am trying to be a Texan."

"You don't have the accent for it. Say, 'I luv yew, Jacib.'"

"I luv you, Jacib."

"We'll work on it some more," he said.

Arina made friends with the dogs, peace with the house, a pact with the mountains. She would let them have Jacob if they would let him return to her.

They took walks and rides every day, and it was lovely, but Jacob needed a job. He liked the peace of the mountains, but he didn't want to be tracking animals when he was fifty, sixty. Maybe his education and experience would get him a job in a research lab or a university. He interviewed for faculty positions at Sul Ross University and Fort Davis High School. He was offered his old job at Parks and Wildlife relocating lions, but he didn't want to leave Arina alone or be alone.

Arina noticed his restlessness. "Go to the mountains if you need solitude," she said.

"Parks and Wildlife tells me every time a cat is seen anywhere. Game wardens check out dead animals. The Highway Patrol reports sightings. The tiger is out there somewhere, but until there's a sighting or fresh sign I'm waiting for the second bell."

One day Barry Windom called. "Thought I might catch you at home," he said. "Ran into a student pilot who was practicing touch and goes. Said on his cross-country from Del Rio to Ozona he saw something too big for a hog, too fast for a cow, between Red Bluff Creek and the dry fork of the Devils River. I've worked for a rancher near there, Paco Rooney. He has some exotic game under a high fence. He said you were welcome to camp on his place, look around."

"Maybe it was one of the exotics."

"I checked with Paco. The exotics are deer or antelope. He doesn't have any cows, and it's too dry for feral hogs."

"Where is the ranch?" Jacob asked. He knew it was beginning again, the mingled thrill and anxiety of the hunt, and there was nothing he could do about it. It was a feeling he neither encouraged nor denied.

"About twenty miles west of Loma Alta off Highway 277," Barry said. "Not much at Loma Alta except a store and a couple of gas pumps. Paco said he would leave keys and a topographical map in an envelope at the store. He lives in Del Rio. Yellow Bluff is the name of the ranch."

"Do you think the student pilot will talk to the press?"

"Nobody wants to talk to a student pilot because all they talk about is stalls and their last landing. Are you sure you want to go after it?"

He and the tiger had a predisposed attachment. "I'm sure."

"I'm tied up right now, but give me a couple of days and I'll come help. You won't have to be on the ground with it."

"Thanks, Barry." Shooting it from a helicopter seemed disrespectful.

"Give Arina my love. Sorry I missed the wedding."

"Barry Windom," Jacob explained to Arina. "Someone may have seen the tiger. Probably nothing, but I'm going to call the rancher."

Paco Rooney was eager to talk to Jacob. "I've got a thousand acres under high fence, and I've got axis, sika, blackbuck antelope, Corsican sheep, and the like. I make a little money off of them, along with the native game in season, and I can't afford to lose them. I had a buffalo—bison. This morning I found what was left of it. No ordinary cat killed that buffalo. I didn't get out of my pickup after I found it."

"I know what you mean," Jacob said.

"I've got 20,000 acres on both sides of the Devils River, so if you have to cross over, don't worry about it. Go anywhere you have to; I've already talked to the neighbors. You need a place to stay, you're welcome to the house."

"Thanks, but I'll take everything I need."

"I am going with you," Arina said.

"It's probably a wild goose chase. You stay here and—"

"I am going with you."

Jacob knew that short of locking her in the house, there was no way to stop her. He had promised to take her camping, and here was the chance. Maybe that's all it would be. "Take warm clothes; it'll get cold at night."

Jacob piled his gear on the porch. Tent, two sleeping bags that could be zipped together, cooking utensils, lantern, flashlight, and batteries. *Cap-Chur gun and darts?* Leave them; he had no way of holding the tiger once it was sedated. *The Ruger and plenty of shells.* He surveyed the pile, not wanting to leave anything essential behind, then checked Arina's gear.

When all the gear was assembled, he packed it in waterproof bags. "If we find the tiger, killing it is going to be easier than capturing it. I've always depended on my dogs to help me, and that's what I'm going to do now. What happened to Roy Farley's pack put the fear in me."

Arina put her hand on his arm. "Jacob, I know how you feel about your dogs."

"I guess people are more important than dogs, at least some people and some dogs. I'll call Reymundo. Ask him to look after things while we're gone. We'll drive up to Yellow Bluff Ranch in the morning." He went to select the dogs he would take.

While he was gone, Arina took the last of the urine they had collected and stowed it with her gear.

Jacob tried to make up his mind. He needed at least four hounds—three Walkers and a bluetick. If he took his best dogs he could be out of the dog business for sure. Tigers could be rough on dogs. They could be rough on people too, and Arina was going to be with him. *Okay, Sandy and Tip for sure. Socks and Blue. Bo? Grady? Red? Red was old, slow, and nearly deaf, but his nose was still good, and Red knew they were going hunting. Take him and if he didn't feel like hunting he could stay behind. Hell, take them all.*

Roy Pat worked at day jobs that didn't require ID or a social security number—cleaning garages, repairing cars, clearing vacant lots. He heard that the tiger had disappeared in Mexico, had died after being wounded by Bump, had been killed by a rancher who buried the body to avoid prosecution by the Feds. "Where is it buried?" he asked.

"I can't show you the grave, but I can show you the ranch it's on."

Roy Pat did not believe it. The tiger had wrought havoc wherever it went, destroying families, unsettling cities, turning America into a jungle. And television, that godless false witness that turned shameful people into idols and called on people to worship them, had proclaimed the tiger a victor over God-fearing men, fear victor over faith, chaos over order, blind ferocity over courage. God had called him to kill the tiger, and when the tiger was dead, peace would return.

One day while unloading a truck, Roy Pat overheard a driver say he was half asleep when he almost ran over something big and orange. Woke him up for sure. If it was a dog, it was the biggest chow he'd ever seen.

"How big was it?" Roy Pat asked.

The driver thought his credibility had been questioned. "It wasn't no damn dog, I'll guarantee you that. It was as big as a cow, but no cow ever jumped like that."

"Where was it?" Roy Pat asked.

302

The driver coldly surveyed Roy Pat to show that his answer was an indulgence not to be repeated. "Near Loma Alta."

"Where's Loma Alta?" Roy Pat asked another worker.

"Highway 277. Some eastbound truckers take it as a short cut from I-10 to Del Rio. Not many cars."

The next day, Roy Pat took his bag to a truck stop. He hung around until he found a driver delivering ice to Quemado, Spofford, Brackettville, and Fort Clark Springs. At Fort Clark Springs, the driver introduced him to a trucker headed for Del Rio who offered to drop him at the junction of Highways 90 and 277. Roy Pat left without saying good-bye to the family that had taken him in. It wasn't the Christian thing to do, but it was best for them not to know when he left or where he went. When he took care of the tiger he would send money to them for the church.

"Hailee, you interested in a story about militia in West Texas?" one of the station reporters asked her. "A ranch woman said she could feel them watching her, following her. She was so frightened, she ran in the house and called the sheriff."

"Probably some cowboy looking for a date."

"Some man said they stalked him, too. They were in camouflage, and he caught a glimpse of orange."

"Orange camouflage?"

"That's what he said."

"Where was it?"

"Val Verde County."

Hailee consulted a map before checking for other stories about stalkers. Some teenagers on a desert blanket party saw something that chased them into a car. It wasn't a man, they said, more like an animal. Hailee went to the news director.

"There's no story," he said.

"Nobody has seen the tiger since it killed those people at Eagle Pass. If we got there first, confirmed there was a tiger stalking people, there'd be a story."

"There's no blood."

"If it's the tiger, there will be blood, and we'll get it on tape."

"That's a hell of a long way from Houston."

"I want this story. I'll take vacation time if I have to."

"If you don't get a story, don't expect me to approve a lot of expenses."

"Said and done," Hailee said. Now all she had to do was talk Tony into going with her. No one had gotten a picture of a live tiger loose in Texas. He could be the first.

Jacob and Arina drove to Sonora then turned south on 277 and did not stop until they reached Loma Alta, an hour's drive through rolling hills covered with scrub brush.

Signs on the white wood and stucco service station on the west side of the highway declared: "Loma Alta. Groceries. Beer. Ice. Sandwiches. Milk. Cold Drinks. Bus Stop." Other than a tin barn and a residence, it was the only building in town.

"I'll pick up groceries and the maps to Yellow Bluff Ranch," Jacob said. "The sign says the restrooms are over there." He pointed at a wooden shack near the service station.

"Look, Jacob," Arina said. She kneeled to examine white, fluffy chickens.

"Silkies," Jacob said.

"They are so soft." She held out her hand, and the curious chickens came closer, cocking their heads to stare at her. "We must get some."

When Jacob opened the door of the service station, a striped, orange kitten ran out and jumped into Arina's lap, startling her. Jacob laughed. "An omen," he said, reaching to pet the kitten. "A miniature tiger." The kitten hissed at him and raked its claws across the back of his hand.

"Hidy," said the buxom woman behind the small counter as they entered. Strings of graying hair hung down one side of her plump, ruddy face. "You folks need some gas?"

"Just groceries," Jacob said. "Did Paco Rooney leave a package for Jacob Trace?"

"If you're Trace he left you some keys and maps."

"I'm Trace. Got any fresh vegetables? Meat?"

"Shoulda' shopped in town," she said. "We just got canned here. It's all on the shelf. Help yourself. Got some cheese, though. And some Flying D eggs. They're fresh enough. Come from right down the road."

Jacob selected several cans of vegetables from the shelves and placed them on the counter. He added a loaf of bread, a box of crackers, a dozen beers, and a dozen eggs. "Give me a couple pounds of cheese and add a couple of bags of ice. That ought to do it."

"Go up the highway a couple of miles," the woman said, tallying the bill. "Past Vinegarone Creek. Take a left this side of the rest stop. Dolan Creek Road. Yellow Bluff is at the end of it. About twenty miles. This will open the gate," she said, pressing a key in his hand. "This one will get you in the house if you need it. There's no one there, but Paco said you was welcome to it. These maps are for the ranch and most of the county."

As they left, Jacob noticed a truck stopped on the other side of the road. He did not recognize the hitchhiker who climbed down from the cab.

When Roy Pat saw Jacob and Arina, he praised the Lord for putting the tiger in his hands. He went inside the service station and greeted the woman. "Did a man and woman stop here? I was trying to meet up with them but had to leave my car in Eagle Pass." Roy Pat did not lie.

"Headed for Yellow Bluff Ranch? You just missed them. They stopped here for groceries and to pick up the keys Paco left them."

"I guess I'll just have to catch up with them."

"You're going to have a hard time doing that afoot. And you won't know where they are when you get there."

"Any place I can rent a car?"

"Del Rio."

"I just came from Del Rio. I hitchhiked this far, I guess I can hitch a ride to the ranch."

"Except for them, there hasn't been a car on Dolan Creek Road today, and unless it's them there probably won't be one tomorrow."

"You don't have a car you could rent me?"

"If you're just going to the ranch, I guess I could let you have that old pickup out there. It doesn't get driven much anyway. You think ten dollars a day is fair?"

"It's fair with me," Roy Pat said. "And I'd better get some groceries. I don't want to catch them short." He took all the pinto beans she had and most of the canned meat.

"You don't want any bread or anything?" she asked.

"This will be fine."

"I'll fill up the truck for you. I want to be sure it'll start," she said.

"Haven't heard of any strange animals around, have you?" he asked as she pumped gas in the idling truck. "Any deer or cattle being killed?"

"There's exotics if that's what you mean by strange. But they don't kill deer. They are deer, most of them. Least, they all got horns."

Roy Pat was disappointed but not discouraged. God hadn't led him all this way to let him die in the wilderness. God had brought the tiger to him once to show him emptiness. God would bring the tiger to him again to show him that faith could fill the void. He drove down the highway and turned off on Dolan Creek Road. When the highway was out of sight, he stopped the truck, got out his bag, reassembled and loaded his rifle.

When he got to the locked gate at the end of the road, he considered. He could leave the truck, put his faith in God, and go after the tiger on foot. However, he didn't know how far it was to water, and he needed water to camp. Also, he could sleep inside the truck instead of sleeping on the ground. That would put him out of the way of rattlesnakes and protect him from the tiger. He shot the lock off the gate and drove into the ranch.

Arina saw them first. "Vultures," she said.

"*Caracara,*" Jacob said. "Mexican buzzards." He drove down a rough trail through low rocky hills, along the edge of a wide, deep arroyo. Mesquite, prickly pear, and guajilla grew in the rocky soil. Sotol raised spear-like shafts above the brush. Jacob drove off the trail, forced the truck through the brush, and stopped in a cloud of dust.

"There's not much left," Arina said, pointing at the remains of the buffalo. "Whatever it was ate most of it."

After assuring himself that the tiger was not lurking nearby, Jacob opened the door and got out. Green flies buzzed the head of the bison, and Jacob studied it for a moment—not enough left to draw the tiger back—before looking for tracks. "Mostly rocks here," he said. "Look for sandy spots in the arroyo over there."

Arina worked her way down the arroyo. Experience had taught her to avoid thorns on the vegetation and to check shade for snakes. She paused to pick something from a curved thorn on a catclaw. "Jacob," she called.

"It's the tiger," Jacob said after examining the hairs and then pug marks. "Couldn't be anything else. The tracks head toward the river. My guess is he'll stay fairly close to water." He studied the sun. "It's late. Trail's probably too old for the dogs to take, anyway. We'll set up camp at the river and make a few casts at daylight when it's cool."

The mouth of the canyon opened into a narrow, boulder-strewn flat studded with small stands of cane bordering the Devils River. Unable to get the truck to the flat, Jacob parked, and he and Arina walked to the river. The river, no more than forty yards wide, ran clear over shallow shoals and through deeper pools. A yellow bluff rose more than a hundred feet into the azure sky. The bluff towered over a bend in the river, and the water washed quietly against a jumble of rocks that had fallen from the face of the cliff.

The slide had originated thirty feet above the river. It had come from an overhanging ledge that sloped toward the river on either side. A ten-foot section of the overhang had given way. Jacob could see a few hardy shrubs and sotols clinging to crevices in the rock ledge. The shifting of the earth that had caused the slide also had split the face of the bluff. A deep, jagged crack in the sheer wall of yellow rock reached upward from the rubble to the top of the bluff along the downstream side of the slide.

The ledge reminded Jacob of the one where he had captured his last mountain lion. It would be a good place for a cat, even a cat as big as a tiger, to hide, and Jacob scrambled over the rocks to see if the ledge was accessible from downstream. Arina's voice stopped him.

"Jacob, look," she said, pointing to a small red figure on a rock.

"Pictograph," Jacob said, examining the faded lines. "Indian rock art. Hundreds of years old. Fairly common in this area."

The figure was that of a running deer, a buck, and Jacob pointed out the feathered arrow that protruded from a rear leg. "Must have come down in the slide," he said. "Probably an old Indian shelter up there. Maybe we'll have time to look at it."

"May I keep the rock?"

"We'll have to ask Paco about that, but it won't last long exposed to the weather the way it is now. See that split? We called them chimneys and used to look for them to climb. Put one hand and one foot on each side and walk up it. I bet I can still do it," he said, wanting to show off for her. He placed his hands and feet, suspending his body between them, and had climbed a few feet when she implored him to stop.

"You might hurt yourself," she said.

Jacob was glad. Climbing chimneys was harder than he remembered.

Roy Pat wasn't lost because he didn't know where he was going; he was walking point with God. He didn't know where the ranch house was and had seen no sign of habitation since leaving Loma Alta. He followed rough roads and trails across the ranch. The sun was almost down when he saw the brighter green that marked running water. He abandoned the road and drove toward it. It was a creek, but its current was spring-fed and the water sweet. He parked the truck on the low bank above the creek. He placed the rifle on top of the cab, opened a can of meat with his pocket knife, and sat down beside the rifle to eat, spearing the meat with the knife. When he had eaten, he rinsed the can in the creek and drank from it.

He sat on the cab to watch the moon rise and to say his prayers and make plans. "Lord, it is not for us to question Your way but to do Your will. I prayed for You to take the tiger out of my mind, out of my dreams, but You would not. When You brought the tigers to America, even before the plane crash set them free, I knew that it was Your will that I by faith overcome them. Deliver the tiger into my hand, keep my faith strong, and I will hang the tiger's hide on my pulpit to Your glory."

Each day he would scout the water's edge for signs of the tiger, taking one side until noon and the other side back to camp. Then he would move to another location and begin again. He had food for several days, and, if necessary, he could kill game to eat. God had sent ravens to feed Elijah; God would provide for him.

Getting back in the cab he put on an extra shirt and a sweater. It would get cold before morning. He also rolled up the windows so that he would not be jerked from sleep by fangs or claws.

The night was cool but clear. Jacob staked out the dogs and saw that they were bedded down. He did not erect the tent but spread the sleeping bags on a ground cloth over soft silt that had collected between boulders during high water. He built a driftwood fire and heated a can of Ranch Style beans and a can of corn. They ate them with cheese, crackers, and Shiner beer. Neither of them spoke as they ate. Instead they watched the sky that slowly yielded its color until only black was left, pierced by hundreds of stars. Jacob was as content as he had ever been.

Arina listened to the soft rippling of the water. "I remember nights such as this on the Dnieper. On summer nights when I was a girl my father and I walked to the river after the evening meal and watched the stars come out. Once he said, 'You work all your life to find silence.' I thought he was speaking of death. Now I know that he was speaking of moments such as this. I was such a fool I did not know. I am wiser now."

"And happier?" Jacob asked.

"And happier."

"I'm getting too old to chase lions," Jacob said. "I loved camping, even dry camping, the mountains, the solitude. But I liked having someone to come home to. When this is done, I want a steady job, something steady but close at hand. We'll have the mountains, the isolation, a steady job, and each other. We can camp every weekend if we want."

"Jacob, zip our sleeping bags together, please. I want to make love to you under the stars," she said.

While Arina went to the river to wash, Jacob added wood to the glowing coals and zipped the bags together. For the first time in a long time he felt at peace with the world. He wished he had known Arina's father. Jacob was certain he would have liked him. He was showing Arina and her father the Davis Mountains when Arina slipped into the bags beside him. He reached for her as a gift he was eager to unwrap.

Roy Pat was awake before daylight. He opened a can of meat and ate it. When it was light enough to see the ground, he went to the creek and drank all the water he could hold. The rifle and a can of beans for lunch was all he needed. He struck out, humping through the brush, checking animal trails. He spooked deer and saw goats in the distance. Once, he thought he heard dogs. He stopped to listen but did not hear them again. *There shouldn't be dogs out here,* he thought. He walked in that direction until he came to the river. Seeing a wide place where the river shallowed out over gravel, he crossed. He would backtrack on the opposite side.

Roy Pat had heard that in India they tied a goat to a stake

to draw a tiger into range. He offered himself. *Come and get me*, he thought. *Come and die*.

A sound awakened Jacob, and he reached for the Ruger before identifying it. An overheated rock had popped beneath the fire. His movement awakened Arina. "What is it?" she whispered.

"The fire. The dogs would alert us if there was a tiger. Cold?"

"Just the night air."

"It always gets cool in desert country at night. I'll build up the fire. The next time you open your eyes, the coffee will be ready. You want eggs for breakfast? This is my chance to impress you."

She sat up with the connected bags over her shoulders. "I want to watch you," she said.

"I'll boil some eggs for a snack; we may have a late lunch."

"I'm going to stay here."

"Not with a tiger around, you're not."

"The truck is there. I will not go anywhere. I want to examine the rocks, take a bath. Set up the tent, make this less a man's camp."

"I'll leave one of the dogs. You feel okay?"

"I'm fine."

Jacob shrugged. One of those annoying but temporary female things. The country, the climate, the food was strange to her, and she carried a great weight on her mind. She could not go home, and her friend Andrei had been arrested and who knew what else. When he needed her, she was tougher than six strands of barbed wire. When the trail got hot, Arina would be stepping on his heels.

"I may be gone for a while."

"I will be okay."

Jacob tied Bo to the truck on a long leash. Bo would

recognize the approach of a tiger, and he would fight to the death to protect Arina. He picked up the rifle and led the other dogs away from camp. Bo whined and barked, unhappy to be left behind.

Arina washed the dishes, rolled up the sleeping bags, and cleaned up the mess Jacob had made. *He thought he was a good camper.* The thought made her smile. If they camped there for a week, he would make no improvements. She smiled again at the memory of him showing off for her. Didn't he know that she would do anything to keep his love? That trying to impress her only made her laugh that he was such a little boy?

When she had the camp to her satisfaction, she retrieved the bottle of tiger urine she had hidden in her duffel bag. She would leave tiger sign on both sides of the canyon and try to lure the tiger to the camp. She would be safe in the truck, and Jacob could shoot the tiger from the rocks above. She paused, trying to decide whether or not to take the dog. It would be a nuisance and probably would leave its own sign along with that of the female tiger, but she decided to take it. Not only would the dog warn her, Bo would divert the tiger while she sought safety in the trees along the river if she could not reach the truck.

Bo was so excited he quivered when she went to him. She didn't know dogs the way Jacob did, and she was amazed at how eager they were to work, even when that work was to bring a larger and more powerful animal to bay. "You'd better hope Jacob doesn't need you," she told Bo as she led him away. She hoped he didn't need any of the dogs. *The tiger would kill them as quickly and certainly as it had killed Farley's dogs and perhaps*—she forced the thought from her mind. Jacob knew what had happened to Farley. He would see that it didn't happen to him.

. . .

Jacob led the dogs back to the remains of the bison and turned them loose, except for Red. He kept Red on a short rope, tied the leashes around his waist, slung the rifle over his shoulder, and led the way into the arroyo at first light. The hounds checked the tracks silently and continued down the draw. As Jacob suspected, the tiger had continued toward the river. He heard a hesitant, half-hearted bawl, then the hounds became silent again. *Got a whiff, that's all,* he thought.

The hounds worked slower as the arroyo deepened and widened and dropped toward the Devils River. He had reached another part of the river before the sun reached the bottom of the canyon. He worked the dogs along the river without success, then worked his way upstream. The temperature soon would be too high for good dog work, but he had no plan except to work the river until he found fresh sign. He would work one side upstream, then work the other side back to camp before lunch. During the hot afternoon, he would drive around the ranch, hoping the dogs could pick up a scent.

Arina worked her way upstream until half the urine was gone, then turned back toward camp. She would leave the remainder of the urine downstream and on the opposite bank. Then she would nap until Jacob returned, and tonight she would insist they sleep in the truck. She knew he would be angry with her, but if the tiger came to the river, it might encounter the sign and follow it to the camp. The dogs would alert them, she would hold the flashlight, and Jacob could kill the tiger.

When she reached camp, she decided to leave Bo. He had been a nuisance, sniffing at every sign she left so that she had to drag him away, marking the trail they made, startling her every time he jerked up his head to look at something. Besides, she did not want to cross the river with the dog.

She tied Bo to the truck, and again he whined and barked when she left. "Hush," she said, pretending to throw a rock at him. "You'll bring Jacob or the tiger, and either will be very angry to see us."

She crossed the river slowly and cautiously so as not to lose her footing. The first time, she had left sign near the camp and worked until she was done, but she had the dog with her then. This time she would walk until she was approximately the same distance from camp and leave sign as she returned so that she did not have to retrace her steps past the sign. She smiled at her caution; Jacob would tease her when she told him.

Nevertheless, she felt a sense of unease, something she had never felt before. Tigers stalked their prey, silently creeping up behind them and springing without warning. She frequently turned to look behind her. She also knew that tigers sometimes caught prey by crawling into bushes and waiting for a victim to pass. She carefully examined every clump of brush, every rock that could conceal a tiger, and then skirted it.

She stopped and listened, mouth open. She thought she heard dogs baying in the distance and that comforted her. Jacob was nearby, the dogs were on the trail, and the tiger would have no time to think of her.

Roy Pat watched the woman threading her way through the brush and occasionally stooping to pour something out of a jar. *Brush killer? Coyote poison?* When she turned to look over her shoulder, he recognized her. *The Russian woman. What was she leaving? A signal? Something that could be spotted from the air? By UN helicopters?*

From the corner of his eye, he saw movement. That would be the lion hunter. *Had Jacob seen him?* Slowly, he moved his head. He could see nothing, but he knew someone was there, a darker shadow in the shade of the dusty brush. Roy Pat didn't move, trying to blend into cover. He wished he was wearing his cammies. They wouldn't spot him then.

He looked back at the woman. She continued as before, seemingly oblivious of him and Jacob but moving slowly, steadily toward the lion hunter. *Was she trying to lure Roy Pat into the open? Would Jacob shoot him? For trying to kill the tiger?*

With a grace that shocked him, the shadow moved from one shade into another. *That wasn't the lion hunter, that was*—Roy Pat raised his rifle, but it was too late. In two bounds, the tiger was upon the woman. "Drop," he yelled, hoping she would fall to the ground, giving him a shot. Instead, she ran. A claw shot out, catching her boot and knocking her to the ground. With a backward glance at Roy Pat, the tiger grabbed her by the shoulder and carried her, dragging her through the brush.

Again, Roy Pat took aim at the tiger. He could kill the tiger but might injure the woman. *Why had God let the woman get in the way?* He was testing Roy Pat's faith. Raising the rifle Roy Pat fired into the air, hoping to frighten the tiger into dropping her and running. The tiger moved faster. Roy Pat yelled, hoping the tiger would drop her and turn on him, giving him a shot. The tiger did not.

Roy Pat ran after the tiger, hoping for a shot without the woman in his sights. The tiger slowed and turned to face him, holding the woman like a shield. Roy Pat studied the image before him—a tiger with a woman in its mouth. *Did God want him to kill the Russian and the tiger?* He had wanted to face the tiger alone, his faith against the tiger's terror, but God's ways had never been easy to understand.

He could see her breathe, see her eyelids flutter. He was twenty yards from the tiger, and he could clearly see the tiger's intense eyes, teeth stained with the woman's blood. The tips of its ears trembled, and the hairs on its back were as stiff and erect as bristles. It growled low in its throat, growling around the woman.

The woman's eyes fluttered open, and she looked at him. Her shoulder was in the tiger's mouth, her head hung over the tiger's heart. He aimed the FAL at the tiger's heart. At this range one bullet would kill both of them. Taking a breath and releasing half of it, his finger tightened on the trigger.

"Help me," she said, stifling back a moan. "God, save me."

Roy Pat hesitated. *Did God bring him here to save this woman? Instead of bringing the tiger's skin to his church as a sign of God's glory, did God want him to bring this Russian to his church as a sign of God's grace?* The tiger did not move, but its swollen tail whipped from side to side.

Roy Pat took a step forward, but the tiger did not back up. He took another step, another. The tiger's eyes blazed. The whiskers on its lips quivered; its ears were back, its brows contracted. Moving his rifle slightly, Roy Pat fired a shot into the ground beside the tiger, spraying it with dirt. Without warning, the tiger dropped the woman and sprang at him, knocking him down as he fired again.

One swipe of its paw destroyed an eye, ripped away his nostrils, and tore loose his jaw. With one eye gone, the other filled with blood, Roy Pat tried to force the rifle between the tiger's jaws and again pulled the trigger. The tiger's mouth enveloped him, one fang tearing through his neck and into his mouth. The tiger shook him like a dog, then carried him, half-dragging him away. Arina watched in horror, afraid to move. The last thing she heard was the baying of dogs.

The dogs had been cold-trailing, and Jacob's frustration grew as another trail played out. The tiger played tricks with them, crossing the river. *Patience,* he encouraged himself as he worked the dogs across the river. Get this last tiger and he and Arina could go home. Let the government try to deport her after that. The country owed them, both of them, and he would tell them that if he had to.

Jacob was startled by the gunshots. He didn't know what they meant, but they seemed to come from close to the camp. At the same time, the dogs picked up the scent. Jacob fumbled with the snaps on the leashes while the frantic hounds leaped, bawling and straining at the ropes. One by one they raced bawling downstream. Jacob lashed the leashes around his waist and ran after them as fast as he could.

The dogs were sniffing Arina when he saw her. They caught the tiger's scent, and then they were trailing again. He knelt beside Arina, afraid to lift her, afraid of what he would find. *Her heart was beating, thank God*. Her pulse was thready, she was covered with blood, but her heart was beating. Quickly he examined her wounds, finding most of them cuts and scratches from being dragged through the brush. There was a deep laceration above her boot, puncture wounds in her shoulder, a broken collar bone, and perhaps other broken bones in her shoulder.

Wetting his bandana with his canteen, he bathed her face. She jumped and opened her eyes. "Jacob," she said. "I thought the tiger carried you away."

"It's okay," he said. "I'm here."

"I thought it was you in the jaws of the tiger."

"I'm okay. The dogs are after the tiger, but I need to get you back to the truck, back to Loma Alta. They can call for a ambulance."

"No, you must leave me. Please, Jacob. Find your dogs and kill the tiger. You must."

"Later," Jacob said. "I'm getting you to the hospital."

"It is too late," Arina said. "Everyone who has been bitten by the tiger has died."

"We know what we're up against now. The doctors, the scientists will know what to do. This is America."

"You must kill the tiger. My life does not matter."

"It matters to me, Arina, and I'm not—" He stopped in mid-sentence and stood up. He listened intently. "The tiger is backtracking," Jacob said. "Coming this way."

A wide, brushy flat that sloped gently toward rolling hills bordered the western shore of the river. A quarter of a mile away rose the bluffs of the high bank that contained the river during floods. He heard the dogs howling. The tiger had turned on them. The tiger roared, and even deaf old Red howled as the moaning roar tapered in volume and ended in grunts. *Damn, that was close.* A second thundering roar erupted almost immediately. It echoed down the canyon of the Devils, ricocheting off the bluffs like an approaching flash flood.

"It is the mating roar of the tiger," Arina said. "I tried to lure it with the last of the urine."

"My God, you got it on you. Hold on." He picked her up as gently as he could, but she lost consciousness. He ran for the pickup, heedless of the thorns that tore at his flesh and clothing, hearing the dogs returning to the river, fearing the tiger could cut him off.

Roy Pat was tempted to remain unconscious and free of pain, but he knew it was the devil who tempted him. He fought through the pain until he was able to think. His neck and part of his head were in the tiger's mouth, but his hands were free. His rifle was gone, but he had a knife in a sheath on his belt. He fumbled for the knife, pulled it free, and with all his might stabbed it into the side of the tiger. The tiger growled and clenched its jaws tighter, its fangs digging into his neck, his skull until he thought it would explode. He fought the darkness that closed in around him and tried again to stab the tiger, but the knife fell from his hand.

The tiger shook its prey until it was still. Then it dropped its meal, placed one paw over it protectively, and turned to face its tormentors. The dogs skidded to stop their pursuit and scrambled out of the way.

Jacob knew he was hurting Arina, but if he could get to the pickup she would get over it. His lungs burned, his arms ached from the load, but he dared not stop. He plunged into the river. The bottom dropped sharply and Jacob went under with Arina in his arms. He reached for her and felt the Ruger slip from his grasp as Arina struggled under the water. He pulled her to the surface and thrashed until he got his feet under him.

The rifle was gone. He started to dive in an effort to retrieve the Ruger, but as he loosened his hold on Arina, she went under again. He heard the dogs yelping in fear and pain. Movement on a low hill two hundred yards away caught his attention, and he gasped when he saw the tiger running toward them through the sparse brush. Leaving the rifle, he splashed across the river.

When he reached the shore, he looked back and saw the tiger hesitate at the edge of the river and look over its shoulder as three hounds, two Walkers and the bluetick, raced through the brush toward him. The tiger wheeled on the baying hounds, and Jacob looked away, concentrating on not tripping over rocks or roots. He could not watch his hounds die.

Jacob heard a dog yelp in pain and saw one of his Walkers on the ground, all four legs kicking wildly, a dozen feet from the tiger. The cat faced a single dog, the bluetick. The bluetick rushed at the tiger and tried to back away as the cat lunged, but the hound's retreat was an instant too late. The tiger's claws caught the dog just behind its rib cage and almost ripped it in half. The bluetick's body arched through the air and crumpled in a heap on the ground. Jacob saw the hound's intestines dragging as the dog tried to crawl into the brush. The tiger pounced on the dog and crushed its head in its huge jaws. Then it turned to face him.

Jacob watched the tiger standing over the bluetick, and the tiger returned his stare. Jacob prayed that the tiger would stay on the opposite bank and eat the dogs, but without taking its eyes off him, the tiger waded unhurriedly into the water and began swimming.

Jacob was afraid to run but slowly retreated, praying he did not fall. Remembering the boiled eggs in his pocket, he dropped them, hoping to distract the tiger, wishing they were grenades. Without taking its eyes off him, the tiger reached shallow water and trotted unhurriedly after them.

Jacob ran again, but the truck was too far, hopelessly too far. *The chimney.* It was his only chance. But how could he climb with an unconscious Arina? He dropped the blood-stained bandana, hoping to delay the tiger.

He ran for the yellow bluff, skirting the tent, and climbed a jumble of rocks toward the crack in the face of the wall. "Arina, Arina, you have to help me. Arina, please. Please."

"Leave me," she said breathlessly.

"You have to get on my back, hold on with your good arm. It's the only chance."

He shifted her onto his back and tried to lock her legs around his waist. "Don't faint on me, Arina. Don't faint. Hold on."

Bo, still tied to the truck, was frantic, leaping, bawling, snapping at the rope as the tiger destroyed the tent and bedding.

Jacob placed a hand on either side of the chimney, then his feet. With Arina on his back he could move only inches at a time. He was not going to make it. The tiger would bound up the slide ready to attack, tearing out his entrails the way it had disemboweled the bluetick, crunching his spine like a matchstick. He pushed himself up the rock wall, tearing his hands. *Bo. Poor Bo was tied helplessly to the truck. If only the tiger would attack Bo first.*

His foot slipped from a small outcropping of rock, and he almost fell, causing Arina to gasp. He wanted to say he was sorry, but he had no breath, and her arm was clamped around his throat like a garrote.

He was less than twenty feet above the rubble when the tiger walked slowly into view at the base of the crevice. Arina moaned. He wished he had started up the chimney with his back to the tiger; that way, Arina would not see death come.

The tiger crouched to spring. Jacob clawed at the rock, trying to climb higher as the tiger gathered itself to spring. He was spread-eagled in the crevice, staring at the cat, bracing himself against the tiger's claws when Bo appeared behind the tiger, trailing the chewed rope. Snarling, Bo feinted an attack. The tiger turned, and Bo ran, scrambling over the rock slide and circling, staying out of the tiger's reach.

Jacob's arms and legs trembled. He didn't think he could go higher, wasn't sure he could hold his position much longer. Bo had given them a reprieve. Did he dare slide down the rock and run for the truck? The tiger turned back to the chimney. Jacob could not move, could not escape. He prayed that the fall would render him unconscious so that he would not know the horror of being eaten alive. Snarling, the tiger sprang, its claws raking the bluff, gouging deep scratches in the rock inches below Jacob's right boot before it slid back to the base of the crevice. Bo attacked again.

Jacob knew he dared not squander the second reprieve. He forced himself upward despite bleeding hands. *A foot. Two feet.* Another while the enraged tiger bounded after Bo, catching the dog with one giant claw and knocking him off his feet. Before Bo could recover, the tiger bit through his head and shook him before tossing the dog aside. The tiger sniffed the dog, then walked back to the chimney, raising its head to glare at Jacob. It sat on its haunches, waiting for them to fall.

Jacob's muscles cramped. They had to get to the ledge before his strength gave out. He looked up. The ledge was three feet above him, impossibly far. Muscles quivering, he inched his way up, three inches, six, nine. "Arina," he could scarcely breathe, could scarcely talk so tightly did she hold his neck. "You have to reach up to the ledge above you." *Thank God it was on her good side.* "Put as much weight on it as you can. I can't hold you much longer."

If the movement caused her to pass out and she fell, they were doomed, but he had no choice. She groaned as she slowly lifted one arm. If she had a grip on the ledge, he could tell no difference. Scarcely daring to move his trembling legs for fear they would give way, he inched upward again. *Another three inches. Six.* Her head was above the ledge. She slid her arm and shoulders onto it, giving him a little respite. He inched upward some more, and he could feel her trying to crawl onto the ledge. Her legs loosened their grip around his waist, allowing him to breathe more deeply. He stopped to pant.

He heard Arina cry out in pain as she shifted her body from his back to the ledge. Jacob drew a shaky sigh of relief. Even with the lighter load, he was not certain he had the strength to reach the ledge himself. Trying to lock his legs under him, he slipped one arm along the ledge, searching for a purchase, then quickly swung his other arm around while trying to support himself with one leg. Jacob scraped his boots against the wall, searching for support. The toe of his left boot slid into a narrow, horizontal crack in the wall and held. He paused to catch his breath and gather his strength for one last effort, then boosted himself up, grunting, straining. With the bulk of his weight on the ledge, he allowed himself a moment to rest. When his breathing and heart rate were under control, he pulled himself onto the ledge and checked Arina.

She was unconscious. He wondered how much of this ordeal she would remember, if she had a chance to remember anything. They were safe, but the tiger was still between them and the truck. *How long before it was safe to climb down from the ledge?* How long before his muscles recovered enough to allow it? Perhaps he could leave Arina on the ledge, drive to Loma Alta, and call for an ambulance and help. His heart swelled with pride in her. Her courage almost provoked him to tears. Together they could do anything.

Jacob looked down. The tiger waited, occasionally curling its upper lip over its long, yellow fangs and snarling.

Jacob slowly got to his feet and looked down at the tiger at the base of the cliff thirty feet below. The tiger laid its ears flat and hissed. *Damn*, Jacob thought. The tiger seemed almost human, as though carrying out a vendetta against them for killing its mate. He knew better. They were no more than mice to a cat, and they had almost become dinner. When they were out of its sight, it would tire of waiting and leave.

How long could Arina wait? She would survive her wounds, but if the tiger's saliva had infected her, how long did he have before the best medical facilities were of no use? There were excellent medical facilities a few hours away, and she had convinced him she could do anything. He had to find a way off the ledge.

The ledge led to a large overhang. The overhanging rock was blackened from ancient fires marking an Indian shelter with pictographs on the back wall and fine silt for a floor. Jacob had no time to examine the cave. He followed the ledge, finding fresh goat and javelina tracks. Brush grew along the edge of the ledge and in places covered it, but if goats and javelinas could use it, so could they. So could the tiger. However, the bluff dropped straight into the river in front of the shelter. The tiger would have to swim downstream to find the goat trail that led to the ledge, and that was unlikely. Tigers weren't afraid of water, but they weren't as equipped for reasoning as humans were.

Relieved that there was a way off the ledge other than climbing down the chimney with Arina on his back, Jacob retraced his steps to the chimney, stopping to check Arina. She was breathing evenly, and while she was still the bleeding had almost stopped. He looked at the chimney they had climbed. On the other side of it, the ledge led to the top of the bluff. But the rock slide had taken out several feet of the ledge. The tiger could jump across it, but they could not.

He was startled by the tiger's roar. It was not the mating roar that he had heard earlier. It seemed a roar of anger and frustration. Jacob looked over the edge of the ledge. The tiger stared at the bluff. When it saw Jacob, it hissed, baring its fangs, then trotted around the bend in the cliff, out of sight. If the tiger climbed the backside of the bluff and found the ledge, it would also find them.

Jacob heard Arina moan and say something in Russian. "Water," she mumbled, then lapsed into Russian again.

Jacob picked her up and carried her to the shade of the Indian shelter. He laid her gently in the soft, powdery earth on the floor of the cave, leaned forward, and kissed her on the forehead. He envied her unconsciousness. At least she didn't know what they were up against. "I'll die with you," he said. "I don't think I can save us."

The tiger had gone upstream. Maybe it would be attracted to the smell of food at the campsite. Maybe the sight of the truck would scare it away. If it found the trail, it would come this way. It would stop over there, inspect the gap, jump across, kill him, then kill Arina.

Jacob ran back along the ledge and along the trail to a clump of lechuguilla, a ground-hugging plant with wicked, needle-sharp spines as hard as seasoned oak at the tip of each rigid leaf. Using his knife, he cut a dozen of the eight-inch leaves, then continued down the trail until he located the tall, slender bloom stalks of the sotol he had seen the previous day. He cut three of the stalks and hurried back to the chimney.

At the edge of the trail near the slide, he brushed the earth away from the rocks and jammed the lechuguilla leaves into cracks, angling the leaves so that the spines pointed toward the opposite side of the slide. Within minutes he had them all in place.

He picked up one of the sotol stalks, ignoring the barbs on the edges of the dried leaves, and trimmed the small end until the stalk was a foot taller than his height. The center of the stalk was soft and pulpy, but the outer layers were tough and rigid. He reached for another stalk, then stopped and listened. He was trimming the third stalk when he heard Arina scream.

Arina dreamed of sheet ice cracking along the shores of the Dnieper. The cracks were dark and widened into stripes. She was a girl, hatless and coatless in the cold, pounding on the door of her home, terrified by the stripes. Suddenly she could feel the heat of the wood stove in the kitchen. She was inside, and her father stoked the stove until it glowed red, then white. She begged him to stop, but he did not. Her face burned. "Please," she said, "please." Her father's back stiffened. There was something about him that frightened her. Slowly he turned, his eyes blazing. It wasn't her father; it was a tiger. Its lips curled over its fangs; its whiskers were rigid, its tail lashed. Suddenly, it sprang, and she screamed.

Arina opened her eyes and stared into the back of the cave.

She blinked, trying to clear her vision and saw red, yellow, and black figures. Deer, turtles, serpents. Men, or what she thought were men, arms outstretched, some with no heads, others with no legs, some holding feathered spears. All dripping blood. Or tears. Where was she? Her eyes swept along the wall and stopped on the tiger. A red tiger, rearing on hind legs, its erect tail curling over its back.

Tony followed the caliche road back to the highway. Hailee said nothing, so he asked her. "What do you think?"

Hailee turned and looked at him. "Hysterical woman. Probably wanting attention. No self-respecting militiaman would stalk her, and I doubt a tiger would eat that stringy bitch. Did you see what the sun did to her face? Leatherized it."

"So what do we do now?"

"Go back to Houston. Tell the news director the tiger had been there, but we missed it because it took him so long to okay the trip, and turn in our expenses."

"You think he'll go for it?"

"No, but let's make him say no. Stop at that place we passed on the way. I need something to cut the dust in my throat. You want a beer?"

"I'll get a six-pack," Tony said.

Inside the store, Tony spoke to the buxom woman. "Help yourself," she said, when he picked up a cold six-pack, "but you can't drink it on the premises. State law."

"Get much business out here?'

"Ranchers. Truckers. Enough to keep me awake. Had some excitement yesterday. Man and woman came in. Thought he looked familiar and then in the middle of the night, my eyes popped open, and I remembered who it was. That lion man that's been chasing that tiger."

"Are you sure?"

"Sure as sin. And the woman with him looked just like that Russian that was on TV."

"Just a minute," Tony said, going outside and getting Hailee. Hailee asked the woman to repeat the story.

"Where did they go?" Hailee asked.

"Folks out here don't like outsiders meddling in their business," the woman said. "I shouldn't have said nothing. It's just that we don't get a lot of strangers out here, and yesterday we had three."

"Who was the third?" Hailee asked.

"I think I've said about all I'm going to say," she said. "I ain't much for gossip. It was just so unusual. Seeing somebody that was on the TV."

"My name is Hailee White. I'm a television reporter, and this is my cameraman. Tony, get your camera," she said. "We're not interested in gossip, we're interested in news, and what you know is news. We want you to tell your story on network news. This is something the whole country is interested in."

"I didn't dress for no network news."

"You look fine. Mostly, we'll just show your face. And the store, of course. We'll want some shots of the outside. Maybe I should warn you that after this story airs people will be coming to see this place. Curiosity seekers, coming to buy gas or a soft drink."

"I guess we could use the business," the woman said.

Outside, Tony took the camera from the case and shot footage of the store. Little if any of this would ever be aired. Hailee was after information, and she knew how to get it.

When he went inside, the woman was telling Hailee what groceries Jacob and the Russian bought and about the man who came in afterward and bought some things. Hailee asked the woman to retell the story and Tony taped it. It was sloppy, but Hailee was in a hurry.

"Who was the man following them?" he asked when they were back on the road and headed for Yellow Bluff Ranch.

"Probably a print reporter. We've got to get to them first, then get to Del Rio. We can feed the story from there."

Jacob found Arina as he had left her. He dropped to his knees beside her. She was unconscious. He saw the crude animals and shamans drawn by aboriginal inhabitants of the cave. "I'll bring you back some day and show those to you," he promised, his words sounding hollow in his ear. American medicine and technology could save her; he was sure of it, but first he had to save her from the tiger.

He returned to the chimney, to the sotol stalks. He trimmed all three stalks to the same length, then took the dog leashes from around his waist and used all but one to lash the stalks together. The last was for his knife. He was wrapping it around the knife handle and the end of the stalks when he heard the tiger muttering. The tiger came up the ledge. It was in no hurry. It approached slowly, spitting and hissing, ears flattened, yellow eyes flashing. For a moment Jacob was transfixed by the gleam of hatred in the tiger's eyes, then he hurriedly finished tying the knife to the sotol stalks.

The tiger stopped at the edge of the slide to judge the distance it must leap, then crouched low so that it seemed flat on the ground, gathering its limbs under it.

"It's not going to work," Jacob mumbled. "Forgive me, Arina. It's not going to work." Maybe when the tiger killed him, it would forget about Arina. *Maybe*—

Both Jacob and the tiger heard the bell tinkling. Jacob glanced over the ledge. The tiger rose slowly from its crouch and also looked down at the redbone hound sniffing at the base of the crevice. Jacob almost yelled, then checked himself. Red couldn't hear him, but the tiger could. He wanted the tiger to concentrate on the hound, not him.

Red looked up, saw the tiger, and bayed. The tiger hissed at the hound, then turned its attention back to Jacob and the slide. It crouched again. Jacob took a deep breath and faced the tiger.

"Okay, Ivan," he said, as loud as his shallow breath allowed. "Let's get it over with." He gripped the rough spear with wet and trembling hands.

The tiger jumped. Six hundred pounds of snarling orange-and-black death easily crossed the span. It landed on the lechuguilla spines, driving them into its broad pads and spoiling its second leap, the one that would have put the cat on top of Jacob. The tiger roared and spun its body on the brink of the ledge, biting at the embedded spines.

Jacob lunged forward. The knife blade entered the tiger's throat, drawing blood. Instantly, the cat slapped at the crude spear, slamming Jacob into the rock wall and almost knocking the spear from his grasp. He thrust at the cat again, jamming the blade into the tiger's chest as it sprang, and, using the wall for support, pushed with all his strength.

The tiger, already off balance, clawed at the ledge and slipped over, the spear embedded in its chest. Jacob, unprepared for the tiger's sudden fall, released the spear too late. Off-balance and unable to stop his momentum, he stumbled at the edge of the ledge and twisted as he fell, but his feet still slipped over the edge. Two of the remaining lechuguilla spears pierced his thigh, and he winced in pain and clawed desperately at the earth and rocks to halt his slide off the ledge. When he stopped sliding, he was hanging over the crevice from the waist down.

Panting and groaning, he pulled himself back to the ledge and jerked the spines from his thigh, not pausing to stem the flow of blood. He crawled to the edge to look down at the tiger. The big cat lay on its side at the base of the crevice. Its tail lashed back and forth, and the claws of its hind feet ripped spasmodically at the rocks. Blood ran from the wound in its throat.

Old Red stood well away from the tiger, baying. In slow motion, the tail and hind legs of the tiger stopped moving, and Red silently, cautiously approached the cat to sniff at the broken body. Red glanced up at Jacob, walked to the shade of the bluff and flopped on the ground, panting.

Jacob allowed himself a moment to catch his breath, then hurried to Arina. She was as still as the tiger, her face white and clammy. He scooped her into his arms and started down the trail. She neither opened her eyes nor responded.

The trail clung to the side of the yellow bluff for several hundred feet before reaching the shore of the river. He was hampered by the tenacious thorny brush and wild persimmons that had forced roots into the sparse, rocky soil, and the trip took longer than he had hoped. He was out of breath when he reached the end of it, on the opposite side of the bluff from the truck.

Nevertheless, he ran, praying he would not trip. His breath came in wheezing gasps, blood pounded in his ears. When he could run no more, he walked. When the pounding of blood in his ears slowed, he heard the tinkling of a bell and realized that Red trotted at his heels.

Jacob saw a cloud of dust. Even before he saw the car, he knew who it was. Tony pulled up beside him, and Jacob told them they could videotape the tiger, his dead dogs, the body of Arina's savior if they could find him. But no pictures of Arina, and he was taking their car if he had to steal it.

Suddenly, he heard popping that signaled the approach of a helicopter. *Barry!* Barry would get Arina to the San Antonio Medical Center. He turned his head as the chopper blades churned the earth into a whirlwind. He ran to the helicopter and, with the last of his strength, climbed aboard with Arina in his arms. "San Antonio," he gasped. "Call Medical Center. Tell them rickettsia. A virulent form."

As Barry lifted off, Hailee got out to wave. Then she helped Old Red into the car. "I'll see you get home," she promised him. "After we wrap up this story."